KING PENGUIN

WALES' WORK

Robert Walshe claims to have written for a daily newspaper, a public relations office, a scriptwriting enterprise and a small galaxy of advertising agencies.

In reality a number of different writers inhabit the same skin, and *Wales' Work* is a phantasm resulting from that discovery. The rest is a matter of lists and numbers: two passports, Canadian and British; eight countries, four of them in Canada. 'This brief confessional apart, I find myself on the side of those who say that what matters is the poem, not the poet. To hell with the poet; it's probably what he deserves.'

Robert Walshe has lived in Paris since 1971, latterly as the Paris agent of a London bookseller.

ROBERT WALSHE

WALES' WORK

A KING PENGUIN
PUBLISHED BY PENGUIN BOOKS

Penguin Books Ltd, Harmondsworth, Middlesex, England
Viking Penguin Inc., 40 West 23rd Street, New York, New York 10010, U.S.A.
Penguin Books Australia Ltd, Ringwood, Victoria, Australia
Penguin Books Canada Limited, 2801 John Street, Markham, Ontario, Canada L3R 1B4
Penguin Books (N.Z.) Ltd, 182–190 Wairau Road, Auckland 10, New Zealand

First published by Martin Secker & Warburg 1985
Published in Penguin Books 1986

The Michelangelo letter on p. 150 is taken from
Vasari: Lives of the Artists, trans. George Bull
(Penguin Classics, Revised edition 1971, p. 400)
Copyright © George Bull, 1965

Made and printed in Great Britain by
Hazell Watson and Viney Ltd, Aylesbury, Bucks
Typeset in Ehrhardt

For Gian Piera

The First Envelope

I had hoped that by now the transcript would be in your hands so that we could begin with all trumpets flourishing, but it was not to be. All the same, and you will understand, it is a relief to know that the real work will be going on elsewhere. I pass it along to you, you pass it along to the neighbouring drudge, he passes it along to the next, and so on infinitely until we have solved unemployment. You are not to look for evidence of literary application at my end: I can confidently can't I leave the spitand-polish to you. Did I ever tell you that Tom Magguinness once spent three months trying to find an opening line as good as the first sentence in *Pride and Prejudice*, and on the day it came he realized that fifteen thousand others had suddenly gone pale? I helped him out by knocking it back to the level of the others.

Perhaps as a way of beginning I should repeat in greater detail what I have already said on the telephone. I am to send you the material as it accumulates month by month, in a series of envelopes. Each envelope will contain dredgings and salvage of a kind that may or may not be of use to you in writing the official biography of Wallace Marshall Wales: for you to dispose. Wales once had the curious notion of getting someone to write a biography backwards – *The Life of Terence Twerp from Death to Birth* – and I suppose we might try it here. If so, this is the death envelope. For the birth and indeed the early life in general we shall have to go to other sources. No doubt there will come a time to attach dates to events and people to places, but for my part I am content to leave that sort of needlework to the end. Meanwhile think of me as the thumbprint on the doorknob in the corridor leading to the closet concealing the matter locked doubtless in Wales' safe whose combination, we are encouraged to believe, has been immolated with the genetic code of our dearly departed. Never mind, the ashes are in my care.

The obituary is useless. Another idiotic curriculum vitae, as if the man were about to apply for his first job in publishing. I am told seriously that there are private papers, but no one seems to know where they are to be found. All I can say authoritatively is that he was as deeply involved in the blackening business, or should I say, greening, as you or I: he had a lifelong habit of writing his notes in an appalling colour of green ink. So eventually the envelopes will be filled with those, if they can be found, plus the results of research plus whatever else I can think of along the way. My part of it will take an interminable number of months, which may on the face of it seem eternity; but remember I have my ordinary work to dispose of at the same time. I am told that a deadline may be 'imposed by events', mysterious note, and I am not sure I like the sound of it. Whatever happens, you will be offered two years to complete the manuscript. From your point of view, then, the job is more gambol than gallop.

Can you come in fairly soon, Horace, to talk about money? There may be a little extra in it for you this time on account of another quirk in Wales' will. He may have been niggardly with his colleagues, but where his own interests were concerned the taps poured champagne. There is none of it at the club, I may as well warn you, but they've got in a very decent cask of Sabine, aged four years, and the roast lamb no longer tastes of unwashed wool.

Wales versus Wales.[1] This in lieu of the transcript which, they tell me, they haven't got round to typing. When will it be done? Just as quickly as it gets to the top of the queue. When will it reach there? Oh well you know it's very much in demand, it was a very popular trial. I know, I was the star witness; does that make any difference? Naturally it makes a tremendous difference but you know we do have a backlog. I'm sorry about that, how long does it take a backlog of these proportions? To be dealt with? The last one we had took us three years, but you know we are trying to do our best and if you care to put in a word for another typist that might be a good idea. Would it help if I came round and typed the thing myself? That's awfully nice of you, really it is; the snag is that there's only one set of headphones. Perhaps I could rent another. You *are* thoughtful and we *are* grateful for the offer, but unfortunately they've

---

[1] *Wales versus Wales*, Court of Banal Pleas, in which the publishing company Wales & Wales Limited, opposing The Wales Charitable Trust, applies for an injunction to restrain the publication of *Wales' Work*.

stopped making them for our kind of machine, it's a tiny bit oldfashioned you see. Could we send out the recording machine and have *it* duplicated? What a jolly interesting suggestion; it would however mean however inevitably sending it out of records somewhere, you know, *else*, and that unfortunately would be frowned upon. *Frowned* upon! Fraid so. But we do appreciate your suggestions. Most helpful, really. Pity we can't just put it in an envelope for you this afternoon because we'd *like* to you know.

And so what I've done, and there wasn't much choice, was to photocopy the notes I made from memory after the trial, to which for the record I append our subsequent conversation in The Heart of Darkness.[2] You are therefore reading a passage from the journal I keep, otherwise known as the dustbin I fill up, when I have nothing better to do.

I haven't bothered with the dramatis personae. You will detect the voices of the presiding judge, counsels for the prosecution and the defence, and the inimitable vocables of your reporter.

*   *   *

– Can you be so kind as to describe the circumstances leading up to the disappearance, if we may call it that, of Wallace Marshall Wales.

– Objection.

– In other words, please tell us of the events leading to your last meeting with Mr Wales.

– It was my duty, as one of the executors of Wallace Wales' last will and testament, to look after the funeral arrangements. He had insisted on cremation, and had organized all the details himself: the time, the place, the nature of the ceremony. There was to be no service, and no one was to participate other than myself. I was to remain present with him throughout the night preceding the incineration, which was to be carried out at eight o'clock in the morning.

– And you followed his instructions?

– Yes and no.

– Objection.

– I fear you will be asked to answer yes or no.

– Yes, I installed myself as expected beside the coffin and waited for morning.

– What time of day did you begin this watch?

....

[2] Ed.: Robert Racine's epithet for the room in the Wayfarers' Club where he met Horace Bentwhistle to discuss the terms of the assignment.

– About an hour before midnight.

– And where were you installed?

– At the funeral home. There was a small chapel of sorts. A private chapel.

– And what did you see?

– He was laid out in the casket in his dinner jacket.

– In his *dinner* jacket? How do you account for this?

– I can account for very little. By that I mean I don't know why he had specified in his will that he be dressed as if for a formal dinner party, but since he had left all the blacktie arrangements in a conspicuous place in the bedroom with a note of instructions pinned on top, we thought we had better follow his wishes.

– You say 'we' thought 'we' had better follow his wishes. When you say 'we' you are referring to whom?

– To myself and the two attendants from the mortuary.

– What did the note say?

– It said 'Dress me in this. Do not omit the black hose.'

– By black hose I suppose he meant stockings.

– That's what I thought, until I found the length of black rubber pipe.

– Please explain.

– He had left a short length of garden hose in the left sleeve of the dinner jacket. It fell out when I picked up the jacket.

– What did you do then?

– I put it in my overcoat pocket.

– But you told the funeral attendants to dress the body in the dinner jacket?

– I did so at the appropriate moment.

– When was that?

– The following day. The day preceding the event.

– By which you mean the ceremony itself?

– Yes. The funeral, if you can call it that.

– Now, let's be sure we've got all this straight. Wallace Wales had left on the dressing table of his bedroom a dinner jacket with its trousers and black tie. What else?

– A pair of black silk hose, a pair of black shoes, a white shirt, some studs and cufflinks.

– And a length of black rubber hose.

– And a length of black rubber hose.

– Together with the note.

– Together with the note.

– How long was the black rubber hose?

– About two feet.

– How did you get it into your overcoat pocket?

– I rolled it into a sort of circle, like a sausage.

– And what then did you do with it?

– I took it home and kept it there until the funeral. Then, because he had said 'Do not omit the black hose,' I took it with me to the funeral home and slipped it into the open coffin beside the body.

– Can it be said that you were labouring under some confusion as to the meaning of the words 'black hose'?

– I realized that he probably meant the black silk stockings. But as I was not absolutely certain about it I took along the rubber hose as well.

– Why were you so willing to observe a dead man's nonsensical command?

– Objection.

– Why did you bother?

– Force of habit, I suppose. Wales had behaved like that all his life. Besides, as I was the executor of the will I did not wish to be anything but scrupulous.

– Did Wales have a fondness for practical jokes?

– I believe it could be said with some fairness that Mr Wales' entire life was a practical joke.

– You realize you are using the past tense.

– I mean to say his entire life was and continues to resemble a prolonged practical joke.

– Objection. The witness's opinions are of no interest to the court.

– Sustained.

– Can you give the court one or two examples of practical jokes practised by Wallace Wales?

– For the most part he covered them up and other people were made to take the blame. But the answer to your question will emerge as the story continues. It concerns the black hose and the wooden box.

– The black hose *and* the wooden box. Very good. Before we go on to that, Mr Racine, what is your conception of a practical joke?

– I should define it as the acting out of a series of events or *practices* in which the actor becomes the unwitting victim of a prank. In psychological terms the practical joke implies an element of sadism on the part of the originator, and of masochism on the part of the protagonist. Most people go along with it because if you've been made to look a fool, protesting only makes matters worse.

– Yes. Well, let's get back to the ceremony. You mentioned a wooden box. How did that come in?

– I found out about it during my exploration of Mr Wales' bedroom. I was told to look for the box under the bed.

– Told by whom?

– By the other executors, Mr Thrale and General Smallwood.

– And is that where you found it?

– Yes.

– Describe it to us.

– It was a rather handsome wooden chest about eighteen inches by perhaps ten, with a carved lid. The lock and fastenings were of brass, and it had brass handles at each end. It was covered with dust.

– As if it had lain under the bed for a long time?

– Exactly.

– Were there any fingerprints, any displacement of the dust to suggest that it had been handled recently?

– None whatsoever.

– What did you do then?

– I cleaned off the dust with a towel and took the box home with me. On the day of the ceremony I carried it with me to the funeral home as Mr Wales had expressed the wish that it be destroyed with him.

– Was it locked?

– Yes.

– And the key?

– The funeral home attendants found it hanging from a gold chain around his neck when they undressed him.

– Did they give it to you?

– Yes.

– And what did you do with it?

– I put it in my pocket.

– You have said that there were carvings on the lid. What kind of carvings?

– Nothing immediately identifiable. I mean they were abstract rather than figurative designs.

– Now, let's go back to the night of the ceremony, as you call it. You are sitting in a small private chapel in the presence of a man dressed in a dinner jacket. The man, Wallace Marshall Wales, has been prepared for incineration. He is lying in a coffin. Beside him is a two-foot length of black rubber hose. Correct so far?

– Correct.

– And where had you placed the wooden chest or box?

– At the foot of the coffin. It was to travel with the coffin along the short railway leading to the incinerator.

– And since you were to remain there until the body disappeared into the incinerator, how did you pass the time?

– Well, as I had nothing to do – and had forgotten to take along something to read – I'm afraid I dozed off.

– How long did you remain awake?

– About an hour.

– During that hour you had nothing to think about?

– On the contrary, there was a great deal to think about. Unfortunately it was all rather tiring. I could find no purpose at all in being there, or in following the instructions spelled out for me in the will. It was a depressing moment.

– Were you not tempted to open the wooden box? After all, you had the key.

– I was extremely tempted. But I fell asleep instead.

– When did you wake up?

– At about two o'clock.

– What happened then? What caused you to wake up?

– I don't know. I had the impression that something or somebody had tapped me on the shoulder.

– Where were you at the time? Were you still sitting in your chair?

– Yes. I had tilted it back against the coffin in order to be able to rest my legs comfortably on another chair.

– In a manner of speaking, you were stretched out.

– Half stretched out.

– What did you do when you awoke?

– I stood up and looked at Wales. After all, I was supposed to be keeping watch.

– What did he look like?.

– He looked like a corpse. His face was grey. There was a single very tall candle burning at the head of the coffin – no other light. It was all very composed – an arrangement in blacks and whites, with the grey face circled in the candlelight. I was standing at the foot of the coffin, and my hands fell on the mahogany box.

– And?

– And I suddenly found myself saying out loud, 'This is all too damned silly.' I took the key out of my pocket and opened the box.

– And?

– I found the matrioshka.

– You found what?

– The matrioshka or Russian doll.

– Please describe to the court this matri . . . oshka.

– A matrioshka is a painted wooden doll, the top half of whose body can be removed to reveal an identical but smaller doll inside. The next doll can be decapitated in the same manner, revealing yet another identical but smaller doll, and so on. In theory this reduction of the wooden doll might go on to infinity; in practice, however, they are usually quite small, the mother doll containing three others. But this one was enormous – the largest I'd ever seen. It was so large, in fact, that it very nearly filled the wooden chest. The picture was altogether an extremely curious one, with the dead man laid out in his wooden box and the matrioshka, or icon of fecundity, in hers.

– Is this the matrioshka you found in Wallace Wales' wooden box?

– It is.

– Will the court please enter into the record Exhibit A, one wooden Russian doll or matrioshka. Did you then decapitate the Russian doll, Mr Racine?

– I did.

– And what, if anything, did you find inside? Another doll?

– No. I found a sheet of notepaper, folded once. I unfolded it and found some words written in Wales' handwriting on his own notepaper.

– What did the note say?

– It said, 'From this moment onward, Root, you will do everything I tell you, and I mean *everything*, because if you do not I will disclose your Abominable Secret and your career will be at an end.'

– Who is Root?

– I am Root, sir. Wales called me Root from the beginning of our relationship. I suppose he thought that my adoption of the name Racine was a way of putting on airs. Racine, as you know, means 'root' in French. My original name was Skrzypek.

– And what does Scraw-peck mean?

– Fiddler, sir, in Polish.

– The court will no doubt follow your line of reasoning, Mr Racine, given a little time. Please continue.

– So what did Wales tell you to do?

– To begin assembling the story of his life according to a pattern which he would describe for me as I went along.

– I presume the letter still exists and can be entered as evidence.

– It does, your Honour, and I hereby enter it as Exhibit B. Now will the witness please describe what happened next as carefully as possible and with particular attention to the details of the events that occurred.

– I was standing at the foot of the coffin, reading the letter, with the opened box and matrioshka immediately in front of me, when the body began to move. With infinite slowness, as if in the performance of one of the rituals of Hatha Yoga, he first raised his arms until they were perpendicular to the body, and then just as slowly sat up. As he reached the sitting position the arms – with equal deliberation – began to drop toward his sides, and at the same time the eyes began to open so that by the time the arms had reached their nadir the eyes were fully open and staring at me.

– What did you do?

– Nothing. I could neither move nor speak. I believe I had even stopped breathing.

– Continue.

– He then removed the white handkerchief from the breastpocket of the dinner jacket and began wiping his face with it; the normal fleshtones soon began to emerge from underneath what must have been greasepaint or makeup of some kind. At which point, realizing that he was perfectly alive and well, my strength returned to me and I somehow managed to compress into a single word all the loathing, indignation, and horror I felt at that moment.

– You swore?

– No, but it was the same thing. I shouted his name at him. It came out of me with enough force to break down the walls. They must have heard me on the West Bank.

– Go on.

– He then began speaking in his normal voice and in his normal manner as if nothing whatever had happened. 'Who was the silly ass who put this length of rubber hosepipe in my coffin, Root? What in God's name does one *do* with a length of rubber hosepipe in one's coffin, water the daisies?' He then threw it at me and hit me on the chest. I backed off while he climbed out of the coffin.

– Was there any more conversation?

– Not much. I hadn't yet collected myself. He added a few words, nothing of great significance. As he was climbing down he said, 'I recommend hard beds. It's been years since I've had such a good rest.' Then, as he was about to go out the door, he said, 'By the way, I should take that letter seriously if I were you,' and disappeared.

– You mean he went out of the room.

– Yes, closing the door as he went. I rushed after him but couldn't see a thing: there were no lights. But I could hear his footsteps. He was already at the farther end of the corridor.

– Did that give you the impression that Wales knew his way about the place?

– It did. I gathered up the box, the length of hose, and the matrioshka, and followed, but by the time I reached the exit he was gone. He had vanished into the night

– Out of sight but not, I gather, out of mind.

– I have not seen him since. Nevertheless Wallace Wales lives on in my mind as if he were present in this room.

*   *   *

I looked up from the paper and reached for my glass. It was empty: I must have drained it during the long reading without being conscious of doing so. Horace (you are reading this, remember, over my shoulder) had meanwhile lighted his pipe, and it had gone out.

– What do you make of that?

Several matches were struck, manipulated, extinguished before the reply came.

– If you ask me it sounds like a load of golden buggery. You know what I mean.

– Poe.

– More than that. It sounds to me as though – to put a fine point on it – you'd been screwed. May I change over to whisky?

As nobody ever came into The Heart of Darkness I went out in search of George, ordered two glasses of whisky and a jug of water, and returned.

– You see, it didn't strike me that way because Wales was like that, one had learned to expect it of him. I realize of course that anyone looking at it from the outside would have to agree with you. But all that is of no interest; what matters is that the court pronounced Wales dead.

Horace receded briefly behind a puff of smoke.

– Try that one out on me again.

– We might have had a chance if it hadn't been for that damned length of rubber hose.

– What became of it?

– I am ashamed to say I chucked it in the dustbin.

– So?

– So I threw away the one piece of tangible evidence that might have proved I was not dreaming.

– Yes, but what about fingerprints? On the coffin, for example. On the doorknob. On the matrioshka.

– In the first place, the coffin was burned.

– *With nothing in it?*

– I am coming to that. The prints on the doorknob were obliterated by my own and afterwards by God knows whose else. The matrioshka had my prints on it but not his: he must have polished it. All this came out during the trial. To reduce it to its bare bones – if I may be so indelicate – what happened was that the mortal remains of Wallace Marshall Wales were delivered to me the next day in a handsome bronze casket.

– Another bloody box!

– We sent it to an analyst who confirmed that it was, indeed, a collection of chips of charred bone, ashes, and dust. There were also a few lumps of gold in it – presumably melted-down studs and cufflinks and teeth.

– Pah! Multiply that by six million.

Very long pause.

– The dust sounds odd. Could it have been, what shall we say, an administrative mistake? They do that sort of thing in hospitals with babies, why not at the other end?

– We thought of that. In any case we were not able to shake the defence. For them Wales went into the furnace at eight o'clock in the morning in wood and came out the other end in metal.

– Who put the lid on the coffin?

– One of the attendants. And when he did so the body was inside. According to his testimony.

– The mind positively crepitates with disbelief.

– Doesn't it just.

– Tell me something, Robert – and I want a straight answer. How do you know you did *not* dream all this?

– The rubber hose hitting me on the chest. Thump. But for that

– Hmmmmm. Let me think about it. You are not hiring me because you think I'm a writer of thrillers.

– We know you are not a writer of thrillers, Horace.

Background notes. There was a time when his 'cell', as he insisted on calling it, was lined with books on three sides and up to the ceiling on each. Nothing atypical there: one talked about, negotiated for, and accumulated books just as a wine merchant might accumulate bottles of wine. But imperceptibly or almost, because it happened over a period of months, the books began to disappear from the shelves. We were all pretty much underawed by that: once one has filled the shelves the neverending war with clutter is engaged. Had Wales decided once and for all to place himself on the winning side? No one dared to ask. The prevailing notion was that he had taken them home.

I suppose he had emptied an entire wall before the first of the eggs appeared. It sat there, large putative offspring of some antediluvian beast, on one of the shelves where the books had been kept before. Closer inspection showed that it was not exactly eggshaped, but subtly flattened at top and bottom and polished smooth as a billiard ball. White marble, I guessed, or something very like it. Once, when Wales was not in the room, I touched the stone; it swayed silently from one side to the other and returned in diminishing movements to its horizontal stance. Silently, because a runner of red cloth – is there such a thing as red baize? – had been laid along the length of the shelf.

Each time Wales returned from one of his periodic disappearances (recapitulation to follow), another monstrous egg would take its place on the shelf until in the end there was a collection of seven in the room, all waiting placidly like a tribe of Humpty Dumpties but for what? How little we know about one another; how very little we really knew about Wales. There we were leaping about him like marionettes on a string, without ever pausing to ask ourselves what made us move, so entranced we were by motion itself. Or is there even greater health in not wanting to know?

Eventually there was nothing in the room but his long refectory table and chair, two other chairs for visitors, and an immense palmate plant. The bookshelves were taken away – all but those supporting the eggs – and the entire room was repainted white. Beyond the table an accordion of French doors looked out on the courtyard, and as the carpet in the room was the colour of grass, one was given the impression, when the doors were thrown open in the summer, that whatever went on there went on outside. All a bit austere even so, and in a strange way unnerving, because we knew that the calm was apparent, that nothing or very little of Wales was expressed in that peaceful décor, and that one day it would all be taken away like props on a stage to reveal the books, grime, and fearful clutter of the real world once more.

Wales, as you know, was not a confiding person: a direct question about the marble Humpties would only have provoked a dusty answer. Julian Cragg once volunteered to ask one of his friends at the Archeological Museum about them, but we knew this was an empty promise: Julian was far too absorbed in his own intrigues to concern himself with Wales' eccentricities. And so we let sleeping eggs lie.

Toward the end the collection was augmented by another kind of stone object: bellshaped, this one, rising to a point or spear at the top, and considerably taller than the eggs. One might think of a Prussian military helmet without the aperture for the face. Mars. 'In his lifetime,'

Borges writes, 'he suffered from unreality, as do so many Englishmen.'[3] Though Wales was no Englishman we assumed he had become infected with the disease. My own theory is that he picked it up at Oxford.

We never found out what Wales did with the books: they were not in the flat when I went in with the people from the bodyshop. It's hard to imagine him selling them. They were first editions, most of them signed by the authors, all of them published by Wales: his own lifestory filtered and refracted through the pages of other people's work. He may not have read them, but having approved first the synopses and later the blurbs, he knew what was in them and they were, after all, his children. What does a man do with his offspring when he chooses to go along with one foot in one world and the other in another? Do they follow him about in cardboard boxes?

The private papers were even more baffling, because not even Philippa Fox-Taylor knew what was in them and they, too, had been cleaned out. All his life, it seems, Wales had written notes to himself and then squirrelled them away in a safe hidden behind a reproduction of a medieval map of the world from Hereford Cathedral – world concealing a world. No one but Wales knew the combination, so that when he was gone the general wisdom, meaning Julian Cragg, felt obliged to organize a safebreaking. God knows how, but they dug up a professional burglar who came in dressed in a business suit and opened it – to use Philippa's phrase – 'with the tips of his fingers.' But it was bare as Mother Hubbard's cupboard. Crestfallen Cragg. He had good reason, I suppose, because he was the only one of us who had ever read Wales directly, and it was an experience he was not likely to forget. During the week of the final boardroom row (more about this later), Cragg stole into Wales' room after hours and began going through the drawers. Wales walked in as people will when they are not expected and found him there on hands and knees, if you can imagine it, like a child caught stealing the jam. It seems that no words were exchanged: Wales simply kicked him through the French doors without pausing to open them beforehand. Cragg had plaster on his face for days afterwards, and far from being ashamed of it went round behaving as if he had been one of the conspirators in a plot to destroy Hitler, narrowly escaping with cuts and bruises – and indeed his life. You see, he had discovered that Wales and Selwyn Bream had been siphoning off money, mostly from the enormous profits of the Bedside Bible, into the holding company, and doing it without saying a word

....

[3] *Tlön, Uqbar, Orbis Tertius*, New York, 1964.

about it to the Board. Whether Bream was fully aware of what he was doing or just countersigned because Wales told him to is of little importance; Bream was seldom sober, and when he was, he was said to be on his way to Australia.

The other thing Cragg found out was that Wales had been amusing himself with the ladies, and that his inamoratas, or some of them, had favoured him with the sort of letters for which the pulper would have been too kind a fate. He kept them in cigarboxes, so that instead of smelling of various shades of perfume as they do in the pages of Victorian novels, they smelled of cigars (no mean bloodhound, Cragg). You will want to know who the ladies were and how they came by their enthusiasm for our former chairman; unfortunately I can't ask Cragg. Anyway the evidence is gone, and it is by no means central to our task. As long as Alethea was alive, Wales was, from all accounts, a devoted husband. I do not propose to sweep the affair with Helena Brown under the carpet, but it was all very *managed*, if you know what I mean, and none of us, Helena excepted, ever felt that Wales' attitude toward Alethea had in any way been altered – 'attitude' being, for the purposes of our story, a spiritual thing. I very much doubt that any of the subsequent throbs got much of a grip on him. He wasn't that kind of man. For him, freedom was an absolute undilutable and indivisible, to be practised not merely discussed.[4] Alethea succeeded with him, I think, only because she had

....

[4] Wales insisted that the idea of liberty had become so debased in our time that the word deserved to be struck from the dictionary. At the centre of the rot was a twentieth-century practice euphemistically known as salaried employment: to him it was on a level with pulling an oar in a galley and he could never really believe that other people were capable of submitting to it. 'What sort of stuff are people made of,' he would growl, 'jelly, putty, or liquid compost? Can you imagine it, there are actually men in this world functioning daily and in our presence who allow themselves to be *told* how much they may earn and how much they may not earn, at what age they may begin working and when they must cease? Can you believe that there are individuals who consent to be *told* what work they shall do and what work they shall not do, not to mention when they shall do it and how, and go on so consenting throughout their entire lives? My dear sirs, it is not to be believed *and they are not to be saved!*' By which time, fully aware that he had been speaking to his own galley slaves as if they were a public meeting, he would begin tugging the end of an eyebrow so violently that one feared for its tenure. Time passed, and we began to experience unemployment as a plague of worldwide dimensions; would Wales modulate his song? Not a bit of it. Survival for him, and by natural extension for everyone, passed by signposts labelled initiative and selfhelp. All those who refused to practise that cardinal creed merited their fate – to be given over into the hands of their masters – because they had allowed themselves to become servile, interested, and false.

the means to buy space and retire to the furthest ends of it when the going got rough. She was the one with the ivory tower.

Cragg's story of the cigarsmelling loveletters may not sound plausible until you hear another. I once had to go with him to Paris to negotiate the rights to a Catholic encyclopedia; there I was able to observe him at work firsthand. It was Saturday morning, the agreement had been signed the day before, and since it was the weekend we decided to profit from the fine weather by exploring the Left Bank on foot. We went along the river a distance, then turned off into the rue des Fils-du-Calvaire. I can remember, some distance along, walking by a bakery that exhaled the smell of Marcel Proust's buns. Wales then spotted a boutique which astonished the Puritan in both of us: it was called *Le Mons de Vénus* and specialized in mirrors and lamps and various objects of mildly erotic art. Nothing more scandalous than Leda being had by her swan. Wales smoothed an eyebrow and assumed that tight, semirepressed smile that was invariably the prelude to mischief. 'Come,' he said, 'this is worth investigating,' and led the way into the shop.

– Bonjour, Madame, he said in his atrocious French, we've come all the way from Grande Bretagne to investigate your famous course in Alpinism. I trust you will be able to help us complete our research.

The woman was naturally dumbfounded – whether by the accent or by the proposed 'research' it was impossible to tell – and in the normal course of events I suppose the conversation might have stopped there in a desolation of malentendus. But as it turned out we were not alone in the shop. There was a short burst of feminine laughter, and a tall woman wearing Chanel – the suit – emerged from the door at the end: ravenhair falling diagonally across the forehead, defiantly made up, approaching Wales' age within, I should guess, six or seven years but not showing it much.

– I have an idea you're not going to find what you're looking for here, she said. I'm not even sure you're in the right country.

– Nor am I, said Wales. Perhaps we could repatriate ourselves over a glass at the King George.

She studied him with the disinterest that people contrive without effort when they know they are of the same caste, and accepted with pleasure. I excused myself and left them to their adventure.

He did not return that weekend: he made an excuse of some kind and returned three or four days later looking remarkably fit. She had assumed, he said on his return, that he had been looking for a travel agent.

*   *   *

End of envelope. I apologize for the quality of my scrawl: virtually illegible, I am well aware. For a time I toyed with the idea of running it all through the typewriter, but then I discovered a quirk in my machine which makes it impossible for the thing to make a black mark on white paper. Every typewriter I have known has a mysterious small key with three dots beside it; the central dot, I am told, is for making stencils. Well, my machine now behaves as if it were permanently adjusted to the central dot. You get the mark of the keys incising the paper, white on white, and that's all. To read what I've written you'd have to screw up your eyes and slant the paper toward the light. I never did trust machines.

The Second Envelope

Somehow I must restore calm: this Wales business has been spinning in my head like a toy in space. The task, I suppose, will be to bring it back to earth and dismantle it, carefully numbering the pieces as we go. But that will take time. God damn him, Horace, he knows I have a wife and my work and a life to get on with, and yet he is quite prepared to use me to accomplish any purpose he may care to undertake. What if he is mad? I should not, then, if I could prove it, be obliged to follow his instructions. But he is legally dead. No one can be dead *and* mad at the same time, though Wales seems to have accomplished it. Shame's Voice. Infernal. How could he possibly know that I should want a haircut on that particular day and at that particular time? Does he have a room somewhere opposite the house where he sits watching with binoculars? If he is not there himself, somebody must be doing it for him, watching, following, waiting for the moment. The most unremarkable moment. If one did not know that Wales was like that it would be enough to drive one out of one's socket.

What happened was that I had decided to have a haircut after lunch: the wisps were down to the collar and getting longer by the minute. Sausages and mash and light ale at the pub in Ascent Street: nobody there but a halfdozen advertising men going on about cigarettes as if they were Vitamin C. Could one of them have been a spy? If so he'd have had to follow me across the triangular square behind Wales' flat, long since let, past the school and the din of children behind a wall (battery chicks greatly amplified) into Diary Street, past Stokes' then left along Cumberland Row to Trimble's, where they fold you in and fold you out as if you were a length of the royal linen. As usual they gave me Benson the Silent: we've been silent together now for more than five years. What kind of conversation can pass between a barber/hairdresser and his

17

client once he discovers that you come from Saskatchewan and you learn he lives in West Wittering, Sussex?

He was well into it when the boy came in carrying a brown paper parcel.

– This is for you, sir, he said, and stood there waiting for a tip.

I can remember struggling under my sheet to produce a coin, which finally I did, and he deposited the parcel on my lap. It was the size of a shoebox, done up with string. I set the box aside until Benson had finished, and carried it back with me to Tricorn Square, hoping to find an empty bench in the sun. One of the three seats was occupied by two women in identical flowerpot hats; the others were empty. So I sat down in the second sunniest position, untied the string, removed the paper, took off the lid, and found – God save us! – another matrioshka just slightly smaller than the first. Same naïve drawing of face and costume, same bold colouring: clearly the offspring of the one Wales had placed in the wooden box. It all came back: the long, dismal night beside that ghastly furnace with Wales' ashen face encircled by candlelight, the depression, the weariness, the tap on the shoulder, the opening of the wooden box; the you will do everything, *everything* on account of your Abominable Secret; the appalling erection, the wiping away of the paint, and the thump of the hosepipe – two resurrections in one event. Horace, I swear to you I lived it all over again, there in those marvellously peaceful surroundings with the immaculate lawn, green even in February, and the chestnut tree, and the women gossiping under their flowerpots, to the point where once again I felt that same thump on the chest and literally looked along the bench and down at the lawn, convinced that I should find a ridiculous length of hosepipe beside me. But it was all imagined, and I was fully awake. I reached into the box and screwed off the doll's head. It was Wales' notepaper again – grey vellum with the address at the top, handwriting in that same vicious shade of green:

> I trust you have dealt with the first envelope. There is a manuscript waiting for you on the Isle of Wace. Go down there at noon this Saturday and collect it. Then proceed with the following envelope à la mémoire du Maistre.

I now see clearly that my one chance to go about my own life in the ordinary way (my own life!) came then: I should have torn up the paper and walked away with my head up – the devil take it, and me, and Wales, and the world. But I didn't, and I lost it. If you are to follow me at all from this point, I must go back and put down what I felt from the beginning about living in this Tokyo-on-Thames, about the *impossibility* of living in it, and of the particular terrors that working for Wales & Wales struck into me with gongs and twangs and blows of the Master's stick. I can follow Wales readily enough when he describes existence as a heap of buildingblocks that we are free to construct or assemble into meaningful (or meaningless) shapes and structures; where I quarrel with him is in the description of the blocks themselves. His is the viewpoint of those who believe there is some basic order somewhere to which we must become sensible and attuned, and furthermore he believes, as befits his background, that it is the prerogative of the élite (in all probability himself, viewed in an infinity of mirrors) to discern and exploit that order. The building blocks, therefore, are uniform in size and shape and smoothness; if not, one had to proceed as if they were or the house would fall down. Well, I was prepared to go along with that, or any other nursery image, so long as it didn't cost me a fullscale metaphysical enquiry.

When I came here a journalist in my twenties, I was what? Simple hayseed? Irenic optimist unencumbered with guile? I had managed to define myself well enough in my writing; for the rest I was, I suppose, largely indescribable. But it didn't matter; these were the people who had invented the rules. You were not going to be clouted on the back of the neck while you were busy pulling up your shorts. What mattered was being out of money. That was decisive, because it meant that I could not buy the time to write myself into the black. Therefore I braced myself to accept the inevitable. Hard work and good old Saskatchewan spunk would make up for it in the end.

Protest, defiance, resistance, dissent[1] – to most people the natural response to any shoulder to shoulder predicament – to me seemed not only a waste of time, but proof of failure to find a purpose. Amused politeness, suppressed passion, jollyjoviality, the relentless pursuit of the frivolous – all these I tried to soak up into the sponge of second nature; but what the devil did the man mean by Sweetness and Light? In short, Horace, I was made to be muscled all over the shop. How was I, creature of limitless skies and uncluttered landscapes, Tom Sawyer crying out to be rewritten by Evelyn Waugh, to accommodate myself to this labyrinth of caste and velvet cunning?

Soon it all came out. I was not going to be able to knock banks together at breakfast and it was unforgivable. There were no uranium

---

[1] To me, the characteristics from which all aggressive attitudes emerged were vestiges of the unevolved. I was mistaken in considering them vestigial.

mines, no chains of newspapers in my bags. My careful book of cuttings only made them snigger. For the privilege of breathing the decomposing air at Poets' Corner or the thrill of gazing up at the squalid warehouse where the Globe Theatre once stood, I had to begin again. That, or go back with nothing more to show for it than a collection of crested coffeespoons smuggled in with the socks. Not good enough. So I installed myself in a cheap boardinghouse near Keats' Walk, and took a job as a proofreader, vowing that I should never rest until proofreaders became kings: promising myself, in other words, that I should not remain in *that* particular job a day longer than I had to. I learned once more to be insignificant. I learned to *accept*, and went on doing so like Bob Cratchit until someone noticed that I had published a poem in *The Auditor*. It was not one of my best efforts and I sincerely hope it will never be exhumed; but one of the junior editors of MacFarlane and Broad liked it and wrote to ask if I would care to read manuscripts. Why not? The first one I read, luckily for me, was excellent, and I was able to fire myself up a bit in writing my report. That led to other assignments, and by the end of the year, when I learned that Wales was short of a desk editor, I had a plausible file to show. I got the job not because of what was in the file, but because of James Clutterbuck's fondness for graphic art. When the girl led me into his office I felt very much at home because – remember? – the walls were covered with lithographs: an interesting if eclectic collection. I spotted a Pasmore, a Friedlander, a Hayter, a John Piper, a Marino Marini, and as I was busy looking at them rather than at him, he asked me what I thought of them. Well, it so happened that my favourite lunchtime diversion from the beginning had been to cultivate the small galleries nearby – and as Malraux might have it, they cultivated me, within the limits of the possible. The conversation with James therefore developed as freely as conversations do when professional matters are not at stake: neither of us touched on publishing at all. At the end of ten minutes of this, he managed to convey the impression that I interested him as a potential designer of dustjackets, and I was asked to ring Helena Brown: at that time she had a vague responsibility for personnel. But even then I knew I was in. People who liked his lithographs were *his* people: the rest would fall into place. I sometimes wondered, as the years went by, if everyone else in Wales & Wales, and for that matter in companies throughout the country, had not been hired in the same insouciant manner. If so, I said to myself, we should all end up in some American technocrat's study of the performance of the British economy since the war, with extremely bad reviews. To me it seemed a society without shapes or edges, and living in it was a business of floundering about in a sea of cottonwool. The major political parties were Tweedledee and Tweedledum; they pretended to oppose one another, but once they were in power they pulled identical tricks out of the bag. Mistakes were made – and at all levels – but one seldom found out who made them; even the sacrificial goat could look forward to a quiet retirement in his pasture of peers. *What did these people believe?* It was extremely bad form to ask and even worse to care, and I must confess, Horace, that in the end I cared as little as the next man. The white rabbit turned brown, and melted into the hedge.

Let us then attribute my presence at Wales to a fusion of eccentricities – theirs for having looked at me with one eye shut, mine for failing to ask myself why they did so. I knew I was useful; why was this usefulness of such slender interest? My dear friend, it took me years to find out. The penny finally dropped at the time Jeannine and I began looking for a house. If you show an interest in a thing, the price goes up, and if the rule applies to houses it is all the more true, here, where people are concerned – which brings me back once more to my odious comparisons. The ordinary American manager says to himself, 'If we show an interest in that guy he will become more and more useful to us'; his British counterpart an ocean away is saying, 'If we show an interest in that bloke he will cost us more money.' Knowing that, why the hell did I stay? Patience, Horace, we are getting there. You see, my theory is that the Julian Craggs of this world are a new virus best brought into focus by comparison with Wales himself. One felt it was an honour to work for him; after all, he represented publishing, and generations of it, in the grand sense. His cultural roots went back to Samuel Johnson and forward to the Educational Press. When the name was mentioned at a book fair, in a lecture hall, at a cocktail party, you could tell from the way people arched their oyeses (oewyeses?) that to them Wales was in some way set apart. The name projected an aura,[2] and Wales, the man, gathered it about him like a royal robe. How could anyone resist him? During the early days in Great Conduit Street a brisk goodmorning from Wales was worth more – a lot more – than the promise of a raise/rise from Selwyn Bream, and of course they knew it. Wales' job was to lift you up, Bream's to hold you down. My life was strung out between them, pulled this way and that, subjected to the most unbearable tensions – and it never snapped, or seldom. I became, without knowing it, Pavlov's dog. Can you imagine the humiliation of it? Not easy to

....

[2] WED[3]: (Path.) symptom preceding epilepsy and hysterics.

21

convey yet I must succeed, Horace, if you are to understand what I did next. Reserve this word 'humiliation' for special study.[3] It may be the key.

There is a manuscript waiting for you on the Isle of Wace. Go down there . . . You see, there was always a manuscript waiting for me somewhere. In all the years I knew him, Wales never turned one over to me himself. If it did not come *down* from somewhere I had to go *down* to collect it; I sometimes wondered if an original manuscript had ever passed through his own hands. Selwyn Bream brought them *down* from the country (he read them too, in a manner of speaking), Helmut von Gildenkrantz brought them *down* from Belgravia, and Angela Dulcimer-Smith brought them *down* from the fourth floor of the annexe. Sooner or later they all came *down* to me because – unfortunately for me – I exuded the stink of work. Racine the masticator; Racine the nerveless digestive gland; Racine the alimentary canal. Feed the stuff in one end and it comes out the other end a book.[4] You will ask why complain, isn't this what publishing is all about? Perhaps so. Every activity calls for a method. But the *manner* of the method – that's what makes the difference between heaven and hell.

I don't know if it was Wales who discovered 'creative conflict', or Julian Cragg: it is said to emanate from Harvard. Cragg may have brought it back with him from one of his excursions to the other side, rather like Columbus bringing back syphilis, or Sir Walter Raleigh the noxious weed. It was the philosopher's stone of the smooth new breed of business managers, the ones who laughed so hard at their own jokes, and as an expert in the matter I can tell you that jokes of the kind those people had in mind were invariably made at the expense of someone else. Whatever the origin of the idea, it fit the temperament of Wallace Mars Wales like a second skin.

You were lucky to come and go during the Clutterbuck era. Before Cragg took over completely – that is to say, in the pause that followed the aborted bloodbath – there was an interregnum during which he shared the managing director's office with Harper Cabot; it was during that period that the *cahncept* was debated behind closed doors and then slipped in between the shoulderblades with the appointment of Jeremy Chesterton, Angela Dulcimer-Smith, and Freddie Fear, whom we in the lower orders have taken to calling the Trilogy.

. . . .

[3] Pushed to extremes, the word can mean 'mortify', which in turn once meant 'to render death-like' (WED).

[4] The digestion metaphor is Wales', not mine.

Let me tell you about Harper Cabot 3rd. I am sorry you never had an opportunity to meet him: your analysis of the man would doubtless be more objective than mine. Harper was one of those Americans who felt his prestige in some way threatened by a society in which Dukes and Duchesses and Lords and Ladies seemed to stand taller than men from Texas. His answer was to play the oneupmanship game back at them with as many cards as he could muster: old Boston family, *the* Cabots, you know; Harvard as a matter of course; rich wife, all the right clubs, the principal one of which had its rooms in Washington, DC, and was painted white. He came in after Wales had gone to New York to make his arrangement with Cabot and Raw, an uncomplicated proposal in which each side declared willingness to offer the other first refusal of foreign rights. Cabot had been sending infections like *The Miracle of Monogamy, Somebody Up There Loathes Me,* and *Finding Yourself in Your Face* – instant bestsellers in New York – and since it was too tedious to explain why they were of no interest to the British market, Wales invited Cabot to come over and sit in. It was an opportune moment, because Harper's wife had just then decided she wanted to install her son in a British prepschool: she wanted the boy to grow up with short pants and a broad A. We all thought Harper would be with us no longer than a few weeks, and as the months went by we began to wonder just how indispensable he was to the management of Cabot and Raw.

You really must see the man to grasp the nature of his charm: is there not some anthropomorphic relationship between skulltypes and character, muscle and manners? Harper had one of those heads that grows straight up from the shoulders without the intervention of a neck – square at the back, closecropped at the top, small eyes pinching the nose like the friendly animal we all devour at breakfast. There was a considerable bulk of shoulders and chest sweeping down to even more substantial hips and backside, the overall effect being that of an athletic pear. He had the habit of going about the office with his hands in his pockets, so that when he came toward you what you saw was largely an expanse of trousers pulled up to reveal the ankles, and all of it coming at you like a sail. He was a lexicon of Madison Avenue slogans, all so numbing to the brain that I can remember precisely two, and only one of them has any relevance here – 'Run it up the flagpole and see who salutes.' Novels, for which he had a general aversion, were dismissed as 'sleeping pills'; other genres were known more favourably as 'pep', 'dope', and 'speed' (sex manuals, investment analyses, formulas for personal – read 'business' – success). Curious that Cabot and Raw should have published so many passably good novels.

Harper's chief mission in life was to make himself liked, so that when he hit the other guy nobody could possibly take offence. He wanted everybody to call him 'Harp'; Wales of course called him Cabot, or 'the Italian ham',[5] and never once went into his room in the months he remained with us.

Moot von Gildenkrantz, who was something of a student of genealogy, came in to see me one day with a large reference volume in his hands.

— I'm an idiot, he said. I went through all the Cabots in the International Who's Who before I realized I must have been looking in the wrong book. I finally found him here — and he showed me the cover of *A Compendium of Small Businesses in the Middle West*.

— He comes from North Dakota. His father was a dealer in agricultural machinery and is listed as an entrepreneur. So much for Boston.

You know how these publications are produced: the entrant is encouraged, within the limits of plausibility, to write his own blurb. The word 'entrepreneur' is pure Harper: he could not bear to think that people would identify him as the son of a tractor salesman. (One wonders what euphemism Harper Cabot 4th will come up with to describe his nonshareholding father. Nonshareholding, according to Wales, because when his wife bought him the partnership in Cabot and Raw she took the precaution of keeping the shares in her own name!)

In all fairness it must be said that Cabot's presence among us was tolerated, if not encouraged, by Wales himself. Wales needed him because of James Clutterbuck, who was then seventyseven and showed no sign of wanting to go. You may have heard that James had begun to lose his memory: he confused Lady Moira with Jessica Birdwell, and began talking to people about 'that promising young chap Bekorgakov' ten years after he had won the Fermentora Prize. Wales couldn't bear to deal with it himself; you know how much Clutterbuck had done to get the list back into shape after the war. So he got Cragg to send round a memorandum announcing the appointment of Harper as joint managing director *pro tem*, and before we knew what had happened we were pouring champagne in dear James' honour and wishing him a pleasant time in his rosegarden. Our aristocratic American came to the party, too,

. . . .

[5] A mixture of etymologies drawing on the French *cabotin*, untalented actor, and the Italian *Giovanni Caboto* who, anglicized as 'John Cabot', discovered Newfoundland in 1497. Wales had few scruples about practising this kind of tomfoolery.

and one could not help wondering if he would have felt more pleasure, or less, if the rosegarden had been a place called Omsk. Wales said there were to be no speeches and then made one, bringing tears. The following day there was no sign of him in the house; nor was there of James, the man who had made literature possible for at least fifty of the finest authors on our list. Three months later he was dead.

(That reads too much like cause and effect; what really happened is a story in itself. He did absent himself for a day, but the day after that he was back in his place. Wales walked by the door of his room and thought he had glimpsed a ghost. Finally he summoned up the courage to go in and offer the usual pleasantries of the morning. He emerged minutes later looking somewhat shaken: James had forgotten that he'd been fired. Not only that, he went on forgetting it for the next three months! I must say Wales took it extremely well; he simply accepted it as a *fait accompli* and left the remedy to the course of time. One day, in midafternoon, our resident Petrarch's head fell down and we found him there in his room, collapsed over his papers. Memoirs, we were told. Nothing has been heard of them since.)

As for Cabot and Cragg, those two began functioning together in sin long before they were officially recognized as a married couple. There was no way of knowing what they were cooking up until the others arrived – the Trilogy – and they did, and our world has not been the same since. It was Wales who first called them that, of course, and it stuck because Philippa then passed it along to us. He also called them, less frequently but interchangeably, 'The Work in Three Parts'. It would be pleasant to be able to say that a resistance movement developed, or a repetition of the gods succeeding the Titans; unfortunately it all worked itself out on a rather more modest scale. On paper Jeremy Chesterton was brought in to replace James Clutterbuck as editorial director, Freddie Fear to take over production, and Angela Dulcimer-Smith, sales. The editorial side had been handled, since Clutterbuck's decline, largely by Peter Glyffe and myself; Humphrey Pall had dealt perfectly competently with production; and there was very little about sales that was not already known to Helena Brown. Why, then, the Trilogy? How could the house bring in a living for so many people and, worse, how could any of us consent to work for any of them? I was finished, I felt sure of it; Humphrey and Helena were the only ones who showed no real concern. Helena we understood: she had been Wales' playmate in the old days and was accordingly invulnerable. But Humphrey had every reason to be alarmed and wasn't showing it. Von Gildenkrantz, who viewed us all with a lofty tautological disdain, put it down as a case of 'British upper lip prematurely stiffened by rigor mortis.' He thought, reasonably enough, that people whose jobs appeared to be threatened by administrative fiat should react. Moot did not bother to do so on his own behalf, because like Helena (and as Lady Moira's protégé) he was out of range. But he openly wondered about the rest of us and our apparent lack of guts. Apparent or real?

Shock! The papers, the papers missing from Wales' table in the house, have been found. Double shock: they're about as useful as an old laundry list, or so my preliminary tastings compel me to believe. One folder actually contains a stack of Brummell Row invoices going back to 1937. No trace, so far, of the cigarsmelling ladies, and I am not optimistic about them because none of it was in boxes.

This is a real blow – the random nature of the material, I mean. I was counting on it to supply the buildingblocks of our enterprise, but if I can't make sweet Fanny out of it, what conceivable use can it be to you? Instead of writing *about* Wales we shall now have little choice but to write *around* him, as though the man had already dematerialized and become elevated to the status of a spook. No need to hector me with your famous lecture about the Goncourts[6]: it will all be preserved even so.

What happened is that Thrale called one morning to say that Mrs Carruthers, Wales' housekeeper, would be calling in for the keys to the flat in Ascent Street: she was to be allowed to go in and shroud the furniture in sheets. Eventually it would all be taken away and sold, but that could wait till they had disposed of the lease. She tottered in and tottered out, staring dismally at me the way old people often do, as if in horror at the thought that younger generations would have to live it all over again. Two hours later she came back and deposited the keys.

At lunchtime, for want of better to do, and with the vague hope of finding, you may well ask – an envelope with a return address? an unripe banana? a moist bar of soap? a crumb of toast? – I went round to Ascent Street and let myself in. The curtains were drawn, enclosing the gloom. I groped for the lights and heard, as I was feeling my way along the wall, plock plock plock plock: are grandfathers' clocks immortal? Finally, and much to my relief, I touched a switch. I had found my way into the

---

[6] Ed.: Edmond and Jules de Goncourt maintained that the significance of an age could not be grasped by the historian unless he had at his disposal a dress pattern and a menu of the period under examination.

sittingroom; it was now robed in white. Wales' ancestors were still there on the walls, posturing in varnish. I tried to think my way into his skin, to ask myself what he'd have done had he wanted the papers to disappear and, to look at it the other way, where he might have put them had he wished them to be found. The third possibility – that he might have considered them without interest – seemed to lead nowhere. If so, why had he removed them from his table in Great Conduit Street?

Instinct, or was it simply a desire to get on with it, led me into his study. I drew back the curtains and the light fell on his desk. Nothing in the room was dressed in sheets: it was all leather, wood, and books behind glass. The writing surface of the desk was of inlaid green leather, gilt at the edges. An antique globe of the world, waisthigh, stood in one corner. Apart from the straightbacked chair at the desk, the only other objects in the room were a reclining leather chair and its footstool, and a teatrolley on whose lower shelf had been accumulated a battery of drinks: whisky, brandy, claret, port. An amber liquid, twothirds consumed, slumbered in a cut glass decanter. I made a mental note of the level, and just then there occurred what the French so neatly call a *déclic*: 'But then he's a poet,' I quoted to myself, 'which I take to be only one remove from a fool.' *The Purloined Letter*. Only one remove. I walked the three steps that separated me from the desk, opened the excessively obvious, the top righthand drawer, and found it: a veritable sea of paper, and every scrap of it covered with that snotgreen scrawl – green of envy, green of springtime, green of nausea: at last, I said to myself, we shall find out.

There were papers in all but one of the drawers; in that one, the usual clutter of envelopes, paperclips, and inkpots to which I paid no attention, and a small canister of spiced tea to which I did. Why on earth should it not have been kept in the kitchen? With that one rattling round inside me I went out, elated all the same, and bought a couple of plastic garbage disposal bags. After work that evening I returned, crammed the papers into the bags in no particular order (they were in no apparent order in the desk), and took them home with me on the train. You have noticed, I suppose, that the papers were unattended throughout the better part of the afternoon, and that it would have been entirely possible for Wales, or anyone with a key, to have crept in after me and taken away the ones that mattered.

(I mention this only in Pavlovian obedience to one of Wales' more ominous injunctions: '*Leave no stone unturned; you may find that one of them conceals your grave.*')

The following Saturday morning, my first morning of free time, I spread out the contents on the floor of the gardenroom in a state of high excitement – and what a waste of good adrenalin! I'd have been better off using it on the bicycle. Bite on this:

Faenza/Francs-Bourgeois.

The young man who appeared at the door on the dark winter morning to ask: 'What kind of man is this Mr Magguinness?'

Flying Buttresses. A collection of verse by that most famous of self-effacing Anglo-Saxon poets, Anon.

Work in Regress.

Carnets de Sennelier à l'Italienne formats 32 × 24, Frs 36, 40; 24 × 16, Frs 25, 20. Papier d'Arche. Alternatif 1/8 Jésus Grain-Fin 28 × 18.

And so it goes, a long list of cryptic notes and phrases without structure or sequence or point. The two references to Tom Magguinness appear to be quite gratuitous. In a word chaos.

Priorities for the immediate future. Each is to be assigned a strict time-limit. All will be short and published, if at all possible under the Wales imprint.

1 A sociological thriller based on the rich man in Laon turned thief. Model, Sciascia. Find out if anyone else is doing it. Legal aspect.

2 Alternatives. A study of communities formed in reaction to a society gone wrong. Hay-on-Wye. Pugwash. Brera. Chigi in Siena. Or single out a village to be re-created from the ruined state and chronicle its progress.

3 Erotic fairy tales. A Child's Garden of Curses. Priapus. Freud, Marx, Einstein as erotic fairies. The Swiss Family Freudian. Crusoe and Friday.

4 Assemble the skeleton of the book. What is the underlying myth? Read Frye. Define it. De Beauvoir on Sade. See Harriet.

Now if you read that as a memorandum addressed by Wales to himself, it begins to make a certain amount of sense. Sciascia, for instance, is probably Leonardo Sciascia, the distinguished Sicilian author. But how are we to account for his presence here? Did Wales have Italian friends? I have never heard of any, but how else to account for the references to Brera and Chigi and Siena? And the erotica: boggles, doesn't it? Wales of course was never sufficiently intimate with any of us, Helena excepted, to leave grounds for the suggestion of a suspicion of interest at the back, or should I say, bottom, of his mind. All we knew or at least assumed, was that pornography was to be given short shrift: certainly you will find none in the backlist. Erotica are another story. They do creep in, but they have more to do, I think, with the general unzipping of the times than with any declaration of policy on the part of Wales.

But erotic fairy tales! I don't know how imaginable the idea is to you, Horace, but if I know my Wales he was capable of dredging up a manuscript strong enough to turn a pederast pink. I almost regret he didn't stay behind long enough to see it through the press. Can you hear the din? Good God, we'd need bomb shelters.

Assemble the skeleton of the book. Was he writing one, feeding an idea to someone, or piecing together some long lost manuscript discovered in fragments in a dark corner of a forgotten attic? Just at the moment I can't see him writing it himself: he has always said that a publisher's responsibility should be confined to throwing his authors the occasional piece of raw meat; the animal was then left to get on with the chewing.

What is the underlying myth? Yes, indeed, and what lies above it? Frye must be Northrop Frye, the Canadian critic, because he writes about that sort of thing, I think. De Beauvoir has written about Sade, but more than that I can't say. *See Harriet.* Well, if he wanted to see Julian Cragg's wife about all that, one can suppose the conversation might have taken a fairly lively turn. Why don't we give it all up, Horace, and write fiction?

There is more of the same, or similar. This, for instance:

> *Sage was right; in concluding with* Finnegans Wake *Joyce bowed to the unrepeatability (?) of death. But had he lived, where would his work have taken him? Along what exponential curve of invention would it have ascended/descended?*

Interesting speculation. But it surprises me that it occurred to Wales to pose the question. My impression is that his interest in the modern movement had hauled up about the time of Rudyard Kipling.

> *Pilling's Irish jailbird. Reading and writing. Cat biscuits in a jazz factory. Pilgarlic.*

That could be Oscar but my money's on Sam. John Pilling writes about Beckett at the University of Reading and locks him away in vaults. As for the rest, frankly I am meeaaoowing foxtrots.

> *Batrachomyomachy: burlesque version of the Iliad once thought to have been propagated by Homer in his declining years but subsequently discovered to have been the work of an obscure classicist from the Isle of Wace. Hideous Greek corruption for 'the war between the frogs and the mice'.*
>
> *The Adversary. Christ versus the law. Christ versus institutionalized paranoia.*
>
> *Economics as Fiction. A critical study of the work of Smith, Ricardo, Marx, and Keynes as manipulators of themes in the manner of Jane Austen, George Eliot, Joseph Conrad, and Henry James. Model: Leavis.*

Correct me if you think I am reading too much into this, but it seems to me we are entitled to observe a tendency to stand on toes and tread them into the ground with a delicate twisting motion of the heel.

I then came upon a folder with a very rough drawing of an empty glass scrawled on the outside. Underneath the scrawl, handprinted in hateful green, *Boissons Fortes, 1958–1968*. An occasional notebook with a jocular title? Jottings for a funny book by Tom Magguinness? My dear friend, there was nothing in the folder at all. And yet the other papers were there, in a pile, on the floor, substantial, inescapable, pressed between my sweating hands. I had used up the whole of a Saturday morning on them and could make no sense of them at all. I went upstairs and poured myself a jigger of boisson forte. Jeannine was astonished to see me doing it so early in the day.

There are few things in life I loathe more than the stupor that sets in when you realize you have been led up a blind alley.

*   *   *

The questions you put to me in your letter are all perfectly good and understandable. I balk at none of them but the last, and I propose to deal with it before we go any further.

The Abominable Secret, as Wales so charitably named it, has already caused me more misery than I can afford to remember. I don't expect you know that I have been to prison on account of it – yes, *prison*. Two weeks in a space large enough to house a wasted cadaver in a morgue, and I was not alone. I shared it with a pair of Platonic lovers who never washed, and I am delighted to be able to tell you that when they had anybody, which could not have been often, they had each other.

You will remember that during the trial I was obliged to produce Wales' message, the one he left in the matrioshka: '*From this moment onward, Root, you will do everything I tell you*' etc etc '*because if you do not I will disclose your Abominable*' etc etc. Naturally enough, counsel for the other side wanted to discredit my testimony and kept pressing me to tell the court what it was that Wales had been able to hold over me as a threat. The court upheld his right to pose the question, I refused to answer and was sent up for contempt of court. This was a development which amazed everybody: we all thought it was Wales who was on trial and it turned out to be me. Flashbulbs and peering cameras. Pandemonium. I became the anticelebrity of the day by seizing the defence counsel's file and hurling it at the press. Frontpage blizzard of paper shown flying out of the hands of your outraged witness, oneword headline the full width of the page:

ABOMINABLE!

Were *they* telling *me!* At the end of my two weeks with the Platonics I was brought back for a cosy chat with His Lordship (one wonders why we couldn't have had it earlier) and I told him *in camera* what I thought he wanted to know. It was not the truth. But it was good enough to get me out of there and into the nearest available hot bath, which I poured myself at the Wayfarers', together with a tall whisky, in separate vessels. I had to get the stench of that place out of my nostrils before going home to Jeannine.

It was not as bad as it sounds. They let me take my World's Classics edition of *The Pilgrim's Progress* with me and I pretended to absorb myself in it like a passenger in a railway compartment. Pretended, because I had to struggle, hour after hour, with a depression of a kind that made it almost impossible to focus on the page. Depression alternating with rage. Rage of helplessness, rage of disbelief. All of it hopelessly obscure to anyone who has not lived it, but it is the best I can do. The Abominable Secret must remain the property of Wales and myself alone, for no one in his right mind ever made a news bulletin of his own grief. What is privacy if not that? Think of it, if you must, as my original sin, and of Wales as the 'divine' blackmailer. But for God's sake don't put it in the book!

*　　　*　　　*

Sorry to have uncorked myself like that: I am still a bit emotional about it. On with the other questions.

There are three executors of the will – myself as literary executor, Aubrey Thrale, and Bertram Smallwood,[7] the retired general who, with Wales, represented the holding company on the board of Wales & Wales. They are both Wales men from hairroot to toenail – a loyalty that developed between them, if I understand it correctly, during the war. I can't get my hands on the will itself (Thrale sees no reason why we should meddle to that extent), but I can resume briefly, insofar as I can fathom it.

As Wales was childless and Alethea died before him, there were no family beneficiaries. Small sums were left to Mrs Carruthers and to an obscure clergyman in the North, but that was all there was of a personal nature. The bulk of it, including a majority shareholding of Wales & Wales Limited, was handed over to the Wales Charitable Trust. So we are left with three legal entities: the holding company, the publishing company, and the trust. Thrale is now chairman of the trust, Smallwood chairman of the holding company, and Cragg chairman of Wales & Wales. Where between heaven and hell I stand in all this remains to be seen because, though I am still senior editor, under Chesterton, of Wales & Wales, the responsibilities of the literary executor, according to Thrale, are continuing, and they are a matter for the trust. So far those responsibilities have included the wake – a job Thrale delegated to me because both he and the general were 'unavoidably detained elsewhere' – and this pile of effluent that may one day, accomplice willing, become the biography of Wallace Marshall Wales. Thrale has said nothing, but I am left with the uneasy feeling that another thunderbolt is about to descend. After all, *'From this moment onward, Root, you will do everything I tell you . . .'*

As for why he singled out *me* – Robert Roberd Rot Rut Rote Root Radish Racine[8] – to carry out his purpose rather than someone like

. . . .

[7] Wales called him 'Birnam Wood' – appropriately, because as we shall see, the holding company provided the cover for a small army of other activities.

[8] Ed.: If Robert Racine's real surname is the Polish equivalent of 'fiddler', his right to the name 'Racine' is questionable, to say the least. The linking Middle English 'Rote' (medieval musical instrument of the violin family) does supply one of the root-forms of the name 'Root', but branches off to 'fiddle' in the 14th c. Unless 'Rote' is regarded perversely as metonymic, a more honest claim can be made for the name 'Robert Fiddle' than for 'Robert Racine' if the reader is not predisposed to read significance into the shared meaning of 'Roberd' and 'Root', both of which in medieval times meant 'robber' or 'highwayman'. Thus our narrator might have

Chesterton or Angela Dulcimer-Smith, I can suggest two answers, and I am sure of neither of them. There was no visible bond between Wales and myself, neither of sympathy nor of intellectual inclination: he seemed to regard me with the same indifference – contempt would not be too strong a word – with which he favoured everyone else. If anything separated me from the rest it was my immediate dislike of Julian Cragg. Shortly after Cragg was brought in as managing director (this was before the arrival of the Trilogy) I went to Wales and offered my resignation. I hedged, of course, by asking to be shunted off to WEEP[9] where I should be more or less out of reach. That seemed to amuse more than it offended, and he persuaded me to stay on with the argument that if I did I could expect 'interesting developments'. No more was said. He knew my curiosity would get the better of me, and it led to one or two small privileges such as the trip to Paris. Cragg left me more or less to my own exploits because he was too busy battling with Wales.

The second reason is that Wales seemed to have a streak of sadism in him that needed to be expressed from time to time. The sequel to the Paris trip will do as an illustration. You may not know that in recent years all the expense accounts in the house, down to and including small chits for tea and paperclips, passed across Wales' table. My Paris account was waiting for him on his return, and early that morning Philippa called me into his room and retired into her own, closing the door behind her. Ominous. Wales then launched into one of his famous monologues: it went something like this, and I assure you my account of it is not far off the mark.

– In law, he said, at any rate in the few parts of the world where British traditions still prevail, we allow ourselves the luxury of the presumption of innocence. Nowhere else does it apply. By the tenets of the Christian faith itself, life is a long remission of guilt. A man would have to be singularly unperceptive not to see that his business, foreordained by centuries of gentlemanly precedent, was to relieve his neighbour of his cash – and not necessarily in exchange for anything of value. In this house, ever since I assumed the chairmanship, I have invariably proceeded on the assumption that a man is guilty until proved innocent.

---

done well to have named himself 'Robert Roberd' if 'Robert Robber' were thought to go down badly. In any case, Venantius Fortunatus, who rescued the original Celtic *chrotta* in the 16th c., would scarcely have been overjoyed to learn that his devotion to original texts would lead to so dubious an issue.

[9] The Wales Elementary Educational Press.

Tell me that you have never tried to rob anyone and I shall listen to you with the most profound disrespect. We are born thieves and we shall die thieves – one on either side of the cross. Your Paris account is reduced precisely by the half that you have been unable to justify by means of receipts. Better luck next time.

No, I did not hit him. What saved me was that I had thought of a better idea. I snatched up the piece of paper he handed back to me, strode out of the room, down the corridor, and up the stairs, stuck a piece of paper in my typewriter, and pounded out another version, this one revised upward by a third. I then put it in an envelope addressed to Wales himself (bypassing the people in accounts), and left it in the basket for the boy. Awesome. I was so furious I scarcely knew what I was doing. A strange phrase kept repeating itself in my head as I smashed the typewriter: Pull down the walls, pull down the walls – as if I could. As for Wales, he had found out my limits, but did I know anything more about his? Had I placed the Abominable in jeopardy? Two days of hell followed until the brown envelope was delivered from accounts: at one moment I even contemplated going back to him with an apology. Had he tried me again he would rapidly have discovered my melting nerve, but it never came to that. Something like a bond of complicity was established between us, unspoken of course, and now when he launches into one of his famous charges it is often prefaced by some such placatory phrase as 'I think you will agree, won't you, that ...' Everything seems to have been made secondary to the 'interesting developments' whose unfolding we are still waiting for, without much patience.

I never heard another word about the expense account. And yes I did get the money; Jeannine and I went out to dinner on the extra third.

Curious, the above: notice the unconscious use of the present tense? As if at any moment Philippa might come into my room with a summons from the chairman for 'Bright and Cheerful'. Wales likes/liked calling me that because, as you may have noticed, nature has ordained in putting together the parts of my face that I should look permanently glum. As a student of words he knows/knew that 'Robert' is Old English for 'famebright', and that before Root meant *racine* it meant 'cheerful'. He plays/played that game with everyone in the house: Selwyn Bream is 'The House Fish', and Julian Cragg 'The Roman Rock' or sometimes 'The Roman Candy'. Once when he had just returned from a trip to New York he referred to Cragg as 'The Climbable Allday Sucker'; I got it, but I doubt anyone else did. Angela Dulcimer-Smith becomes 'The

Lord's Piano': he'd have done better to emphasize the colour of the Smith. But 'The Blackeyed Queen' for Jill Sullivan is excellent, and so is 'The White Goddess' for Liz Gwynne. He also occasionally refers to me as 'The Famous Fiddle', which is every bit as plausible as the other. Poor Philippa. She has to translate all that nonsense,[10] and it can't always be done simultaneously.

I am not addressing myself to your question, your anxiety, about this past/present dilemma. All very natural, and I sympathize to the full especially as you see yourself running the risk, if he returns, of putting in two years without a publishable result. But what is to stop you changing the names and publishing it as a *roman à clef*? I don't expect Wales & Wales would buy it, but imagine the glee of some of our esteemed competitors: you would have them queuing up outside your door. So don't lose heart. One way or another you will come out of it well. I wish I could be so sure for myself!

Speaking of names I have just reread this all the way back to the beginning of the envelope, and I realize that you will find it all but incomprehensible. No faces, no voices, no identity cards – they might be the opening lines of any dreary old opus whose author had decided that what he must do *now* was to establish the characters. But how else was I to bring you into Wales' postClutterbuck environment short of converting myself into Charles Dickens? Come to think of it – and what a marvellous idea! – all the editions of Dickens I have ever seen had, at the beginning, a list of characters or CHARACTERS that one could consult as one went along, and what would we have done without them? URIAH HEEP, a clerk in the office of Mr Wickfield. MR EDWARD MURDSTONE, the stepfather of David Copperfield – and so on into the story. Let's try it here. I'll type it out on a separate sheet of paper so that you can pin it up on the wall. The order is not consequential; all hierarchies are despatched to the woodshed to be chopped into fine kindling for the new alphabet which, my eager imagination tells me, we are about to impose. I may have forgotten people and others, in the nature of things, have yet to appear. For all I know some of them may never appear. Anyway, once you have taken your swipe at them they will all fall into place, won't they? Here goes:

. . . .

[10] Some of these phrases – you will recognize which – eventually made their way into the titles of books.

ALBERT, keeper of the code.

HILDA AXELROD, flinthearted personnel manager, successor to Helena Brown.

LILI BACKHAUS, née BAUM, divorcée, pianist.

WALTHER BACKHAUS, Lili's unforgivable husband.

NOEL BALDING, literary agent and friend of Robert Racine.

DR JASON BALDWIN, mentor, administrator, author of psychosociological bestsellers.

SALLY BATES, book designer.

BORIS BEKORGAKOV, man of letters. Prix Fermentora 1952, Nobel Prize 1964.

YURI BEKORGAKOV, photographer, son of Boris.

MALCOLM BELL, novelist.

BENSON THE SILENT, hairdresser.

JESSICA BIRDWELL, novelist.

CAROLINE BREAM, daughter of Selwyn Bream; director of the Wales Elementary Educational Press (WEEP).

SELWYN BREAM, company director, retired.

HELENA BROWN, onetime director of sales and paramour of Wales.

HARPER CABOT 3rd, American publisher and scion of Harper Cabot 2nd, etym. dub.

MRS CARRUTHERS, Wales' housekeeper.

JEREMY CHESTERTON, editorial director of Wales & Wales under Julian Cragg.

JAMES CLUTTERBUCK, to remind you of his role as first English language translator of the work of Boris Bekorgakov.

HARRIET CRAGG, bestselling novelist and wife of Julian Cragg.

JULIAN CRAGG, publisher, megalith, and managing director of Wales & Wales.

ANGELA DULCIMER-SMITH, director of sales under Julian Cragg.

FREDDIE FEAR, director of production under Julian Cragg.

PHILIPPA FOX-TAYLOR, Wales' then Cragg's secretary.

GEORGE, bartender at the Wayfarers' Club.

HELMUT VON GILDENKRANTZ, editor and protégé of Lady Moira, friend.

PETER GLYFFE, editor.

ELIZABETH GWYNNE, editor of the 'Mothers' Help' series.

MAXIMILIAN HERDER, composer, author, friend of Robert Racine.

MARGOT HERDER, wife of Maximilian.

HOKUSAI, Japanese artist of the Edo period.

BURTON LOCKE, art collector.

THOMAS MAGGUINNESS, author, humorist, friend of Robert Racine.

MICHELANGELO, sculptor and poet.

MILDRED, proofreader composite of sandpaper and silk, sometimes known as Mildew.

LADY MOIRA, the Baroness Threshold.

MOSES, son of Levi, Jewish prophet and poet.

HUMPHREY PALL, production manager.

JEREMIAH PEACH, poet and train conductor.

MRS PEACH, his inspiration.

PIPICACA, dogs.

THE PRIME MINISTER, a bookseller's Neville Chamberlain in hobnailed boots.

JEANNINE RACINE, wife of Root.

GENERAL BERTRAM ('BARNEY') SMALLWOOD, Wales' colleague; chairman of the holding company.

JILL SULLIVAN, secretary.

SUZANNE, sister of Jeannine Racine.

TIM SWARBRICK, editor.

AUBREY THRALE, Wales' other colleague; chairman of the Wales Trust.

WINIFRED WALTERS, Thrale's secretary.

I have just pinned it up in front of me on the wall in the gardenroom, above the table where I like to work on clement days, and I am amazed at my handiwork: any one of the names is enough to make the pen leap forward automatically on the page. But don't panic. There may be exits and entrances, but none of them will be 'developed' – your province entirely. What interests me about people is everything we don't know about them, which, when all's said and done, is everything we think we know about them.

The Third Envelope

Overnight ferry to the Isle of Wace. Extremely heavy weather: the boat is creaking, the stewards are damning and blasting, the crockery in the dining saloon has all come down with a smash. My stomach seems to be made of castiron, but the man in the bunk above retches steadily into his tin cup. At intervals the boat hits things, or things hit it, with a dreadful bang. School of blind whales? No matter as long as we make it in a single piece; but for Jeannine and the cats I'd be tempted to say no matter point final. One lives for others and in spite of others. Because of Jeannine, in spite of Cragg; because of Wales, in spite of Thrale. Thrilling Thrale, the handcuffed pixie. Wales wasn't the only one who could deal out blows under the chin.[1]

It would have been nice to have been able to bring Jeannine, but there wasn't enough money. There is never enough money. Remind me to speak to Thrale about emolument for the literary executor – grind it out of him if need be. Wales could not have assumed that I would do all this just to pass the time of day, or could he? Since the blackmailing appears to have succeeded, he may conclude that it is I who should do the paying.

Horace, I want you to understand that I am not on my knees – far from it. Jeannine and I could sell the house and just get the hell out. I could change my name and grow a beard and we could rent bicycles on Fermentora. But I refuse to panic. After all, I have not been invited to throw everything overboard, I have been invited to collect a manuscript *à la mémoire du Maistre*. We shall see what Thrale says once I have

....

[1] Ed.: *Soubriquet*, 15th-century connotation. Racine appears to have caught etymologisis from Wales.

38

accomplished the present mission. Meanwhile – creak, crash, bash, retch – reminds me of a pathetic line I once jotted down on a piece of paper as I was trying to scrub a kitchen floor:

> smile, floor, smile, he sweats
> and the cloth smacks, smears, whacks
> and the black, base floor only smirks
> and says me smile's for a lady.

The words effaced themselves, I am glad to say, in a wash of dissolving ink as I went along. And now the sea has taken the trouble to scrub the dirt off the side of the ship, not knowing that it is not the ship that matters. The dirt is not on ships and not on floors, it is inside all of us, and it may be that we shall never get it clean. Still, there is time, and as sleep will not descend I may as well occupy myself with this, my search for order in chaos, at least until the wretch aloft misses his cup. Where to begin? Shall we try to attack it point by point? One, Wales detested Cragg yet tolerated him. Why? Two, Cragg brought in the Trilogy and Wales stood back, allowing them to pour his reputation down the drain. Why? Three, one of the foremost publishers of our time and place, the publisher's publisher, Wales, slowly and deliberately made all the wrong moves, and having made them disappeared before the game could be played out. Why? Four, to what extent are Cragg, the Trilogy, the holding company and the trust, you and I and the rest of them in the house the instruments of his purpose? What was his purpose? What *is* his purpose?

(Fascinating monograph to be written on the inventor of the questionmark, one Interlinneus, crookbacked Basilian monk of the fourth century of our era. How did civilization proceed before him??? Are there arcane languages to be dug up in which the questionmark never appears but is simply indicated by a repetition of the opening phrase are there.)

I wonder if you will agree, before too many layers have been scrubbed away, that it would be wise to proceed as in the apocryphal biography of the Hon. Terence Twerp: that way I shall be able to deal with material which is still fresh in the memory. For the rest, we can set up a system of five boxes, one for each decade of Wales' life, and throw material into them as it is revealed or reconstructed. The method is the archaeologist's: dig, scrub, classify, and glue the pieces together. If Wales wishes to end up as a pickpocked statue with half his limbs missing, that is his risk and our pleasure.

Back to the episode of the disappearing books. I now see that Wales began his housecleaning at, or almost coinciding with, the moment when Julian Cragg arrived. As Cragg's influence became felt, more books disappeared and Wales spent less and less time in the house. It was as if, after a lifetime of reading synopses, he had finally decided to square accounts by reading the books themselves.

(I have no way of establishing this: Mrs Carruthers told me she never once saw him read a book in all the years she was with him. What, then, did he do when he was not eating or sleeping or hobnobbing with friends? According to Mrs C he used to sit at his desk staring out over Tricorn Square in the direction of a particularly fine old birch tree behind the church. From time to time he was seen writing his notes. I blush to think that he must often have noticed me sitting there reading manuscripts during office hours; in those days I had no idea he had a window overlooking the square).

I have not dealt with the aborted bloodbath, Cragg's first move. It was designed evidently to establish his authority and diminish Wales'. Those of us who were fired – Tim Swarbrick, Humphrey Pall, Helena and myself – were to be rehired the following week on Cragg's terms. No mention of Peter Glyffe or Helmut von Gildenkrantz. We never found out what Cragg's terms were because Wales countermanded the whole thing in a fine fury the following day, controlling himself only just enough to save a vestige of Cragg's face. It would not have served his purpose, it seems, to let Cragg walk out so soon after his arrival.

> There has been a misunderstanding at the executive level, and a failure to read the mind of the chairman. The administrative changes envisaged in yesterday's memorandum are hereby annulled.

That was all Wales' memo said, and it was a bad moment for Cragg – almost as bad as being propelled through the window. But it was quickly and conspicuously oiled over. Wales invited Cragg to his room that same day, and all was cordiality and bland smiles for at least a week. Tim Swarbrick and I resumed breathing; Humphrey never believed in it in the first place. Moot made sardonic jokes, and Helena carried on as if nothing more substantial had occurred than a tentative tweaking of her finelyturned bottom.

She was not to concern herself about her bottom until some weeks later. Wales was more and more absent, and he had said no more about it to her than to anyone else. I expect that was a source of sadness to

Helena: after all, they had been more than close, and she responded by doing her work well. No one ever orchestrated a literary lunch more grandly than Helena. But as the days passed, Wales' remoteness began to worry her just as it did us. 'I am suffering from a severe case of the Pees and Dees,' she said to me one day, meaning the weekly executive meeting at which we proposed our ideas and the Trilogy disposed of them. For the first time I noticed that lines had begun to etch themselves into her face, and when she moved it was not quite with the bounce of earlier days. 'So am I,' I replied, and it was the truth. (We got along well, Helena and I, why not confess? Had I been a less highly developed prude I might have played Oedipus to her Jocasta; but neither of us was made for the tragic muse.) 'Everything I suggest is automatically squelched,' she continued, 'have you noticed? I thought it would be a good thing to have a party for Horace Bentwhistle's latest, but no go. They want the money spent on athletes and film stars. Can you imagine all that bleached hair billowing about in the same room? Yes, I suppose you can.'

Somehow it had escaped Helena's attention that we had all had the same treatment from the Trilogy, I suppose because we got it separately: von Gildenkrantz the first week, myself the next, and so on, divide and rule. At the beginning it didn't concern me much because Wales had approved a substantial backlog of work which I then had to follow up. Von Gildenkrantz was the first to be cut down for the simple reason that he had so little to do. Moot went in one morning and found he had to wait half an hour before he could see them, as if he had gone out to the dentist. 'I am shot down in flames,' he said, slapping his files, 'in flames completely. Do you know what they want me to do? The men in the life of Heidi Schmucke!' And he stormed out promising to have words with Lady Moira.

My turn came the following week when I was called in supposedly to give them a rundown on work already in hand. They had acquainted themselves with that, of course, and because it already bore Wales' imprimatur they did not dwell on it. No, I was there, it seemed, mainly to be jollied up with coffee and sticky buns, the sticky buns being the inspiration of Angela whose metabolism, as she explained it herself, shunned vinegar and cried out for sweets. You see, it was by no means clear what our new relationship was to be; nobody had taken the trouble to define it. Chesterton, as editorial director, outranked me, but he was behaving as if he was unaware of it. Angela and Freddie now outranked Helena and Humphrey Pall, but they were not about to offend 'the workers' because they had no wish to do the work themselves. The whole thing was a ridiculous game of blind man's buff, and no one, least of all myself, appeared to know who was blind. All we were able to grasp, really, was that they were Cragg's men (let's be fair from the start and lump Angela in with the boys), that Wales tolerated them as he tolerated Cragg, and that they would function as a sort of directorate or layer of cloud interposed between us and the gods. Much as I hate the thought of revising Harper Cabot upwards, I feel I must include him among the reigning powers; after all, he was the Cabot of Cabot and Raw, and he must have backed Cragg's initiative in bringing in the Trilogy as a way of propagating precious Creative Conflict, you see, in the placid backwater of Great Conduit Street. What transpired then over the sticky buns was a sort of triangular congratulatory session in which they agreed among themselves how splendid it would be – wouldn't it? – if the list could be made more dynamic, more modern, more *more*. After all, tastes and reading habits were changing at such a vertiginous pace – were they not? – that no publisher could afford to stand still. Bibles had built Wales, and thank God for that. What could we think of that would do for today's list what the Bible had done for it in the past? Wasn't there some new direction we might pursue, something that would bring fruit because it was already rooted, invisibly, in the culture of our time, something we might count on to lift the list out of the choirstalls and carry it in triumph to the launchingpad?[2]

All this was argument developed by Angela: she had been delegated by the other two to send up the rocket and was relishing the assignment. Was it not Churchill who said that a man could go anywhere in this country if he could speak well in public? If so and even so, Angela had learned the lesson. Jeremy Chesterton was a mere pipesmoking don beside her – the pipe, for reasons of intellectual economy, was deliberately allowed to get in the way – and Freddie Fear was a marionette who dropped puns the way rabbits drop turds. But Angela was the real article, a disappointed Prime Minister who at all costs must never allow the disappointment to show.

– In a word, she said, licking a dab of icing from a long and singularly crooked forefinger, what is the religion of our time? If we succeed in isolating it, we shall have no great difficulty in finding someone to write its Bible for us. Do you not agree, Freddie?

Freddie disentangled himself from his heap at the bottom of a chair.

– Amen naturally, dear Angela. Amen and the Lord be praised.

. . . .

[2] Angela's mixture, I assure you, not mine. Chesterton managed a faint smile.

At which point all three of them looked at me, Chesterton tamping his pipe, Fear chuckling and winking wisely, and Angela coughing modestly into her cup. My silence may have put them off. In the end Angela got up, a performance in itself because she reaches up like a polevault, and virtually as thin.

– Well, I think that's the big assignment, she said. Meanwhile Jeremy will have to freshen up the list a bit, won't you Jeremy?

– Something like that, said Chesterton, and the meeting broke up.

Is it not the rhinoceros that defecates all over the countryside, hoping that by so hanging out his signs he will ward off territorial threats? This one, if I may melt the three of them down and pour them into the same shapeless hide, had unloaded at the door of my room, blocking the corridor and all the entrances and exits of the house. Wales & Wales had once stood for quality. What would happen now, I had not the least doubt, is that Chesterton would go for popularity – not twenty times out of a hundred, as most of us do, but all the way through the list. And that is precisely what happened. In place of Graham Grand we got Malcolm Spinks, the motorcar racer who came back to thrill us all after being burned alive three times. There was much furtive talk of the eventual emergence, country by country, of a *World Anthology of Party Jokes*. Jessica Birdwell was quietly dropped: quietly, because Chesterton hadn't the guts to tell her that one of his new readers had left the typewritten copy of *The Fertile Stone*, her latest, in the waitingroom of a birthcontrol clinic. Underground Occupations became a series called Top Dog, profiles of the monumentally rich – and so on all down the line. The rationale was Angela's, the execution Jeremy's, and Freddie threw in ideas for titles as they went along, notably *Rags to Ritzes* which owes its success more, I think, to the lady's pudenda than to the genius of Mr Fear.

It was eventually made known that the Bekorgakov anniversary book or *Festschrift*, as the pedants like to call it, had been 'postponed' in favour of *The Seven Charms of Adolf Hitler*. I was certain that Wales would come down on them, but no, nothing happened, nothing was said. It was at this point that I learned that Wales had not been seen in the house for several days. Unobservant? You may think so, but you must understand that I was to refer all new work to Chesterton, and as the old already had Wales' approval I had less and less reason to go into his room. It was Philippa, finally, who told me about these remarkable absences of his. A day here, a day there, eventually two and three in a row. Curious, to say the least, on the part of a man who had never failed to appear on any occasion except for trips and rare bouts of 'flu. Was he ill? Philippa said he showed no sign of it; on the contrary, he moved with the same brisk step and went about pumpumming Beethoven symphonies under his breath with the usual zest. And then toward the end, when he did come in, it was for the purpose of closeting himself with Cragg for half an hour behind closed doors. Even so, evidence of Creative Conflict could clearly be heard. Finally when he learned of the loss of Jessica Birdwell's typescript, he mounted one of his furies (sound travelled well when the windows of the courtyard were open) and Chesterton was obliged to ask the lady for the manuscript copy. *The Fertile Stone* was added to the list, and Jessica is with us still.

During all this time – and I am speaking of the three months preceding Wales' disappearance – nothing whatever was said about the 'interesting developments' that were supposed to make up for the various knocks I'd had to absorb. The Trilogy had come in over my head and Angela was telling us all what to do and how to do it. Freddie Fear, now responsible for production, was systematically proposing titles and making them stick. Chesterton, nominally editorial director, went along as if editorial policy had become the responsibility of sales. How long would it be before some intolerable unpleasantness were assigned to me? Would I then go back to Wales with my resignation or would I try to brazen it out?

The questions came very much to the fore with the suspension of the new poetry series. New poetry, as you know, was my dada, and the series had become the best of its kind. Some part of Wales' reputation had come to depend on it, in the upper echelons at least. I was now faced with the prospect of having to close it down, and that meant not just loss of face for me but worse: loss of friends. Loss, one might also predict, of one's place at the banquet table of the Muse, for like any other activity in life, poetry is politics. As the notices went out I began, for the first time in my life, to lose sleep. The telephone rang more frequently, and the voices at the other end were less cordial than they had been before. It was then that I began to understand what fragile things we are, and how brief our day can be. You see, Horace, I had never really been challenged. Until you reach a certain threshold of age, salary, position, prestige, your future is never really in doubt: you are there to be used, and as long as a minimal competence is obtained, some employer, *any* employer, will be there to use you. Such was my story, and in normal times when massive unemployment is not here to haunt us, it is universal. But one day something in the air (condensation of a ghost's breath on the mirror?) takes it upon itself to breathe elsewhere, and you are lost. The how and the why are beyond you, invisible, inaudible, impalpable – beyond imagination. And so your dreams turn sour and some of them begin to stink of the grave, you are wrenched awake at four o'clock in the morning and your wife begins to grumble about your fading interest in sex. Is there an answer? You say to yourself of course there must be an answer. If there is a challenge you are required to respond. Muscle meets muscle; a contest ensues. I suppose there are people whose entire lifestrategies are based on the assumption of winning (as if, in the end, one could); in my case, when they took the poetry away from me, it was the opposite possibility that occurred. It was as if everything I represented had been locked away in a steel vault for safekeeping; now, from one day to the next, the steel was reduced to something malleable, glutinous, and cheap.

So, and inevitably, I arrived at the point where it all boiled over, and I went in to see Wales again. He was not there. He had not been seen for days. Philippa tried to reach him at the flat and he was not there either. I had gone in full of fire and attack and there was no way of releasing any of it. The following day I came down with 'flu, and it kept me in bed the better part of a week.

Ten days later, the disappearance. I was deprived of the only force against which I could exercise my strength. I had been pushing against a wall, the wall was removed, and I fell off the edge into space. I am still there, spinning, whirling, turning in my sleep. Do you remember Byron: 'To withdraw *myself* from *myself* . . . has ever been my sole, my entire, my sincere motive in scribbling.' I could no longer bring it off. I had taken up another existence. I had moved all my belongings into an unfamiliar apartment. A name was lettered on the door. It was written in a language I could not read.

*   *   *

We filed off the ferry in a headsplitting screech of seagulls: my fellow passengers had progressed beyond green into grey. I had had two hours of sleep. I fell into a little café off the waterfront and felt slightly better after coffee and a raisin bun, though the boat still rocked underfoot as I went along in the direction that had been pointed out for me by a kind woman in the street.

A la mémoire du Maistre. There are various Waces in English history reaching back to medieval times; in this century one of them was Dean of Canterbury. That much I had learned before my departure. But my Maistre was clearly a Frenchman. Magister, maegester, maistre, maître, master, mister. The word *maistre* enters the stream of the French language about 1080, and appears as late as Rabelais, veering off in

1532. So we situate our man between 1080 and 1532, an interval of a mere four and a half centuries. Child's play, my dear Watson. If anything was known about him at all it was doubtless to be discovered at the central library, and it was in this direction that I now turned my steps.

Maistre Wace was indeed known to the librarians: he had achieved some renown as the author of historical epics in the style of Geoffrey of Monmouth, whose contemporary he was. Geoffrey is thought to have died in 1155, and in the same year a work described as an 'adaptation' of Geoffrey's history was attributed to Robert Wace, himself.

There was more, but to go further would have led me into an extended engagement not only with the matter of Britain, but with the matter of Troy and the sons of Aeneas as well. As I paused over the reference wondering what to do next, the librarian came up to me and said, 'He was perhaps the chief literary product of the island. A plaque was dedicated to him, Lord knows when. You will see it on the wall when you go out.'

I thanked him and went out into the small square facing the library, a particularly pleasant place with trees and tubs of geraniums and a seagull sitting on the head of a laurelwreathed hero brandishing a scroll. Himself? The library is a splendid Renaissance style edifice with white window surrounds set against the dusky rose colour one finds on houses in Italy. On the wall, more or less in the centre of the building, cut into a rectangle of stone, was this:

À la mémoire de
MAISTRE WACE
poète Normand du XIIe siècle
qui naquit dans cette isle
JE DI È DIRAI KE JO SUI
WACE DE L'ISLE DE GERSUI
ROMAN DE ROU

It was eleven o'clock. I decided to buy a paper and read it, during the hour that remained, in the pub at the corner of the square: the pubs on the island open early. But I made more progress with my pint than with the newspaper, because along the way it occurred to me that Wales, himself, might appear at noon, and what the devil would I say to him if he did? Panic. Every thought that occurred to me was immediately wiped out by another. I was totally at sea, knocked this way and that by the relentless washingmachine of the waves.

At five minutes to the hour I was back in the square. There was a bench immediately opposite the Wace plaque; I sat down on it and waited. Just as a bell somewhere nearby began sounding the hour, I heard a door close behind me and footsteps come down the steps of the library and across the narrow pavement that separated me from the building. I turned and saw a girl coming toward me with a paper bag in her hand. What happened then, or did not happen, is difficult to explain. She was extraordinarily beautiful, one of the most exquisite beings I have ever seen. She smiled – can you picture Garbo greeting me there in the sunshine, or Helen of Troy? – and handed me the paper bag. 'I was asked to give you this,' she said, and walked away from me without another word. Within seconds she had disappeared through an archway leading to the parish church at the end of the square. I peered into the paper bag: it was she, none other, granddaughter of the first. Finally – it seemed hours though it could not have been more than a minute or two – I threw off my paralysis and ran after her. The courtyard of the church and the small passageway alongside were empty. The church door was locked. I could not find her in any of the streets leading off at the other end.

On my way back to the square I stopped, once more fastening myself to reality, to read a notice fixed to the wall at the entrance of the church: *Every Saturday coffee and biscuits in the Church House.* A passerby directed me to the house itself: it was closed. I returned to the library, to the same person who had looked out the reference to Robert Wace, and asked him if he had seen an extraordinarily beautiful girl in the library at noon: not an eyelash, though I could sense a certain wariness in his reply.

I went back to my bench and opened the matrioshka. Same grey vellum notepaper, same green handwriting, new message:

Put on your bulletproof vest. Next stop Vindobona.

There was nothing more to be done on Wace's island. I looked up from the bench and noticed that the pub where I had waited for noon to arrive was called The Battle of Gersui. I could not help wondering who had lost that one and how many, if any, of the warriors had survived.

The Fourth Envelope

Just as a matter of interest, have you asked yourself how in God's name we are to proceed? Am I going to be required to travel round the world waiting on public benches for the next injunction, and the next one after that? And what am I to do while we are waiting, interview everyone in the house and everyone he knew outside? And if I did, what would it be worth? Does Wales actually *want* all this? Where are you, Interlinneus, in this my hour of need?

I am counting on you, Horace; your memories go back further in time.

We have agreed, have we not, that I am to concentrate on the immediate past, the parts that I know more or less firsthand. But what about the present, what are we to do with the here and now? What if Wales has taken it upon himself to torture us indefinitely – obstacle piled upon obstacle, matrioshka pursuing matrioshka, green on green? All very well and good for you to counsel patience, and you are right to remind me that we are being paid. But I am not as conveniently removed from all this as you are. I tell myself there hasn't been time to put down everything that needs to be said, but it isn't the truth. The truth is that I can't bear to put it down. It's too much like death. Listen, Horace, listen to this. He has invented a way of stopping the entire house. Not even Cragg has been spared. Cragg, who seemed so invulnerable, so doubly protected: Easter Island stone, we had all assumed, held erect by the terra firma of Harriet's millions. How wrong we were.

I can try to explain. But before I do so I intend to go to Thrale. The whiphand, the visible whiphand, is now his. He must know a great deal more, and it's time he spoke up. For instance, why will he not let us see Wales' will? Why has he sat there, impenetrable, while Wales & Wales has very nearly ground to a halt? Are you listening up there in the North?

Authors still rush up to the door in their clanging ambulances; diagnoses are made, forceps applied. Then why is the result so sickly and thin?

I shall have to see Thrale and make him talk, that's all. If he refuses I will take the matter into my own hands. Wales is there, you know, lurking somewhere in the foliage, sneering at us, shovelling us into his pit. If not, I am what the court says I am: some kind of fool taken possession of by a pornographic dream. Provisionally, at least, I intend to believe in myself. Wales is there, somewhere, playing on his heap of dung. I am going to find him.

Two days later. Thrale's secretary says he is out of town and I must wait. Very well. Back to the bedpans. What was it, a postdisappearance loss of confidence on all sides? Not a bit of it: there are enough manuscripts in the house to support the place like pillars, and some of them are bound to be worth saving. But how shall we get to any of them now, beyond a few layers at the top? Painful as it may be, I am obliged to take you back to the Harper Cabot days, to the contamination following which, one now sees, nothing could ever be the same.

One of Cabot's ideas seemed to have been worth pursuing. It surfaced as the result of Harper's natural snobbery. He was the kind of man who systematically weaselled his way into racquets clubs wherever he went – and he'd have gone for polo if the people he wanted to meet had played that. To give him credit, he went about it methodically, beginning with squash lessons which gave him a convincing technique, and moving along through friendly games with good players to the level of tournament play. Eventually he got close to certain individuals in the American diplomatic corps who played regularly at the club in Panda Place: good business, that, because with their help he was able to gain access, through the various foreign embassies, to some of the best printers in Czechoslovakia, Romania, and Poland, whose prices undercut ours in the AngloSaxon world by margins that were extremely worthwhile. Before long most of the colour printing coming out of Cabot and Raw was being done over there. Nothing much new in that; everybody does it in Holland, Belgium, Italy, Yugoslavia; what was so brilliant about going farther afield? The answer in a word was quantity. In the end Harper persuaded them to print not only colour in the bleak world of the commissar, but blackandwhite as well.

Cragg learned about this and naturally was interested in following. But as the pipeline had been set up in the first instance to function from New York, it was thought best to send our own typescripts to Cabot and Raw, and from there on direct flights to Prague, Bucharest, or wherever.

And so, you see, the editorial staff of Cabot and Raw got a good sniff at our prepared manuscripts before they went off, and more and more of them were to their liking: they even went so far, surprise, as to buy *The Fertile Stone*. We should have known it would go that way: the advantages of the edited over the unedited are obvious, and an immense temptation to those of us who live buried under mounds of the raw material. Cragg was delighted, Cabot's editors were delighted, and wheyfaced commissars in Gdansk were gradually turning pink with their unexpected afflux of Americaninspired vodka.

Enter Wales. I quote his memorandum directly from the files: it was addressed to the managing director, the Trilogy, and the senior editors.

> It has come to our attention that an increasing number of books bearing the Wales imprint are being produced in the American language, a development which can only be attributed, it is to be hoped, to collective oversight. As we in this country have not yet ascended nor descended to the status of a colony of the United States, I ask you to ensure, henceforth, that our work be expressed and presented to our readers *without exception* in the idiom of Her Majesty the Queen. Titles already published in American are to be sold forthwith to Cabot and Raw or remaindered on the other side of the water. Those for which demand remains steady will be reprinted.

Panic. Cragg, whose precious balancesheet had taken a direct hit, spoke to no one for a week, not even to the Trilogy. Chesterton had to make an inventory of everything that had been proofread by the devils of Cabot and Raw not only while Harper was with us but, to be safe, of all the books we had bought from America before his, Chesterton's arrival. Angela was obliged to analyse the performance of the entire list title by title, and Freddie was actually observed in action, stoking up the boiler. It was the first serious work they had done since they came into the house.

Chesterton put in a very difficult ten days in coming up with his answer, a list of no fewer than one hundred and eightyseven titles, some of them spread out in various stages of production between New York, Bucharest, Prague, and Gdansk, others already mouldering in the depository. Fortunately or unfortunately Angela was able to demonstrate that only a third of them were worth reprinting, but that still left us sixtytwo titles to proofread from guggle to zatch. The result was that everything else we had scheduled had to be put back, which soon had the authors snapping at us like demented poodles. Chesterton pressganged all of us into proofreading service – Angela, von Gildenkrantz, Glyffe, Pall, Swarbrick, Liz Gwynne, Jill Sullivan, Sally Bates, myself – and there was this curious pause during which nothing could be heard throughout the house but the silent mastication of American prose. One of the wags – I suspect Swarbrick – fashioned a plausible Uncle Sam out of bits of old cloth and hanged him in effigy from the tower; it dangled down into the courtyard in front of Harper Cabot's window and caused him to retreat to the safety of the squash club until the antiAmerican wave had washed over. And it was a relief when it did. We had lost, in all, the better part of two months. Faces had begun to grow blank with tedium, and because there was nothing to talk about everybody stopped going to the pub.

Throughout all this Wales maintained his usual detachment and, when he was there, went on pumpumming Beethoven symphonies as if nothing had occurred. Philippa told me he went into a huddle over the accounts with Selwyn Bream, once. Apart from that, there was no outward sign of concern or further involvement with the British Secession, as it came to be known, affectionately, to us all, and under the stress of the moment I actually began to feel some sympathy for our fellowsufferers, the Trilogy. Freddie's puns had dried up and Angela appeared to have been given not only pause but (pass this along to Magguinness) menopause. Chesterton wore the same stained and threadbare jacket throughout the episode, as if he had retired from the house in favour of the garden, hoping that somehow things would grow better there. What happened, of course, is that they grew worse. You know what happens when a publisher remains absent from his desk for a week, whether from 'flu, holidays, or too much devotion to the taps. The manuscripts pile up. The proofs pile up. The letters pile up. Now ask yourself what happens when, in effect, you are absent from your desk for two months. Sheer cashgripping anal bind. Not fun.

As for the rights and wrongs of Wales' diktat, there was not, below the level of the Trilogy, a word of discussion: it was taken for granted that the American language would be cordoned off on the south side of Great Conduit Street and permitted no deeper incursion into the British psyche than the toy department of Gordon's Breeches and Hats. How the American toy industry had managed to penetrate Gordon's in the first place was not a matter for topical discussion.

I expect it would cost most of us, Wales included, no great investment in linguistic pride to admit that the English language is pretty much a painted lady – not a bad reflection, come to think of it, of the English mind itself. I have always felt this was its chief glory. Let a little foreign influence creep in under the skirts: what better way – fast in, fast out – to dispose of it? In similar circumstances the French, urged on by the Academy and the President of the Republic, stiffen their backs, throw up the barricades, and lob dictionaries at all passing offenders: verbal version of the Maginot Line. The American language, I have come to believe, is a succession of trains passing through. Remember what trains were like when we were small boys, all huffs and puffs and sniffs and whooooooooooahs? The American language is like that, whooooooooooah one day and zap the next. How long did it take to ingest, digest, and excrete such abominations as 'I'm *into* computers' or such infantilisms as 'hippie', 'yippie', 'junkie', and 'grass'? Of course there is more where all that came from, and on the next train. But it will not remain in the station very long. What does remain is selfcorrecting, a collective memory of the good noises, huff, puff, sniff, whooooooooooooah. The bad stuff trickles out of the toilets as we go along. Then am I saying that Wales is wrong? Not at all; find inconsistency in it if you like. Ecoute, we do not even know what individual words stand for; subjective experience has so coloured everything that the best we can manage is an impressionistic blur. All the more need, therefore, for those influences that try to create and maintain the illusion of the welldefined. Like Wales I am for the dictionary and against gabble, but I want to know what the dictionary is used for. I am not sure that Wales cares, unless Celtic disdain and managerial fascism can be translated as expressions of concern.

When I arrived in England I spelled colour 'color' and called a car's bonnet a hood. I soon fixed that. What has not changed and cannot be replaced, is the longing I feel, whenever I find myself watching a cricket match, for a hotdog with slops of oily mustard on it and hot coffee in a paper cup. A cup of tea and a slice of railway cake will not do. And that, I fear, is language: not words in museums but the odour given off by them as a function of their time and place.

Forgive the digression: all I meant by it was to say that as usual I am for Wales and against him, just as I was and remain in what became a far more serious affair, though it began simply enough as another linguistic jape. Again I quote directly from Wales' own memorandum which followed the British Secession at an interval of three months.

I have come to the conclusion that far too much proto-crypto has been creeping into our published work as the result, no doubt, of what is sometimes called the exertion of the educated mind. The English language, I must remind you, is a modern tongue of predominantly Teutonic origin. Accommodating as it may be, you cannot bend modern English to fit the angularities of Attic Greek, or its derivatives. Yet I have noted references in some of our latest work to cases of 'chthonic phthisis' (a mis-spelling, I hope, of a more plausible phrase) and an increasing fondness for 'synapses' and even 'sphenoid' writing. None of this, I am sure you will agree, is particularly synchronic. Indeed, were we to allow the practice to flourish, it would lead inevitably to early synchrondrosis of the reader's mind, not to speak of the passably literate world in which we live. Accordingly I must ask you to eliminate all vocabulary of Greek origin from manuscripts, proofs, and forthcoming editions of work already in print. Your praiseworthy efforts in expurgating American influence from the list persuade me that this is entirely feasible.

The day the Greek Injunction came down we were sitting in Chesterton's office, wondering what to do next, when Harper burst into the meeting, flapping his sails. 'Jesus,' he said, 'what are we going to do about Gloria Hymen?' There was a moment of silence; then everybody, the Trilogy, Peter Glyffe, myself, and even Harper began to laugh. Glorious Gloria's latest, a number called *Sex Through Nine Innings*, had long since passed a million on the New York bestseller list, and Cragg had bought it. Liz Gwynne was two-thirds of the way into her 'translation'. Now, if we were to follow Wales to the letter, we should have to translate Gloria. It was too absurd. Absurd and paralysing (Gk *paralusis*). I carried my tea back to my own room and began thumbing through the dictionary, making notes as I thumbed. This is what came of it, my reply to Wales.

It appears that we are going to need to compile a list of Greek words eliminating, in the first instance, the offending *lexicon*, for use as a temporary procedural guide. I wonder if, as a way of getting on with it, I may have your comments on the following. Eventually, of course, it can be arranged for convenient consultation in the order of the alephbeth.

Testament. Apparently the word has come down to us as a mistranslation of the Greek *diathēke*. To be on the safe side I suggest we use 'dispensation' as in 'The Old Dispensation'.

Genesis (Gk *gignomai*). 'The First Book' offers advantages, but it might lead us on monotonously to 'The Thirty-Ninth Book' and beyond. I suggest 'The Creation'.

Exodus (Gk *exodos*). Departure.

Leviticus (Gk *leuitikos*). We shall have to fall back on the Hebrew.

Deuteronomy (Gk *deuteronomion*). The Second Law.

Pentateuch (Gk *pentateukhos*). The First Five.

Pentecost (Gk *pentēcostē*). Literally 'the fiftieth' as in 'The Festival of the Fiftieth Day'.

Psalms (Gk *psalmos*). We cannot use 'hymns', which is also Greek. The only remaining possibility appears to be the phrase 'Sacred Songs', though the Latin *sacer* may be suspect: we do not have an etymological dictionary of Latin in the house.

Ecclesiastes (Gk *ekklēsiastikos*). Speaker, if there are those among us who dislike the sound of 'preacher'. 'Clergyman' is contaminated.

Prophet (Gk *prophētēs*). Revealer, as in 'The Revealer Isaiah'.

Messiah (Gk *Messias*). 'The Anointed' would seem to be less contentious than 'The Deliverer' or 'The Liberator'.

Gospel has its feet in the Old English 'godspel', which to my mind is far more euphonious (sounds better). Can we not, while we are about changing things, change this too? I do not know why some translators favour the expression 'good news'. The burden of the news, in the light of what went on at and since Golgotha, would seem to have been almost unrelievedly bad.

Epistle (Gk *epistolē*). Letter.

Apostle (Gk *apostolos*). Missionary. Travelling salesman.

Epiphany (Gk *epiphaneia*). Manifestation.

Eucharist (Gk *eukharistos*). Supper.

Evangelist (Gk *euaggelistēs*). The ideal substitute probably does not exist; it would appear to be an amalgam (mixture) of teacher, preacher, and writer of the Gospel. I suggest the neologism (new word) 'Godspeller'.

Hebrews (Gk *Hebraios*). Jews.

Jew (Gk *Ioudaios*). We shall have little choice but to fall back on the word *y'hudi* from the language of 'the people from the other side of the river'.

Israel (Gk *Israēl*). The original *yisreal*, 'striver with God', is obviously too close for comfort. We shall have to devise something like 'Godstruth' or 'Godson'. During any period of feminist ascendancy the latter might prove dangerous, and doubtless the Moslems would object to the former. Suggestions, please.

Christ (Gk *Khristos*). Anointed, as in 'Jesus Anointed'.

Jesus (Gk *Iesoûs*). Saviour, as in 'I believe in Saviour Anointed . . .'
God. Teutonic to the mists of time. We are saved.

> This, of course, is only a beginning as the original translation
> of *The Bedside Bible* comes from the same Greek that supplied
> the raw material for the Authorized Version. It will therefore
> have to be examined word by word by a committee of Greek
> professors of God enjoying special competence in the English
> language. You will not need to be reminded that the *Septuagint*
> was originally thought to be the work of seventy Palestinian
> *y'hudi* who were shut away on the island of Pharos for a
> period of seventy-two days. This was later found to be false.
> The Old Dispensation was translated by Egyptian *y'hudi*
> who, for all we know, took seventy-two years or longer to
> complete the job. I am not sure that Wales & Wales Limited
> is suitably equipped to follow their example.
>   I have nearly forgotten to say that the word 'Bible' itself
> is Greek and will have to be purged. As the Greek noun was
> used to describe a roll of papyrus *(papuros)*, I suggest that we
> retreat to the Teutonic word 'scroll', which seems to have
> an affinity with the Old French *escroue*, or 'screw'. Thus *The
> Bedside Bible* becomes 'The Bedside Scroll', and nobody will
> know the difference.

I sent copies of this to the entire editorial staff – the same list of people
to whom Wales had addressed his own memorandum – and it made me
the house hero for a day. Von Gildenkrantz dealt me a hearty Teutonic
clap on the shoulder, and even Angela favoured me with a sympathetic
smile, as if to commend me for a particularly apt demonstration of the
art of harakiri. Then Wales came back with this, addressed to the same
crowd.

> Your 'Saviour Anointed' sounds a bit dated, unless the
> application of shaving-lotion were thought to produce rever-
> berations in the contemporary mind. I myself am doubtful
> about it as I consider shaving-lotion absurd. One way of
> dealing with it might be to return to the Aramaic and try to
> reconstruct a likeness suitable to our own time and place. I
> am certain that the sound of it would in no way resemble
> what has been given to us by the Greeks. This is as it should
> be, because the message of the book, or scroll, as you call

55

it, is one of discovery and rediscovery implying a work of translation and retranslation forever amen. As long as forever lasts. Meanwhile, thanks to your researches, we are reminded that all present complications are the fault of the pedants and the Greeks. For my part, I have always regretted that the Saviour was not called something simple, like Sam. In the interests of that same simplicity – which ought to be made the watchword of the enterprise – I suggest we translate Jesus Christ as *The Leader* whenever it is not possible, after the famous example of Rider Haggard, to call Him *He*.

As for the rest, you are clearly working along the right lines and are encouraged to continue. I rather like the idea of *The Bedside Scroll.* I do not believe that a committee of seventy God-seekers or seventy linguists would be any more useful than a committee of seventy dishwashers, who, after all, are experts in getting things clean. If each of you will take a letter of the dictionary at a time, I have no doubt that the offending vocabulary can be made to disappear within a year. You are not asked to put anything in, you are asked to take Greek out – an operation which is faster, easier, and, as you will discover, infinitely more satisfying than any effort to burden the language with lumber, old or new. Once that is complete you will find our own excellent tongue rushing in like Shakespeare to fill the void.

P.S. On re-reading the above I find that it rests on an alarmingly thick layer (I was about to say 'sub-stratum') of Latin. I am not at all happy about this, and I propose to come back to it once we have dealt with the earlier malady.

You can imagine what that led to: mutterings behind closed doors, Cragg grimfaced; the Trilogy stopped speaking to me once they had decided that I should not have gone to Wales over their heads. Even Helena, Helena of the beatific calm, confessed to me that she could no longer read Wales' mind. By this time Cragg had probably realized that a direct confrontation would serve no purpose: he had had too many of those. Two days went by in which nothing happened, but there was the feeling of an explosion in the air. What form it would take and when it would go off, no one could tell. No one, that is, but Cragg. I tried to guess what he would do: total blank. If we are all meant to be political animals in one degree or another, I had to admit that I was deficient in those particular genes. And yet, and yet. Was I not at the centre of the storm? I, guileless, pacific me?

What I was unable to calculate, you see, was the strength of Cragg *vis à vis* Wales. How is one supposed to know these things if one never gets to see the books – I mean the ones that balance the debits against the credits, the scruples against their lack? I ask you, Horace, and please tell me before it is too late, how do men strike *deals*? How do they become sufficiently calculating to know, as in the relationship between Wales and Cragg, that what matters is not the other man's face, or his accent, or his family background, or what he knows about business, but what he can *command*? I put the question to you in all innocence, because one knew in advance that Wales and Cragg would hate one another's guts. Wales, the unaristocratic aristocrat; Cragg, the climber. Wales, the indelicate rapier; Cragg, the butcher's cleaver. Wales, the finedged diamondcutter; Cragg, the massive stampingmachine. One needn't have been any great student of human nature to understand that they could never live together; then why in God's name did they consent to it at the beginning? What did they have in common? We were about to find out.

On the third day, Harriet came into the house. The news travelled with the speed of electricity: Philippa to Liz to Sally to Moot to Peter Glyffe, and then to me, as if they all expected me to light up like a bulb. Most probably I did, for it was just in that split second, with the mention of her name, that I was able to answer my own question for the first time. What they had in common was Harriet. Harriet's fluvialalluvial energy, Harriet's annualperennial bestseller, and, for all I knew, Harriet's extravagant milkies, those splendid projectiles proud enough, even in repose, to bore holes in the observer from the far side of a literary luncheon. How, you will want to know, could it have escaped me? Well, I suppose it was because I hadn't yet had time to think of Harriet as one of ours. She and Cragg, after all, were part of the new wave. We have not yet actually produced anything of Harriet's; B.C. she was always on somebody else's list.

Liz Gwynne wanted us all to go into her own room where sound rattled across the angle of the courtyard like dice in a tin cup. I didn't much like doing it, but went along with them all the same. It was a short meeting. Cragg said something lost in the shuffle of bodies jockeying for position at Liz's window. Then Wales came across loud and clear.

– I must remind you that I am still the proprietor of this house.

57

If I wish to publish a work in white leather with a pink ribbon round it and sell it to defrocked priests as *The Bedside Screw*, that, I think, is my business.

— Jeremy, Cragg shouted, you will witness that!

Silence from Wales. It may be that he realized he had gone too far. It may be that, having said something so certifiably mad, he realized he had no choice but to disappear.

*   *   *

Thrale's office is in one of those monumental piles in Gullet Street, third floor overlooking the park. I don't suppose you've ever been there: the place stinks of clubland in a dark sort of way, wood panelling, elephantine leather chairs, books behind glass. There are two vast urns on either side of the inner door leading to the room where he works. Olive jars, perhaps; souvenirs of a holiday in Tuscany, and badly cracked, as if he had demolished them with a hammer in order to fit them into a suitcase, and then reassembled them with glue. Funereally empty. I know, because I peered into them, imagining that I might find Wales crouching in the one and his missing papers in the other.

A hospital matron ushered me into Thrale's den. He was sitting behind his desk with his elbows resting on it and his hands pressed together in the manner of a praying pope. There were no preliminaries of any kind. I had tried to prepare myself the night before by rehearsing my questionnaire with Jeannine, but as I sat there trying to make sense of the wax effigy in front of me I felt my guts dribbling down my legs and sliding away from me on the parquet floor. Finally words came, as from the hinged jaw of a ventriloquist's dummy.

— I've got to see Wales.

— He's dead, you know.

— Then why does he continue writing notes to me in green ink?

— *Green* ink?

— You know, the ink he always uses. And on his own notepaper.

— We've closed the flat. Does it have the address of the flat on it?

— Yes it does.

— Hmmmmmmm. Well, evidently he is not there.

— Evidently.

— I do not mean to imply that he is somewhere else. You were in court with the rest of us. He was pronounced dead.

— Yes. And I was pronounced a fool for insisting that he is still alive.

— It would be unkind of me to comment on that.

– You have not answered my question about the messages in the matrioshka.

– Matrioshka?

– The Russian doll.

– Ah, yes, Exhibit A. Well, it may be some kind of practical joke.

– We went into that during the trial. Anyway if it's that, who else could be doing it?

– Cragg?

– Cragg does not write in green ink in Wales' handwriting.

– I suppose not. What do they say, these messages?

– The first, you will remember, said I was to do everything I was told or else. The second told me I was to go to the Isle of Wace. The third told me to put on my bulletproof vest.

– Any sign of the bullets?

– Yes. Cragg has ordered me to stop the production of the Greekless dictionary and the bedside scroll.

– I see. Well, I shall speak to him about that. If necessary we shall apply for an injunction ordering him to produce them. You are to continue annihilating the Greek.

– Cragg will fire me.

– He can't. You are under the protection of the holding company and the trust.

– What's to stop him stopping my salary?

– We will get an injunction ordering him to pay it.

– You don't know Cragg. If nothing else avails he will close up the entrance to my room with bricks and mortar. While I am inside.

– I suggest you climb out of the window.

– And climb back in at ninethirty in the morning?

– We have to maintain a presence at Wales and Wales, you know. A bridgehead.

– I hope somebody will tell me when deeday arrives. Or is it to be called doubleyouday?

– The latter. And by the way, it is upon us.

– What does that mean?

– It means that we are about to execute his will.

– All of whose executors are entitled to know its contents but myself.

– I'm afraid that's so. But you will learn about it as you go along. There will be a letter for you in the post in a day or two. It satisfies the first clause in the will, or will do so once its provisions have been carried out. You are the executor of this part of the testament. I have an idea you won't find the job all that unpleasant.

– You don't seem to understand that Cragg will not allow any of this work to go forward.

– I promise you I'll deal with Cragg.

– All right, I'll take your word for it. But how can you be so sure that I will go along with all this? After all, you are treating me as if I were to serve as some sort of drainpipe or digestive tract, as Wales would have it. Why should I accept instructions from a man whom you insist on describing as dead?

– Because of the Abominable Secret, as it's called.

– If he's dead, who will divulge it?

– He left it in a sealed envelope. I don't know what it contains – that is to say, I don't know what the secret is – but I am empowered to open it and act upon it if you fail to carry out your part of the bargain. I hope we shall be able to avoid going that far.

It arrived as promised, two days later: a meticulously worded note from Thrale asking me to proceed with the work, the burden of which was specified in detail. If you will read the memorandum I then sent to Cragg and the others you will need no further explanation. None, at any rate, that I myself can supply.

In my function as literary executor of the testament of Wallace Wales, I am obliged to issue a number of directives, and also to make sure that they are carried out.

1. *The Wales English Dictionary*. We are to proceed with the WED in such a manner as to leave blank spaces on the page wherever a word of Greek origin was used before. The purpose of this is to lend visual substance to the claim that ours is the only English dictionary in existence. It will also facilitate the work of those pedants who will insist on knowing which words we have taken out: they will be encouraged to buy both editions and refer to them side by side. A promotional campaign will be put in hand to make the advantages of the new WED known to the widest possible public. Production costs will be kept to a minimum by the simple expedient of pasting white paper over the expurgated words, and reproducing the result in facsimile.

2. *The Bedside Scroll*. We are asked to resume work on this project forthwith, proceeding along the lines already described in the exchange of memoranda between Wales and myself. A promotional campaign will be put in hand to make

the attractions of the new Scroll known to the widest public possible. At the same time Mr Fear is asked to give us a costing for a limited edition of one hundred copies printed on a continuous roll of fine parchment and mounted on two sticks for the convenience of the reader.

3. *The Wales 20th Century Biographical Dictionary* is to be re-named. The word 'biography' is dead; long live Wales' 20th Century Lives. We are to edit the new dictionary of lives in such a way as to break it down into three volumes to be named, respectively:

> WALES' 20TH CENTURY LIVES
> I – Ignominious Behaviour
> WALES' 20TH CENTURY LIVES
> II – Loathsome Enterprise
> WALES' 20TH CENTURY LIVES
> III – Terminal Disease

Lives I will resemble the dictionary in the sense that it is essentially a work of expurgation. We are to go through the twenty-one volumes systematically eliminating childhood. We are specifically required, as in the dictionary, to substitute white space for all excised material.

Lives II will expunge all adult activity from the record, leaving intact only those passages that refer to youth and old age. Of the three lives this one will display the greatest amount of white space.

Lives III, the third panel of our three-panelled picture,[1] excludes all references to old age which, in most dictionaries, is dealt with summarily. This accordingly is the edition that

....

[1] Before Wales got us all thinking about Greek I should have used the word 'triptych' in place of the phrase 'three-panelled picture'. No winners either way. What prompts this note, however, is the typewritten document sent to me by Thrale: originally the third edition was to be subtitled *Pathological Symptoms*, but then Wales noticed that both 'pathology' and 'symptom' are kneedeep in Greek, and he changed it in his own evergreen handwriting to *Terminal Disease*. This of course reinforces my conviction that he has not himself become the victim of any known terminal disease. Wales asterisked his editorial correction to refer to a note of his own at the bottom of the page: it said 'See semiology.' I did. Before the pedants got their hands on it, the word meant 'branch of pathology concerned with symptoms'.

displays the least amount of white space. I am not sure what Wales intends us to infer from this other than that our treatment of the aged, and perhaps our attitude to ageing as a process, has somehow, like youth and maturity themselves, become a blot upon our performance. Be that as it may, it is not our purpose here to speculate about his motives; our purpose is to produce three new editions of the defunct Biographical Dictionary. As with the English-language dictionary, a promotional campaign should be roughed out now so that we may be sure we have reached a common understanding about what we are trying to sell before the work begins. Librarians and pedants are to be encouraged to acquire all three volumes, as they are complementary. The production aspect may be dealt with as before, by means of paste-ups and facsimile.

It would be a task of some proportions to describe my state of mind the day I put that particular explosive into the internal post. Not comforting: I had the feeling the thing might go off in my own hands. But where else did my interests lie, with Cragg and the Trilogy? Unthinkable. We lived under the same roof, in the same cage, but I was not prepared to admit that hyenas and putative birds of paradise had any language in common. Jeannine and I had long talks about all of this, of course, and we had concluded that it was better to go along with Wales, unimaginable as that might seem, than to become the playthings of Cragg and company. Better the devil known than the devil abhorred. But what an incongruous bloody mess! If I had not had Jeannine and the cats and my sanctuary, the garden, I am sure I should have gone mad. As it was, they tended me. So when Philippa summoned me to see Cragg I was serene, or nearly. He made me sit there for some time without saying a word while he read some sort of document, but it did not shake me. I sat opposite with my hands resting on my thighs. I looked down at my hands: there were traces of the garden in them, and one of them had been scratched, lovingly, by Ozzie. (As a kitten he used to sit on the windowledge, elegant and erect as an Egyptian god, birdwatching. This prompted me to name him Ozymandias which became, in the shortened forms, 'Ozzie' and 'Oz'.) I was thinking of him when Cragg raised his voice. Cragg, by the way, had installed himself in Wales' room and was sitting behind Wales' desk with the pacific green of the courtyard stretching beyond him. The eggs were gone and the walls were once more lined with books and cabinets and clutter. He picked up a paper, my memorandum, between two fingers, as if it had previously been applied to the backside of a Walloon at breakfast.

– What is the meaning of this?

I don't know if I've ever mentioned this: Cragg (so appropriate is the name) has one of those jaws that makes you feel as you look at him that you are in the presence of a wall or rock, an unclimbable rockface carved forbiddingly in the shape of an Easter Island head. We all know that these megalithic men stand on the same precarious sand that stops all of us from plummeting into the void; no matter, they are nonetheless aweinspiring, and the worst of it is that they know it.

– What is the meaning of this?

– You know as much as I do. Ask Thrale.

– I have asked Thrale. He hasn't the faintest idea.

I felt I was turning another colour. Not white.

– What do you mean, he hasn't the faintest idea?

– He does not consider himself responsible, I am glad to say, for memoranda you choose to concoct and shoot round the house like the bullets of a drunken cowboy.

There are occasions, don't you think, when terror will stretch only so far; it then snaps back on its own elastic and becomes a joke. I decided there was no salvation in letting myself be bullied by an Easter Island sheriff, and jammed another bullet in my Smith and Wesson – if that's the gun the slingers use.

– Of course he's not responsible. He's only the bartender.

– Aubrey Thrale? Don't be absurd.

What do bartenders do when the shooting starts? They duck behind the bar. That evidently is what he is doing now.

– Stick to the point. Thrale didn't write that memorandum.

– Nor did I. It was dictated to me.

– At the point of a gun, I suppose.

– In a manner of speaking.

– It won't wash. Wales is dead. Thrale had no hand in it. I have instructed Jeremy Chesterton and the others to disregard this . . . this indecency.

– My instructions are to proceed.

– Then I must ask you one of two things. Either to submit to a psychiatric examination or to leave this house immediately.

What would a man who *needed* a psychiatric examination have done in the circumstances? He'd have turned Cragg's table over and tried to bury him under a mountain of books. He'd have smashed the window, torn down the curtains, set off the fire alarm, peed on the carpet like

Sigmund Freud. I did none of these things. I simply laughed. Laughed in his face. I laughed, Horace, until the tears came and the tubes clogged up. I then got caught up in a fit of coughing which went on until I was nearly exhausted. Then I began laughing again, and I was still laughing when I went out of the door. By this time the miracle had occurred. That great prognathous megalith, that implacable stone mask had fallen open at the jaw and begun to tremble.

The following morning when I came in at the usual time I found my door locked. Fortunately my room is on the ground floor: I went outside, hoisted myself up to the ledge, and by dint of an ungainly acrobacy of arms, knees, and toes, managed to slide breathless and dustjacketed through the unlocked window. Then I called Thrale.

The Fifth Envelope

Bekorgakov has admitted in one of his essays that his reading of Ovid has not greatly changed his perception of existence. Who has failed, Ovid or Bekorgakov?

A literature that does not explode our habits, our lassitude, our mechanical or ideological ways of seeing things, is not literature at all, and not even variation on the theme. We have a right to expect it to shake people out of their skins. The old skins (pax vobis, Jonathan) are masks concealing the unspeakable.

*　　　*　　　*

Problem of identification. What would you do in Wales' place, hole away in Mount Athos? Dig a bunker under Pen-y-fan and prepare for the end of the world? All we have to go on is ignorance – all of us with perhaps one exception, Helena. See her. Find out what she knows. Make a list of all possible sources of information and check them one by one. Wales would not hole away in Mount Athos unless for the sport of smuggling in a female pubic hair. Study the literature of disappearance, example *Majorana*. And the Italian publisher who was blown up tied to a television mast: Wales, I know, was fascinated by him.

Begin with Helena.

Notes for Horace. There wasn't time to begin with Helena, I went to Hietzing instead. Wien no less; Vindobona. No, not for the Austrian authors on our list: we only have two of them and they're both dead. I was ordered to go there by Wales, or rather I consented to go there as the result of the last matrioshka. I now have a row of four of them on my windowledge at home, standing there in descending order like mother and offspring waiting in a queue for a taxi.

That, incidentally, is the way it was delivered. I was reading my paper at the station, too late to walk across the park to Great Conduit Street, and I must have been thirteenth or fourteenth in the queue when a taxi pulled up beside me to the general astonishment, and the driver called out my name. 'I've been sent round to pick you up, sir,' he said, and invited me to get in. I opened the door of the cab and immediately and most literally got the message, for there on the seat waiting for me was my fellow passenger, matrioshka number four. This time he hadn't even bothered to put it in a bag. More nauseous green ink inside:

Meet the Painted Lady at the junction of the Danube, Po, Elbe and Weichsel. March 4th.

On the way to Great Conduit Street I slid open the window separating me from the driver and asked him who had given him the wooden doll.

– Wooden doll, sir?

– This.

He turned and inspected the matrioshka. Either his eyesight was bad or he was reading a microdot.

– Yes, it does look like a wooden doll, sir, that's right.

– It was left on the seat.

– People do odd things these days, sir. If you knew what some of those blacks and Irish leave behind, you'd think you 'ad a roobish 'eap for 'ire.

– Who hired the taxi in the first place? Who told you to drive up to me in the queue?

– I was instructed not to say, sir.

– Was it a tall gentleman with a narrow face and a grey moustache?

– I'm afraid I can't say, sir. I'm awfully sorry, sir. You know 'ow it is.

Yes, I knew how it was. Wales, or somebody doing his work for him, had paid for his silence. All the same, when the driver let me out in front of the house I thought I would try. I offered him a fiver for any information he might give me, the merest straw.

– It's no good, guv. I'm only doing my job. Cheerio!

And he drove off without asking for the fare.

I thought of taking the number of the taxi, but you know I have the wrong eyes for that, and by the time I'd got out my glasses he'd made off round the corner. Don't laugh, Horace, I'm only short on technique. Perhaps I should read thrillers, but Wales didn't like them and there are none in the list. I haven't so much as read a Sherlock Holmes since I was a child, which must be two or three million thrillers ago.[1] Where do I begin?

That evening Jeannine and I had what by now we had begun to call our matrioshka conference, and we decided I should go. I could have done nothing of the kind, of course, had Thrale not given me the money. What happened was that I got on the telephone to him to complain about Cragg, and we had another of our intimate conversations.

– I have instructed him, he said, to put the key in the lock. Has he done so?

– Yes. But everybody in the house has stopped speaking to me, as if I had come in covered with plant lice.

– Plant lice? What's wrong with the other kind?

– Wrong colour, I suppose. Anyway they have stopped speaking to me. They meaning Cragg, Chesterton, Dulcimer-Smith, and Fear.

– No great loss, I take it?

– You seem to forget that I have work to do. The biography, the dictionary, the Bedside Scroll, and now the truncated lives. No one is going to lay down a red carpet.

– You will just have to get on with it yourself.

– Behind their backs, I suppose.

– In your place I shouldn't want to count on their help.

– Another thing, I have been instructed to go to Vienna.

– Vienna? By whom?

– I've been hoping you might tell me that.

– Tell you what?

– Who wants me to go to Vienna.

. . . .

[1] Wales may have despised the genre but he was by no means indifferent to the phenomenon. He once asked me to find someone who would be willing to produce a dissertation on fictional violence as a safety valve for the twin explosions of population and technology. 'The meaning,' he said, 'is plain enough. The more people we produce, and the more machines, the more we shall be inclined to dream of killing one another. What I should like to see examined are the conditions that drive us to proceed from dream to action.' Harold Melanchthon, the anthropologist, was at the point of signing when he was knocked down in the street by a van delivering flowers. He never recovered.

Pause. Then:

– I'm afraid I know nothing. Was it the Green Monster?

– Precisely. Another matrioshka, this time planted in the back of a taxi.

– Curious. Well, I suppose you'd better go.

– I can't. I haven't got any money.

– Not to worry, this sort of thing is provided for. You got the money for the other trip, did you not?

– Yes. Three weeks later.

– Well, I'll have Winifred send round an air ticket and an advance. When will you go?

– A train ticket, please. As soon as possible. I shall need enough money for a week.

And so you see, dear friend up there on your blasted heath, if you want to travel round the world on somebody else's cash, what you must do is to find Wales, persuade him to give his literary executor the sack, and take over yourself. Tempted?

Schubert Express. First class this time, small cabin to myself. Flask of scotch for comfort, ice tinkling in a jug, bed made up ready to be leapt into. Remarkable what a word in the right place will do. Why the train, you will ask, when it takes half a day to get to Lutetia and another seventeen hours to Wien? Precisely for that reason. If I could arrange it my way I'd go the entire distance on foot and live ten times as long. I am being perfectly serious: listen to what I have managed to pack into the day. It began with a longish whiff of sea air, the spectacle of hordes of nubiles on deck with operative parts described in Druidic blue, Calais to Paris in the same compartment with the greatest actor in the Kingdom (no less!) who, I regret to say, fell asleep, jowls drooping over a typewritten manuscript, and so remained all the way to the Gare du Nord. (Privileged circumstance: I was able to observe that great actors come equipped with mouths stretched infinitely wide to facilitate the escape of Shakespeare.) Seven free hours: place des Vosges for a word with the ghost of Victor Hugo, then a prowl round les Halles, or what's left of it, where in a chaotic bookshop I found and bought, to start me thinking about Vienna, an essay on Karl Kraus – and if you think you're prolific remind me to tell you about *him* one day. Quiet dinner on a white tablecloth amid brass rails, mirrors, flowers in pots – *ris de veau* with Alsatian Riesling – and back by a leisurely progress along the rue St-Denis where the girls, some of them very fetching indeed, line up in corridors all the way to the Gare de l'Est, and so to bed. Find me on earth the purveyor of haste who can offer up a programme to beat that!

Early morning, beyond Salzburg. Lili. Lilith. Lilitu. Stupid that a memory extinguished or virtually so for sixteen years can still provoke that same yearning, straining, pounding sensation – or is it? For some infancies there is no end in sight. Herder's description; yes, there is that. And recent. Can it be true even remotely? Three children, divorce, succession of lovers, Lili gone plump. And Wales in all this: calculation or accident? 'I am stopping in,' he had said, 'on my way to the country.' On a Sunday when he knew we should be there. 'I want to talk briefly about French translations. A cup of tea would be welcome.' And characteristically there was not a word about translations; all he did was walk about the house, sniffing. He sniffed his way up the garden and from one end of the terrace to the other. 'I take it you put in quite a lot of time tending all this, or is it Jeannine?' Then up the stairs and along the row of books, which he passed without interest. Jeannine couldn't take it and fled to the kitchen. 'Who plays the flute?' Finally it was the turn of the pictures: a brief inspection of the Fresson prints, a lengthier pause before the Uppsala poster with his nose practically in it – and then the portrait of Lili.

– Mmmm. Who's that?

– The love of my life. That is, before Jeannine. A lady named Lili Backhaus. I met her in Vienna a number of years ago and did the painting.

– I didn't know you painted.

– I don't, unless someone thrusts the materials at me. That's what happened on this occasion.

– Vague likeness?

– Not particularly flattering. In life the lady is, I think it's fair to say, quite beautiful. Also I made her hair red. Lili is as blonde as a Valkyrie.

A brisk interrogation followed. How had I met her, where was she now, what did her husband do, and her own career, what progress had she made since? I filled in as best I could from my distance (think of it!) of half a generation, together with what I had learned from the world-travelling Herder.

– Who's Herder?

– The composer. We publish his books. *Ariadne's Needle. The Pasture of the Minotaur*. Among others.

– Oh, that one. Haven't read a line. Is he good?

– Extremely.

– And it was Herder, as I understand it, who introduced you to this . . . Lili Backhaus. She might have chosen a more felicitous name.

– Her husband's fault, of course. When I met her she was Lili Baum. No accounting for taste.

– You didn't care for the husband? Bit of rivalry there?

– I had every reason not to care for him. She married him. I could never really believe he was good enough for her.

– By the way, what were you doing in Vienna?

– Ostensibly I was there to write. Herder had preceded me and I moved into his flat. Then I met Lili and forgot about the writing. She was a fulltime job. I was happy to be employed.

– What was Herder doing there? I take it Herder is not Viennese.

– No. He was born near a saltmine half a Siberia away from me. He went to Vienna to write music in the atmosphere of Mozart, Beethoven and the rest. Which is what he did with great diligence while I tried to pursue Lili.

– Unsuccessfully, I take it.

For a moment I thought I would tell Wales everything – how I had written letters to her, sent flowers to her, taken her for long walks in the Wienerwald, to the opera, to glorious concerts where all the applause seemed to have been misdirected to the conductor and the orchestra on the platform, instead of to the exquisite creature beside me – but Jeannine came in with the tea. We manufactured footling conversation for ten minutes and then he drove away in his archaic Bentley.

– What was all that about?

– Good question. We were supposed to be talking about translations.

And that, incidentally, was the one occasion in my life when I felt that Wales and I might have pulled down the walls and come to know one another – on the pretext of his curiosity about someone else. Of course it was not to be. The walls were made of the kind of glass which is transparent on one side only.

The hotel. This is the way it happened. I called Lili's number in Hietzing the minute I had installed myself in my room only to be answered by a woman, presumably the maid, who spoke not a word of English. But we jabbered at one another in our neighbouring languages and I understood that I was to call back in the evening.

I have never explained, have I, how I managed to decipher Wales' message about the painted lady at the junction of four rivers: not

70

difficult, my dear Watson, for anyone who knows Vienna. The only place in the city some might expect Wales to study with close attention – and he might have learned about it from any guidebook – is called *Freyung*, 'the freeing place', so named because fugitives in medieval times were able to take refuge there in the Monastery of the Scots. The minute one hears or reads the word *Schottenkirche*, one wants to know how the devil the Scots came to install themselves there: my guess was that Wales had posed the question and found, much to his amusement, that the monks who established themselves there were not Scots at all, but Irish – in a word, Celts. That made Freyung Wales' place, and you have only to read a paragraph farther in the guidebook to learn that somebody named Ludwig Schwanthaler had designed a fountain for the square in 1844 and set it up outside the church. It is called 'Austria Fountain' and is described as an allegorical representation of the four main rivers of the Empire.

My first thought, once I'd spoken to the woman, was to go there, to Freyung, and – thrilling stuff – verify my deduction. I proceeded along Kärntnerstrasse and the Graben to Freyung where indeed the fountain still presides: one of those forgettable creations with a saucer in midair and figures writhing toward the top. I had no reason to suppose that it might have disappeared; even so I was relieved to find it there. Nothing else had changed. The Schottenkirche was still clothed in Maria Theresian ochre, and the burghers, I am glad to say, had not brought back the stocks and gallows where, according to the book, they used to detain and string up traitors who failed to make it to the sanctuary. Traitors to whom and for what? Precursors of Harry Lime, at any rate.

I continued my walk, and the city, which had gone by in a blur before, began to come back into focus. The Hofburg, the Albertina, the Opera, the miniature Parthenon in the Volksgarten. One pleasant change: the new underground railway has given them the excuse to banish cars from some of the streets in the centre. One can now weave in and out among the sleepwalkers in the Kärntnerstrasse without falling over them. I had a glass of wine and a sausage in the cellar below the Albertina, and then installed myself in a coffee house to read the essay on Karl Kraus. It was a place I'd often gone to in the Ring, populated in midafternoon by middleaged people who never worked, but sat there as part of the décor reading newspapers on sticks. Reading the *same* newspapers, I began to believe, that had been given to them a generation before. I ordered coffee with whipped cream and applied myself to my reading. Vienna early in the century, when Kraus saw it as a testing ground for the destruction of the world – a conclusion any of us would have found inescapable had we been exposed that early in the day to the sound of Schoenberg post Verklärte Nacht. I tried to attune myself to this sombre vision, but somehow it failed to fit the whipped cream, and a vision of another kind, a wraith of flying hair and whirlpool eyes kept drifting in between the lines, drawing me down and down into the memory of an offering perpetually withheld. The waiter said 'Bitte?' and I awoke.

*   *   *

– Robert! *Wunderbar!* Where are you? What are you doing this very minute?

I gripped the telephone and summoned up my voice from the centre of the earth.

– I am at my hotel, Lili, and dying to see you. Can I come up? I can get a taxi in two minutes.

– No, I'll go to you. We are supposed to meet at Freyung by the fountain.

I could hear the water raining down from an immense distance, over traffic, over the beating of my heart.

– Are you there?

– Lili, how did you know about that? Who told you to meet me there?

Laughter. Hers, not mine. Cascades of it. *Schönbrunn.*

– I'll see you there in half an hour.

*   *   *

The lamps were already lighted when I set out from the Ring; one plunges from the dazzle of the Opera and along past the immensities of gloom that make up the courtyards and passageways of the Hofburg at night. I don't suppose it took me more than fifteen minutes to reach that curious jumble of angles pretending to be a square, and of course I was early. I walked round it three times trying to decipher the language of the statuary: the four rivers were not clearly personified as others are in the immense fountain opposite the Bibliothèque Nationale: you must remember the French version from your days there as a worm. Then along the few steps leading out of the place to Am Hof, an authentic square, and beyond to the old City Hall. There I turned back, not wanting to risk being late even if it meant waiting the rest of my life,

72

which, by now, is what it had begun to seem. Lili, divorced, a free woman; lovers, so Herder had said, or was it no more than idle talk? How was he to know? Was it Backhaus spreading spite? Backhaus exhibiting the authentic jealousy of a disappointed spouse? The jealousy I could believe, the authenticity much less. Backhaus has a lot to account for in my life. Now that I think of it in the light of the cool thereafter I can see that it was Herder's fault, really, for being so conscientious about his work. I had gone there to visit him, to work alongside him, to learn. He may not have known it, but I always felt I had something to learn from him. I had read music since childhood, but the thought of writing it had never properly installed itself in my head. Oh, I had ventured some juvenilia – a short piano prelude, an even shorter waltz – before I came to my senses and resigned myself to the distance between us, the distance, let's say, between my own modest scribbling and *Finnegans Wake*. The trouble was that Vienna was new to me and already a wellthumbed streetmap to him. Also he had plunged himself into a programme that, as I was to find out much later, established foundations for his first ten years of published scores, and refused to dislodge himself from it. So he handed me over to Backhaus, genial welcoming Backhaus, with instructions to ply him liberally with cheap slivowitz; the slivowitz, he was sure, would unlock Vienna for me and keep me out of harm's, that is to say the muse's, way. And it worked. I soon found myself collecting invitations from distinguished ladies who knew all there was to know about literature in Europe: that Sartre was queer and Shaw impotent, that Gertrude Stein went to bed in the summer with a hotwaterbottle. There were diplomats' soirées and concerts in the Konzerthaus and afternoons at the openair skatingrink next door where I displayed my Saskatchewan hockeyplayer's lumberjack style. Backhaus presided suavely over all this, my 'coming out' in Vienna. I supplied the slivowitz and the cash. In retrospect it seems fantastically frivolous for someone supposed to be there to absorb the sonorities of Goethe and Grillparzer, and even if it went no further than the tabletalk of Johann Eckermann, I was said to be, *seen* to be, serious in my pursuits. But the real pursuit was Lili. Backhaus introduced me to her at a party: I can still remember a first snapshot of gaiety and green eyes against a background of chamber music and sober tapestry and gilt.

– She's nice, he whispered, go after her.

And effaced himself in the direction of a dusky beauty from Acapulco.

I had planned to stay with Herder for a week, but the days stretched into weeks and the weeks into months. Not because of Herder, even less to soak up the cultural advantages of Vienna. Because of Lili and entirely because of her. I gave up only when my money began running out.

Backhaus' family had left him a large flat in Hietzing, and to make ends meet he rented one room to Herder and another to me. In the evenings and at breakfast we shared the kitchen, the sittingroom, and a sympathetic nurse named Elsa, who doubled as Hausfrau for all purposes but the nutritive: we took our meals together at a jolly Gasthaus in the neighbourhood. Backhaus was never there during the day: there was some fugitive pretence about studying dentistry but no evidence of progress in the direction of the professional world. Lili came and went often at the end of the day after she had put in four or five hours at the piano: have I forgotten to say she was a pianist? Yes, and I have never heard anyone play with greater sensitivity, especially Bach. What she did when she met me explains why she never went on to become a concert artist in the grand manner: she found it no great loss to put aside her work. She was capable of working hard for three or four days at a stretch; then she would lose interest and come to see the Innocent Abroad. I was available, you see, an excuse to get away from the grind, and she assigned herself the task of showing me round the city. And she transformed Vienna for me simply by being there, or should I say she transformed me, because the city itself floated in and out of my consciousness like an indifferent film: there were details I managed to grasp but never the whole. All this time I was bound by the unspoken: I could have her as sister, friend, coquette. Muse, if my interests were strong enough to sustain the role.

She knew I had fallen in love with her, and it was of the smallest apparent concern. Pleasing, perhaps, but something that happened as a matter of course every two or three weeks, each time with a different buffoon. She kept me at a distance – kept me, *tortured* me! – by confiding to me her impressions of the others. She had a particular hatred for oily hair, and, at the other extreme, for socks that fell down round the ankles. She could not abide men who talked nonstop, nor those who strutted about, as she put it, 'on thick thighs'. I offered few of these liabilities; my legs were thin and athletic, my hair wandered about untamed, my socks were disciplined with suspenders. So why was I making so little progress?

– You've got to be ruthless, said Backhaus, making vigorous gestures with a fist. Ruthless. Women like men who are hard.

– I can't do that, Walther, I replied. She's not like that at all. She is interested in higher things. For God's sake, she goes about with *beads* in her fingers. How could I dream

The beads were perhaps an overstatement, but she did take me to

74

mass with her on Sundays, to a different church each time, and if there is a reason for living in Vienna it is surely that: Haydn, Mozart, Beethoven performed by full orchestral groups where, elsewhere, one hears tinny tintinnabulations on an electric organ. Still, she did carry a rosary with her, she did finger it in a distracted way, and she did manage to convey to me the idea that she was not to be taken trivially but in earnest, once and for all.

Backhaus continued to cavil. According to him she was waiting for it, yearning for it, imploring the tactician in me (where?) to make the right move.

— Try flowers, he said. Women turn into putty when they stick their noses into flowers.

I tried flowers, forgetting that putty turns hard with exposure to the air and that flowers wither and fade.

Years later Herder told me the story. I had misread the moment completely. Lili's coquetry, the coquetry of any beautiful woman for that matter, was a *performance*, said Herder, an invitation to the spectator to rush up the aisle, climb slambang over the kettledrums (with perhaps a delicate turn at the oboe in passing), mount the stage, seize the fair lady, and bend her to his will: prolonged tutti and general applause. If you like, a musical version of Backhaus' own thesis, but with an important difference. Herder's was the humour of hindsight, Backhaus' the sardonic comment of intimate knowledge. Three months after I left Vienna, Backhaus and Lili were married. They had been having an affair all the time I was there. Herder learned about it from Backhaus long after the event, and marvelled at the innocence of the spectator. But why? Why should Backhaus have wanted to play so cynical a game? Because, it seems, he was unsure of himself and unsure of her. I was to be the test. And I failed as litmus paper because of my pious hesitations.

— Why don't you try putting your hands on her? he had ventured, desperate to take the measure of her resistance, and perhaps for the first time in my life I felt a deep loathing for another man. But I got over it, and her, as one does. When at long last I boarded my train to Venice I was already aware that my sorrows would be short and less than terminal. I had never visited Italy. The excitement of going there for the first time (which I felt I had to conceal) very nearly compensated for everything.

I never saw Lili again. But whenever Herder returned to Vienna he naturally met Backhaus and picked up the thread from him and from other old friends who knew her. And so we knew a little. Divorced. Children. Lovers. The story of the century: too banal to provoke comment. But as I waited there by the fountain I began to wonder.

Plump? Possible. Career abandoned by default? Probable. Lovers? Discriminately, no doubt. What bothered me more than anything was the implied knowledge of Wales' message. He must have spoken to her: there was no other way. He must have remembered the painted lady and gone out of his way – far out of his way – to find her.

There were six streets leading into Freyung; it seemed to me that she would be most likely to enter the side nearest the Ring. If not, she would come in from the Graben and Am Hof. I positioned myself with my back to the fountain and turned my head nervously toward one entrance, then toward the other. Tennis. A cat crept along the wall of the church and vanished into a shadow. From all sides came the sounds of night: heavy doors on hinges, a bell marking the halfhour, footsteps on the pavement, more footsteps, yet no one entered the square. Once more I began walking around the fountain – once, twice in widening circles, and when I came back into the light she was there waiting for me.

– Lili! Schönbrunn!

We held each other, swaying, turning, dancing on silent feet, until I began to regret that she was wearing an overcoat.

– Where did you come from? I looked for you everywhere!

– From the gallery beside the coffee house. There. That passageway in the dark. I wanted to surprise you!

We began walking aimlessly into the night. Not much was said. I wound my arm tightly round her waist and pressed my lips into her neck, and held her, and held her again, and tried to make love to her in a courtyard. We realized, half way into our fumble, that there were better places for that, and took a taxi to Hietzing. There, in the same apartment where Backhaus had had his way sixteen years before, I took my sweet revenge.

*   *   *

Treason? Not to myself. And let me say, before stones are cast, that there is a sense in which it was not to Jeannine, either, although in other circumstances it might have upset our applecart. For such is the risk we all take, knowingly or not, when we enter into that pretence of stability and possession called wedlock – lockup of the wed.

Jeannine and I were not innocents when we began sharing one another's lives; we were simply tired of living alone. Scratch beneath the surface of any relationship, particularly those that are, for one reason or another, delayed, and you will find the same motive: the desire to avoid solitude, the fear of forever remaining alone, desire coupled with fear.

We never succeed entirely, for there is a sense in which we remain separate between the same sheets, but we do not entirely fail. There have been periods of trial and stress, and one came to regret the loss of time in which to dream, time in which to await those parcels of experience, those unheralded moments or 'special deliveries' which are the raw material of poetry. I knew I should write very little afterwards. But it was a smaller sacrifice than you might think. Poetry is no longer an activity for the gifted few; it is now thought to be accessible to anyone who buys the right kind of machine.[2] We lost our faith when it became clear that nothing was more important, this side of the looking-glass, than a television jingle, and that the Shelleys and Byrons of our day all thumbed electric guitars. We have not stopped altogether, those of us who live on the other side, but we no longer know how to make mythologies of it; we have lost sight of the collective dream; inspiration has withered away to the dimensions of the ninehundredpage blockbuster. And so, rather than run after chimeras, many of us retire to our gardens, hoping as we work among the shoots and tendrils that it will all blow over in a century or two. To each bard and balladeer his time and place; ours is underground, beneath the weeds.

Now the chief curiosity about all this, for our present purpose, is that it makes living together thinkable. And Jeannine made it all the easier by making none of the usual demands. There were to be no children: each of us was already the child of the other. Money was not to become an obsession. As for the demands of the flesh, Jeannine – perhaps because she was born French – expected that one day we should cease to excite one another, or at any rate that we should begin to excite one another less. At that moment we should let nature inform us and try to accept its information without prejudice or fear. 'If ever you feel yourself becoming involved with someone,' she had said on our first day together, 'all I ask is that you break away for a holiday – and take me with you.' It was understood that she would do the same. Neither of us had ever felt the need, and life went on. An element of risk was always present, but somehow that made it a better challenge: there was, in the arrangement,

- -

[2] Machines for 'writing' type, machines for 'reproducing' sound, machines for 'capturing' images, machines for 'processing' thought. Among contemporary poets, Herder is one of the few to have grasped this unpleasantness; even when he wrote music for electricity some overpowering instinct or truth made it impossible for him to neglect the constant, the raw factor without which poetry is nothing – the human voice itself. Ignore it and you have forgotten Moses, and Homer, and Shakespeare, and mankind.

something of the notion that its right to continue – especially in the absence of children – had to be earned. I had opportunities outside the curriculum, but seldom the time. She, living in the country, had time but few opportunities. And so the balance was maintained.

My adventure with Lili, for all these reasons, was something we had come to expect. Inevitable and refreshing as a glass of champagne – and as *passagère* in its effect. Goddesses, when they are possessed, cease to be goddesses: a metamorphosis occurs: they become lovers, mothers, friends. Confidantes at times. And thank heaven for that, or the strain would break us all. Besides, once we had accepted one another in that particular way, there was no further need for secrecy. I found out from Lili why I was there.

– It was only three weeks ago. Someone, a man, telephoned me from the Sacher. He said he had seen the painting you had made of me – you remember? The one with the red hair. He invited me out to dinner.

When Lili began to blush I knew what was coming. I listened all the same; it was like peering through a keyhole in a sordid hotel.

– He said you were well, and married, and doing good work. He talked about you for a long time – as if, well, as if he had a special interest in you.

– Special interest?

– Yes. In bringing you along. Almost as a father speaking of a son. Or perhaps there is not that much difference in age between you?

– Only if he had started early. He looks younger than he is. So Wales wants to bring me along, does he? Did he tell you how he has chosen to go about it?

– Not exactly. He said something about your poetry, that it was very good but that it kept disappearing before publication. Accidentally or not accidentally, no one knows. And it seems that you leave a lot of it on trains. Can that be so? Also he told me what he thought I should do when you came. He said he thought I should not – how did he put it – that I should not play mouse and cat with you.

– God damn him, what right had he to talk to you that way! As if I couldn't, *we* couldn't look after our own lives. Mouse and cat indeed!

– He is a very charming man, you know. It was impossible to resist him.

– What on earth do you mean by that?

– Well, you know he has such marvellous manners. I will tell you a secret, Robert. He reminded me of you. Not as you are now, but as you will be.

– You are talking nonsense, dear girl. How is anyone to know what I will be like twenty years from now?

– You will be like Wallace, I am sure of it. With grey hair at the sides and initials on your shirts.

– Wallace? Not Mr Wales? Wallace?

She laughed uproariously.

– Nobody says mister any more. Not after you have been to bed.

I wanted to strike her. I came perilously close to doing it. What was I supposed to be, another Backhaus? Another expendable? Less. Worse. Backhaus became her husband: I, even in my moment of glory (glory!) was never more than a promise of Wales to come. I had been treated with derision. I lost my head and ran out of the flat without uttering another word.

Return journey to Paris. But I didn't give up, Horace; I can credit myself with that. The following morning I called her and made some sort of apology, enough to make it possible for us to meet again. Neither of us had slept much, so we agreed to go out together for a long and restorative walk in the gardens of Schönbrunn Palace not far from where she lived. Schönbrunn, beautiful fountain. That, you will remember, was the name I had given to Lili in the old days, in homage. Now I thought of it in another context: Elsa and Herder and I were walking back to the apartment from the Gasthaus in a mood of hilarity – had we drunk more slivowitz than usual? – when another definition of the name occurred to me: *beautiful woman sitting in a watercloset*. Herder translated for Elsa, and she laughed until tears came, and toppled me over into a snowbank. It was this second construction of the word that came to me now as I approached Lili in the courtyard of the palace, and suddenly good humour was restored. I kissed her on both cheeks, and we set out arm in arm – for all the world as if nothing more serious than one of life's small hiccups had come between us.

– You see, I explained to her, I was jealous. Tortured, ravaged with jealousy.

– I know. It was wicked of me, but I couldn't help it. I adore being cruel to men. It's a sort of revenge, don't you see?

– Revenge for what?

– For everything. Disappointment. The pain of having children and seeing them go away. Revenge against life, for being born. How do you think I felt when I knew he would take me and then go away? And you, Robert, you also will go away. You are all alike. Fading outlines in an album of photographs, that's all.

– But you said I would be like Wales twenty years from now. I can always come back.

– Yes, but what will I be like? Will you want me then?

Her eyes shone and I almost found myself unable to reply. But I did.

– You will always be beautiful, Lili. Always.

– You are lying, Robert, but I love you for it.

So you see, we were able to talk freely because, for the first time, there was nothing left to conceal. When that happens – and it happens so rarely – we talk in monologues. She told me about herself, I told her about myself. I learned more about Wales from her than I had really expected to know, yet none of it really leads us to the man.

– It was as if, how do I put it . . . he made me think of the first Christians, the ones who were forced to hide from a world that hated them. One day here, one day there, a life underground, shadows everywhere. Instead of going to a priest to confess, he came to me. He said he was weary of it all – of what, I never found out – and that he had left everything behind him, and closed the doors. Everything and at the same time not everything. It was as if the past had become useless, of no interest; his whole existence, *our* whole existence had to be remade. Of course what he said about that was said differently: I am only telling you what I gathered from a word here and a word there. I asked him what he wanted, why he had come to me, and he replied by looking out of the window in the direction of Schönbrunn. I couldn't understand: he didn't even smile. Then, I said, why do you want to go away if you have found what you are searching for, and he said it was to find some more. Some more what, sex? More candies for the greedy male? And he replied, 'You ask so many questions. If any of us knew, there would be no more questions. The experts in these matters tell us that we have been given four ways of rooting ourselves in one another. Eros is one of them. Without it the house would fall down, at one corner if not entirely. At the same time we must live with a paradox, this: there is only one moment that passes between a woman and a man – the first. The rest is repetition.' Yes, and though he said he was weary of it all, he did not give me that impression. Not at that moment. Perhaps he had taken some strength from me, I don't know. All I can tell you is that I am sure he will go on as he said he would, for a long time.

– Did he say he would come back?

– No. Anyway that is the one question I never ask, otherwise there would be no surprises. But I want him to come back, Robert, in the same way that I want you to come back. We must all stop being so weary, and so pale, and add a drop of generosity to the recipe.

That was all. By that time we had reached the monument they call the Gloriette, from which one looks down on the palace and the city's distant splendour. Napoleon had stood there, and Marie Antoinette, and Mozart. It is the kind of place meant for apotheoses out transfigurations, but none occurred.

I found myself wondering what it was that caused us to expect so much of one another. We had become, Lili, Backhaus, myself, even Wales, the tiny figures an architect once placed in the maquette of an imperial palace to impress his imperial mistress. Matchstick figures meant to represent human beings. Had Wales stood there, too, wondering how our silent gods, the trees, had become reduced to splinters? Lili did not know. Wales had said nothing to her about what he had seen while he was in Vienna.

The Sixth Envelope

Awful torturing feeling that I had forgotten something essential, the one detail that might have brought it all into focus. As if the whole enterprise depended upon a single question, the one it had never occurred to me to ask.

Dear Lili. Unfinished business about Wales. Forgot to ask whether he . . . Dear Lili. While we were walking in the gardens on the way up to the folly I meant to . . . Dear Lili. At Freyung, in the joyous confusion of our meeting, there was a moment when . . .

Make a list of everything seen and done and thought. Something will leap out and announce itself.

> *Westbahnhof. Mariahilferstrasse. The Bristol. The Sirk. The Ring.*
> *The Karlsplatz. Kärntnerstrasse. Stephansdom. Our Lord of the*
> *Toothache. Our Lord of the Grüss Gott and Bitte Schön . . .*

The corner room between mine and Herder's (material for an entirely separate work) was occupied by a photographer, and not just any photographer. Yuri Bekorgakov. Such was my ignorance at that moment in life that I had never heard of his father. But once I had satisfied a number of conditions (had I read *Entrances?*) I was taken along to meet the great man at his apartment in the Innerstadt. By that time I had absorbed a brief study of the Bekorgakov canon borrowed from the library of the British Embassy. The last thing Bekorgakov wanted to talk about however was his own work. What fuelled him was the city itself, its gossip, its pallid intellectual life, its decrepitude and irreversible decay. He held court in an immense chair with wings at the level of the head, serving Turkish coffee in small black cups to keep the conversation going. 'Karl Kraus was absolutely right,' I can remember him saying, and I can still hear his words and the way he enunciated them, punched them out from under the enormous underbrush of his white moustache, 'Karl Kraus was absolutely right. We have created all the conditions we need to bring down the curtain on the civilized world. Why wait for events? They have all taken place here already. Wittgenstein destroyed philosophy, Schoenberg killed off music, and Klimt perverted painting into decoration. What have they left us to live for? I'll tell you what in a single word. At 19 Berggasse an old man determined that what was needed to save us was a reinstatement of a practice that humanity found perfectly respectable before the arrival of Moses. Incest. Freud dusted off the skeleton and renamed it after a Greek. What was he doing, absolving his ancestors? What God hath wrought!'

There was more in this vein, and one day I must put it all down for the pedants.[1]

For Horace. The problem, if I may refer you back to yourself,[2] is to find out how to make our exit from this vale of tears without spilling too many of them. At the moment I must tell you the auspices are not favourable. No need to say more about my *états d'âme*: they are in the vale and you will not benefit from a drowning.

There was a short memorandum from Cragg on my table the morning I returned, announcing to the staff in two sentences that I was no longer senior literary editor of Wales & Wales. The reason given was that the duties of the senior literary editor were 'clearly in conflict with those of the literary executor of the late W. M. Wales.' Peter Glyffe was appointed to take my place.

I rang Thrale immediately: he counselled calm, and observed that in the circumstances Cragg's move was less than a surprise.

– The important thing is to maintain our bridgehead. I am counting on you to do so.

– Let me remind you, Mr Thrale, that the Second World War ended

. . . .

[1] Since I may never get round to it, weighed down as I am with all my other responsibilities, I must tell you about the visit of Athol Potts, the American critic, who remarked after a brief preamble on the use of the phonetic disjunctive in the poetry of the Ming dynasty: 'I do not believe there is anything in the universe of print that has escaped my attention.' Bekorgakov regarded him benevolently for an instant and replied: 'I am so glad. You will spare some of us a great deal of trouble, Dr Potts, by telling us what you have learned.' Athol laughed nervously, wiped his upper lip with a carefully folded handkerchief, and then *began to tell us!*

[2] Bentwhistle's *Notations and Annotations*, Wales & Wales, 1971, page 74.

some time ago. I now need evidence from Wales that my new job is worth going along with.

– It seems to me the evidence you are asking for is contained in the envelope Wales gave me to hold in safekeeping. Whatever happens, you know, your salary will be maintained. I have seen to that.

And so I had no choice but to return to my duties: this, the Greekless dictionary, the truncated lives, and the papyrus scriptures. I had scarcely had time to ask myself what to do next when Angela came into the room. She went into her number without even troubling to ask me about my trip.

– I am glad to say that Julian Cragg has approved my promotional approach for the party jokes idea. We then had to ask ourselves who in the house would seem to be best equipped to take over the editorial responsibility, and the answer was clearly you.

– Me?

– You seem to have become the expert on dictionaries and encyclopedias and the like. Anthologies are not far off.

– They are not far off when they are concerned with poetry. That used to be my responsibility. Anyway, as I am no longer senior literary editor I see no reason why all the fun should come to me.

– You are still, so far as I am aware, a salaried employee of this house, and Jeremy has asked me to hand over the file. We can work out a timetable at our next committee meeting.

And so there it was, jokes for poetry, salt in the wound. Have you ever looked up the word 'salary'? It comes from the Latin *salarium*, money given to the Roman soldiers so that they should have the wherewithal to pay for their *sal* or salt: saltmoney for the long march. Henceforth I am considered to be worth my salt if I prove myself capable of gathering jokes at all four corners of the world and bringing them back to Rome. There is another rather hoary expression that seems appropriate: one is 'made of salt' or 'not made of salt' as the case may be, meaning that one can or cannot go out in the rain without dissolving. It is now raining hard and the gutters are full.

Peter Glyffe found the courage to stick his head in the door and say, in some embarrassment, that what had happened could not have happened to a better guy. Impossible to tell whether he meant me or himself; I gave him the benefit of the doubt. Moot then came in and offered to resign; I cooled him off by asking him if he had Lady Moira's permission. I am not sure he liked that very much, but you know I don't really give a damn: I wanted him to know that I was prepared to answer for myself and in my own way.

Helena rang on the internal telephone.

– We're all counting on you to dig in and make the most of it, ducks. You are still top dog as far as I am concerned.

– Helena, sweet heart, I've got to see you. You are mixing your animals.

– Animals?

– I mean I've got to see you. It's important.

– Yes, but when? I'm on my way out to see Julia Goldwater. She's given birth again, I fear.

– Well, when you can. As soon as you can.

– I'll ring you back. Promise.

And she crackled me an electric kiss. Do you hear me, Horace? There are still plants in the garden that flourish in darkness. It must be so, or none of us would know what it means to have friends.

Michaelerplatz. Kohlmarkt. Peterskirche. Von Hildebrandt. Pestsäule. The Teutonic Knights. The Doorway of the Giants . . .

The following day two boys in blue overalls came into my room and began loading my books into boxes. I asked them what the hell they thought they were doing, and they said they had been told to transfer them to a room in the basement.

– Told by whom?

– Mr Cragg's assistant.

– Which one? We are all Mr Cragg's assistants.

– You know, the long blonde with the teacups in her shirt.

I went out in search of teacups. Philippa was not in her room. Cragg was not in his. What does one do in an earthquake to escape the shattering walls? I ran out of the house, entirely unaware of where I was going. A car hooted at me violently and I realized I was in the middle of the street. It was raining. I went back inside and collected my umbrella, then flagged a taxi and asked the driver to take me home. I could not have faced the train.

– Cost you about twenty quid, guv.

– That's all right, go ahead.

The city and the green belt went by in a blur. Jeannine paid for the taxi out of the housekeeping.

*   *   *

I gather you have been titillating Jeannine on the telephone with your impeccable French. What a wretched way to meet: voice without face, handclasp without hand, nauseating syrup all round. I had always thought the telephone the ultimate machine for manufacturing hypocrisy[3] till television came along. Anyway it's your fault for neglecting to invite us up for a weekend. Seven years, do you realize, have gone by and you still haven't got the measure of my luck. I agree when you say better books than invitations, and understand, but that doesn't stop me wishing you'd taken up some more sociable trade, like washing windows. That way we might at least catch the occasional glimpse through bleary glass. Meanwhile I've had to tell Jeannine that you took up writing because you were not presentable in public. She now thinks of you as some sort of furclad troglodyte or Shakespeare with a double nose. Olfactory into factory, and be it on your head.

Well, then, since you are unlikely to listen to these strictures however wellmeant, I'd better tell you about Jeannine, because without her the roof would fall down and the work would not go on. You are not to picture her as one of your blinding blondes; she was dipped, instead, in colours of the earth and made warm. See her as the sort of creature, if you will, to whom with whom any discerning man would be happy to unfold his burdens and take his rest. She has been the place of my confessional, and of my repose, and I sometimes wonder if it hasn't been unfair of me: I have all too seldom been hers. For the details: brown hair and eyes, Mediterranean skin, good bones, wellorchestrated teeth. The written word is no better than the electronic fog, because what she is, essentially, is a smile – wide, welcoming, and utterly unironic. An understated personality become statement by means of a smile. Sometimes, when I feel low and more useless than usual, I can pull myself out of it by promising to make her laugh before we go to bed. And then, in spite of everything, it begins, trembling, flirting with the corners of the mouth. She looks at me, I look at her, and it floods out – sillynonsensical laughter that builds and builds for no reason – perhaps as a challenge shared, as defiance, release. And when it subsides, all but that marvellous heartwarming smile, we both feel better because we know that we have touched one another in a world where touching is no longer one of the tools. But then we're odd sods, we are, and we don't repent.

We have few friends, and we never go out to manufacture amusement or to have it manufactured for us. Turn that round and you'll have us

....

[3] This is one instance where I feel I must object. I might have said 'cant' (WED[3]: words used without being meant), but the Latin offers none of the lovely glutinous quality of the Greek. That is the point, surely: use Greek whenever you are determined to be ugly. 'Prognathous megalith' in, most definitely.

sounding like Polonius. We are both earthcreatures: nothing in us is automatic, gleaming, or smooth. We cling, we burrow, and climb as slowly as Gunter Grass' snail. Do you see? We have become wound around one another and nothing will tear us apart.

– What happened? she said, putting first things first.

– There's been another catastrophe. I want to work in the garden for a while.

– In the rain?

– In the rain.

– Well, then, let me know when you'd like tea.

You must understand, I know nothing about plants. That may sound bizarre, I suppose, coming from someone who spends half of his free time in the garden; if so, I accept the indictment cheerfully. When Linnaeus invented his names, so my theory goes, he was responding to a need. Gardeners were farmers, or most of them were, and their performance had to be improved or people would starve. Two centuries pass and you get farmers raising pigs and chickens on assemblylines, dilettantes like me who don't know the difference between a fruit and a vegetable, and more people starving to death than ever before. Progress. But let me defend myself as best I can. The garden is the only place we have left where sanity prevails; wherever you look you find purpose in it, and even in the most badly tended of natural economies nothing is out of place. Nothing is out of place because every living thing in it – every weed, every slug, every fern or shoot or toadstool – has earned its right to be there, and earned it simply by being itself. Think of it! An entire universe beneath our feet, aspiring to grow beyond our knees and beyond them to heaven, a universe incapable of ambiguity or dissimulation, where nothing but integrity reigns. No, my friend, there is nothing there in the earth beneath us that is not utterly and perfectly itself.

And so I come along, humility clothed in rubber boots, to prod here and pull there, and I am never sure that what I am doing is a help or a hindrance to the plants, but I can tell you this: it certainly helps me. The hands grow tough, the face turns brown, and muscles harden in the legs and back. Invariably the cats come down from the house to nose about, and if there are no mice to stalk they stalk one another. A moment comes when Ozzie leaps up to the lower branches of the birch, knowing that I shall come along with a twig and play poke: now in the ticklish part of the ribs, now between the ears, now at the tail, and his paw sweeps the air in wider and wider circles until he loses his balance and comes perilously close to a fall. Then I sweep him up on my shoulder and he rides there, purring in my ear, with his enormous fox's tail flying, as we go up the flagstones to the house and tea.

— You are soaking wet. And the cat is filthy. Absolutely disgusting, both of you. I'll put the kettle on and you can tell me what happened.

I have never been able to give a moment's thought in the garden to Wales, or Cragg, or anything to do with Great Conduit Street or what purports to be my work. There, I learn what it means to create the world in seven days. I also know, when I leave it, how it came about that God should have been so disappointed with his creatures as to acquiesce in their Fall.

*   *   *

— We could sell the lawnmower to Neville Raikes.

— Better sell the rake to Neville and the mower to Moira.

— Do you think we'd get anything for the compost heap?

— You realize of course that we are talking about selling the garden. Well, I won't have it. We can sell the books and the furniture and for all I care the house, but we are not going to sell the garden.

— We can always live in the garage and buy a birdbath to use as a bidet.

— Jeannine, I know what we are going to do. We are not going to sell a thing. We are going to dig in and fight. I am not quite sure how we are going to do it, but at least I know what we are fighting for.

And that was how we decided that I should not risk everything by quitting my job, though we did consider it earnestly. It was the garden that tipped the balance, not the unspeakable secret. No one was going to take Eden away from us.

Next morning I went to work in my new room in the basement. Moot was the first to come down. He nearly collapsed when he saw me seated at my table on a pile of lectern Bibles: someone had seen to it that my chair was lost in the shuffle.

— This is not permanent, Moot, I assured him. There are people above who are going to regret this. Do you know what de Montherlant said about belief in the human enterprise? We can all expect to find talent and courage and so on, but where can we find *the absence of meanness*? That, he said, *that* particular absence, would give us reason to believe. Well, we are going to have to live without it. The problem is one of learning to take measures without ascending to their level.

— It's true, it would not be practical to descend to it. Robert, if there is anything I can do

– Yes, Moot, there is something. Arrange a meeting with Lady Moira.
I want to ask her a few questions about Wales – for the biography, you
know.

                    *   *   *

– We could set up a bookstall on the Seine and live in an attic and write
poems.
– Have you ever seen anybody sell a book from a bookstall? They are
there to decorate the city for the tourists.

                    *   *   *

*Michaelerplatz. Montezuma's treasure. The House of Habsburg.
The Order of the Golden Fleece. The lance that pierced the side of
Christ.*

I want you to know that the lance that pierced the side of Christ has
now made its way from its storehouse to Great Conduit Street for
further employment. Do not accuse me of promoting myself: it pierced
other sides before and after Golgotha. I am only the latest in a
longsuffering line. And what a line! Have you read Interlinneus' *Lives of
the Martyrs*? Inasmuch as ye sow love shall ye reap horror. Not to be
taken, I assure you, with hot chocolate before bed.
To resume. I got my chair by the simple expedient of removing it from
Glyffe's new room (my old) when he was out, and sat down to work
surrounded by books piled in total disorder on the floor. Distracting, you
might think. A certain lack of ambience. A naked lightbulb hung from the
ceiling and in ordinary circumstances I'd have hated it, but as there were
no windows I was not all that much opposed. During my first lunch hour I
went out and bought myself a Max Ernst poster for the wall facing me and
a coloured Japanese lantern in the shape of an accordion. I pinned up the
poster and fixed the paper lantern over the light and – will you believe it? –
actually stood back to admire the effect. Let me admit at once that I did
not stand back far: the room measured, by my reckoning, only five metres
by four. But the lantern cast a pink glow over the grey walls, and if the
poster failed to split me with laughter, it did provoke a grim smile. My first
morning in the boileroom (as I had now come to think of it) was dismal and
I accomplished nothing; but my newlyacquired artifacts were all I needed
to break out of my spiritual prison and transform the room, in the
afternoon, into a place where work could be done.

The first thing I did was to lay out a progress chart; it took me most of the afternoon. I had resolved, from that day, to count on no one in the house. When I needed paper I should buy my own; when a letter needed posting I should post it myself; and I decided to bring in my portable typewriter, now repaired, and do my own secretarial work. From there it would be a short step to the purchase of an accounts ledger: Thrale could not expect me to get along without petty cash. My plan was simple. To get back at Cragg I had decided to publish Wales' work and to publish it without help. Decided? You know that I was obliged to do so. All the same, Horace, something happened that afternoon in that tiny cell that had not happened before. I was in prison and somehow felt free. It may also have had something to do with a correct identification of the jailer.

At any rate the miracle occurred, and it was as if I had cast off an old pair of shoes, a pair which had never really fit but which I had nonetheless felt obliged to put up with for years, and replaced them with new. I had never before had to lay out type or buy paper or negotiate print, but I felt strangely calm about it, as if I had been meant to be a oneman publisher from the beginning. Wales, Cragg, the Trilogy, and all the others had been injected unnecessarily into the stream of events and would now be ejected as foreign elements. The stream would flow and bear fish once more.

My new euphoria, out, in which I had managed by some incredible conjuring trick to separate the activity from its consequences, lasted exactly one afternoon. That afternoon. The following morning they sent in the carpenters and began partitioning my cubicle into two small spaces, the one about a third the size of the other. I hurled myself up the stairs and ran pellmell into Teacups.

– This is hopeless, Philippa, they are trying to board me up in a closet.
– Can't stop now, love; ring you back later.
– You can't, I shouted after her. There is no telephone.

I went back down and stood in the doorway, paralysed by the scream of the electric saw. Finally I realized that I should accomplish nothing by staying there. I collected my umbrella and left. As I stood in the drizzle outside the house, trying to hail a cab, I wondered if I should ever see Great Conduit Street again.

*   *   *

– What do you advise, Mr Thrale. Can you see how I am to maintain my bridgehead, as you call it, in a basement room with no windows, no

90

telephone, no secretarial help, no production and accounting services, nothing?

– Hmmmmmmm. We shall have to organize our counterattack.

– You have a plan.

– Yes, but it needn't concern you for the moment. You will find, however, that it will play itself out to your advantage.

– I admire your choice of verb. Meanwhile I am to go on working in my timecapsule as if nothing had happened. As if the launching would never occur.

– I'm sorry, but that, too, is part of the plan.

I stood up and placed my hands flat on the table in front of him, and peered down into the smooth mask of his waxen face.

– Mr Thrale, I've had all I can take and I intend to take no more. You will have my resignation in the first post tomorrow.

All that happened is that he blinked as if struck full force by a feather, and then took up his prayingpope attitude. After a long moment of silence, he resumed.

– Tell me what this means. Are you resigning from Wales and Wales or from your position as one of the executors of the trust?

– If driven to it, from both. I had made up my mind to go forward as executor of Wales' will, but Cragg has made that impossible. I'd rather have Wales' madness than Cragg's – don't ask me why – but I can see no way of serving the one without being humiliated by the other. Impasse.

A thin smile melted its way into the wax and Thrale began to look almost human. He reached for the telephone. It crackled and he spoke.

– General Smallwood, please.

I'd rather have Wales' madness than Cragg's. Chew on that for a minute. Ask yourself how in the name of God I had managed to arrive, spontaneously it must seem, at that particular verdict. You may be certain that I had no intention of resigning when I went in to see Thrale; yet, as I think about what happened now, it had all the marks of the prearranged – as if someone had taken the trouble to expose the concentric circles of my years in publishing and trace a pin along the last millimetre of the outermost line. It may have been the most important millimetre of my life. I feel now as I did then, that I could not have offered a better answer if I'd worked at it for weeks. But was it mine or was it not in some way what was expected of me? What is Wales trying to say to us: have you worked it out? What are we to make of a Bible in the form of a toilet roll? What meaning do we read into the banishment of Greek, the effacement of childhood, adult life, and old age in sequence from the palimpsest, sorry, slate of twentieth-century affairs? What's so sordid about the twentieth century, I mean for him? Why ignominious behaviour, loathsome enterprise, terminal disease? Why a series known as *Wales' Lives* inside a performance crying out to be called *Wales Dies*? Conclusions, please, and if they are not the same as mine we have a quarrel on our hands.

> *Kohlmarkt. Christkindlmarkt. Hoher Markt. Neuer Markt. Gustav Klimt. Egon Schiele. Oskar Kokoschka. Dürer. Rembrandt. Fragonard. The Duke Albert of Sachsen-Teschen. Fasching. Opernball. Nationalbibliothek und Kapuzinergruft. Schulerstrasse 8. Rathausstrasse 7. Berggasse 19.*

Finally it was language that saved me or damned me, we may never know which. It came to me early one morning after more wrestling with sleep: I was trying to read the text on a package of pantyhose that Jeannine had left on the table by the bed (we never did get round to installing one of Wales' white calfskin glories there, I may add); to my astonishment I found it was printed in some sort of macaronic – a language, at least, that was unknown to me. Had she been indulging in a furtive adventure with a PaysBas diplomat? Or was it another of the curiosities of modern communication, socalled? I tried reading it aloud, and it reminded me for an instant of the famous dustjacket bearing the words Dylan Poems Thomas Poems:

ONZICHTBARE
panty
STRUMPFHOSE
transparent bis zur Taille
PANTYHOSE
allsheer

I should perhaps explain that I was in bed and that Jeannine was beside me curled up in the sheet. Dawn was breaking over the valley. My thoughts, suddenly arrested by the ridiculous text, leapt back to an image of Hitler screaming at the multitudes from a platform in Berlin: *Onzichtbare! Strumpfhose! Pantyhosenallsheer! Transparent bis zur Taille!* Frenzied applause several millions deep. But why the English 'transparent' and the French 'Taille' – size, after all. *Size!* That was it. I knew then what I should have asked Lili before I left her. Without disturbing Jeannine I eased myself out of bed and crept downstairs to my writing table, where Nefertiti lay in a black blot on the chair. I lifted her up without waking her, replaced her on my lap, and wrote my letter to Lili. A week later:

Dear Robert,
How funny you should ask such a question so late in life! No he was not tall, rather he was thick if you know what I mean. Thick in the shoulders and thick in the waist. Not enough for it to get in the way. He was very strong and not very gentle. He had a lot of fur on his head – correction, hair. Will that do? Let me know if I can any more help.
All my love,
Lili

And that, dear friend, is how I learned that the man who had preceded me at Lili's was someone who was 'thick in the shoulders and thick in the waist'. Someone with a lot of fur on his head. Wales, I am told, went bald in his twenties.

The Seventh Envelope

You may not have noticed, because I've given you no better than condensed versions of what went on between us, that Thrale's conversation is strewn with military clichés: all bridgeheads and counterattacks and deployments of forces. General Smallwood is the reverse. My theory is that his background as a writer of didactic military histories has taught him the value of originality. Be that as it may, the Birnam Wood is very different timber from ours and, for that matter, from Thrale's. A tall man, at least as tall as Wales, with that unspoken and indefinable air of command one associates with Eton – 'one' meaning myself, because I have never been able to distinguish an Old Etonian from an Old Clodhoprian, and I don't suppose I ever shall.

The General and I once had a conversation that made me wonder if I should ever find it in me to shake off Saskatchewan. On this occasion he was wearing his politeness like a medal.

– How many yahs, he said, have you been living in England?

I replied naturally in my original accent which, as you know, comes out flat as a postage stamp and adheres.

– I've been heer ten years. I mean, ten yahs.

– Better than, what was it, Toronteaow?

– Chronna. Yes, in many respects better. But I miss the space. We don't have much of that heer. I mean, we daen't rally have enough of it hyah.

– It's true, we daen't. I always think, howevah, that anyone feeling claustrewpheaobic can always shove off in a sailbaet. Plenty of Atlantic aet thah, you knaew.

And saew foth and saew on. In the battle of the diphthong the General was never going to be on the losing side.

I am not trying to say that Thrale is not one of them – far from it. But why should his language bristle with militarisms while Bertram's is heavy with birdwatching, the lore of antiques, and last night at the thyatah? Is Thrale a frustrated general and Smalltalk a disappointed ballerina? One never knows. The real question is Wales, who is/was clearly the boss: why has he chosen to throw me into this bearpit? Well, perhaps I am overshooting the mark so far as they are concerned; all I can say is that when I am in their presence I feel very much alone and very much encircled, and if they had not yet thrown another bear into the ring with me I could not help feeling that it was only because they hadn't yet found the time to go out and catch one. But as you will see from this, the circus is not to be delayed much longer.

We met at Thrale's office: I have never been so privileged as to be invited to the General's. The hospital matron greeted me abstractedly, as if I had walked uninvited into one of her dreams,[1] but managed all the same to open the door between the olive jars. Thrale rushed forward, hand outstretched, face positively shining with approval. I felt he saw me as someone who had just descended from his camel to report the taking of Akaba.

– So glad to see you, dear boy. Bertram has not yet arrived. Nothing so comforts the military mind as the thought of others lined up to await its pleasure. How are you getting along down there in the boileroom?

– The usual amenities are not provided. By the way, how did you know it was called the boileroom?

– Haha, good shot don't you think? Everything that goes on below decks. Power that turns the screw

– I have a feeling the power may be elsewhere. Did I tell you they sent in a carpenter and partitioned me off into a corner?

– You don't say! I thought it was already a corner.

. . . .

[1] Unfortunate soul, plain as a potato. Thrale later related her story in that clinical way of his to explain, I suppose, the peculiarity of her manner. He had kept her at the office one night until nearly ten o'clock, and because it was so late he offered to drive her home; they were to meet at Thrale's car after he had downed a reviving pint at a nearby pub. Thrale had rented a parking place below the icecube that disfigures the street opposite his own Victorian building: one of those subterranean caves with whirring fans and cetacean shapes looming out of the darkness. And there he found her slumped against the bonnet, dress ripped down the front, a beatific absence in her face. Thrale thought he could hear a man running up the ramp, but clearly the first task was to help the girl. He gathered her up and drove her to a hospital where she remained under observation the better part of a week. She is called Winifred. Winifred Walters. She has gone about in her dream ever since.

– It's now grand enough to accommodate a table, a chair, and an umbrella. If Cragg knew that I've been keeping my umbrella in the space between the table and the wall, he'd send in the carpenters to shrink the place even more.

– What have they done with the other part?

– Stacked it full of unread manuscripts. The proofreader comes in from time to time to remove a sheaf from the top of the pile. It's a farce: proofreaders don't read manuscripts.

Thrale leaned forward across his table, elbows asunder, thin smile splitting the wax.

– Things are pretty well seized up at the house?

– We've been struggling to catch up ever since Wales ordered us to draw the line on the American. Some of the backlog may be due to the methods of Mr Cragg's team of technocrats. There is a fine flow of patter, but the work doesn't necessarily follow.

At this point General Smallwood came into the room carrying a drinking glass. I had seen the man on no more than three or four previous occasions – twice at literary cocktails celebrating new books about antiques, another time at an exhibition, whose catalogue we eventually published, of paintings of country houses. With Birnam Wood, I was about to learn, there were never any preliminaries: no goodmornings, no howareyous, no sorrytobelates. He went straight into it as if the last meeting had never ended and nothing had happened since.

– Which way to the water?

– Through the door, first on the left.

He returned and seated himself at Thrale's table: the drinking-glass was half empty. Irrelevant detail, you may think, but why, if one wanted a glass of water to drink during a meeting, would one begin with it half full? Why, indeed, my dear Watson, unless it were half filled with vodka? I made a mental note to examine the profile of the General's hip pocket when the meeting broke up. Meanwhile there was a conversation to follow, and it was no simple task. For them, no doubt, it was standard fare, for me, an undecipherable cant of crossreferences, unidentifiable allusions, and disassociative puns. Ordinary functional communication is not good enough; how could it be when the object is bafflement and 'fun'? Of course, they themselves are never baffled: they have invented the rules. But what advice do you offer the outsider, should he laugh when they laugh – forever two seconds too late – or plunge himself directly into a trance? I sometimes make the mistake of trying to penetrate these arcana, but inevitably a moment arrives when I fall behind and my face betrays me. And of course they adore that; they are one up and they can see you suffering for it.

All this by way of explanation for my failure to produce a useful account of the meeting. The truth of the matter, Horace, is that a conversation went on at that table lasting an hour, and though it went on in the English language I am at a loss to tell you what it was about. I am not exaggerating as much as you might think. Let me throw you a bone, the one about the 'liquidses', invariably presented as a double plural. When Wales began acquiring companies, the main requirement, we are led to believe – the only requirement so far as I can tell – was that they produce something wet. There is a company that makes corn syrup, another that bottles mineral water, still another that produces a generalized sludge for making gravy. And of course there is a whisky company and a gin company and for all I know a vodka company. Come to think of it, that may explain why Harper Cabot was able to persuade Wales to buy print in Poland: he might have had his labels done cheaply at the same time. Whatever Wales touched, you can be sure that General Smallwood and Aubrey Thrale touched with him – and transmuted into solid cash. One day they bought into North Sea oil and that put them up among the Arabs. Don't ask me how they found out about it in time to get in before the mob; they did. So if they talk about money at all, as I imagine they must, there is so much of it that they no longer refer to it in ordinary terms. The references are all about 'spirituals' and 'nonspirituals', 'heavies' and 'lights', 'drips' and 'flows'. I simply put on my glazed look and let it slide over. What did it have to do with me?

Eventually Thrale translated something about a lemonsquash company into semimeaningful digits.

– I suggest we go for twoandahalf million.

– Better twoandthreequarters.

– Twoandtwothirds if we can get it.

– Who on earth drinks the stuff nowadays? Terrible waste of good water. By the way, where does the water come from?

– The tap, I suppose.

– Whose tap?

– We shall have to look into it.

And so it went on, only it was worse.

– What about the paper and ink?

– Oh, that. Yes, well.

– Bad news. Hadn't we better give it another knock?

– Not an implausible idea.

– Send in the digger?

– I expect it will come as something of a surprise to Mr Cragg.

There was a silence and they both looked at me. It occurred to me that they had been talking about us – about Wales & Wales, I mean – for some time. The 'paper and ink'. What was I supposed to say?

Smallwood went out for another glass of water and returned. It was still half empty. He downed it at one go and began making noises that reminded me of a mastiff growling in his dreams. It occurred to me then to try to say my piece – before he recovered.

– I'd like to bring you up to date on the work I've been doing. As you know, I am one of the executors of the trust.

They looked at me as if struck by nervegas. I can't pretend that I was not encouraged by the effect.

– There is, first of all, the Work in Regress.

General staring silence, if silence can stare. In my opinion it did. He did, most certainly.

– I thought you knew. 'Work in Regress' is the universal publisher's cliché, meant to be a joke, for any project that makes negative progress. Goes backward, if you know what I mean. It takes off on 'Work in Progress', provisional title of the last book written by Shame's Voice.

Staring silence part two. Energetic swallowing action on the part of the General.

– 'Shame's Voice' is a pun on the name of James Joyce.

The General bounded in his chair.

– I take your word for it, but who the devil is James Joyce?

– Never mind that, Barney, said Thrale. It would take us another meeting to get to the bottom of James Joyce. Go on, Robert.

– I don't know if the General knows that I've been getting messages in wooden bottles.

– That, too, would run us into another meeting. Perhaps we could deal with it in overall terms?

– I thought wooden bottles went out with the spinning jenny, said the General, or thereabouts.

– I am sure you are right, said Thrale, but that's another issue. What Robert means, I think, is that he is not making any progress with the biography.

– Whose biography?

– Wallace's.

– *Wallace's*? I'd have thought that would be fatal.

– In what sense? The man is dead, you know.

– Oh yes, I see what you mean. Yes, I'd forgotten about that.

– You were saying, Robert.

– I was about to explain that it is impossible to get on with it because so much of the evidence is gone, and the private papers appear to be without interest.

– The evidence! said the General, bounding again. Good heavens, we wouldn't want you to go into that, would we? I mean, that really would be fatal.

– He is not thinking about the same thing, Barney. Do go on, Robert.

– The private papers are impossibly cryptic, and Cragg won't let me look into the house files. As you know there were no surviving relatives, and so far his closest friends have been less than helpful: Helena Brown keeps avoiding me, and Helmut von Gildenkrantz has had to postpone my interview with Lady Moira three times. The Lady Moira interview doesn't much worry me because she doesn't know me, but Helena has always been kind to me in the past and I can't understand why she won't see me now. That leaves me with you, Mr Thrale, and you, General Smallwood. Perhaps you would care to advance the plot, as you were both on intimate terms with him, and for many years.

– I can't think for a moment why Wales should want us to do any such thing, said the General. I thought we were sworn to secrecy.

– Just so, replied Thrale. All the same it seems to me that Robert should continue trying to patch something together as he goes along on the supposition that a purpose will emerge. Of course I know the purpose because I have been privileged to read the will, but I am not allowed to disclose it.

– You are inviting him to go ahead with what he's got, which is practically nothing.

– The assignment, as I see it, is to record what happens. The story, or biography if you like, will develop as we go along.

– May I say, said the General, that this is the first time I've heard of a biography of events. What else is on your plate?

I ignored the question; in fact, I barely heard it, for I was on my feet, roaring with rage – torrents of incoherent, uncontainable, irremediable rage. I have no idea what I said to them. I simply shouted until I had drowned them in it and then walked out, banging the door so hard behind me that it rattled the olive jars.

*   *   *

The following morning I called Thrale and apologized: I had to. He said he understood and probably would have done the same in my place. I was to continue filling up my envelopes even if, for the present, the material seemed unpromising, and to press on with the Greekless dictionary, the revision of the *Lives*, and the rolledup Book.

The Word is law.

Wales may want to efface Greek from books and eliminate it from the language, but let me ask this: how can he hope to obliterate it from our minds? Decapitation? One can only hope that the idea hasn't occurred to him. Meanwhile, during my labours, I have begun to accumulate a Greek vocabulary, and some of it has begun to feed my curiosity. For instance, the word *agapaxia* – do you know it? From *aga*, 'too much', and *paksein*, 'to feel', and thence to the medical dictionaries where it is presented as 'congenital mental hypersensitivity characterized by *an excessive reactivity of the mind* to events of all orders, happy or unhappy, but especially to those which are vexatious or contrary'. My ics. And of course there are pills to deal with the excess. Yet there was a time when sensitivity was thought to be a precious thing; can you imagine poetry, or pottery, or psychology, or an activity beginning with any other letter of the alephbeth chosen at random, proceeding from an insensitive mind? Continue stuttering over the p's and you arrive, inevitably, at politics in the bad sense, and it is my undoing. Tell me, you who look down on all of us from your septentrional heaven, why must we meddle with one another in this meretricious way? Which of us is the whore – Smallwood, Thrale, or myself? Dark images lurk and nothing will banish them. And so on the slightest pretext – *slightest?* – I explode. Thrale says he would have done the same in my place – merde! The nearest he's ever come to an explosion was the moment Wales accused him, during the days when Thrale vetted our manuscripts for libel, of 'systematically wanting to throw books into the fire like Adolf Hitler'. But all that happened was that he paused to polish his glasses. Then he rephrased his objection.

Do you know how he refers to me now when we speak on the telephone? I am now his 'dear boy', as in 'My dear boy, you must learn to take these things with a pinch of salt.' I wonder how old he thinks I am. Christ, even my *cats* are octogenarians!

*   *   *

According to Helena, who at last has consented to see me, it all began when Wales lived at the top of the house. You will remember this period better than I can possibly relate it: Alethea was still very much alive and, as she put it, 'living in sin' (though she had been married to Wales for

100

twentyfive years), and Helena spent half her time nipping upstairs – at Wales' request, she would have us believe – while Alethea was out canvassing to save the children. Curious, when you think about it, from all points of view. Alethea wanted children but couldn't have them; Wales could have had them but didn't want them; Helena wanted Wales but could only have him in bed. All this against the backdrop of a population explosion destined to change us all from pink to pale chocolate in the space of three generations – unless in the meantime the pink race in its entirety can be funnelled through Great Conduit Street, in which case it will end up black.

Helena says Alethea knew, and Helena knew that she knew, and Alethea knew that she knew that she knew, and it was all they could do to avoid comparing notes. And they remained perfectly good friends – more, I think, on account of Alethea's tolerance of Helena than the other way round. Anyway if they stopped short of gossiping about Wales to one another, Alethea seldom hesitated with me. 'What do you suppose he sees in her,' she said to me one day at one of our literary cocktails, and for a moment I thought she might really want to know. Then, answering her own question with that saintly smile of hers doing most of the work: 'The truth, of course, is that he sees her as a fencepost. You know how men are, don't you Robert, being one yourself; they must have something to rub up against, like a horse bothered by flies. If he hadn't found Helena he'd have needed to be fed tranquillizers, or sprayed with DDT.'

If we are to believe Helena there was no recourse to either until some time later when Barbara Button came into the house and blundered in on them, thinking it was the upstairs ladies' loo: Wales had forgotten to lock the door. During the two weeks that remained of the lady's cisAtlantic tour, Wales transferred his attentions to the Button perforce, so Helena says, to save her for the list, and nothing was the same again. Wales and Alethea moved to Ascent Street, and Helena's years of darkness began. Presumably Wales had had enough of unlocked doors. One might suppose as well that he had had enough of unlocked ladies but for subsequent events, which we are coming to.

The years go by. Alethea dies. Helena goes about in widow's weeds as if death had occurred not to Alethea but to Wales. Wales 'dies'. Helena begins showing signs of life. Then one day in the middle of the night, the doorbell rings (brace yourself, this is the news), and there he is, umbrella at the slope, moustache at the twitch, eyebrows flying.

– But you are supposed to be dead!

– I am. You are dreaming. May I come in?

And within minutes Helena found herself once more on the couch, this time doing it with a corpse.

* * *

So you see I was not wrong and I am not as mad as the court would have us believe. You can imagine what I felt when she told me. Wales the living corpse: present tense in the guise of the past. First outside confirmation of what I had known, from the matrioshkas, all along. That much was exciting; the interrogation that followed, less so.

– Listen, Helena, you've got to help me.

– What is it this time, money? God knows it can't be the other thing.

– Of course I adore you. You know that. You've got to help me find Wales.

– I'm doing what I can, you know. I've told you all about my lovelife: what else is there to say? He didn't tell me where he's staying and it didn't occur to me to ask.

– What, you didn't want to see him again?

– Don't be silly. There was just no point in asking. Wallace never confided in me before, you know; why should he begin now?

– Helena, dear sweet *thing!* You did sleep with him, didn't you? In the years gone by and now again, bringing him back from the dead. Wouldn't that entitle you to certain small privileges – conversation, for example? How are you darling after all these years? Nothing?

Poor soul. Wounded eyes staring at me out of a streetmap. I was not enjoying myself much but I had to go on.

– I'm sorry.

– Oh, not to worry. It's just that it's all so difficult to put into words. I'm not really sure I can.

– Try. Please try, for my sake. You know how much this means to me.

– I'm not trying to hold anything back . . . Well, yes I am. It seems so absurd. Makes me look such an awful harlot.

– Are you afraid I'm going to rush straight off with it into print?

Her eyelashes began to flutter; I knew that she knew.

– I know it must seem strange, but let me try to explain. It's a question of feelings, you see. We never did have what one might call a close relationship. We *impinged*, if you follow me, but we never really got to *know*. There was this tacit understanding which had the effect of closing the shutters and casting everything into darkness. We already knew more than enough about one another's professional lives, you see, living together like that for such a length of time; it seemed wrong somehow to go further. I mean, we talked about books constantly, and authors, and about people in the house, but insofar as *intimate* things were concerned, well I'm afraid we did tend to leave those out. I had a terrible fear of treading on Alethea's toes, you see. She presumably knew what he *thought*; I only knew what he *did*.

– But Helena, darling, the man entered your life and then went out of it. Then he was said to have died. I said he was still alive and the court called me a liar. Now he has reappeared and come back into your life. Are we not entitled to know a little more? Just a modest bit more, a hint perhaps, some sort of what next – if only, for God's sake, because we have *served* him?

By now she had begun to mutilate a handkerchief and I was beginning to feel very low indeed.

– I agree, she said quietly, we are entitled to know more. But we can't get it simply by asking for it. He never played that way in the past, and he certainly isn't going to begin doing so now. After all, he is trying to cover something up, isn't he? If not, why the elaborate fuss about dying and having it proved in court?

– Why indeed. Tell me, did you know he was alive all along? Or did it come as a shock, if shock is the right word, to see him standing there at the door?

– The truth is that I was scarcely able to remain standing. I literally fell into his arms and was carried straight off to bed. He poured me a small glass of brandy, and for a moment I feared it had become a doctor and patient routine, if you know what I mean, and he *did* ask me how I was feeling, and when I said ever so much better it began all over again as if no interval had occurred and nothing in life – or in death? – could be so natural. I mean I really didn't stop to think about it, thank heaven, we just went on and it was heavenly.

– And then?

– And then I got up and made us a cup of tea.

– In books that's when things begin to happen – over cups of tea.

– Well, he did ask me how things were getting along at the house and I said I thought only a gangster could do what Cragg was doing to the list, and that I couldn't *bear* Angela Dulcimer-Smith, and he said women never *could* put up with one another, could they? and I said I'd always got along rather well with Alethea, bless her, and he said hmmmmmmm.

– And?

– I'm afraid there wasn't much more. He put on his briefs and gave me a peck and then went out of the door.

– But what else, for God's sake, what was he up to, where was he going, when were you to see each other again, and so on into the night!

– Oh, but we never did that sort of thing. All the deciding was left to him. You see, if ever I'd become the least bit pushy I'd never have seen him again. Ever.

– But you never did see him again! On two occasions!

– That's what I mean, he keeps coming back.

– You're expecting a return engagement.

– I'm expecting a return engagement.

*   *   *

Your turn; I'm speechless. Have you ever heard of a movement known as Women's Liberation? Is it conceivable that I am the only person alive at the end of this agonizing century who knows that women exist in their own right and are not merely here to be used? Is it possible that women do not know it, or care? I have always believed it was right to give them the vote, though it seems to have changed nothing; now I'm beginning to wonder if we should not have invented some sort of qualifying test.

There is one other crumb, a comment Wales made in passing when she tried to explain what Cragg and the Trilogy were doing to the list. 'So far,' he said, 'I have managed to get through life and beyond without murdering anyone. I consider that a triumph.'

*   *   *

Perhaps I'd better tell you what Cragg and cohorts are doing to the list, now that we've touched on it. First and foremost, Siberia. They sacked seventeen authors including Malcolm Bell[2] who, as you know, is no slouch, and not only on the page. At the Strathmore literary luncheon the other day he kept breaking into Harriet's speech with the cry, 'I'm out of print! I'm out of print!' Cragg, ever the accomplished shit, eventually leapt up and said 'Will someone please lead the gentleman out and introduce him to a printer.' Mild pandemonium, Malcolm menacing Cragg with sugartongs. 'Fat lot of good that would do,' clanged Bell, 'your blockbusters have dried up all the ink!'

....

[2] If ever I have a word to say again about the destiny of the house you can be sure that Malcolm will be back where he belongs – high up among the roofbeams.

They were going to give Magguinness the boot, too, until he consented to go along with what he calls 'the Performance'. The Performance is the new routine in which the author is required to become his own salesman. I am not talking about writing signatures in bookshops. It all began when Harper Cabot sent Angela a teeshirt celebrating the publication of Gloria Hymen's latest, which is called *Tail*, and is already thundering to the top of the New York charts. You've guessed it, the title of the book was printed on the shirt, front and back, and Angela took particular pleasure in tying the sleeves round her waist and letting it fall over her skirt like 'Just Married' at the back of a country wedding. One up for Angela. Before we knew what had happened, Magguinness was required to do the same. I mean, to wear a teeshirt, a lapelbutton, and plastic belt, all three displaying the title of his own book.[3] Tom naturally said no thanks, but Angela raised such a howl about it that he shortly found himself gracing Cragg's carpet. There he learned that not only was he going to have to wear his decorations while autographing in the bookshops; he was also going to have to expose them during his appearances on the ladies' lectureclub circuit *and* on television.

– Consider yourself well off, said Cragg. We might have asked you to go round with the reps.

I learned about all this first from Helena, because she is organizing the lectures, and then from Magguinness himself who, despite having to visit me in 'debasement' (his), still comes down from time to time to confide. I asked him why on earth he had put up so dismal a title in the first place, and he replied, hand on heart, It wasn't me, it was Freddie Fear. I wanted to call it 'Before I Turn Over'. Much more distinguished, don't you think? The next book I write is going to be about the publishing business, I assure you. Fortunately I know nothing about it.

– Fortunately?

– Because you can't sue Alice in Wonderland for libel.

Seven out of ten. The real problem is that he looks exactly like Gregory Peck and can't bear to go through life unseen.

What this amounts to, for the list as a whole, is that it is undergoing a gradual process of Cabotization. When Harper was with us he observed, rightly, that the assemblyline had somehow become automated without our seeming to notice – programmed to produce endless iterations about gardening, country houses, and cats, with the occasional bedroom diary or treatise on horses thrown in for variety. I was held to be

. . . .

[3] *Kiss Me Before I Turn Cold.*

responsible for the procession of books about cats, to which I pleaded guilty: how was I to subsidize my poetry series without them? 'I'll tell you how you can do it,' he replied. 'Get back to basics. What are the real motivations of people today, what makes them tick? Take them apart piece by piece and whaddya find? You find sex. You find health. You find money. You find sex. All human life is there. Build your list around sex, health, and money and you'll never look back. And besides,' he added, smiling like W. C. Fields, 'you'll have fun.'

I won't say that Cragg and the others pretended to be impressed by this argument. They said nothing, but went away and did it. Freddie, who it seems has always considered himself a fountain of ideas for titles, was the first to grasp the crosscultural possibilities: *Sex and the Country House; There's Money in Your Garden; Stretch your Way to Lasting Health* (subtitle: That's the way your cat does it!). Chesterton, who seemed to have adopted a policy of going along with everything that Cragg approved, merely put on his bland face (Helena's word for it) and began assigning authors to themes. And that is how the publisher of Samuel Johnson and the Holy Book in twentyeight versions ended up pushing a list which horrified Wales and caused Helena to describe Cragg as a gangster.[4]

Wales wasn't the only one to be horrified. Noel Balding came in one day without warning and asked to see me: you may remember him as one of the new generation of literary agents. Philippa brought him down to the boilerroom where he found me sitting on my work in three parts; I did that to solidify the glue. I gave him the chair and placed it at the entrance to my cell.

– I'd heard that strange things were going on at Wales to the power of two, he said, but I'd no idea it had come to this. Can you live with it?

– Scarcely. I'm hanging on because the plot hasn't unfolded.

....

[4] Monica Mead, *Sex and the Fat Man*; Monica Mead, *Sex and the Thin Man*; Harold Upps, *Sex and the Fat Woman*; Harold Upps, *Sex and the Thin Woman*; Monica Mead, *The Thin Man's Fat Time*; Harold Upps, *The Thin Woman's Fat Time*; Monica Mead and Harold Upps, *Sex Bargains of the Western World*; Harold Upps and Monica Mead, *Sex Bargains of the Eastern World*; Monica Mead and Harold Upps, *Sex and Your Bank Account*; Harold Upps and Monica Mead, *Our Sex* etc etc all imported from Cabot and Raw. From this modest beginning the list flowered to include Cissy Narkos' *Finding Yourself in Your Face*; *A Golden Treasury of Business Deals*, by Paul Haddam; *Watergate Down: Richard Nixon and the Art of Power Maintenance*; *Your Baby's First Bank Account*, by the omnipresent Upps and Mead; *I'm OK, Adolf's OK: The Secret Papers of Martin Bormann*; *How to Make Love to a Hermaphrodite*; and *The Case for Battered Husbands*, by F. J. Clough, the only British writer on the list.

– Whose plot?

– Wales', I think.

– If I may say so, that sounds less than conceivable. How can a dead man be expected to busy himself with it?

– I don't know, Noel. It's complicated. Obviously I haven't given up or I wouldn't be here.

– So you've been kicked downstairs and the Chesterton gang has been installed. Three for the price of one. I hope the new list is none of your doing.

– Noel, really! Fortunately they think it's clever and want to keep the credit for themselves.

– Meanwhile what does that leave you with?

– The unspeakable. I may tell you about it one day. For the moment, silence. And yourself, what have you got that's going to put breath back into the poetry of the land?

– Well, I've been studying the list. It's no bad thing, let's admit, to leap from Dr Johnson to *Sex and the Fat Man* if what you want to do is to make money. And what you want to do is to make money. But surely it's a mistake to drop the animals; after all, that's what poetry is made of, isn't it?

– That's the way I did it. We've given up the poetry series, you know.

– No, I didn't know. Pity. Still, you've had a good run. What I'm thinking is this. If Wales and Wales must throw out the bathwater, they might at least hang on to the baby. Let me tell you about the common cow.

– I am reaching for my powdered milk.

– This is serious, I tell you, and it's going to do some publisher a lot of good. So why not Wales and Wales and specifically why not Robert Racine?

– About as specific as you can get. I am mooing.

– Unbelieving bastard. Listen, the world is full of cows. We eat them, drink them, make them into shoes. There are more cows in India than there are people and they're all sacred. There are cows in Uganda, cows in Patagonia, cows in sausages, cows in glue, and the French transform their milk into a different edible turd for every day of the year. But who, I ask you, who on this cowinfested earth knows what a cow is? Why it has four stomachs and nine balls. Why flies adore it. Why bullfighters fight it. Why it shits pancakes. You see the possibilities?

– No, but I'm beginning to smell them.

– Racine, you are not only a tit, you are a cow's tit.

– I am honoured, dear Noel.

– Yes, and you might have been situated elsewhere in the anatomy. I hope you understand I have put a lot of work into this. I've even written a threepage synopsis.

– Tell me, Noel, what sex is a cow?

– Female, idiot. Everyone knows that.

– Just as well. One wouldn't want to end up calling it 'The Common Bull'.

Balding was at the point of launching the back of his hand at me when Cragg went by on one of his heavyfooted patrols.

– Who was that? he said, leaning back in his chair to follow the bulk of our chairman as he receded into the darkness of the corridor leading to the stairs at the far end of the house.

– That was Cragg.

– What's he doing down here?

– Checking up on me. Probably on you, too.

– Sinister. Listen, Robert, you've got to get out of this . . . abattoir.

– I know. The trouble is, I've been given, shall we say, a special assignment. I'll tell you about it one day. Meanwhile I keep having these ghastly dreams. There is a procession. Von Gildenkrantz and Peter Glyffe are carrying a body on a plank. They go out the door and down the steps. They lay it down on the pavement and hail a taxi. The taxi drives it away. Later it comes back from the other direction. Glyffe and von Gildenkrantz come out. They unload the body and carry it into the house on its plank. They come down the stairs and turn into this room. They prop the body against the wall and go out. There is a large book lying open on the table. I turn over the page and begin my day's work.

The Eighth Envelope

It seems to me that for our present purpose humanity can be divided into two camps: those who take life in hand and those who are taken in hand by life. The takers and the taken. Most of us go along with membership in the second, on the assumption that it will be possible one day to break out. Lion's head, goat's body, serpent's tail?[1] But what are we without our illusions?

Since this is about to become the three hundred and thirtythird literary form spawned by this cancerous century (Biography of Events, if we are to believe the unexpurgated General), I may as well tell you that I am prepared to witness most of them and even to be dictated by them in order to go on. But one day I will find Wales. That will be my event. That day, friend, we shall throw out all the plastic bags and toiletbooks and wooden mums and begin again on my terms. That day you will learn from *me* how this story is to unfold.

Meanwhile Wales has set out on what Helena describes comisadly as his 'nocturnal mission' – sadly, because it appears for the moment to exclude her. The mission consists of knocking on the doors of all the ladies in the house (a little suspension, please, of disbelief) and then having his wicked way with them one by one. Now don't rush off and throw this in the fire; it's been confirmed. By no less an authority than Liz Gwynne.

Liz, I should tell you, came into the house three years ago to build up what we called the 'Mothers' Help' list – everything I couldn't do and Peter Glyffe couldn't do and von Gildenkrantz wouldn't touch because he's too grand. Books about having babies and wearing clothes and

[1] Ed.: Racine's contortion avoiding the Greek 'chimaera'.

making quilts out of bits of dungaree. On paper she was under me, but I soon let her go her own way; she had no need of my help. A striking creature, to put it mildly. Tall, outcurving. Less beautiful than Philippa but infinitely more disturbing. If it hadn't been for Jeannine and my scruples about company incest I'd have been in there years ago tearing up the passes at the palace gate. Since the pedigree of names may not be among your central preoccupations I must explain that Gwynne, in Welsh, means 'fairwhite' and Elizabeth comes from the Hebrew meaning 'my God is satisfaction'. In a phrase, the White Goddess herself, or not far off.

One evening just as I was putting on my coat she came down and invited me out for a drink. We walked up Ascent Street to The Brass Monkey and ensconced ourselves at a corner table away from the crowd. She threw open her fur coat, and heaved a thigh in my direction.[2]

— You'll never guess, she said, smiling all over.

— You've been taken up by an Arab prince.

— Better than that. It's Wallace Wales. He's come back. I mean, you were right all along and the court was wrong.

— You won't mind if I pretend not to be surprised. What did he do, come down the chimney?

— It was all very ordinary, really. The doorbell rang in the middle of the night. I let him in. What else could I do?

— How did you know it wasn't someone else?

— I have one of these judasthings, you know.

— I can imagine.

— I mean in the door. I could see him there in the hallway ruffling his moustache.

— So you let him in and he threw you on the couch.

— Well, I didn't have much on. One thing sort of led to another.

— It's the saaaaayme the whole world overrrrrr; it's the poooooor wot gets the blaaaaayme . . .

— Are you disappointed in me?

— I am pretending not to be furious. Why couldn't it have been me?

— It's your own fault, you know. You might at least have tried.

— Oh God, Liz, you know I'm not the type. How do people deal with the guilt?

. . . .

[2] Literally true, but I am obliged to credit Tom Magguinness. 'Why is it,' he said to me one day, 'that women in novels always heave sighs? Why can't they occasionally heave thighs?'

– By not admitting any, I suppose. Anyway what was there to lose? You can't do much damage by having an affair with a dead man, can you?

– What if it was a dream?

– It wasn't, you know. It was much too interesting for that.

– At any given moment there are three billion people in the world doing it in unison: there must be something in it. But Wales. Liz Gwynne. Yes, I suppose that is interesting. But in what way?

– You are curious, aren't you. Well, I'll tell you. He had a small deck of playing cards in one of the pockets of his waistcoat. On the back of each card was the silhouette of a man and a woman making love; and each card was different. He spread them out in a fan on the bed and said which one will it be? I covered my eyes and drew at random.

– And studied the diagram before you began.

– We did, and decided it was much too athletic. So I drew another and it was the right one.

I hid my face in my pint.

– You are jealous, Robert, I can tell.

– No I am not jealous! No I am not jealous! No I am not *jealous*!

I admit I was a bit loud. People in the pub turned round to look at me, and Liz covered her confusion with both hands. When she recovered – and it didn't take long – she drew herself close to me, smiling her lovely Cheshirecat smile. An arm crept round my waist; fingertips wedged themselves under my belt and began wriggling sensuously south.

– Can I help it if all the nice men are married?

– Wales is not married and Wales is not nice. And this is no place to be doing that. They are all looking.

– Well, then, she said, pulling me into range with her disengaged hand, let's give them their money's worth.

And we did.

Patter of applause from the bar. I extracted her hand, straightened my shirt, and led her out the door and into the night. We walked into the darkened lane leading to Tricorn Square, and there in the alcove of a stolen statue, enfolded in furs and perfume and melting mammaries, I had *my* wicked way. We were both pleased as kittens. I called Jeannine and said I would be late. Then we went along into the lights and had dinner.

*   *   *

And what would you have done in my place you old prude? You know damn well what you'd have done, and you'd have thanked your blighted stars. As for me, why be less than honest. I can't even offer the excuse of having wanted to get on with the Wales matter; the only matter I cared about was Elizabeth Gwynne's. Twinges of guilt came later when I made my way home at the end of the evening; at the moment there were none. I mean, it had happened, and there was nothing to be gained from not enjoying it all the way to the port and cigars.

Back to Wales and *his* enjoyment, damn him. This next part, preceding the port, I followed over *rognons de veau* with a fascination heightened by experience.

– Well, and so he gathered up his deck of cards and we poured ourselves a couple of snifters and began to talk. What an extraordinary adventure, I said, searching rather desperately for something to say, and he said yes, wasn't it; should have thought of it years ago. Did, in fact, but didn't want to make it seem a condition of the job. Anyway I said, you had invested your coins in other parking meters hadn't you, and he said hmmmmmmmm. What next? Well I said I didn't quite know where to begin, and he said don't but I did anyway. How were we to *read* it all, I said; the funeral and the trial and Robert's disgrace, and the way Cragg and the others had been allowed to wreck everything that had been built up so patiently and so well over a span of generations, and he said what we must do is to stop reading things altogether and wait for events. What events? The kind that unfold the way flowers open themselves to the sun, and he laughed and began feeling me up in any number of places, distracting man. And of course he did – distract me, I mean. All I could do, really, was to lie back and let everything happen. *Again.* And it did. Can you imagine it? Wallace Wales the gentleman's gentleman, old enough to be my grandfather, going on like a young buck on his first honeymoon.

– Where is it all going to end?

– Exactly, she replied. That's what I'd like to know. Because it hasn't ended yet. Not if Helena has anything to say about it.

I put on my best innocent face.

– Helena came into my room and said she simply had to talk to me, would I mind if we went out for tea? So we went out and hid behind a potted palm like conspirators, and you won't believe this, Wales has been to her, too!

What was I to register, astonishment, disbelief, horror? I fell into a sort of seizure, and somehow contrived to catapult one of my kidneys into the gravyboat. They couldn't have done it better in a French farce.

– Let's go over this again slowly. Am I to take it, quite literally, that Helena has also been favoured with a, what shall we call it, visitation?

– Precisely.

– Before or after?

– Before or after what?

– Before or after his visit to you?

– Before.

– Good God! How do you feel about that?

– A little less chirpy. But then I said to myself pull yourself together, girl, and try to look astonished. Which I did; I mean, I did my best.

– What happened chez Helena – apart from the obvious?

– Not much. He came in the middle of the night

– You must learn to edit yourself, dear girl.

– He came in the middle of the night and . . . I see what you mean. But there wasn't much else, it seems. No playing cards, no promises, no clues.

– How does Helena feel about his visit to you?

– I didn't have the heart to tell her. She learned about it from Philippa.

– You told Philippa and Philippa told

– I suppose it came out when Philippa was telling Helena about her own adventure.

– There are no secrets? I mean to say, can I now assume that Helena and Philippa will know that *we* . . . and come to think of it, when do I go and see Philippa?

– Isn't it a giggle?

*　　　*　　　*

Frankly, I don't know if it is. When you think about Wales' daisies one by one – Helena, Philippa, Liz, Sally, Jill, Hilda, Winifred, and who knows if it will end there – I am not at all sure it makes sense. Helena, yes, for historical reasons. Philippa and Liz, yes, for every kind of reason. Sally and Jill – one would be churlish to complain. But Hilda Axelrod, Winifred Walters? Loooooooooooong paaaaaaaaaaaause. You haven't forgotten them, have you, or could you forget them? Hilda the Hatchet? Carpark Winnie? The one a catalogue of payslips, spiralbound, the other a misery of trepidation and tears, and not a sexhormone between them that wasn't sealed away among the mammoths, glaciers ago.

Have you ever sat in a public house, alone, watching couples? The beautiful people tend to collect near the bar close to the lights: they are on show, and if you are not close enough to hear what they are saying you'd swear you were watching a toothpaste commercial with the sound turned off. Then, a lightcircle away, you find the tables where they are still amusing themselves, but in a more restrained way. These are approaching autumn – late thirties, midforties – some of them still attractive but not working at it so much. Colleagues at the office. Solid. Worthy. Seldom averse to having a go at the office party. Now cast your eyes farther back, to the outer circle. Not much chirruping there. A cast of sagging jowls and depending buttocks, mercifully covered, the latter, with cloths drab enough to send a stockbroker into mourning. Among these you will find, once or twice a year, the Hilda Axelrods and the Winifred Walters, alliterating dullness, dribbling platitudes, extruding caution, work, and woe. *How could he?* And yet it seems confirmed. By the grapevine. Daisyvine if you prefer. I spilled out *my* disbelief to Magguinness, in whom I sometimes confide under stress, and he said something that's been nagging me since: 'Maybe they got their vines crossed.' Incorrigible but worth more than a passing thought. Liz will know, and Philippa, the one no more than two seconds behind the other. But if it makes them look in any way foolish – and it does – we can't count on getting the truth.

Philippa I am saving till later on. Don't expect me to blurt out all my goodies in a single breath; I have my envelopes to fill, you know, and I intend to do it at my own pace. From now on your pleasures are to be measured out with coffee spoons, and if you don't like it you can go lick your salt.

Later. The preceding petulance was the fault of Jeannine (who does not see these lines and does not ask to see them) for reminding me of another happy event of which this is the biography out account. Yesterday on the way home I lost another sheaf of poems and I have been scolded for it. Seventeen manuscript pages. Hoot of the train hurtling into the night with my immortalities aboard. Tiresome. Somewhere in the railway system a ticket collector sits hunched over my scrawl, wondering how to go about making himself rich and famous. There is no hesitation in his mind about doing it; the question is, what are they to be called? And what is he to call himself – himself? Do you see him sitting there in the dim light of his cabin, goldrimmed, pillboxed, the kind of man whose trousers reflect the slide of a thousand seats, feeling his way among the blots and blurbs for the magic that will transmute them into money? What were the great ones called, *Looking Out Over Battersea Bridge; Lake Isle of Whatsitsfree; Paradise Bust?* But all that's been done and none of it fits. Look for a key phrase. Anything that leaps out of the page like a fire extinguisher on a brass rail. Zaza zaza zaza zunk. Zaza zaza zunk. Thin soup before the skates, zaza zaza zunk. London pool too small for tears, zaza zaza zunk. The trail spills down a Kentish hill, zaza zaza zunk. Hangs his Christ upon an easel, zaza zaza . . . would that work? *Christ on His Easel?* Nobody would buy it. *Kentish Hill?* Pleasant, pastoral. A bit dull. *Too Small for Tears. Soup before Skates.* Wot's the blighter drivin' at anyway? Woy cawn't 'e do it simple loike? Troy anuvver. You will hear the clashing tongues, zaza zaza zunk; here a message stretched on space, zaza zaza zunk. Once more the catapulting sand, zaza zaza zunk. Clippery cloppery green sheen, zaza zaza zunk. Breathing breathing drops of menace, zaza zaza zunk. Left right left right, the soldier's plaster growling clamour, zaza zaza . . . Cor! Ayn't gonta ge' us tovve topuvvepops 'is woy, izze? And he flushes the whole bleedin' mess down the public drain where they fly, shitdaubed and sodden as birds floundering in an oilspill, out into the unforgiving night.

Why do I do it, Horace? Why does anybody do it, unless for money? And since poems are not things to be wrapped up in plastic and sold from a supermarket shelf, you can put me down as Dr Sam's blockhead. A blockhead, though, who repents, and repents seven times. Uselessly. Pointlessiy. But what if I should walk out of the house one day with someone else's posies under my arms, in order to leave *them* on the train? Don't you see that this seemingly gratuitous act, my leaving a clutch of inconsequential papers on a train one day, and another and another seven times over, could become grassfire, a *movement* in which publishers' readers everywhere might rise up united in their condemnation of the blighted page, and march all the manuscripts off to hell? And do you realize, you who practise so lovingly and so well, that if all of it were consumed tomorrow, and assumed in smoke, that the world would go on *in precisely the same way as before?* Now you are beginning to agree with the others; you are thinking, yes he's gone over the edge. Wales has pushed him. But wait, Horace, before you send round the men in the white suits, and consider this. If we all stopped writing at one another (we who no longer write *for* one another) we might resume talking. And if we resumed talking we might learn to listen, and if we learned to listen we might like what we heard, and if we liked what we heard we might once more take care of what we said, and if we took care of what we said we might begin speaking poetry, and if we began speaking poetry we might want to repeat it to our friends, and our friends might want to repeat it to their friends, and so back to Homer and Gilgamesh and beyond. We could begin all over again, every man his own Pierre Menard – ultimate folly, world without end. We could also abstain. With innocence made new we might – just possibly we *might* – feel no longer impelled to pick up our pens and start up our presses to make asses of ourselves all over again to the end of time.

We are ahead of ourselves. The forces of reiteration will not be disarmoured overnight. Let us suppose, while we are waiting, that our railway attendant is literate and impressed. Like many another contemporary critic he can make nothing of my poems; this proves to him that they're good. With pencil poised over clipboard in earnest application to the conundrum of names and their reluctant correspondence with things, he licks the tip of it, flourishes wrist and elbow, and writes:

Tragicommas and Tragicomas
by
Jeremiah Peach

Cautionary tale. The part to note is that our friend is not likely to be of two minds. Either the manuscript is considered incomprehensible and worthless, or it is seen to contain the droppings of a giant. We shall just have to watch the bookshops to find out.

The following Monday. Incredible lassitude. Abandon hope all ye who enter. Have you ever asked yourself why people exert themselves when the purposes they serve are so seldom their own? Superfluous question. Only the lords can know purpose: the rest of us, serfs to a man (Magguinness: serfiettes to a woman) must plod along in darkness without maps, without lamps, without destinations. Why do we consent? I have addressed myself to this drunk sober, awake asleep, gurgitating regurgitating, and the answer comes back with the monotony of a frog croaking in a desiccated well. No one who breathes is exempt. Each of us is bound to it in his own abominable way. And so, whenever I place myself in readiness before the empty page, the tension returns – the desire to blacken it at war eternally with the obsession to leave it clean. Only now, toward noon, am I beginning to emerge from our scarifying weekend. I found myself shouting at Jeannine as if she were a wall, *the* wall, the one I long to run against with my head lowered and my horns drawn in.

When finally I master myself and the stain begins to flow, it all moves forward as if someone were dictating it with a gun. Assault. And absolutely effortless. What uses up the years is the time it takes to destroy the world and reassemble it before one addresses oneself to the task.

The destruction first, and the injustice. Why is Wales doing this?

Why has he set out to destroy the printed page? For what else can it mean – these Greekless referenceworks, these blottingsout of black by white, these scriptures never folded, never cut – if not a mad attempt to annihilate us all? But he had been part of it himself, a mover and a shaker, he had inherited Samuel Johnson, he had done everything for the printed word except to perpetrate it himself. Is that the key? To believe so would be to admit that civilization itself had become monstrous. But Shakespeare isn't monstrous; nor is Mozart; nor is Jacopo Bellini. One tries to hold them up, and others, as candles in the encroaching darkness. Small comfort to know that the possibility of greater light exists somewhere above, on the other side, beyond.

Notes from this side. How does the writer proceed with his account of events when the events refuse to occur? In the absence of useful advice I have gone back into the Old Dispensation to take the measure of the offending Greek, and the awful thought occurs to me that I may have to learn the language itself in order to be certain of its excisions. For one never quite knows: languages, too, have closed lips and eyes.[3] What is one to do, for instance, with the recurring *sabbath?* Hebrew, one supposes, until the Greeks twisted it into *sabbaton* and the irremedial *sabbatikos* for sabbatical, and how did the *y'hudi* write that? I think of Herder and his fascination with languages: nothing would delight him more: return to sources. His forebears, like mine, were driven away from, or abandoned for reasons of necessity, their own roots. And it's precisely this that bedevils all North American expression: none of the languages we work with is indigenous. Language, like a tree, grows out of the soil and accumulates at once horizontally and vertically. The vertical line is the spectacular one; the other inches forward in concentric rings like geological time. Herder and I came into the world second-generation Canadians whose language was more vertical than horizontal, all sap and no grace, and so we had to set out to invent one of our own. Interesting to speculate what might have happened if the European colonists had lost, and been forced to adopt the speech of the American Indians: Mammon displaced by Manitou. What we can say, I think, is that none of the imported European tongues carried the poetic charge of the languages they displaced, because they were there for a different reason: the fur trade was not a hymn of praise to the spiritual qualities of the pelt. Later, in the *akadēmos* and all the *technikos* that it poured out, out, an unconscious

....

[3] Ed.: Periphrasis avoiding the Greek 'mystery', sb[3] and sb[4]: WED.

confession of inadequacy emerged. It took the form, on the one side, of a multiple reliance upon cant sb.[4], the use of language for the purpose of selling goods. Everything in the marketplace had to be new and now, but words and meanings were old and then. Deathrattle of an old language, birthpangs of a new minus the concentric rings. This may explain what Wales is trying to do. Part of it, at any rate. The limits of my language mean the limits of my world.[4]

*   *   *

But the means, the means! They have taken away my secretary, my telephone, my space. All I have left is this uttering, muttering, stuttering machine, useless to all but two of my fingers. Have you noticed that Wales has stopped sending me matrioshkas? At least they had the merit of catapulting me out of this place, out of the present and back along the rutted roads of the past. I enjoyed that backward journeying. It got me nowhere, but it did leave me with the feeling that one day a message in a wooden dummy would lead me to a destination of sorts, back to my own origins; even, with luck, back up the stairs. Send me another, Wales. Send me another wretched mum made pregnant with your green priapic finger, out, and I'll follow you to Patagonia and back if you will pay the ticket. Anything to get out of this dismal hole. Did I say that Cragg has shut off the electricity? It was off when I came in on Monday. I crept round the basement and tried the other switches, as many as I could find, and they all worked. They must have brought in an Einstein to tinker with the wires. But you know, these trials A. D. Wales, if I may dignify them that way, have changed me in some measure: there is a higher proportion of rubber in me now. What I did was to walk out to a giftshop, the one in Crofters Market, and buy myself a battery of candles – six of those multicoloured monoliths fat enough to sit on a table without additional support. Now they are guttering away in the gloom in front of me, and frankly I find them rather cheering. One day, if ambition seizes them, they may take it upon themselves to lick a tongue or two at the stacks of paper next door and warm up Cragg's backside. Meanwhile, whenever he agitates himself on the floor above, the ceiling shudders and my coconspirators dance with glee. I may yet buy another row of them and found a school of basement Christians. The bill for the first six has gone off to Thrale.

....

[4] *Tractatus Logico-Philosophicus.*

More grapevine. I had never been on a horse before. Fortunately mine, a grey, was elderly and docile; the other, Philippa's mount, had flaring nostrils and vengeful eyes, and cantered sideways, snorting, while she struggled with the reins.

– I shall have to give this one something to think about, she said. I'll be back in minutes.

She cut her riding crop into the horse's left flank, then smartly into the right, and thundered off into a lane dividing the forest.

Ten minutes later she reappeared, bearing down on me at the gallop, and a blizzard of blackbirds wheeled offstage screaming. In a panic, and needlessly as it turned out, I steered my mount hard left into a bush which the animal declined to penetrate – needlessly, I say, because Philippa had successfully dealt with her animal's malevolence, and brought him up under perfect control, sides heaving, foam falling from his masticating mouth. She gasped with laughter.

– What on earth are you doing pointing yourself into that bush?

– Never mind that. Tell me how you make this thing go backwards.

– Hold on. I'll pull her out for you.

She dismounted, pulled the grey back to the path, and tethered it to a tree.

– Off you get, she commanded, and I slid off the horse and fell into her arms. Had I not I'd have collapsed into a pile of burnt roots.

– Do you know, she whispered, and there was delight in her eyes, that's exactly the way it happened with Wallace.

And that, dear friend, is the way my weekend at Gathering Hall began – exactly the way it had happened with Wales. In truth that part of it must have happened somewhat differently – probably the other way round – because Wales, as you know, is/was an excellent horseman and would have dismounted rather than fallen. Whatever the method, the result was the same. We did not proceed, Philippa and I, from one thing to the other immediately; instead she led me in the direction of her own panting steed, climbed expertly aboard, and held out her hand.

– Come on, get up behind. Don't stand there, heave!

And somehow with much leaning and lurching and careening into the stirrup, I managed to insert myself into the half of the saddle she had left unoccupied.

– Hands around my waist.

I obeyed with pleasure.

We set off through the forest at a walk, and Horace I must tell you I have never known anything so sublime: the easy rocking motion of the horse beneath us, Philippa's slender body swaying gently against mine, her hair caressing my face, the smell of crocuses and the horse and the good earth around us. The horse stopped, she leaned her head back against my shoulder, and my hands strayed blissfully among the teacups.

*   *   *

— That's exactly the way it happened with Wallace.

Well, no, not exactly. She told me then and there how it happened with Wales, and I must say it put my pedestrian manners to shame.

— At any rate it *began* the same way, with the two of us on the same horse.

— The black or the grey?

— The black. You see, when you ride well, you are never much drawn to the ones that are virtually in retirement. You've got to feel that the animal under you wants to give something of itself.

Irritating. That Wales and I should find ourselves sharing the same woman was all very well and good, and not unprecedented, but something made me want to draw the line at the beast.

— Tell me, I don't expect Wales would ever be so gauche as to fall off a horse into a lady's arms. How did it come about that you both ended up

— On the same black charger?

— Precisely.

— Well, it happened that way because I let him take the black — normally my horse, you see. But I just couldn't see him on the grey. Sorry. He rides rather well, you know.

I was at the point of remarking that I had heard that story from any number of ladies, but managed to abstain.

— Which means that Wales had to invite *you* to

— Precisely. I thought he did it because he was tired of hearing me complaining about the grey.

— Not the best of theories, that one, but go on.

— We came to the same sunny clearing; you know, the one where we

— Yes, I know. And?

— And that's where it began to get different.

— Different. Is it ever different?

— Listen. The first thing that happened was that he pulled off my boots.

— You were still on the horse?

— We were still on the horse. It was a performance, but we managed.

— And then?

– And then . . . well, I don't know *who* did it, really, but somehow I had got myself out of my jeans and the rest and

– And?

She looked at me rather furtively, as if expecting to be struck.

– And then we went riding.

She threw her head back and tolled with laughter. Finally, covering her modesty with both hands, she peered at me over fingertips.

– Honestly I'd never experienced anything so heavenly in all my life.

– Mmmmmmmm. Tell me about the horse. Was it going along at the gallop or at the trot?

– Don't be vulgar. You're jealous.

– You're damned right I'm jealous. Here, turn round on this filthy black horse and we'll find out how much fiction there is in all that, and how much truth.

And we did, Horace. Once we had stopped laughing, we did.

*　　　*　　　*

Later.

– When we first came to the clearing in the sun, he stopped to take it all in – to breathe it all in, really. It is rather beautiful, don't you think? Then after a moment I heard him murmur the words 'heaven of light'. What do you suppose he meant by that?

For me, it was a reflection about the ending of a world. It was about the passing of the centuries, and of the years: a moment of sadness in the life of a man no longer young. I could not reply because I knew what he meant.

The Ninth Envelope

Dustbin. And what if the only important truths were to be learned, as Graves would have us believe, from goddesses? Where, then, would *they* go for instruction? Plodding unromantic that I am, I confess to the suspicion that he may have grasped no more than half of the equation – enough, however, to be getting on with.

Leave it to the pedants; what matters is the speech of the senses, the *feel* of the thing, always. How to write about it, what to say about it, is it possible to try? The girl meant nothing to me. We had spent our previous moments together passing one another in corridors. We had never eaten together, let alone slept together. I had never heard her speak of her father; her mother might have been the woman who brought in the tea. An ocean and two thousand miles separated her country from mine. What mattered, to be deliberately vulgar, was the smell of it. The horse. The decaying moss. Wild flowers and garlic. An unidentifiable perfume in her hair. The rest was a juxtaposition of bodies, and not to be underrated for all the ugliness of the Latin: we were swept up to the sky and beyond like soaring, captivated birds. Fate, accident – blunder? – had led us to the same doorstep, to the care or mercy of identical men: Wales alive, Wales no longer alive. So we rode off into the forest and welded ourselves into the hide of a horse, and soared aloft like the centaur sprung from the clouds.

This time there were no twinges of guilt: one might claim progress. All Jeannine knew was that I had spent a night at Gathering Hall in search of Wales, and that Wales had visited Philippa as he had the others. Moreover – and it was this that justified everything – there was the new matrioshka which I took home with me in triumph. Triumph tinged with relief, because it meant, I felt certain, that I was not to be handed all the way along the chain of daisies. Relief because the real need is at home, yes, with Jeannine and also with my creatures, the plants, the trees, the humming insects, the dozing cats, the sun glancing off the glistening trees after a shower. We are poor things, all of us, beside our blades of grass. What are we if not their weeds?

Horace. You are rapidly becoming a bore with all your questions. No, there was no problem in being absent from the boileroom; it was the weekend, and anyway that's what Cragg wants. Yes, of course Jeannine knew where I was and approved of my going. No, I did not tell her of my own adventure; I confined myself to the musical ride of Philippa and Wales. Yes, Wales did visit her unannounced, driving up out of nowhere in the Bentley the weekend before. No, he did not say where he had come from nor where he was going; a secretary, it seems, does not pose questions to her posthumous boss. Yes, I did ask why not, and it seems she felt it would not have been proper; riding is one thing and Wales' private itinerary another; after all, we are safer on a horse. Besides, curiosity is not terribly much a characteristic of the breed, except where sexual intimacies are concerned. Helena and Philippa and Liz found out quickly enough about all that, but what else have they learned? That Wales still uses the Bentley, and I agree with you that it's a substantial clue. But what do you expect me to do, get them to send out a police bulletin? If I did go to them for help – the man is dead but we've seen him driving round in his car – they would send for the nearest psychiatrist out shrink, and I'm not sure they'd be wrong.

Philippa did come down the following Monday morning to favour me with a cuddle: she found me at work in front of my candelabra and said I looked terribly romantic. Since then we've gone back to passing one another in the corridors as if nothing whatever had occurred. In one small detail, however, she was different from the others: she did promise to let me know if Wales should ever want to go riding again. That much she felt she owed me. Perhaps the promiscuous poet is getting somewhere after all: for you to decide. For you, Horace, and for events: they will go marching on independently of us all. I mean the latest matrioshka, fifth in the row. I am coming to that. But first let me reassure you about the vexing matter of Wales' appearance which, as you will remember from Lili's account of it, was of a thickset man with fur on his head. I did quiz them one by one – Helena, Philippa, and Liz (haven't had the heart to speak to the others), and it was Wales all right. No fur, no bulging waistline. The same piercing blue eyes and tickling moustache. So we are left with the problem of the man in Vienna, whoever the hell *he* was.

Matrioshka Five. Our blessed stars. But hold on, there's another hurdle that must be gotten over. What would you say if one were to try to make claims for Wales as a thinker? Not as a thinkerthinker in the horrible DescartianHegelian mould, but as a generalist observer with axes to grind. Well, we are going to have to examine that possibility now, and believe me I am as astonished as I know you will be yourself. Everybody knew Wales had a mind, but the notion that he might actually have exercised it on matters surpassing routine is not one that would have occurred to me. I mean, the impression he gave all of us – and I have checked with Moot and Philippa and Peter Glyffe – was the reverse. All that, one was led to infer, was for the workers; the correct attitude was one of sovereign indifference. How little one knows.

What happened was that I realized, a little late in the game perhaps, that I hadn't finished my homework. *Leave no stone unturned: one of them may conceal your grave.* The stones, or gravestones if you prefer, are the papers I took home with me from Wales' desk, the extraordinary jumble in the plastic bags. Priorities for the immediate future, erotic fairy tales, flying buttresses, batrachomyomachy, and so forth – we never did make it cohere, and it may be that I gave up too soon. What are we to make of this?

> *There is something unforgivably glutinous about German sensibility: any poet capable of describing Beethoven as a 'sweet sensation of death' deserves to be drowned in a vat of black molasses. In other words, he was mouthing the fashionable nonsense of the moment, and fashion invariably destroys. What kind of merit could have been attached to the music criticism of a Coco Chanel or a Christian Dior had either of them been foolish enough to express themselves in that idiom? And why go so far afield for an example when almost any music critic will do? These things are wordgames: one might just as well play Scrabble. Music stands at one threshold of perception, the verbal arts at another. They cannot be made to pass through the same sensual doors. Hence the perpetual failure of opera to convey a purely poetic message; what one gets is a vulgar wash of dramatic intention, and only at the cost of studying the book. Nothing in our appreciation of poetry can substitute for concentrated attention to the text or to the voice reading it. The moment it is set to music it plays second fiddle. I am not sure that the organs of perception are not dominated more by sound than by any other stimulus, for sound, organized as music, is imperial in a way that images are not. Even at the cinema,*

> *where music serves purposes that are not its own, weak pictures*
> *are constantly saved from oblivion by backgrounds of seductive*
> *sound.*

Listen, Horace, if you had seen that in print somewhere, would you ever have attributed it to Wallace Marshall Wales? Imagine it, Wales on poetic intention, Wales on perception, Wales on the imperialism of musical sound! You may argue that he did publish poetry after all, and criticism, not to forget the didactic dandies of Oxbridge and Camford, but we both know that if he read any of it, which seems unlikely, he most certainly never talked about it outside the house. How, then, are we to believe that he exchanged confidences of that sort with the naked page? And yet there it is, half a page of notepaper torn at one edge and covered with the inimitable green scrawl. There is no date. It must precede the Greek Injunction, surely, or 'poetry' would not have been spared.

I then dipped into the plastic for another scrap and came up with this, which seems to have been preceded by a page preparing us for the shock, but as the scraps are not numbered I offer it to you, for the moment, in isolation.

> *pay for higher standards of services and higher standards of*
> *living, our various governments have become the victims of their*
> *own humanitarian intentions, so-called. From this observation*
> *it is no more than a short step to the uncomfortable conclusion or*
> *the accepted reality – depending on the viewpoint of the observer*
> *– that governments were never meant to serve the human*
> *purpose. If so, there remains only one other purpose for them*
> *to serve: that of government itself. Has history ever determined*
> *that the interests of governments and governed must necessarily*
> *correspond?*

Here, at least, the tone of voice is present: one can hear him saying that. If Wales had a hobbyhorse, don't you agree, it was the smashing of icons – clay dolls? – and it was no part of our work to complain. But it did make life difficult, because it wasn't possible to know in advance which ones were to be smashed and to whose faiths they might belong. Von Gildenkrantz has always insisted that the man was not serious; you never knew whom or what he would attack next. Moot, of course, is. He attacks the British for having lost the economic war. Another fragment from the same bag:

aimed at a redefinition of economic activity which seems so simple as to make one wonder how the economists have been blind to it for so long. According to Professor J. we must begin thinking in terms of outputs that are marketed and those that are not. Automobiles represent marketed output; the Army does not. Government health services, civil service, state-run schools, and the police are examples of non-marketed activities because they cannot be exchanged for anything else. In the words of Adam Smith, 'Their service, however honourable, how useful, or how necessary soever, produces nothing for which an equal quantity of service can afterwards be procured.' But Adam Smith's distinction is not entirely trustworthy as it makes no provision for invisible wealth: non-material value of the kind produced by bankers, shippers and insurance men, and very different from the activities of the soldier, policeman and schoolteacher in the sense that it can be exported and exchanged for something else. (Consequential question: what is a thief if not an individual who 'produces nothing for which an equal quantity of service can afterwards be procured'? But the thief's intention is to sell what he steals; in this sense, until he is caught and 'put out of harm's way', he is a productive member of the community. The non-productive members are the soldiers, policemen, and school-teachers, not to mention those capitalists, both private and state, who withhold wealth from all possibility of productive investment by risk. Ergo, all soldiers, policemen, schoolteachers, and hoarders of wealth are thieves.)

I am not sure about the *ergo*, which reminds me of Bernard Shaw, but the rest sounds very consequential indeed. Wales, dabbler economist? Social critic? Capitalist anticapitalist? Who would have believed it! Listen to this dated the 25th of September: the year is not given.

O'Connor's thesis which arrived in the post this morning. The natural drive of the religion of buying and selling is the creation of new forms of privilege (all varieties of the New Money, from prints, paintings, and objets d'art to mountains of butter and 'banks' of information) together with new forms of slavery. This tendency may be said to have begun at the moment in history when one man, proving himself to be stronger than another, forced the other to toil for him at peril of his life. The strong bought the product of the weak at the cost of food and terror (the latter being a cost because it is never applied without effort); the weak then 'sold himself' into slavery in exchange for his life. It was not what we call a free-market exchange, but the results were effectively the same as those obtained in the twentieth century, more by carrot than by stick, from a worker on a repetitive production line. Other forms of contemporary slavery might be said to include such devices as compulsory military service and all manner of confined and salaried activity in which the worker supplies the labour without sharing responsibility (amalgam of profit and risk). In avoiding risk a slave might be thought to be better off than his master; until he is discharged his 'social security' is absolute. This, in fact, is the carrot the twentieth century has asked us to grasp, the new-old idol before which the millions genuflect. And as long as the millions remain bent down before their god, the masters will continue without opposition from the serfs. Their silence has been bought.

Another form of contemporary forced labour not widely acknowledged as such is the slavery of women. This, too, returns us to the origins of the human race when it became clear that the males were more muscular than the females and therefore could be counted on to exercise gentlemanly dominion over them. Though the only muscles the male is still called upon to use are those he lodges between his ears, the practice continues to this day. Even in the so-called developed countries women are still the main drawers of water if not the hewers of wood, and their economic value, the value of the tasks they perform as mothers and mistresses and housekeepers, has been placed at five thousand dollars a year – a modest figure when one knows that if women were to withdraw their labour entirely, society would collapse. (The corollary of this – whether human society would continue if the efforts of the male sex were withdrawn – is not something we are likely to hear discussed.)

The second most obvious form of forced female labour is the universal secretarial pool. Though it has never been demonstrated that women are more efficient as typists and filing clerks and telephone answerers than men, or that their docile temperament lends them more naturally to activities of a routine nature, they must necessarily carry this particular burden wherever there are machines with alpha-numeric keyboards and mini-Hitlers who enjoy bending them to the task. But we are now entering an electro-mechanical era in which women as extensions of the typewriter are to be liberated by self-operating and self-correcting electricity. Once this new instrumentation has been disseminated, our battalions of secretary-slaves will be free to go elsewhere. And where will they go?

The logic of our religion of buying and selling suggests that following an inevitable period of uncertainty, challenge and response, a new slavery will be devised for them. There may be degrees of cultivation or gentility required, from the delicacy of the geisha to the crudity of the streetwalker, but in the absence of an unprecedented access of mini-Hitlerian fairplay, our ex-secretaries will be forced to fall back on variants of the oldest profession.[1]

In a world in which the only values are those of the marketplace, massive ex-secretarial prostitution will not be considered a disgrace. Our legislators, in paying lip-service to women's liberation, will stop short of granting it the status of a liberal, or taxable, profession, thereby making it possible for practitioners to claim state subsidies in the form of unemployment benefits. Almost everyone will be rendered happier by this outcome: the secretarial call-girls, because of the guarantee of social security; their clients, because a part of their fees will already have been paid by the state; and the clients' wives, who will be spared the tepid attentions of a world of husbands jaded by the absence of adventure.

Ouf! That, I can tell you, is Wales undiluted, footnote compris. New forms of slavery, new forms of privilege. The new/old religion of buying and selling before which millions genuflect. The new 'liberation' of women. What do you suppose he was trying to do, *write*?

Unthinkable. Converse with himself in the absence of a partner in dialogue? But why did he put it down? Dialogue, at that level of effort, must have a purpose of some kind. You tell me; dialogue out. Meanwhile in one way or another it all strikes terribly close to the bone; I, for reasons of my own, am the first to admit it. And you, my friend and worthy scribe, how many 'authors' have you drudged for during the course of your distinguished career? What price the sovereign selfemployed?

*   *   *

Jeannine, of course, knows about the daisychain, censored version, and thinks it's hilarious. Her attitude is that since none of them is married, what harm can it possibly do? Besides it disposes of fiction, the one that

[1] Wales: There is good historic evidence to show that the oldest profession, commonly attributed by men to the prostitute, was in fact that of the *scribe*, whose task it was to record what his masters told him to record. If this is so, the slavery of woman's body was preceded by the slavery of man's mind. Not much has changed since Sumer.

pretends he is dead. All very good, though perhaps she doesn't know that if she hadn't set out her beautiful corolla for me all those years ago, any one of them, Winifred and Hilda excepted, would have made a bumbler of me in my first trip round the garden. Could it be that the world has given up marriage, and Wales is the first to have found out? Come to think of it, he might have gone to work on the authors. From that angle the prospects are practically unlimited.

You know, Horace, the more one walks round this story the more one is tempted to give credit to Moot. The man is not serious. He is deliberately trying to provoke confusion, laughter, derision – *you* decide. My sides are aching, but for other reasons.

*   *   *

We were talking about the distance between the Philippas and the Winnies and how Wales might have bridged the gulf. Jeannine was as perplexed as I. She had met Winifred at one of our Christmas parties (Hilda invited her because Wales invited Thrale), and after a brief exchange of vacuities fled to my corner of the room. I could see that she was of a mood to be less than kind. 'How,' she said, 'could anyone possibly want to rape a lump of porridge like that?' Unable as I was to imagine what might go on in the mind of a rapist, I found it even more difficult to visualize a less violent approach. She smiled at me maliciously, answering her own question. 'It must have been those centimetres of silk under the sandpaper sheets.'

I wonder if you were ever so indiscreet – stupid is perhaps the better word – as to catalogue your premarital adventures for the benefit of your wife? I did, once, and I am not sure, come to think of it, that it wasn't the ulterior motive at work: I was hoping that she would do the same for me. The ruse didn't work. But I spilled out all my secrets: not a long story as my early pursuits, as befitted the bard in me, usually ran to the sublime. Nonetheless there were episodes; one would be less than human had it been otherwise. The most curious of them took me back to my first days on this side of the water when for a brief period I shared a house in Stobo Street with an Australian art collector named Burton Locke, a splendid man with a welldeveloped taste for exotic women. What he wanted was not a lodger but a guardian. I was admitted rent free on the understanding that whenever he was elsewhere collecting statues – indifferently of the living or nonliving variety – I was to remain behind warding off thieves. The other condition was that within the house we should live entirely separate lives – he with his women and I, when the impulse should arise, with mine. We should meet only in the kitchen at breakfast, where I was to make coffee out of my own pot. During his absences I was allowed the run of the house, a Georgian splendour with all the comforts. A civilized man, my semiabsentee landlord, and as I was making tuppence weekly reading proof, I was only too delighted to battle burglars for him and affect an attitude of detachment toward his ladies. The burglars were the easy part of the bargain, for they never showed up. The ladies were something else. He had an eye for a statue, Burton did, and there they were, lounging about the place in various amounts of drapery – often two or three at a time – painted, unpainted, coloured, uncoloured, bangled, unbangled, and bathed in the scents of Samarkand. I was constantly meeting them on the stairways and in the hall, and they smiled at me indulgently as if to suggest that I, too, would grow up one day and learn to rejoice in the pleasures that to them were part of nature. I tried to get away from it all by shutting the door of my room, but I could not close out the laughter, which ran through the house like electric current, any more than I was able to unpop the champagne. It was the plight of the monk living in closed community with a sorority of party girls: not calculated to advance one to the higher levels.

At the house where I was reading I found myself seated across the table from one of the plainest – to put it generously – of Her Majesty's flowers, called Mildred. My bardic tic was set in motion the minute we were introduced, and she became known to me for ever after as Mildew. To give her credit, she tried very hard, as plain girls do, to please: ready smile in the morning, solicitous attention to the tea, and quantities of sharpened pencils supplied on a quotidian basis. Little by little we came to know each other, a slow process at best when one's mind is riveted to the page, but there are intervals. By the end of our first month she knew where I lived, whom I shared with, how he disported himself with the ladies, and why I felt envious of his stars. What harm could there be, I thought, in confiding with her, especially as my intimacies almost invariably induced a flow of moisture at the corners of the eyes – token of sympathy and possibly even concern? Before long Mildew's sandpaper complexion and asymmetric jaw ceased to bother me. It would have taken a harder heart than mine to shut her out of the printed prison whose confines we shared.

Then of course it happened as it always does in stories: one evening as she was 'just passing by', she appeared at the door and I invited her to come in. What else could I have done? Locke had bolted and I had the place to myself. I showed her into the sittingroom where she stood for a moment with her back toward me contemplating the statues, and for the first time I noticed that she had a good body. In fact, the longer I studied her the more she *became* a body – fullbreasted, generous at the hips, longlegged, and faceless. Perhaps it was the absence of the dark blue smock she wore at work to protect her dress from the ink. Well, would you believe it, I moved up from behind and began telling her what it was that I so liked about statues of women, describing it with my hands. She pretended amazement but made no effort to resist or move away, none; her only protest was a whisper of surprise and delight. And then the miracle occurred. Within seconds we were on the sofa in various stages of undress (there is always a refractory shoelace or a tangled trouserleg to add to the panic nessepas), and my hands found themselves englobing, encircling, caught up in a shock of discovery, for her skin, the skin of her body, was in total contrast to the harshness of her face; it was of such indescribable smoothness that touching her brought on a kind of delirium, more spasm than caress. Of all the women in the world, this curious creature with the sandpaper cheeks and misshapen chin caused my sparkplugs to explode in a way I had never known before. Seismic. At the end we fell back dazed, unable to move or to speak. Eventually we fell asleep, and when I awoke in the gathering darkness I saw that she was staring at me with liquid eyes from an infinity of sorrow. We dressed and I walked her to the underground.

There was a single repeat performance. This time, burdened as I was by the damp and unspoken reproach confronting me each day across the table, I weakened and invited her up, as they put it in those days, 'for a drink'. There was always the prospect of another seismic upheaval, and besides, the memory of the sandpaper above and the silk below – shall I confess the whole thing, Horace, right down to the last pubic centimetre? It was the inner surface of her thighs that drove me out of my mind. They must have rubbed against one another God knows how many millions of times, smoothing, caressing, softening the way for my blundering thundering me. And so once more I found myself a thermometer's breadth from the molten lava when, without warning of any kind, she went stiff. I mean like a corpse, and ambulance bells were clanging in my head. But before there was time to apply finger to pulse, she had shot to her feet and begun bounding up and down on the trampoline bed, shouting 'It's wicked! It's wicked!' and all I could see in the dark was the shape of a black triangle ascending and descending black on black at the level of my shuttering eyes. Eventually she subsided, and without further comment began to dress. A power of speech returned.

– What's wicked?

There was no reply, and she went wordlessly out into the night. End of

131

volcano, end of Mildew, end of Stobo Street – for Locke below had heard the thundering above, and it was such a loss of face that I began looking for a flat the next day. The job at Wales followed at a brief interval, and I left proofreading without a backward glance or a farewell glass, firmly convinced that in all that governed the pulsations of the flesh, prudence was by far the best policy.

When I told the story to Jeannine she was not amused; hence the crack, all these years along the road, about 'the silken skin under the sandpaper sheet'. Don't ask me about the sheet; she may have been trying to say 'cheek'. But it may suggest an explanation for Wales' venturing so far along the chain. His own approach, one might suppose, could have been as impromptu as mine – I am thinking, now, of the wilting daisies at the end – and as pointless.

The trouble with this theory, of course, is that it leaks. Wales' visitations were premeditated – as if he had set out in search of something for which sex was a pretext. What could he have said to them or learned from them that they haven't related to me? Help me, Horace, for God's sake. I am not as cheerful about all this as I may sound. Far from it. I assure you, if this horrid, braincracking, unconscionable mess doesn't sort itself out soon, I am going to get the hell out, secret or no secret, and that will be the end of me.

I seem to have issued that threat before. Can you believe that I have gone along with it now for ten scarifying months? Scarifying, from the Greek *skariphos*, style, cognative with the Latin *scribere*, to write.

The Tenth Envelope

The way to get the hell out without disclosing the worst is, as ever, by following Wales' injunctions; I was about to explain, was I not, when I became diverted by Stobo Street. I still don't know why, really; this is supposed to be an account of *his* events. But what do you expect me to do when nothing occurs?

Before I forget: Cragg has been elected chairman of the Academy of Letters, no less. He now affects breastpocket handkerchiefs, striped trousers, and, I am told, a goldplated inkwell. The smugness that goes with it is quite nauseating to behold, even from a distance. There was a champagne party upstairs to which everyone was invited but me, but it didn't rub any skin off mine because one by one, Philippa, Helena, Liz, and Sally came down with a glass for me, and other encouragement. By the end of the afternoon I was layered with four flavours of lipstick and inhabited by the fantasy that the Academy had elected me chairman and banished Cragg to the hole.

On to the fifth matrioshka, and you are forgiven for thinking I would never get to it. Well, what happened was that this time I insisted on taking Jeannine. Thrale said he would need the General's approval and the General was not in that week: Winifred eventually traced him to Lord Gracey's grousemoor in Scotland, from which came his OK. That gave me time to tell you about life in Stobo Street such as it was lived, and to put down this next part of the adventure.

Go back to the train returning me from Gathering Hall at the end of my equestrian weekend with Philippa. A seedy little man in a conductor's uniform came along and read my ticket. Then he read me.

– Mr Racine, sir?

– Yes. How did you know?

– I was told to look for a gentleman with thin hair, thick spectacles, and his nose in a book of poetry.

– What would you have done if I'd forgotten the book and put my spectacles in my pocket?

– I expect I should have given it to somebody else.

– Given what?

– Ah yes, this.

And he handed me a box wrapped in rather elegant paper covered with a woodcut motif of monks illuminating manuscripts. I opened it and you can imagine what I found grinning at me inside. Mother and offspring all wear the same infantile smile: not even the parent had managed to grow up.

– Where did you get it?

– It was handed to me by a gentleman at Morden Priory, sir.

– Where's that?

– End of the line, sir.

– He wasn't driving a Bentley by any chance?

– Shouldn't think so, sir. Not quite the type.

– What kind of man was he?

– Well, that's just it, sir, it was difficult to tell. He had on a dirty old mac and gumboots, you see. Not the sort of chap you'd expect to see at the Priory.

– Why the gumboots, was it raining?

– No, sir. If you want my opinion he had the gumboots on because he hadn't got any proper shoes.

– Tell me, did he have a moustache and heavy eyebrows?

– No, sir. Cleanshaven, sir.

– Hair?

– Greyish. Longish. You know, a bit untidylike.

– Complexion?

– Healthy. An outdoors man, I'd say.

– Tall, short?

– Medium. A bit on the stout side, I'd say.

– At the waist, you mean?

– That's where it generally begins, sir. Look 'ere, sir, he said, opening his jacket and patting a cavernous stomach, haven't added an inch since I was seventeen. And that was a week or two ago, I may as well admit.

I had more or less exhausted my Sherlocks. One last question occurred.

– Was there anybody with him when he gave you this parcel?

– Yes, sir. There was a young lady with him.

– A young lady? What kind of a young lady?

– Well, sir, she was a very good looking young lady. Remarkably good looking if you want my opinion.

– Your opinion interests me a great deal Mr ah – what did you say your name was?

– Peach, sir.

– Peach! The fruit?

– Yes, sir. You've got it on the nail, sir. Jeremiah Peach.

– *Jeremiah Peach!*

– Your servant, sir.

– Well, damn! What am I to make of that?

– I don't know, sir. People tell me it's an unusual name, but you know if you live with it as I've done for

– Just a second, Mr Peach. Do you by any chance happen to write?

– By all means, sir. Not a fancy hand, of course, but legible enough.

– That's not what I mean. What I mean is – do you write poetry?

– I do, sir, when the spirit takes me. Now, how would you have guessed?

– Search me. A premonition, possibly. What kind of poetry do you write?

– Clerihews and the like. I tried a sonnet once or twice but it's not really my line. Now and again I take off and do a bit of freeform verse, if you know what I mean, but Mrs Peach doesn't much care for it. Between you and me, sir – and I wouldn't want this to get back to Mrs Peach – clerihews are daft. I only write them to please.

– A universal problem, Mr Peach; the problem of the artist's commission. If you write to order for Mrs Peach you lose your freedom just as you would if a publisher asked you to put together a collection of dirty jokes.

– Ah, but offcolour jokes are fun, don't you think? Have you heard the one about

– Yes I have! There is something else I feel I should be asking you, but I can't think what it is. Wait – yes, I meant to ask you if you had ever submitted any of your work to a publisher.

– *My* bits of doggerel?

– Well, you could always send them in and ask for an opinion.

The railwayman pushed back his hat and ran his fingers through his forelock, as if trying to dispose of an unusually worrying idea.

– Do you know, it never occurred to me. It's one thing to write poems for Mrs Peach and something else again to write them for the world, wouldn't you say?

– Yes, but what if Mrs Peach and the world just happened to see eye to eye?

– That strikes me as being very unlikely if I may say so, sir. Very unlikely indeed. You don't know Mrs Peach. And while we're on the subject I may as well tell you what I think of all those young bucks who go tearing off to the nearest publisher the minute they've scratched a bit of paper.

– Yes?

– There's not a man alive who's got what it takes to beat Will Shakespeare.

– No more than anyone will do better than Jean Racine.

– Sorry, sir; who?

– Another of the breed, or would have been if they'd thrown him into a vat with Molière, and stirred.

– In other words, if I follow you, sir, we're not going to see John's like again.

– Not half of it.

– Then why do they try to prove the impossible?

– But that's not what they're trying to do. If you go to sea on a postage stamp you don't sit there pretending it's the *Queen Elizabeth*. Each poet tries to find his own voice: isn't that the task? Not to be like or unlike, better or worse, but to get on with it and say it in one's own way.

– Say what, sir?

Vertiginous. And if he didn't know I was damned if I would help him. The conversation ended there by mutual consent: he had gone on too long, he said, and went off to punch tickets.

Half an hour after I had got down from that train I was on my way home in another. At that point, midway to Grumley, it came to me that I should have asked him to describe the beautiful girl standing beside the thickwaisted man in gumboots. I expect you have noticed that with the exception of Wales himself, the people who deliver the matrioshkas are unknown to us. The boy at the hairdresser's. The taxi driver. The beautiful girl on the Isle of Wace: same one? The tattily dressed character who hadn't got any proper shoes. Jeremiah Peach. You're not going to tell me, are you, that we know *him!* I raise the point now, because two or three days later, in the back room at Thatcher's Bookshop, I came across a slender volume of poems entitled *Tragicommas and Tragicomas*. They were mine, all right, the ones I had left on the train, and attributed – how did you guess – to none other than our modest friend J. Peach. And the publisher? The work called *Tragicommas and Tragicomas* ('collected poems', it says on the jacket) is brought to us under the imprint of the Wales Elementary Educational Press! One might suppose, if Wales is the author of this ghastly stunt, that he might at least have tried to separate it from the house – but no, the Great Conduit Street address is there in its usual place on the back of the titlepage, the ISBN number is given, and the copyright credited to Jeremiah Peach. I am found dumb.

* * *

WEEP has been the work of Caroline Bream, Selwyn's daughter, for ten or eleven years, and if quantity is a measure of success she has fulfilled the task admirably. We seldom saw each other – largely, no doubt, because our responsibilities did not impinge, and moreover she had her offices in the far wing at the shadowy end of the courtyard. Caroline: a tall creature with a pointed nose and a pointed chin and the habit of walking with a forward tilt in readiness, one would suppose, for unfavourable winds. No one in the house called her Caroline.

Her door was closed when I knocked; a piping voice inside nevertheless invited me to go in.

– Yes? she said, craning over her table, eyebrows at the alert.

She had evidently forgotten my name.

– Robert Racine.

– Yes, of course. The poetry series. Do come in, Mr Racine.

– I wonder if I might ask you about this, I said, handing her my copy of *Tragi and Tragi*.

– By all means, she replied, taking the book from me and bending over it briskly.

– Good heavens!

She sat up straight in her seat and riveted me with incredulous eyes.

– It's published by WEEP!

Her fingers began rattling through the pages in search of other, less incriminating evidence.

– Can this be so? But it's quite absurd, Mr Racine. We have always published our poetry under the Wales and Wales imprint. I have no need to tell *you* that.

– Yes, but I am no longer very much in the picture. I am now responsible for dirty jokes.

– Dirty

– jokes, Miss Bream. The poetry series has been taken away from me.

– I don't understand.

– Wales and Wales hasn't published any poetry since the chairman disappeared. Cragg put a stop to it. But now this has appeared – I found it at Thatcher's during my lunch hour – and I must say first of all that I have no objection to the publication of poetry by WEEP, if that is the

137

policy. What I object to, Miss Bream, is the publication of *my* poetry under someone else's name.

– Will you hold on just a second, Mr Racine.

She removed her glasses and dialled a number on the internal telephone.

– I say, have we ever published anything by an author named Peach? Peach, the edible variety. Jeremiah Peach. Jeremiah, the lamenting prophet, Peach the edible . . . Absolutely certain? Now tell me, does this title ring a bell: *Tragicommahs* and *Tragicewmahs*. *Tragi* as in tragedy with an '*i*' in place of the '*e*'; *commah* as in punctuation; *tragi* again; *cewmah* as in knocked out on the verge of extinction. I believe it's a volume of poetry. Yes I know it's nonsense but I'm obliged to doublecheck. Many thanks.

She extracted a bit of lace from her sleeve and polished her glasses with it. Then, having put them back on again, she opened the book and turned directly to the copyright page.

– Yes, it's all there. You say this is *your* work, Mr Racine? I mean the poems?

– Mine to the last coma.

– A pseudonym perhaps?

– Not a pseudonym. And no permission was given.

Miss Bream blotted a bead on her upper lip with the lace.

– Well, then, what we have here, it seems, is a mystery. But I mean a *real* mystery.

*   *   *

Caroline Bream had never gone along with Harper Cabot's Polish deal; she wanted to have her printers under her nose so that she could be sure of meeting her deadlines. The argument was that schools did not wait for books, and of course there was no quarrelling with that. So in the matter of buying print WEEP went its own way, and Caroline's pointed nose reached all the way up to Scotland. The printer in Edinburgh, whom she rang forthwith, insisted that not only had *Tragicommahs* never passed through his hands; *Tragicewmahs* hadn't, either. Then how did he account for the fact that the printing was credited in the book to his company? There was no accounting for it. The whole thing sounded like pure fiction.

– Dirty trick, said Miss Bream as she put down the telephone receiver a second time. Someone is playing us a dirty trick.

The next call, to Thatcher's Bookshop, was similarly unproductive.

138

The bookbuyer had never heard of *Tragi and Tragi*, any more than he had heard of Jeremiah Peach. It was not listed in *Books in Print*, and to the best of his knowledge there were no copies on the shelves. But he would verify that; just a second, please. Two-minute pause while Caroline once more laced up her glasses. Yes, there were two copies in the poetry section. No, he hadn't the faintest idea how they had got there. Somebody must have put them there: the author, perhaps, one of those cranks like Balzac who printed his own, could that be it? On second thoughts, no, that couldn't be it; the book was published by the Wales Elementary Educational Press. Had somebody at Wales left the copy in the wrong basket? Wasn't it a pretty pickle?

-- Mr Racine, said Caroline Bream, and she stared at me with the look of someone who had fallen asleep without remembering to close her eyes.

– Yes, Miss Bream.

– *Who* is Jeremiah Peach?

The Dante Express. Have you ever noticed that the further we go in the direction of what we adore to call 'progress', the smaller the conveniences become? Kitchens are smaller, bathtubs are smaller, there is less and less room for legs at the theatre, and when one is obliged to relieve oneself in a public place one needs to know how to hit the neck of a winebottle from thirty paces. Who are the architects of our smallness? They must be a race of sadistic dwarves, gasping for opportunities to funnel us all down into some underworld where elephants are chihuahuas and eagles have turned into fleas. Has it ever occurred to you, my dear Horace, that the fastest way to create new housing would be to develop a pill to shrink the householder? No tears for the banks, please; we could always mortgage the pills.

But the great Dean has been there before us and we are shrunk and rejoicing, Jeannine and I, in our tiny compartment on the way to Firenze. We have done Dijon, and Dole, and Jeannine is already asleep upstairs as I scribble away in my theatre seat below. It is so small in this place that we bumped bottoms any number of times as we made up for bed. Somehow that made it all right.

No. What made it all right was the getting away. That, and the ladder Moot finally flung down the stairs for me so that I could climb up and meet Lady Moira.

We drove up, the three of us (for Moot insisted on bringing Jeannine), along the river. It was a grand, rambling sort of house, stuccoed and painted Tuscan rose, with a long stable from whose grey tiles grew a profusion of moss and yellow flowers. A long, wellkept lawn swept down from the house to the tiny jetty where Lady Moira moored her rowboat, a vessel she had painted from stem to stern with frolicking mermaids in pursuit of a number of giant seahorses, or viceversa, and I believe one or two of the maidens had actually mounted their steeds and were breasting the surf.

We found her sitting under a huge Japanese cherry tree radiant with blossom. She was wearing a gown one or two shades darker than the blossom; a straw hat cartwheeled over fading blonde hair, piercing blue eyes, and an expression of perpetual amusement: one of those faces that would have reflected astonishment and delight in the face of the worst possible horrors, and probably had. She grasped me firmly by the arm and we set off in the direction of the jetty.

– We're going for a stroll on the liquid lawn, she said. Much better than this one. What I like about the liquid lawn is that no one interrupts. Not much, anyway. Do you know about spinnakers and all that?

– I'm afraid not.

– No matter, we'll use the mechanical propulsion.

At the jetty she knelt to hold the boat and said:

– Step there. Preferably without falling in.

I made my way unsteadily over the mermaids, which swam with their cohorts on the inside of the boat as well, and held it fast to the jetty while Lady Moira followed, hitching up her long skirt to reveal rudimentary shoes and a pair of socks that would have done nicely on a tennis court.

– Go to the end, she ordered. To the end. And raise the anchor.

I reached behind me and unlooped the rope fastening the boat to a post midway along the jetty.

– Well done. We now open the throttle and work up some knots of speed.

She unlocked an oar and pushed us away from our mooring.

– Let me do that, I protested, as she dipped the oars into the water. Please.

By this time, of course, she was sitting in the rowing seat and it was not easy to imagine how we might have changed places.

– I don't know how you're going to manage it, she said, laughing. Anyway don't give it a thought. I do it to keep the pistons moving. Now tell me about the house. Wallace has disappeared and Harriet's granite has taken his place. You are being given assignments, it would seem, *d'outre-tombe*. How are we to read this?

– I was hoping you might know.

She steered the boat into a gentle current which carried us along without effort.

– I have been trying to work it out. It doesn't appear to make a great deal of sense, does it, unless one knows rather a lot about Wallace, otherwise one would have to suppose one was dealing with a sort of demented pixie. Of course, the sexual mania is new. I am told it happens to men at a certain time of life.

Or any other, I thought. A mermaid rose up out of the blue and frolicked me in the groin.

– Wallace was always a great admirer of the Lord. They went fishing together, you know, in Ireland. He absolutely loathed publishing – Wallace, I mean. Detested it and adored it at the same time. Could never fathom the authors. Why do they do it, he kept saying, why do they do it, all that meddling in other people's business for private gain. We had that pompous man J. D. Carrington here for lunch one day, and Wallace came over to fill up the table. Why do you write, Wallace said to him. I write for other people, Carrington replied. But you don't *know* them, said Wallace. How can you possibly write for people you don't *know?* Carrington thought that was a very curious attitude for a publisher, and Wallace then went on to tell us about a shoemaker and his brother who had spent their lives making shoes by hand, choosing the leather and shaping it with infinite care: they knew their clients because they had measured their feet. That continued, and their clients were very happy to have their shoes made so beautifully, until other shops opened to trumpets of advertising and offered factorymade shoes at half the price. And so the brothers could see that one day they would be driven out because people were no longer able to tell the difference between handmade shoes and the others. The point of the story, said Wallace, applied precisely to publishing. And Carrington, who wasn't altogether a fool, said I know that story, it's one of John Galsworthy's. Did Galsworthy know you when he wrote it? No, replied Wallace, he knew my father. End of conversation.

Our own conversation, or to be more exact her part of it, was halted by the waves of a launch that bore down on us and left us bobbing about in its wash. Lady Moira shipped one of the oars in order to hold her cartwheel in place.

– At this point, she went on, one might say the liquid lawn needed rolling.

Why bother with all this detail about a rowboat bobbing up and down on the lawn whose liquid was, in truth, a rather oily green? Because I felt she had brought me into the presence of a man I had somehow failed to observe. Of a Wales who had learned to regard his world with a carefully concealed complexity of love and hate because of the promise and disappointment it inevitably engendered.

The waves subsided and she went back to the oars, manipulating them just enough to keep us in motion.

– Helmut tells me that a number of your poems have begun to appear under someone else's name.

– Yes, and I think I know who it is. But I haven't had time to confront the man. I am not sure what will happen when I do, because I left them on a train and they were not signed.

– Will you recite one of them for me?

Instant anguish; I could not think. What had I ever written that was good enough to address itself to the strong and sanguine woman bent over the oars in front of me? After a pause I plunged in anyway. I did not look at her as I spoke: I was reading invisible lines made visible in the palms of my hands. When I finished her attention seemed to be elsewhere.

– One forgets, she said, that poetry is always a distillation – what the French call *l'eau-de-vie*. It would be wrong of me to ask you to describe the experience that prompted the poem.

She began rowing more vigorously, turning the boat round to head into the current. A lock of hair fell over her forehead. There were lines of irony and determination running away from the corners of her eyes and mouth.

– Yes, I will do what I can to help you with this prehumous posthumous business. Meanwhile read Ecclesiastes and Burton's *Anatomy*. Use your money, as often as you can spare it, to buy pleasure; and come to see me whenever you feel it would help to talk to someone outside the house.

When we had moored the boat we walked back along the lawn where we found Moot and Jeannine playing croquet. Tea was brought to us under the cherry tree. Lady Moira talked of everything and of nothing: of the years when Lord Threshold was still alive, of his friendship with Wales, of her painting and gossip at the academy. Toward the end she became particularly attentive to Jeannine, and took her away from us for a stroll along the river.

*   *   *

– Do you know what she said? She said she thought Wales was trying to bring the house down. She had no idea why. I am to bake the tarts and cakes you particularly like and take you to dinner at the Ritz.

The Eleventh Envelope

Yes, I understand your wanting to know more about Moot. Lord Threshold heard about him at the Nürnberg trials and eventually met him there when he was called to testify: Moot was then seventeen years old. That led to an invitation to England, a long holiday at the manor-house, and the rapport with Lady Moira. What came of it was an adoption in all but name. Wales took him on without even meeting him: Threshold's word was more than enough. Since then Moot has been in charge of foreign rights, and he's been an excellent scout. Frankfurt bookfair, Paris, Milan, Tokyo, New York – whenever Wales didn't feel like going himself. It was due to him, largely, that we eventually became the worldcitizens we are now, although Bekorgakov's presence in the list certainly helped. As for the real question, what happened to him during the war, the best I can do is to refer you back to our reading of *The Death of Tragedy*.[1] You will remember that Steiner concludes the book on a personal note in which he relates two anecdotes: one, of the monastery in Poland where the captured Russian officers met their appalling end; another, of Helene Weigel's interpretation of *Mutter Courage* in Berlin. Of a third, a woman's account of what had been done to her sister in the deathcamp at Mauthausen, he says, 'I will not set it down here, for it is the kind of thing under which language breaks.'

Moot's story is of that nature. Beside it my Abominable and all our Abominables are so much chaff. I very much doubt that the other Racine could have done it justice; certainly it is beyond me. Bref, I have decided that it has no place in the trivial commerce that engages

---

[1] George Steiner, London, mcmlxi.

us here, and I accept full responsibility for its omission – Wales or no Wales.

The road from Certosa. As it turned out, the Ritz was a modest stone house concealed behind a carpet of vines, with the entrance in the cellar and an immense crackling fire at the end of a long table. We shared it with Jeannine's outlaws and an entire party of locals celebrating a wedding – outlaws, because before I appeared on the scene she had narrowly missed marrying an adopted son; it is for this reason that Wolfram and Vera have come to occupy the cornices of honour in the curious structure that makes up our family life. But that is another story and it has no application here. For the present purpose all I need say is that the honorary outlaws, who spent much of their lives tending the family firm in Munich, are now in retirement among the vines and olive groves and are wearing it very well indeed.

So much for the setting – and don't let me forget the excellent *vin santo* that prepared us for our splendid country fare. The aperitivo is served in the cellar: there, already, one begins to feel salvation. To be more precise, the winecellar made me think of the place as a pastoral version of Michelangelo's Biblioteca Medicea Laurenziana, where from the infernal bustle of the streets outside, one passes, via the cloister, into the vestibule, there to be purged and prepared in the one confined yet soaring space for a higher world beyond. In the one case one lives one's purgatory for the sake of books; in the other, for the sake of food. Paradise is a place where one reads food and wine, where one eats and drinks books.

The table at the Osteria Machiavelli, immediately across the road from the house where he wrote *The Prince*, is excellent beyond belief – of that excellence which only naturalness and simplicity can attain. Olive oil, *extra vergine*, on hot bread rubbed with garlic. Smoked Tuscan ham sliced thin as a wafer. Broad beans *al dente* blanketed with freshly ground black pepper. Sausage flavoured with fennel. The house Chianti in its best year, with grainy white cheese. Jeannine and I were glowing, and Wolfram and Vera reflected our pleasure. There is something about faces lighted by an open fire – a special quality imparted; one would count on it to beatify a Borgia.

Our hosts, the outlaws, went to enormous pains to explain to us how to make the most of our time in Florence. We were not to miss visiting the Bargello, the museum of the Duomo, the cloister of Fra Angelico, and all the churches of the saints: San Giovanni, San Lorenzo, Santa Maria Novella, Santa Croce, Santo Spirito, Santissima Annunziata, and

San Miniato al Monte. There was enough for a lifetime and we had five days. Five days and Wales' blessed work to deal with before going back. I deposited Jeannine at Rivoire for the hot chocolate *con panna* (worth the trip in itself), and set out alone for San Lorenzo. For it was work I needed to accomplish alone. Accomplish? It had to be penetrated the way a monk might set out to examine the first discovered manuscript of the *Ars Amatoria* – with wariness and not little of a sense of awe. I walked directly to the piazza del Duomo, where hordes of schoolchildren were being marshalled in squads, and startled a group of nuns by catapulting a loud *buon giorno* in the direction of the campanile – loud, because I imagined it would take a sound with the force of a bell to reach across seven centuries to Dante's friend who had designed it. And who is to say I was not heard? The market at San Lorenzo was very much alive, and I could have passed the best of mornings simply by wandering from stall to stall, for it seemed to me that every material expression of humanity could be found there: accumulations of pots and shoes and printed cloths, shawls and harlequin umbrellas and crumbling antiques – all of it huddled under canvas against the brick walls of the Medicean church, canvas reaching crazily for the sky as if the entire setting – scarves and bags and cameraclacking tourists – was waiting for a signal to set sail and leave me standing there with a handful of pigeons and a yapping dog. Instead, in a lost corner where tables and chairs fell over one another in disarray, my gaze fell on an old bookbinding press, one of those splendid old devices with an iron vise and a turnscrew handle.

A leatherylooking man in a checked shirt and black vest emerged from behind a green canvas flap.

– *Molto bello.*

I tried to pick it up.

– *Molto pesante.*

We exchanged shrugs, and I made my way behind the stalls along the steps leading to the monastery.

Do you remember San Lorenzo? Both it and Santo Spirito, my favourites in Florence, make me think of a Leonardo cartoon, eloquent because unfinished – the mind of the artist laid bare. I have seen a book of sketches for the façade – Michelangelo's and Sangallo's – and one could not have quarrelled with any of the versions proposed. But the Medici pope died, and the money never came forward. All we have, at San Lorenzo, is the simplicity of bare brick rising up to heaven in steps like a ziggurat. I have an idea that was not what the architects had in mind. But inside – ah, my friend, that's where the mystery begins to grip you.

For there, of all places on earth, is the place where Babel might have stopped. Instead it only paused to gather its forces and then went on, on into the void into whose infinitely receding maw we now feed our desperate capsules of hope.

We learn from Hobson,[2] whom I took the precaution to consult before our departure, that the first of the Medicis to collect manuscripts was Cosimo the Elder, and that his father, Giovanni di Bicci, owned precisely three books: the Godspels, the legend of Saint Marguerite, and a volume of sermons in the Italian language. Inflation then set in, and with the help of Niccolò Niccoli, Francesco Barbaro, Poggio Bracciolini, and Cosimo's two sons, intrepid bookhunters all, the library became a collection of three thousand, at which point, in 1571, the Biblioteca Medicea Laurenziana opened its doors. Babel might have been contained there and then because Florence was Athens and Rome rediscovered; Florence was Dante and Petrarch and the new Jerusalem; Florence was the exemplar – I sometimes think, for all time. The library was never designed to go any further: the intention was that it should serve as a monument to the Medicis and the classics they had helped to save. Think of it, Horace, there at the moment when humanity lost touch with its tools, it might, just might have been seen that if we went on to stack books all the way up to the farthest reaches of Galileo's telescope and beyond, they would cancel themselves out just as the Dark Ages had cancelled out learning – and something beyond price would be lost forever. Of course they were not to know that then. Should we never have translated the classics and dumped lorrytruckloads of them into the bookbarns of the world? Unthinkable. But for the rest, I mean the universe of print that ensued – the commentaries, the commentaries on the commentaries; the bibliographies, and bibliographies of bibliographies; the catalogues, and catalogues within catalogues, and catalogues within catalogues within catalogues; the schools and the seminars and the theses and the doctrines and the systems and the programmes and the structures and the codes – is it conceivable? Certainly. We have conceived cancer on a universal scale. But the reverse – the bookburnings of Savonarola and Hitler, the index of the Vatican, the thoughtpolice of the Gulag, the subjugation of poetry by profit? It may be that we are destined not to be users of information, but misusers of it, eternally misled by our gifts.

....

[2] *Great Libraries*, London, 1971.

146

Dark thoughts for a dark season, and much of it in Greek.

I was in another mood when I went up the stairway leading to the readingroom, and as it's been many years since you've been there you will need to be reminded that it has two wings or flights, one on either side of the central stairway, and that the lines of the central steps are curved, as if molten lava had flowed down from the door and hardened into stone. I paused for a moment and caught my breath (the purgatorial function?) before going up the flight on the left. There was a small table just inside the door where a man sat selling catalogues: I bought mine and proceeded directly to the thirtysecond desk as if I had been a reader there all my life. My nonchalance was a fraud; my heart was hammering. I never told you what the last message *said* – the one that led me to the Laurenziana and this moment:

> *Go back and back. Michelangelo will lead you there, where the triple stairway climbs up toward heaven. Gather your wits at the thirty-second desk.*

The desks, you will recall, are arranged in parallel rows on either side of the central aisle: one might more accurately describe them as stalls, because when you are seated you are enclosed front and back: has any designer since that time been so sensitive to the reader's need for privacy? Twentyseven, twentyeight, twentynine, thirty, thirtyone . . . what was I expecting to find, Wales? Not likely, but one never knew. No, there waiting for me on the bench, hunched down in its place like a stunted scholar, was Matrioshka Six. Unwrapped. Unboxed. Grinning. I picked the thing up and wrenched it open. More green ink:

> *Which flight of stairs did you ascend? Consult your Vasari (28th September, 1555) and you will know whether to place yourself among the saved or the damned. Notice also the Abominable Secret before your eyes.*

My legs were rubber; I fell back into the seat. I had been invited – *ordered* – to begin studying the closelywritten manuscript that swam in its glass case there before my eyes, but I couldn't do it, something was wrong, and the shock of it was almost too much for me. For a fraction of a second I wondered if I hadn't gone mad. My hand reached out to touch the part of the seat immediately beside me: cool wood. *The part I was sitting on was warm.*

I stood up. There were two other visitors, a couple who might have been Americans or Germans, and the man at the desk. I clamped the head of the thing back into its socket and walked up to the visitors, who were peering into one of the glass cases. They were startled when I spoke, because the central carpet, laid down for soundproofing or possibly to protect Michelangelo's marble floor, had muffled my steps. I thrust the matrioshka under their noses.

– Have you ever seen this?

Total incomprehension. I tried it in French.

– *Bitte?*

I turned and swiftly negotiated the length of the readingroom to confront the man at the desk.

– *Non capisco.*

He shrugged and smiled one of those pitying smiles the Italians pour out of a mould for foreigners. Then, for no discernible reason, he was on his feet, the smile erased, horror in his eyes. He tore the matrioshka out of my hand and held it to his ear. Nothing. He pitied me again, and with infinite precaution screwed off the top.

– *Messaggio. Per lei.*

And he handed me the green obscenity inside.

I walked the matrioshka back to the thirtysecond desk, and replaced it where it had been left for me – to keep the seat warm. Who had done the delivering this time, Wales? The thickwaisted deputy? The girl with the golden legs? How could the messenger have vanished so quickly from the room, was he still crouching somewhere between the desks? There was only one way to eliminate that possibility, and I did so peering right and left as I walked, stopping also to examine the rotunda leading off to the right. No exit, at least none perceptible to me, and no crouchers farther on.

At the end of the long room one passes through a doorway leading off left into a series of small rooms with manuscripts exhibited in cases; I went straight through to the end and found a small door evidently not meant for public use, because it was locked. But what other way out could he have taken? It was not beyond Wales' powers to persuade someone on the staff to let him pass on into the treasure, in which case they must have passed on together. What else? He might have gone into almost any of the desks between the entrance and the thirtysecond row, and sat there unobserved as I walked by. From there to the stairway and down into the cloister would be a matter of seconds, no more.

You must tell me one day if you have ever learned to work effectively when you are under pressure: I have never really managed it. Some part of it is inevitably left out, missed out, botched. Even so I did collect myself to the extent of returning to the thirtysecond desk. There I tried to make sense of the manuscript on display – the Abominable Secret before my eyes – a letter addressed to Michelangelo by one Giovanfrancesco Fattucci, papal secretary, from Rome, dated 12.VI.1525. The script was written in a firm hand, in the dark brown ink of the time, on the screened paper now called vergé and still occasionally 'made by hand'. The uneven inking left little doubt that a quill had been used. Twelve lines from the top, a small paper patch had been glued over an inskpot and written over, presumably to clarify the writing obliterated by the spot: no papercrumplers in the Pope's pay, it would seem. The letter was carefully penned, but easier to read in the printed catalogue all the same. It explained that the Pope was mightily pleased with the progress Michelangelo was making on the library, and that *His Holiness had indicated his preference for a stairway with a single ramp!*

That was enough for me. I walked out of the readingroom, down the stairway with the *three* parallel ramps, and out into the cloister where I began to breath again. The steps outside the church were swarming with tourists. I made my way through them and back along the streets leading to the Piazza della Signoria. There while I waited for Jeannine to come out of the Uffizi, I drank a large whisky at a table in the sun, and felt ever so much better.

On the other side of the piazza, David was preparing to unwind his sling.

Vasari, Michelangelo, et al. You may correctly surmise that I do not go travelling about the world with a complete set of Vasari bulging from my pockets. There is, however, an abbreviated Penguin edition, a copy of which I found in an immense galleried bookshop somewhere in the neighbourhood of the house that serves as a memorial to Dante. I pocketed Vasari and wandered, in a circumambulatory way, back to San Lorenzo the following morning, noting, as I went, all the references to the *Commedia* I was able to find along the way. There are three on steles in the Palazzo Vecchio, and others in the Via Borgo dei Greci and in the Via Dante Alighieri itself. All the quotations were in Tuscan; I made no effort to translate, but promised to look them up on my return.[3] They were not, anyway, part of the assignment.

. . . .

[3] *Paradiso* XVI, 109–110, the inscription most apposite to the mood I felt, or perhaps hoped for, on my return: *Oh quali io vidi quei che son disfatti per lor superbia!* I have looked at three different translations and can see no way of making our blunderbuss of a language match the beauty of the original. The *sense* of it, don't you agree, is the old saw 'Pride goes before a fall.' So much for old saws.

The assignment was the Michelangelo letter in Vasari's *Life*. I went back into the cloister, sat down on the ledge facing the library, and searched for the letter dated 28 September, 1555.

Giorgio, my dear friend,

Concerning the stairway for the library that I've been asked about so much, believe me if I could remember how I planned it I would not need to be asked. A certain staircase comes to my mind just like a dream, but I don't think it can be the same as the one I had in mind originally since it seems so awkward. However, I'll describe it for you: first, it is as if you took a number of oval boxes, each about a span deep but not of the same length or width, and placed the largest down on the paving further from or nearer to the wall with the door, depending on the gradient wanted for the stairs. Then it is as if you placed another box on top of the first, smaller than the first and leaving all round enough space for the foot to ascend; and so on, diminishing and drawing back the steps towards the door, always with enough space to climb; and the last step should be the same size as the opening of the door. And this oval stairway should have two wings, one on either side, following the centre steps but straight instead of oval. The central flight from the beginning of the stairs to half-way up should be reserved for the master. The ends of the two wings should face the walls and, with the entire staircase, come about three spans from the wall, leaving the lower part of each wall of the anteroom completely unobstructed. I am writing nonsense, but I know you will find something here to your purpose.

Have you found it, the sentence Wales had in mind when he said 'Which flight of steps did you ascend?'

I shall not try to tell you what I thought but confine myself to what I did. I walked directly along the cloister to the doorway leading up the stairs to the vestibule, climbed up and paused once more at the threshold. I then went slowly up the central stairway and into the readingroom. One day we shall look back on this moment and see it as the turningpoint of my life.

The rest was release of the purest kind, and what I saw there in that magnificent sanctuary I saw and noted as much for you as for myself. A page from the sermons of St Augustine. Titus Livius' *Epitome of Sextus*

Rufius. A *Decameron* dated 1348. The Medicean Virgil, fifth century; in uncials, uncle. Ovid's *Metamorphoses*. *The Satires* of Juvenal. A *Commedia* dated 1417, open at Canto XXIV, Purgatorio: *Donne ch'avete intelletto d'amore*. Cicero's *On Oratory*. Poggio's *Historiarum Florentini Populi*. And above all, quintessence of quintessentials, the codex that Petrarcha annotated and kept with him all his life, the *Carmina* of one Quintus Horatius Flaccus, poet laureate and progenitor. Can I begin to tell you what I felt?

Emptus Ian. 1347. Novombris 28

After which, in Latin, he made a list of the works the book contained: The Odes, The Epodes, The Secular Hymn, The Art of Poetry, Sermons, Letters. Throughout the book there are marginal notes in Petrarch's own hand; and as for the most part they are quotations from Latin authors, they are said to throw much light on the contents of his own library. You must know all this, having been there ahead of me, but did they ever let you see the book? I can't help feeling they must have done so; these things have a way of emanating from the page.

I am sending you the Olschki catalogues of this exhibition, of the Michelangelo exhibition of 1964, and the one celebrating the fourth centenary of the opening of the Laurenziana. They will remind you once again of the void separating us from them, and make you wonder, as I did, whether the message will ever fly over the walls of the museum again. Out.

In another of Vasari's essays (read on, it will do you good), you will find the precedent for what happened when, like a drunken sailor, I fell out of the library and made my way down the steps and back into the market. There, where the steps turn at a right angle to follow the wall of the church, I found an old woman in black huddled beside a pair of canaries emprisoned in a tiny cage. The footsteps of five thousand tourists had driven them into a corner where they now hid, feathers askew and palpitating with terror. She wanted ten thousand lire for them. I gave her the money and threw open the door of the cage. Within seconds the birds had become specks of gold glinting in the sun as they disappeared together over the lantern of the Sagrestia Nuova.

The canary woman pressed a forefinger to her temple and screwed.

The Twelfth Envelope

There is a land where flowers bloom in winter, where wine still tastes of the grape, and coffee of the bean. In the morning you walk out of your house and pluck figs for breakfast; the orange tree is so plentiful that it serves as decoration in the streets. At the table one pours oil and lemon over freshly picked salad; the oil is coloured green and the lemon has not yet been embalmed in plastic. Everywhere the sun beats down and reflects its warmth in stone, occasionally in faces. And because for a time the people there were grateful for the natural good, they painted their houses in hues of rose and gold, and so arranged their world that even the rooftops were a celebration. Paradise was not there, but proximate – in books, handwritten; on walls, handpainted; in the lines and lives of poets. And if, before he died, a man were lucky in his gifts, they would cut a bough from the sacred tree and wind it for his crown.

Elsewhere the leaves bend low under their watery burden, and cats slouch about the gardens shaking the mud from their paws.

Boileroom blues. So we agreed on the way back that something would have to be done. Neither of us knew what it was to be, but because the practical direction of our lives has always come from her – the answers, sotospeak – there was no reason to suppose that she would not rise to the challenge now. It was the triple stairway business, in her case as much as mine, that released the furies.

– We can't let him get away with it, Jeannine kept saying, we can't let him get away with it.

I told her about Poggio Bracciolini, Poggio who once, in a quarrel over the use of the Latin language, had tried to murder his critic and rival; and if Poggio could go that far with the living, what was to stop us doing as much with the living dead? In theory nothing, if we could catch him. In practice (and all scruples aside), there was the little matter of money. As you know and we all know, the unemployed are lining up in the streets once more, and some of them are publishers. Balding and von Gildenkrantz and all the others have said I should resign and go somewhere else, without apparently asking themselves what, in the entire world of print, could look more *ex* on a curriculum vitae than a quondam poetry editor now working on a set of Stalinist encyclopedias, a Greekless dispensation, and a worldwide accumulation of dirty jokes. Besides, it's a coward's way out. I may be no great example of bravery under fire (the Abominable, if you knew it, would attest to that), but I am not about to run away. Not as long as the cats are there to wake me in the morning and Jeannine is there to bring me my cup of tea and the garden continues to push out its shoots. And yes, I'd stand below stairs holding up Cragg's carpet forever rather than separate myself from them. Or so I tell myself in my buoyant moments.

From Thrale, nothing but chin up, keep up the good work, happy days etc – dear boy. He knows I have been sending the envelopes as promised, and he seems to think, strangely, that they are of value. I've no doubt I have you to thank for that. But you know as well as I that we are no closer to writing a life of Wales than we are to a life of Groucho Marx. What matter? You have your advance and I my salt. Difficult, if not downright imprudent, to provoke a break in this best of all impossible worlds, don't you agree?

Best? I wonder, and it is the fault of Hokusai. What a fascinating man. We discovered him at an exhibition in the Marais not far along the rue des Francs-Bourgeois from the Place des Vosges: Paris again, and why not? Are we to pass the remainder of our lives jumping each time the Green Monster lashes his tail, or do we retain some scrap of a will of our own? In short, we stopped off on the way back and treated ourselves to an evening at Le Grand Véfour, on expenses: not one small whisper of a boo, I may add, from Thrale: you see how difficult the revolt has become. There, poring over that week's copy of *l'Officiel des Spectacles* (which sounds more like a governmental decree than it really is), we learned about the Hokusai exhibition. That made it possible for us to become acquainted with Katsukawa Shunrō, Katsu Shunrō, Shunrō, Kusamura Shunrō, Sōri, Sōri aratame Hokusai, Saki no Sōri aratame Hokusai, Fusenkyo Hokusai, Hokusai Tatsumasa, Tokitarō Kakō (Sorobeku), Kakō (Sorobeku), Gakyōjin Hokusai, Gakyōrojin Hokusai, Kukushin Hokusai, Katsushika Hokusai, Katsushika Hokusai Raishin, Katsushika Hokusai Tatsumasa, Shin-musashinokuni Katsushikazumi Tō, Hokusai

Saito, Hokusai aratame Taito, Hokusai aratame Katsushika Taito, Zen Hokusai Taito, Gakyōjin Hokusai Taito, Furumekashiku Hokusai Taito, Katsushika zen Hokusai Taito rōjin, Zen Hokusai Katsushika Taito, Katsushika zen Hokusai Taito, Hokusai aratame Katsushika Iitsu, Hokusai Taito aratame Katsushika Iitsu, Katsushika Iitsu, Getchirōjin Iitsu, Fusenkyo Iitsu, Zen Hokusai aratame Katsushika Iitsu, Zen hokusai Iitsu, Katsushika oyaji Iitsu, Zen Hokusai Katsushika Iitsu, Iitsu, Hokusai aratame Iitsu, Katsushika zen Hokusai Iitsu rōjin, Hokusai aratame Iitsu, Zen Hokusai Iitsu rōjin, Zen Hokusai Iitsu Gakyōrōjin Manji, Zen Hokusai Manji rōjin, Zen Hokusai Manji, Zen Hokusai Iitsuō, Zen Hokusai Iitsu aratame Gakyōrōjin Manji, Zen Hokusai aratame Gakyōrōjin Manji, Katsushika Iitsu Manjirōjin Hachiemon, Zen Hokusai Manjiō, Hokusai Iitsurōjin Hachiemon, Katsushika Manjirōjin, Manji, Manjirōjin, and if you have followed me this far you will have discovered that the name Hokusai recurs more often than any other. This was the name a certain Japanese painter and graphic artist adopted in 1799 at the age of thirtynine as a way of paying homage to the bodhisattva Myōken and the cult of the seven polar stars. The other names were his as well, and they all appear at one time or another on his work. I have listed them deliberately (deep bows of apology from the waist) to illustrate the difference between our crass Occidental selfseeking (make me rich, make me famous; I want it *forever*) and Hokusai, who tried so earnestly to efface himself behind his work as he went along.

In one sense we have Wales to thank for all this – not for Paris, but for the impulse to see the exhibition. Hokusai wasn't even a name to me before Wales' note about him floated, by some crazy miracle, to the top of the pile. As you know, I have been more or less defeated by Wales' jottings – defeated full stop would be a better way to put it – but this one, perhaps because of its incongruity with everything we knew about Wales, really made me want to know more. I read it as the 'programme note' of an exhibition he must have seen some years ago. Possibly many years ago. We have no way of knowing when Wales became interested, nor why.

> *Date of birth 1760. Place, rural zone on the left bank of the river Sumida, district of Honjo, Edo (Tokyo). Parents unknown; the child therefore enters without a name. First given name, Tokitarō. Adopted at age three by the family of Nakajima Ise, artisan, maker of mirrors for the military government. Aptitude for drawing and painting evident at the age of five. Known as Tetsuzō at the*

age of nine. Apprenticed to a wood-engraver at thirteen and at the same age engraves his first six pages, illustrations for text of a humorous novel. At fourteen engaged as clerk by a public library, teaches himself illustration by studying books that pass through his hands. Admitted, at eighteen, to the studio of the famous painter Katsukawa Shunshō – as Katsukawa Shunrō. Becomes known as portraitist of actors, print designer, illustrator of mediocre books. At the death of Shunshō, 1792, younger rival, Shunei, named head of the studio; Shunrō expelled. Mortification. Crisis of maturity. Now named Kusamura Shunrō; little work accomplished in following three years. In 1795 at age 35, acclaimed for his illustration of a book of poetry. Now known as Sōri. Turning point: freed by appreciative amateur poets from routine of actors' studios, commercial publishers. Works privately with immediate success during next four years producing prints, illustrating albums. First serious imitators. Long a faithful Buddhist, now confirms adherence to sect of bodhisattva Myōken, incarnation of North Star, by choosing the name Hokusai, 'Workshop of the North', as secondary name. Other later names – Tatsumasa, Taito, Raishin – derivations from same cult of the seven polar stars.

Nota bene winter of 1798. Abruptly renowned[1] as Sōri, nevertheless confers the name upon a gifted pupil in favour of Hokusai which now becomes his primary name. Even so Hokusai used concurrently with several others: Tatsumasa for illustrations; Tokitarō for popular works of fiction; Sorobeku for prints and books of a commercial nature. Another secondary name, Fusenkyo, adopted in 1800. Then at age when most contemporaries begin falling into decline, his work enters period of extraordinary development; comments on this ironically by sur-naming himself Gakyōjin – 'the madman of painting'. Fame, reclusion. Emerges twice from private world to paint Buddhist temples in public seance. Severely criticized in 1810 for kabuki poster in which he gives actors sickly appearance. Abandons name Hokusai as a result, giving it to insignificant pupil. Renames himself Taito, again after one of polar stars. Encounter with artist Bakusen: lifelong friendship begins. 1820 celebrates 'second cycle' (end of first sixty years, beginning of second?) adopting name Iitsu (sic) meaning 'one year old again'. More prints for private sale, more

---

[1] From Latin re(nominare) – nominate.

book illustrations. 1827, stroke, paralysis. Cured by own remedy.[2]
Death of wife. In seventies completes collection of prints known as
'Thirty-six Views of Mount Fuji', another important series
showing waterfalls, others of bridges, birds, 'ghosts'. New series of
one hundred views of Mount Fuji followed by projected illustration
of one hundred poems, classics. 1836 native city gripped by
famine. Drawings and other work traded for rice.[3] *Publication of*
A Hundred Poems *interrupted with completion of twenty-*
seventh illustration. 1839 destruction of lodgings by fire. Destruc-
tion of materials, files of drawings, sketches. Second great crisis of
maturity, diminution of output. Beginning age 82, during two
years that follow, draws a lion each day: way of 'keeping hand
in'. 1845 completion of several paintings for temple province of
Shinano. Dies 18th April 1848.

What makes it all credible, coming from Wales, is the dryasbones
ending. 'Dies 18th April 1848.' Brief homage? Hats off for a minute's
silence? Not on your life. Turn the page and get on with it. So much for
Hokusai.

There is here, Wales apart, a paradox worthy of consideration, and I
draw it particularly to your attention because, as you have never been
much of a pictorial thinker yourself, it would naturally escape your
gaze. I can only do this by way of an autobiographical reference. I don't
believe I have ever visited a city, major or minor, anywhere, without
going to see its principal art galleries, churches, libraries, and museums
out, together with the more modest storehouses that tourists do not
always find. They represent, after all, the memory of our world. When I

[2] Edmond de Goncourt, *Hokusai*, Paris, 1896: 'At the age of sixty-eight or
sixty-nine, Hokusai had an attack of apoplexy from which he recovered by treating
himself with "lemon mash", a Japanese remedy whose composition the painter
had from his friend Tosaki with, in the margin of the prescription, sketches
representing the lemon, the knife for cutting the lemon, the pot in which it was to
be cooked. Here is the recipe of this lemon mash: "Before twenty-four Japanese
hours (forty-eight hours) have elapsed following the attack, take one lemon, cut it
in small pieces with a bamboo knife rather than one of iron or copper. Put the
lemon thus cut into an earthenware pot. Add one *go* (quarter of a litre) of extra good
sake and simmer until the mixture becomes thick. Then in two doses drink the
citron mash, from which the lemon-seeds have been removed, in hot water; the
medicinal result will follow at an interval of twenty-four or thirty hours." This
remedy cured Hokusai completely . . .'
[3] A useful expedient, but not all the artists and publishers of the day had the same
luck.

was a child our teachers paraded us out of the school to observe a ritual in which a group of fading men wearing medals would lay wreaths of poppies on a memorial tomb; we called it Remembrance Day, and were advised never to forget the dead who, to our young imaginations, were luckless ghosts – faceless names at best. That is one kind of collective memory – our memories of kings and queens and conquerors and slaughter, of those debaucheries of management known as war. My own Remembrance Day is elsewhere in the calendar. I celebrate it each time I pass through the doors where the treasure is kept (read 'valuables' for treasure, 'storehouse' for museum?) – yes, *celebrate*, for what else do you do in the presence of a Donatello or a Vermeer, you raise up a prayer, you give thanks not just to those who produced the work, for they are all dead and past care, but for the work itself, for evident glory, for its desperate defiance of the barbarians at the gate. This you celebrate and remember, and your life becomes a long voyage in search of excellence. Once you have set out there is no turning back; the ticket is one way. And you are forever grateful because along the way you are reminded and reminded and reminded that humanity has always been more than the sum of its warriors' bones. In my journeyings I have trodden the familiar paths that lead from Toronto and Henry Moore to the Whitney and the Guggenheim, the National and the Tate, the Louvre and the Palace of Tokyo, the Albertina and the Uffizi and the Prado and the Maeght. If there was a picturepalace of any kind within reach of my bank account and my feet, I went there and gloated over the stores. For you see, Horace, I owned them. They were mine because some sweaty bugger like myself, give or take the miracle of a gift, had put on a pair of workman's overalls and stuck his finger into the clay. Or the paintpot or the inkpot or the glue. I happen to favour the writing finger, but that was an accident of birth. What little I have done might have been accomplished, had Carrara been my home, with a hammer and chisel, and with infinitely greater promise of endurance.

Along with all the others who went before me, I discovered Dürer and Delacroix and Hieronymus Bosch, and why, out of hundreds, I should list only these escapes me completely. But to return to my paradox: explain to me how, in the immensity of space between heaven and hell, I have managed to traverse so many kilometres of Kultur without once falling at the feet of Hokusai? I am ashamed to think that Wales – who from all accounts was never known to have looked at a picture in his life – was there before me. Listen, Horace, what can I say? The son of the mirrormaker was an infinity of mirrors. Thirty thousand individual works are attributed to the man and all the names we know he used. If he

157

worked every day between his fifteenth year and the year of his death, he would have worked twentyseven thousand, three hundred and seventyfive days. There was more work in his life than there were days. We do not know where his work ended and that of his pupils began. We do not know exactly how many names he used, how many drawings were destroyed by fire, how many have disappeared. We know only that the man was immeasurable and unmeasurable and beyond measure – the tautology of a tautology of a tautology, and out all three. He was an orphan in his own life and unaccountably remains an orphan to our Occidental blindness. And yet the catalogue says that examples of his work have been collected by the museums of eight Western countries and countless individuals all over the world. What are they, who are they, robberbarons simpering over their treasures in the secrecy of their miserable vaults? I have no words to express the shock, the gratitude I felt in the presence of this Japanese 'madman'. Wales knew about him and did not send us to him. Why? I tell you, Horace, if there is any humility left in us at all, it kneels before the memory of Hokusai. In rags. With an empty bowl.

Having looked at more than four hundred paintings, illustrations, and prints, we fell out of the gallery in a state of repletion approaching exhaustion and beatitude. We went along the street not knowing where we were going, nor why, and found ourselves once more in a corner café at the Place des Vosges. There, with good beer and choucroute to restore us, we found the courage to resume our journey. We walked aimlessly round the square investigating rare books and antique shops as we went, and eventually, under the arcade, found a small art gallery showing more of Hokusai's prints, the result of a private collector's timely visit to Japan! We stormed into the gallery like prospectors in a goldrush and once more stood before the master. They were as good as the others we had seen before.

On the way out we bought yet another catalogue, this one of the exhibition marking the twentieth anniversary of the gallery; Hokusai had been shown there as long ago as 1955, which may explain how he came to the attention of Wales. We studied both catalogues on the train – ah, the blessings of nineteenthcentury locomotion – and were virtually experts by the time we returned. Experts! Let's say that we arrived with a little less ignorance in our baggage and a grain of hope. If Shunshō was Hokusai's Wales, a lesson may seem to emerge. *A man who wishes to be free must contrive to get himself thrown out of school.* Yes, but. The trouble with it is that Hokusai contrived nothing: he was.

If the references are complete, Edmond de Goncourt was the only

Occidental writer to have ventured into the life, and it was published nearly half a century after the painter's death. De Goncourt's sources tell us that on his deathbed Hokusai said this:

– If heaven would give me ten more years . . . If heaven would give me only five more years . . . I could become a really great painter.

*   *   *

We bought four postcards for you. There wasn't enough time to look for a post office, so I put them into the subenvelope enclosed. You will notice, I hope, that they all depict poets. The one sitting alone under the shelter contemplating the stillness of a lake by moonlight is, of course, a Japanese version of yourself. The thatched hermitage in the wilderness, shows two poets at a window – one of them, me, contemplating the world outside, the other, you, contemplating the other (through the inter-mediary of these lines). The woman on her knees is a poetess washing her manuscript so that she may prove to her admirers that she is good enough to write another; in those days manuscripts didn't grow on trees. The fourth postcard, of a fisherman contemplating the moon, is Hokusai himself; selfportrait. Now you know what a great man looks like – as vacuous as you or me.

Expect no Hokusaical conflagration from this source now that we are back. I write a few more stingy lines each day on my suburban train. Occasionally I leave them behind for Jeremiah Peach. What will remain of us? Faces peer at me out of a picture passing in the night. Years ago I was one of those faces. I was the small boy with the brown eyes and his hair in a fringe over the forehead, pressing his nose into a white circle against the windowpain. Sic.

Parisian Paradox Number Two. Or the superiority of cats. As usual we stayed over with Oncle Louis and Tante Berthe who have a fine and spacious apartment in the rue du Coup d'oeil. From there, morning and evening, Oncle Louis faithfully descends in order to walk the dogs, a pair of incestuous black poodles known, will you believe it, as Zizi and Tutu. Brother and sister, and that doesn't stop them a minute. Oncle Louis, gripped by *la grippe*, was immersed in bed, and I was delegated to walk the dogs. Walk? I am of a mind to invent a new verb. Sniffpisstrot. Trotsniffshit. These two were prodigies if not superprodigies of the kind, the one spurring on the other to greater and greater effort, like olympic athletes or salesmen selling encyclopedias door to door and in tandem. By the time I had returned Zizi and Tutu to their matrimonial rug by the fire, I had equipped them with names more appropriate to their condition. Pipi and Caca. And I refused to recant.

Fortunately Berthe was amused. She told us that when Louis took the dogs out for a walk he invariably wore white gloves.

With that little warmup out of the way, I can now bring myself to face your question about Matrioshka Seven and how it came into my possession. The two stories I fear are dismally related. My own habit, in the pipicaca department, is to wait in the morning until I am installed in the boiler room: I am rather slow to get moving, you might say. The one good thing about working in the boiler room is that the lavatory, my *private* lavatory I'll have the world know, is situated just along the corridor from my room: quite an improvement as the previous convenience was in the annexe immediately below Angela. On the morning in question I was at the point of effacing the adult accomplishments of Paul von Beneckendorff und von Hindenburg, and had gone so far as to cut a piece of white paper to the appropriate size and shape, when nature called. I lifted the lid, and there it was. Floating. Silly grin up. I lifted it out and ran it under the tap. Someone had sealed the joint between the two halves with candlewax to make it waterproof. It said:

> *Proceed at leisure to the second prize in the contest of the two cities,*
> *and thread your needle through the doughnut.*

Childish business. Surely he must know by now that it will take more than boggery to finish me. Outch.

The Thirteenth Envelope

Or sending bottles out to sea. You realize that this has become our purpose, don't you? It's not good enough any more just to write verse: it has to be *sent* somewhere or it's not verse at all. My messages to you all go out in cacacoloured bottles; I throw them out as far as I can and watch them bob up and down on the waves. I wait. Nothing happens. A bottle of another colour, blue, is washed ashore. I race toward it as hard as I can go, to catch it before the tide sweeps it away. Do you see the trail of footprints panicking across the sand? Mine. I reach down, pick it up, hold it to my ribs hoping it will hear the tintamarre of my heart. I wrench out the cork, and carefully, carefully, with small finger intruded, tease out the paper – will it never come? – my feet in the waves, my hair in the wind; thin cord of flesh strung out between heaven and earth – and what do I read? Questions. Nothing but questions. What does Thrale know? Why won't he let you read the will? When will they move you out of the boileroom? Any more activity in the daisychain? Who could have put the thing in the toilet? Questions, questions, and never any answers. God send me Friday.

On the way to work this morning a mad thought occurred to me. The latest matrioshka was, in its pornographic way, a bottle floating in the sea. What if its message, what if *all* the messages were a stifled cry for help from a drowning Wales? I have tried to read them this way and I must tell you I have failed. They are all do this, go there, take that, and wonder at your own abasement. Wales' mind is nothing but a long injunction and he is beyond help. We are all beyond help, all those of us who have complied.

So many bottles, so much sea. They were digging up Bulford Street this morning; it was raining as ever, and part of the street was awash with

161

mud. They had cordoned off the mud, of course, so that none of it would contaminate our feet. There was a square of mud in the pavement, fenced off, and in the middle of the mud, a pair of men's black shoes. They were not old shoes; you or I would have been happy to wear them to a funeral, or to a wedding. One of the shoes was upright and filling up with water; the other was lying on its side. In the mud. In the rain. They had filled the hole and the mud was there waiting to be resurfaced with bitumen. He had not put on gumboots and disappeared into a work-man's trench, no. He had taken off his shoes, a man like you and me, and stepped out into the mud. Then, after a lifetime of going about his business in the city streets, he had gone away, earth clinging to his socks, mud seeping into the spaces between his toes, gone away. But where? We watch him receding from us, becoming smaller, then infinitely small, a dot stepping over the line of the horizon and disappearing into the universe. Years later a bottle floats back to us and is washed in by the waves. We pick it up and remove the cork. A small voice inside – very small, very faint – sighs 'Telephone bill. Pay the school fees.' and dies away.

The place they had cordoned off in the street, I realized, was exactly opposite Byron's birthplace. Byron of the club foot. Bizarre.

*   *   *

– Mr Thrale, I said this time, will you not let me read Wales' will? I am one of the executors. An executor has the right to read the will he is asked to execute.

– I appreciate your question. In this instance it is impossible. Wales has expressly stated that you are not to read it.

– When did he say that?

– He didn't say it, he stated it in the will.

– How am I supposed to be able to execute instructions that I have never read?

– In your place I shouldn't worry about it. You are carrying out your part of the bargain.

– How can you be sure?

– Well, you are maintaining the bridgehead and sending material to Horace Bentwhistle. Occasionally you are invited to go larking off to Vienna or Florence or some such exotic place. That is all part of the bargain. It satisfies the provisions of the will.

– You have read it yourself?

– Naturally.

– Then, Mr Thrale, you must know the answer to the fundamental question.

Long pause. Dance of eyelids, slowmotion. Background of insect-music: Anton Webern.

– Why?

– Ah my dear boy, there you are mistaken. That is the one question I cannot answer. That is a question whose answer is not even to be found in Wales' will.

*   *   *

I sit here, the light from my row of candles licking at the pages of my prayer, the pulse of willingness at my fingertips, heavy as a penitential psalm. I sit here waiting for a voice that will tell me to go out from this hole and redesign the universe, for God knows the maps we find in our pillarbooks and archives out from centuries past have got it wrong. The mapmakers have traced out another universe, unknown to me, somewhere in the space between invisible continents, unprinted lines. Antimatter parading as the real thing. Horace, we must begin again.

The vision of the vacant shoes continues to haunt me. The shoes, *scóh, schoen, schuhe* (cogn. with shade, sky), the black shoes with the laces trailing in the mud. I say to myself, if only they will dig up the earth beneath them they will find a man like you or me who had once worn shoes like yours or mine, and then, on an impulse, decided not to wear them. He had stepped down into the hole waiting for him there in the street, handed up his shoes, and clawed at the sky until it shattered and fell down on him in shards. He is still there waiting, wondering if there will be anything left of him when he is exhumed, breathing through a straw. The worms gather and gnaw. They do not gather in the earth around him, they are inside, *inside*. The mud presses in against the straw, the breathing stops, the worms work, and prosper, and comfort themselves in slime.

That is one streetmap. In another a man like you or me is walking along Bulford Street at dawn before the shops are open and the shoppers have come out; we do not know why he is there alone nor where he is going, nor can we explain the darkness that gathers over him as he walks. He looks up. It is not a cloud. It is an immense bird of the kind that digs holes in the street and masticates buildings; its nauseating yellow beak reaches down and down toward him, widespread, salivating tar. He turns, runs, slips on the mud, falls. Glop. Nothing is left, once the giant bird has done its work, but the shoes. In the gastronomy of the yellowbeaked pterodactyl, shoes, beneath digestion, are spat out like unwanted pips or blown out with a cosmic fart. And oh the clacking of the carnivore's teeth as it settles back on its haunches waiting for hunger and the next feet that step inadvertently toward it wearing shoes, *schuhe, schoen, scóh* (cogn. with shade, sky) in infinite procession, waiting and salivating the accumulated decompositions of eternity. My friend, you will never walk safely again.

Bottom of the dustbin. Philippa had no idea what he wanted; I was simply to go up, and at once. I snuffed out my candles and followed her up the stairs trying to concentrate on the blur of hips and swaying skirt before my eyes. It was the only easy work of the day. Caroline Bream was there ahead of me: she had her hair pulled back in a bun and sat leaning forward in her chair as if in readiness for a fast getaway or an even speedier genuflexion. Neither of them said good morning nor offered me the other chair; I sat down in it anyway, and waited for Cragg to speak. He was working his way through a pile of books on his desk – 'tasting' them as they say below stairs. I, for my part, think of dogs sniffing lampposts, cacapipicaca. Why? I mean, another poet might think of claret or champagne.

Cragg wore his unpleasant face, in my judgment the only one he possessed, and contrived to place black bars between us in the guise of a pinstriped suit. Black bars separated by parsimonious chinks of light.

He closed the book with a snap. For the first time in my life I saw that a book was not merely an accumulation of paper set against a hinge: it clamped shut like a beartrap. Unaccountably, miraculously (you explain it; I am at a loss) my mind catapulted back twenty centuries to the moment when three officers of the triumvirate cut off Cicero's head because it had spoken out against tyranny, and his hands because they had written philippics against it. Only in my version, which for all we know may be the truth, they cut off his hands first.

Philippics out. Speeches.

What happened next blotted Cicero out and replaced him with two possibilities, both appallingly present. Either I had leapt clean out of my skull, or Cragg was trying to drive me out of it. He spoke; the phrase that fell on my ears could not have been dug out of *my* imagination with a claw.

– Variations on the Word of God.

In some distant corner of the universe a clock could be heard ticking, ticking.

– What does that mean to you, Mr Racine?

The clock no longer ticked; it had become lodged inside the cage of my chest and was hammering at it with fists.

Break down / the walls! Break down / the walls!

He picked up another – I swear to you all this happened in slow motion – opened it, snapped it closed. Never once did he glance at the pages.

– The Wales Universal Book of Famous First Lines. What does that mean to you, Mr Racine?

Break down / the walls! Break down / the walls!

– The Wales Universal Book of Literary Inscriptions. What are we to make of that, Mr Racine?

Break down / the walls! Break down / the walls!

– The Wales Universal Book of Prefaces. The Wales Universal Book of Acknowledgments. The Wales Universal Book of Footnotes. The Wales Universal Book of Appendixes. The Wales Universal Book of Indexes.

Jaws. Jaws. Jaws. Jaws. Jaws.

– You have no comment to make about any of this, Mr Racine? I am afraid silence will not befriend you. Try your memory on this one, the Wales Universal Book of Books, or Numbers. Nothing to say about Numbers?

Break down / the walls! Break down / the walls!

– Well, in that case we shall be obliged to give you something to talk about. Something, shall we say, in a more personal vein.

The books were now heaped on the table in total disorder. He nevertheless managed to extract another volume from the bottom of the pile, and held it aloft.

– You may recognize this.

Upcurling nose, downcurling mouth.

– It is called *Tragicommas and Tragicomas* and is attributed to one Jereh – miaaaaaaah Peeeeeeeeeeechchchch. What do you make of *this* putrefying fruit, Mr Racine?

The clock stopped. The fists stopped hammering. I looked at Caroline Bream: she was staring at the book. Cragg let it fall on top of the others and she jumped.

– Mr Racine, get out of my sight. You will hear about this.

I regret to say that I do not know what happened next. I can only tell you what happened centuries later. I found myself in a dark cell, lighting candles. On the table in front of me were three volumes of a work of reference, one of them open at the letter F. A piece of white paper, the size of two thirds of a page, had been placed on the opened book. Beside it lay another book with a white cover and semiyapp edges. Many of its words had been blotted out with black ink. The page heading had been blackened out and over it had been written: THE PREACHER. My eyes fell on the page and I began reading.

> All things are full of labour; man cannot utter it. The eye is not satisfied with seeing, nor the ear filled with hearing. The thing that hath been, it is that which shall be; and that which is done, is that which shall be done; and there is no new thing under the sun. Is there any thing whereof it may be said, See, this is new? It hath been already of old time, which was before us. There is no remembrance of former things; neither shall there be any remembrance of things that are to come with those that shall come after. I, the Preacher, was king over Israel in Jerusalem. And I gave my heart to seek and search out by wisdom concerning all things that are done under heaven; this sore travail hath God given to the sons of man to be exercised therewith. I have seen all the works that are done under the sun and, behold, all is vanity and vexation of spirit. That which is crooked cannot be made straight; and that which is wanting cannot be numbered. I communed with mine own heart, saying, Lo, I am come to great estate, and have gotten more wisdom than all they that have been before me in Jerusalem; yea, my heart had great experience of wisdom and knowledge. And I gave my heart to know wisdom, and to know madness and folly; I perceived that this also is vexation of spirit. For in much wisdom is much grief; and he that increaseth knowledge increaseth sorrow.

My hands were still attached to their wrists. I reached across the table for the pot of glue I had left sitting among the candles, screwed off the lid, and with the brush underneath it applied paste to paper. I then effaced the childhood of Sigmund Freud.

Sequel to the bottom. Jeannine listened to all that the same evening and as usual was the first to make any sense of it. The next step – and I don't know why I didn't think of it myself – was to go back to Thatcher's Bookshop to the same shelf where I had found *Tragi and Tragi* and see if the others were there. If not, I must look elsewhere, according to the way

166

books were classified in the shop. *Variations on the Word of God* would presumably be found among books on religion, *The Wales Universal Book of Famous First Lines* and the others under literary reference. We were temporarily stumped by *Numbers* (The Book of Books) but comforted ourselves with the thought that the shop assistants, for once, might know something. Then, because she feared that weeks would pass before I got round to it, she offered to go off in search of Jeremiah Peach.

The books first. You will remember how Thatcher's is laid out: not difficult as bookshops go, and there, under P for Poetry, in spite of everything, were three copies of *Tragi and Tragi* – even because of it, who knows. I pocketed two of them: after all, they were mine. No sign of *Variations on the Word of God* under religion, so I moved on to literature and criticism and struck paydirt. *Famous First Lines* was there, two copies strong, among the anthologies out. I glanced at it briefly and it was more or less what the title implied, beginning with A for Al-Jahiz[1] and going on to Z for Zweig.[2] Along the way I came across P for Peach, Jeremiah, and wondered how the hell *he* had managed to become famous, but who am I to quarrel with my own handiwork? *Literary Inscriptions* came next – no problem – followed by *Universal Acknowledgments, Universal Prefaces, Universal Footnotes, Universal Appendixes, Universal Indexes*, all together in the same section of the shop though separated by works of a shall we say more traditional nature. The WEEP books were all robed in royal purple with titles reversed in white. They were evidently designed by someone who knew how to make books: good paper, margins, distinguished type out characters out print. A distance below the level of the Rogers Book, one might admit, but not brutally off the mark either. Compactly bound reference works meant to be read – not, as you are well placed to know, the easiest thing in life to achieve. I examined the colophout titlepage, read on overleaf, and went through the pages at the end but could find no acknowledgment either of printer or designer, rare thing in a book published by Wales. Could that be the assignment: dismantle the printers, having previously disintegrated the Word?

In bookshops, you may have noticed, the shop assistants invariably

<hr>

[1] Ghailān son of Kharasha said to Ahnaf, 'What will preserve the Arabs from decline?' – *Kitāb al-Bayān* (The Book of Proof), 860?

[2] The most certain measure of all strength is the resistance that it overcomes.
— *Freud*, Stefan Zweig, 1932.

gather in defence committees of two in order to ward off the possibility of having to speak to the customers. I went up to one such committee and hesitated, hoping for a break in the conversation. No such break.

– Excuse me.

– If they index those, none of us will get a penny, mark my

– Excuse me.

– Surely the answer would be to index everything. You know, all of us going along at the same infernal clip

– Sorry to interrupt.

– There's bound to be a Beecher's in it somewhere about the sixth

– AAARGH!

Guarded inspection of intruding exhibit.

– Sir?

I opened my mouth. At first nothing came out.

– Aaargh. I am looking for a book called Variations on the Word of God published by Wales. I have looked and it is not under religion.

– Variations on the Word of God?

– Variations on the Word of God, you say?

– Variations on the Word of *who*? You don't happen to have the name of the author?

– Just a minute, it strikes me that I have seen something of that nature, yes. Would you care to follow me, sir?

The man led me on a zigzag course among the tables at the centre of the shop to a shelf arrayed with dictionaries and encyclopedias. There he took up a backwardleaning stance, chin vised between thumb and forefinger, in order to inspect the titles without benefit of visual aids. The forefinger shot out and fell on one of the volumes. It was a bulky business.

– Yes, that's it. Volume one. Volume two hasn't come out yet.

He handed me the book and returned to his place in the committee. Volume one? Yes, volume one, as described in the dustjacket, was 'the indispensable companion to volume two in which all references originating in the Greek language will be rigorously eliminated. By consulting the two volumes side by side the reader will be able to see at a glance the extent to which the septentrional English language has been debased by an incompatible meridional tongue.'

Variations on the Word of God, volume one, was none other than the standard Wales English Dictionary one thousand five hundred and twenty pages strong. I paid for it with the others by cheque, and sent the bill to Thrale. That evening I took them all home in a Thatcher's bookbag and showed them to Jeannine. Neither of us could find a word of God in any of it.

Jeremiah Peach. Jeannine got on the train to Morden Priory as promised and let him punch her ticket. Then she punched him. I mean quite literally, and it must have been a scene. What happened, it seems, is that she quite calmly invited him to follow her to the end of the car, to the part where the corridor takes a bend leading to the washroom – all this on the pretext of talking about *his* poetry in private. There she stood up to him, or shall we say he stood up to her because she must be at least a head taller. It went something like this, breathing downward.

– Who put you up to your dirty little game?

– Dirty little?

Thin volume of *Tragi and Tragi* fanning Peach's nose.

– Who put you up to the idea of publishing my husband's poetry under your own name?

– Er, uh, you mean

– You know what I mean. Come on, confess!

Sharp blow to the Peach pectorals, twohanded attack. Backward lurch through the door of the washroom, *Tragi and Tragi* flying flapping into the basin, Peach declining into the toilet.

– Come on you nasty little man! Whose idea was it?

Foot trampling on the flushbutton, pssssssh psssssssh, cuhchunk, cuhchunk, cuhchunk, cuhchunk. Steel against steel against wood.

Doorslam, buttonclick. Peach rising, absorbing another twohander to the lapels, falling back into the toilet. Imploring eyes. Terror breathing upward.

– Don't do that, ma'am. No need to be violent.

– Well, then?

Psssssssh psssssssh, cuhchunk, cuhchunk.

– I told Mr Racine about the man and the girl. He already knows

– Their names! Their names!

– I can't . . . speak.

Release of strangulating necktie. Return of eyeballs to sockets.

– They never introduced themselves. I never found out who they were. Don't . . . do that ma'am. There is no reason to be violent.

– How much. How much did they give you?

– The money for a fur wrap. For Mrs Peach. Fifty quid.

– Fifty *quid*? It must have been mouse. Cash?

– Cheque.

– *Cheque!* Hah!

More attention to the pectorals. Friendly readjustment of collar and tie.

– I'll be back, Mr Peach. You will get the cheque out of the bank. We will read it together one week from today. Like a poem. Remember, Mr Peach, one week from today. You will cooperate like a nice little man or else you will go to jail. You understand?

Admonishing French finger. No finger on earth admonishes like the French.

– I understand.

Buttonclick. Exit terrorist Amazon. Last glimpse of Peach bending over, wiping hat with toiletpaper.

Battle of the Books (cont'd). In my confusion with the curators at Thatcher's I had forgotten to look for *The Wales Universal Book of Books*, otherwise known as *Numbers*; that problem remains unsolved and I shall have to go back. The others fit together in a curious Chinesepuzzle sort of way, it seems to me, because if you put together a book of prefaces, a book of acknowledgments, a book of literary inscriptions, a book of famous first lines, a book of famous last lines, a book of appendixes, a book of indexes, and a dictionary of the English language attributed to God, what do you get? For want of a better place and a more likely procedure we set them in a row on the windowledge in the bedroom next to the matrioshkas, and studied them from a comfortable position in bed. What, in effect, was God in his infinite variety trying to tell us? Interesting, by the way, to look up a name at random and follow it all the way through. Under 'Swift', since lately we have been talking about shipwrecks, there is this:

> The author of these Travels, Mr Lemuel Gulliver, is my ancient and intimate friend; there is likewise some relation between us by the mother's side. About three years ago, Mr Gulliver growing weary of the con-
>
> *– Prefaces*

> Benjamin Motte, the London printer of *Gulliver's Travels*, was a cautious man who saw risks of prosecution in the text of the first edition (1726) and accordingly proposed an expurgated version. The task of restoring
>
> *– Acknowledgments*

170

MY FATHER had a small estate in Nottinghamshire; I was the third of five sons.

— First Lines

I dwell the longer upon this subject from the desire I have to make the society of an English *Yahoo* by any means not insupportable; and therefore I here entreat those who have any tincture of this absurd vice, that they will not presume to come in my sight.

— Last Lines

The Scriblerus Club

Swift to Pope, September 20, 1723: 'I have often endeavoured to establish a friendship among all men of genius, and would fain have it done. They are seldom above three or four contemporaries, and, if they could be united, would drive the world before them.'

— Appendixes

Swift, Jonathan; Prefaces 373; Acknowledgments 119; First Lines 236; Last Lines 179; Appendices 184; Variations 1240; Lives 1667 vol 17. See Drapier, Gulliver, Scriblerus.

— Indexes

swift, a., adv. (-er, -est, -ly), n. [OE *swifan*, move quickly, cf. ON *svifa*, cogn. with SWEEP]. Fleet, quick rapid. (N.) kind of long-winged insect-eating bird; kind of lizard.

— Variations

No *Inscriptions*: Swift leaned on nobody but himself. I expect you have noticed the similarity between the insectivorous lizardbird and my nightmarish creature that farts shoes. Accident, my dear Watson, pure accident. Could Clutterbuck have known what my imagination would be doing forty years on? No more than I, forty years later, knew that lizards lay under 'swift'. Not bad, all the same, as correspondences go.

What we must do, if we are to save ourselves, is to imagine all this on the same shelf with the *Lives* and the three ages of man effaced, the *Bedside Scroll*, and the detergent dictionary. The two last named will be

Greekless; the *Lives* so far remain impure. Chew on that for a day or two and let me know what kind of taste it leaves in the mouth.

Meanwhile I have discovered a use for the matrioshkas, and I am rather proud of it. Ever since Matrioshka Number Two made them a family they have stood there with their heads in the trees waiting for other matrioshkas. Then came the books from WEEP, and as books will, they had begun to fall over on their sides. Eureka out. Jeannine is a late riser; often I leave her unmolested of a Saturday morning while I get on with unimportant things such as these notes or important things in the garden. On this occasion I fed the cats, stole down to the garage, bestrode my wheel, and pedalled silently off to the gunshop just off the high street in Grumley, three miles away. There I asked the shopkeeper for five pounds of shot – you know, the small black beads they load into shells. No shot. I should have to buy the shells and take them apart, hoping to avoid an explosion. Fine. I ordered two hundred: Thrale would pay. And then, while he was packaging the shells, I began inspecting the guns which stood there gleaming under glass: beautiful things, really, bluestockinged on glorious carved butts. Again I said to myself why not, Thrale would pay; I only needed to edit the receipt. And that, my dear Watson, is how I came to be the owner of a magnificent doublebarrelled murderweapon which now reposes in its case in the winecellar behind the cylinders of handmade paper I once bought for my poetry manuscripts and never used. Jeannine knows nothing except that, having fretsawed the matrioshkas down the middle and closed in each half with quarterinch plywood, I was able to fill them that same weekend with gunshot and convert them into bookends. I ask you, is there any limit to the fertility of the truly creative mind?

Dustbin. Bad news from Baker Street. As promised, Jeannine got on the train to Morden Priory hoping to read the poetic cheque. Another man was on duty; he thought our Peach had been transferred but could not be sure. Death, retirement, illness, taxes – any of these was possible or all of them at the same time. The new man was only temporary, and weren't we all. He suggested she call the personnel office at HQ. She did. A buttery voice at the other end explained that Jeremiah Peach had gone into retirement, ma'am. Not the confiding sort, you know, but in all probability he has retired to his cottage in Poke Stoges. Yes, it's a small village in Hunts; anybody at the local pub will know where Mr Peach's cottage is, ma'am. So Jeannine, who never lets go, got on the train to Huntfordshire. At Poke Stoges she was directed to a small rowhouse with a FOR SALE sign rising up from a post attached to the picket fence.

She copied the number, telephoned the agent, and learned that Mr Peach had gone off to Spain with Mrs Peach. Forwarding address? Try Mr Peach's solicitor. She tried the solicitor who told her in a scratchy voice (she's always been good at voices) that Mr and Mrs Peach were travelling on the Costa Brava and probably would remain there, travelling, for some months. Was she interested in making an offer on the house? Pay Peach for pinching our own poems? Sly bastard. For the first time since I've known her Jeannine was dumped, but really dumped, and I can tell you, friend, that when Jeannine says she is at a dead end there are not a great many destinations left. Even so we kept the solicitor's number, neither of us knowing remotely what further use we could make of it.

Philippa brought Magguinness down to see me the following day. There I was, gluepot in hand, candles fighting their flickering war with obsolescence, and I even had to go along the corridor in search of a chair. 'What are you doing down here in the sticks spelled Styx? Intolerable. We must get you back up the stairs. Tell Cragg I intend to set up a committee of authors . . .' Not a word of it. Magguinness never sees anyone in the great and inconstant mirror of public esteem but his own good self.

— What new, Thomas? Is the book selling?

— You mean you don't know?

— How am I to know? I've been booted off the editorial board. Nobody shows me the figures any more.

— Oh yes? Well, they're not kissing. Cragg says I will have to go out and sell the book myself. You know what that means, don't you?

— More talkshows?

— Talkshows! I've done the talkshows. Cragg wants me to hire a balloon, pull out the plug, and plop down in the middle of the Queen's garden party, signing books as they show me to the gate.

— The dulcimer touch of Angela Smith, I take it.

— Yes, but Cragg bought it. What do I do, change publishers? You know this book cost me an arm and a leg. I was counting on it to see me out.

— My dear Thomas, where you and I are going there are no pensions for the infirm and no villas on the Costa Brava. We might have seen that some distance before the end of chapter one.

Neither of us could face The Heart of Darkness, so I took him out to lunch at Keen's and sent the bill off to Thrale. We did not much enjoy our meatless Friday. On the way back we nosed into Thatcher's (I was about to say 'by some mechanism of shared masochism', and I am on

Wales' side there) to find out how things were going. Adolf and his *Seven Charms* were still number three and Harriet's latest, *The Mud Bath*, was closing in after sixteen weeks. *Kiss Me* was nowhere in sight, and falling fast. Tom was naturally not overjoyed, and I had to bolster him with a pair of doublewhiskys at the nearest pub. What else was I to do? When there is nothing enheartening to talk about one drinks, and the phenomenon has penetrated the entire economy. Drinking is up and book sales are down. There was a time, as your own experience will confirm, when a bestseller sold fifty thousand, and doubtless that's still true of *The Seven Charms*. But *The Fertile Stone* was on the list, too – for five weeks – and it never got beyond seven thousand. The only thing that can save us is a gross inflation of the price of beer, and by gross I mean enormous, because the price of books alone went up seventythree per cent in the past year. Do you realize what that means? It means that all the papermakers and the inkmakers and the printers and the delivery-truckdrivers and the warehousemen and the secretaries and the editors and the clerks and the salesmen and the nonselling booksellers have decided collectively and simultaneously that *they come first*: the cost of books to the reader is a matter of trivial importance. After all there are the libraries, and the libraries will continue as long as we pay taxes; the libraries, the universities, and the rich. If ten sheiks will each pay five thousand pounds for a camelskin edition of Ali Baba in gold leaf, why worry about selling ten thousand copies of a cheap edition to children? Who cares if the havenots still read, they are all plugged into the electricity: less dangerous to the powers than the printed word. And besides, there is the toiletpaper press. Get somebody to write a block-buster to the right formula of slugs and slits and sleazies, auction it off in New York, and you will comfort yourself at Keen's for five years while waterclosets worldwide roar acclaim. Never underestimate the power of the human intellect to *descend* . . . but how was I to say any of this to Tom? I say it to you, Horace, because I know you have given up reading newspapers. Has anybody told you that the government has put a stop to our cosy world of price cartels? From now on the market decides. Decides what! You know the answer to that one as well as I do: it will decide in favour of the toiletpaper press. Come to think of it, I did throw in that particular observation, hoping that Tom would infer that I had inferred that his work belonged higher up. But it didn't wash. He knew that *Kiss Me* belonged farther down; what infuriated him was that it hadn't made it big down there like some of Harper Cabot's friends. Why, he kept asking me, why? I gave him a hypocrite's out liar's reply. You have been too charming, you have tried too hard to please. In a world of nasties one has no choice but to speak to them in their own nasty language. A gentleman's jokes will no longer serve; it's the Greek they want – coprophilia – and it fits. Pure twaddle, but I had to say something. Poor Tom. What will we do if he does fall down on the Queen's garden?

Footnote to First Lines. I have forgotten to mention a detail that students may find significant. I needn't remind you that publishers do not assemble reference books out of thin air: they assign an editor or editors to the job and credit them on the titlepage. The WEEP books are no exception. *Prefaces, Acknowledgments, Inscriptions, First Lines, Last Lines, Appendixes, Indexes, Footnotes*, and *Variations* are all the work of the same editor, none other than your one and truly Robert Racine. Each work is prefaced, naturally, by the editor, and there are blurbs on all the dustjackets. A single blurb chosen at random will give you the tone of the enterprise as a whole.

> From the time of the first cuneiform tablet, scribbling man has fought the losing battle of the Opening Sentence. Losing, because seldom in the history of literature does an author's second sentence measure up to his first. It is on the composition of the first sentence – as often as not of the preface or the acknowledgment – that the conscientious author may expend days, weeks, and sometimes months of creative energy leading, in some instances to the suspicion that he might have been better off to have abstained. For this volume Robert Racine has selected a thousand famous first lines, leaving the reader to judge in each case whether the author should not have stopped there. The preface, a remarkable essay in literary exposition, examines the career of Sir Adrian Hurdle, the one author in the history of English letters who managed to confine himself to a single opening *phrasis*[3] in a lifetime of starts, all but one of them false.

I am now clothed in Polish printer's pink.
Went back to Thatcher's and turned the shelves upside down looking

---

[3] I read this as a lesson in the use of the transliterated Greek. OK in that form it seems, but not when corrupted into a form of English.

for *Numbers*. Zero. Arabic, in case you are wondering. Then I confronted the person responsible for buying, a bearded man in a pintsized cubicle at the back; he had never heard of it, nor had he ordered any of the others. No sign of them in *Books in Print*. No invoices from WEEP. He would have to ring Miss Bream about that. Yes, he would certainly have to ring Caroline Bream and find out what was going on. Caroline? I wished him luck and said I hoped he would find out, at the same time, if she had any copies of *Numbers* locked away in her vault.

The Fourteenth Envelope

It was good to read your letter and to learn that life elsewhere moves along more or less unperturbed. Is it possible that I am the only dark cloud in the Bentwhistling universe? I am both sorry and glad. We all need to be worried about in one degree or another of desperation, and there are not enough people who do it conscientiously. If it were left to me I'd invent an entire class of occupational worriers, people prepared to write letters regularly, and why not for a fee, beginning with the formula 'I have been worried by your long silence.'

I'm joking. Your letters are marvellous – the more so because the telephone has rendered them obsolete. Who apart from ourselves writes them any longer? Curious, isn't it, to think that pedants and perfume-sniffers will work over them one day – yours, I mean, not mine. What begins as private exchange ends up as indecent exposure. Never mind, they will stretch tortured minds into a semblance of humanity.

The three weeks I should have taken have spread themselves, I hate to admit, into this ridiculous length of time. The worst part now is the thought that Wales may know what we are doing, and what he is doing, and that by letting the work slide this way I have proved his point about the management of money and time: we are always eager to spend what is not truly our own. Let me explain, if I can, according to our agreement, the series of events.

The most obvious way of getting something done might seem to be to set about doing it. The other way is by reading books. Understand me, Horace, we have tried the obvious. We have travelled from Wace to Hietzing to Firenze to Lutetia to Morden Priory to the basement of the world. We have obeyed. We have unchastened daisies. When nothing works, what do you do? You try something else. We are trying to find out where Wales is hiding. Could it be, it occurred to me to ask, that he has hidden himself in *Numbers*? That there are signposts in the text, clues clear enough to lead us if not literally to the place then to a better grasp of his purpose? Too much to hope for? Maybe. But why has he drawn it to our attention? Doesn't Wales' new version, the one we can't find, refer us back in some perplexing way to the original?

You, I know, read in an orderly way. You must, or you could never have accomplished so much. I, for my part, have accomplished nothing, and left it on trains. I have learned, nevertheless, to proceed, and I do so by means of an act of faith. There is no other way of explaining it. Perhaps you experience a similar feeling even within the orderliness of your approach: the eagerness that drives one along, the quasicertainty that the next book, the next chapter, the next paragraph or footnote or subordinate clause will be the one that marks the end of the search, the missing piece, the longawaited answer or truth revealed, the Word. And so one plunges in and discovers Infinity. Within Infinity, events. This is the way they fell.

I said to Jeannine:

– Look, all of this has got to mean something. If it doesn't mean something in Wales' mind we must make it mean something in ours. If we fail we are lost. We can't allow ourselves to fail. It must be written somewhere, and edited, and committed to print. This is what our lives must mean. If they do not mean this much our lives are meaningless. But our lives must mean something otherwise

– All right, she said. What do you intend to do?

– I intend to look for him in the Word.

– Which word?

– Precisely. That is precisely the problem.

It was at that moment that I determined to investigate what seemed to be the last remaining hope, the possibility, however faint, that Wales had edited or rewritten the fourth book of Moses to supply us with a sequence of sorts, a code. A definitive Book of Wales. At the same time my bones warned me that any misinterpretation on my part, any bad faith or failure of nerve, would exact a price. I looked for courage in precedents, and found a measure of it in this:

> As I walked through the wilderness of this world, I lighted
> upon a certain place, where was a den; and I laid me down in
> that place to sleep: and as I slept I dreamed a dream. I
> dreamed, and behold I saw a man clothed with rags, standing
> in a certain place, with his face from his own house, a book in
> his hand, and a great burden upon his back. I looked, and

> saw him open the book, and read therein; and as he read, he
> wept and trembled: and not being able longer to contain, he
> brake out with a lamentable cry; saying, 'What shall I do?'

According to my father, who read these opening lines from *The Pilgrim's Progress* to me when I was too young to read them myself, my grandfather, a pious Victorian, used to open the Bible in moments of despair and consult at random. It was impossible, in his way of thinking, not to find some fragment of truth which would see one safely over the next obstacle and lead one back to the path from which one had strayed. It was a tradition he had learned from his grandfather, who had learned it from his grandfather, who in turn had learned it from the Puritans. It occurred to me to try it now as, God knew, all the other expedients had failed.

> Now rise up, said I, and get you over the brook [x]Zered. And
> we went over the brook Zered. And the [y]space in which we
> came from [z]Kadesh-barnea, until we were come over the
> brook Zered, was thirty and eight years, until all the
> [aa]generation of the men of war were [bb]wasted out from
> among the host, as the Lord swore unto them. For indeed
> the hand of the Lord was against them, to destroy them from
> among the host, until they were [cc]consumed.[1]

So much for grandfathers. What did fascinate me, what has always fascinated about this particular edition, a goatskin glory preceding by many years my experience of Wales, was the abundance of references and subreferences: the [ff]'s and [gg]'s sprinkled throughout the text in minuscule, rather like insects buzzing about a vegetable patch in [ss]Saskatchewan. If you take any one page and trace them all to their respective sources, and to the sources of their sources, you can easily lose a week and never find out what has become of it. The real fun comes when you read it aloud.

> And there appeared another wuwonder in heaven; and,
> behold, a great red bebedragon, cecehaving seven heads and
> dedeten horns, and seven eeeecrowns upon his heads. And
> his tail drew the third part of the fufustars of heaven and did

---

[1] *The Fifth Book* 2: 13–22.

geegeecast them to the earth; and the bebedragon stood before the woman which was ready to be delivered, huhuto devour her child as soon as it was born.[2]

I was reading that aloud – my second random selection, other end of the book – when Jeannine came into the gardenroom.

– *J'en ai marre de toi et de ton babil. Ralbol.*[3] In God's name why don't you go out and chase something?

Having got that far I was in no mood to defer.

– I have been chasing something and you have been watching me chase it.

– Then what conclusions have you come to? I can't see how reading that sandy old book will help you to arrive at any conclusions.

– Dusty. The trouble with women, I remarked bitterly and in the plural, is that they have no intellectual curiosity. No nose. Did you know, for instance, that Moses' father married his aunt?

– Whose aunt?

– His own aunt. The sister of his father.

– A likely story. How does that lead you to Wales?

– Well, I didn't write the book.

– All I want to know is why you go on reading it? Why do you waste your time?

Sackcloth and ashes. If I could get my hands on one or two of the Seventy or indeed on any of the subsequent sinners, I'd give it to them, the meddlers, for the trouble they have caused. Look, they weren't even able to get the titles right. *Bemidbar*, the Hebrew title, means 'in the wilderness' in place of which they wrote 'numbers'. Why? Then the Greekhating Wales went to work and construed it as *The Book of Books*, as if none of the rest of it mattered. Why? And what about the fifth book, *Deuteronomy*, did Wales know that it, too, was a mistranslation? The Greek means 'the second law'; the Hebrew title was *Debarim* meaning, God save us, 'words'. Miserable scribes! Phatuous pharisouts! Nobody but Nobody was to be trusted. In short, Horace, if the business can be shortened, there seemed to be two possible lines of investigation: *Numbers* meaning the census and *Numbers* meaning wilderness. I was counting on wilderness because Wales' business, and it's not easy to follow, was words. Bunyan, dear old John again, reminded me that the

. . . .

[2] *Revelation* 12: 3–4.
[3] I'm fed up with you and your gabble. To the teeth.

180

word 'pilgrim' means 'person journeying to a future life', and who was Moses if not one of the first of those? And listen to this, my best Sherlockery, I think, to date. The word pilgrim comes from ME *pelegrim* from OF *pelegrin* from L *peregrinus*. And what does L *peregrinus* mean? It means 'stranger'. And what does Wales mean? You've guessed.

Leave no stone unturned. One of them may conceal.

> And the Lord spake unto [a]Moses in the wilderness of Sinai, in the [b]tabernacle of the congregation, on the first day of the second month, in the second year after they were [c]come out of the land of Egypt, saying, Take ye the sum of all the congregation of the children of Israel, after their families, by the house of their fathers, with the number of their names, every male by their polls; from [d]twenty years old and upward, all that are able to go forth to war in Israel: thou and Aaron shall number them by their armies. And with you there shall be a man of every [e]tribe, every one head of the house of his [f]fathers. And these are the names of the men that shall stand with you: of the tribe of Reuben: Elizur, the son of Shedeur. Of Simeon: Shelumiel, the son of Zurishaddai. Of Judah: Nahshon, the son of

and so on into the tribes. If ever you find yourself in the grip of insomnia, read your way into the first chapter without skipping a line of the census. Your head will be nodding before the end of Issachar's count, and glad of it.

Ninethirty, Great Conduit Street, collided with Cragg on my way in. Exaggerated gallantry: stand aside for the wouldbepope of publishers. Furious opening, slamming of the door. Brass doorknocker rattatting on its hinge. Click of lock, thud of bolt.

Red sentinelbox, traffic island outside Strathmore Hotel.

– Helena? He's done it again. Would you be a dear and unfasten the windowlatch in the stairwell?

– Two minutes, ducks, I'm putting on the warpaint.

– Never mind the warpaint. If you put it all on you won't feel like giving me a goodmorning kiss.

– *Darling*, wherever have you been throughout history? Kisses are *never* distributed first thing in the morning. Two minutes.

So I walked back the long way round. Clickclack of heels on the way to work. Legs carved out of nylon, swinging along as if life had its purpose in the office. Black tubes in pursuit. One two three over and in. Helena already gone up the stairs. Back to the catacombs etym. dub., scratch match, invade the gloom. Dark business on the best of days. Still and all, no agenda, no deadlines, no yessirno sir, nothing but the selfimposed grapple with *Wilderness*. Selfimposed? How quickly we learn to comfort ourselves. My notes nevertheless.[4]

And the Lord said to Moses, these are the men who shall do the work for you. Elizur, Shelumiel, Nahshon, Nethaneel, Eliab, Elishama, Gamaliel, Abidan, Ahiezer, Pagiel, Eliasaph, Ahira.

> As the Lord said this, Moses did that.
> General assembly. And the numbering began.
> Children of Reuben, fortysix thousand five hundred.
> Children of Simeon, fiftynine thousand three hundred.
> Children of Gad, fortyfive thousand six hundred and fifty.
> Children of Judah, seventyfour thousand six hundred.
> Children of Issachar, fiftyfour thousand four hundred.
> Children of Zebulun, fiftyseven thousand four hundred.
> Children of Joseph: of Ephraim, forty thousand five hundred; of Manasseh, thirtytwo thousand two hundred.
> Children of Benjamin, thirtyfive thousand four hundred.
> Children of Dan, sixtytwo thousand seven hundred.
> Children of Asher, fortyone thousand five hundred.
> Children of Naphtali, fiftythree thousand four hundred.
> Six hundred and three thousand five hundred and fifty male Israelites aged twenty and over, all fit to go forth to war. All present and correct.
> No counting the dead without counting the living before-hand.
> The tribe of Levi set aside to camp round and serve the tent of the priests.
> Rectangle of Levites containing
> the tent containing
> the holy place containing

....

[4] Ed.: In his fascination with the biblical account of the wandering of the tribes of Israel and Moses' 40-year government of them, Robert Racine went so far as to supply Horace Bentwhistle with what amounts to yet another revised version, albeit condensed, unauthorized, and highly personal. We see no reason to present more than short extracts here. Although Racine thought he had found in *Numbers* a parallel between Wales' matrioshkas and the 'box within box' construction of the Hebrew tabernacle, readers less addicted to the arcane are likely to find more significance in Moses' habit (as it also seems to be Racine's) of falling on his face.

the sanctuary containing

the ark of acacia containing

the tables of testimony containing

the words of the law written with the very finger of God.

Box within box within box within box within box within box within the mind of God.

World without end, amen.

Arrangement of the camp round the tent. Every man in his place, tent pitched beside his standard bearing the banner of his father's house.

Judah to the east. Reuben to the south. Ephraim to the west. Dan to the north.

As they encamp, so shall they set forward.

Forward out of slavery.

Forward toward the milk, the honey.

Men, women, children, slaves.

Two million? Three million? And their goats. And their cattle. Pots. Jars. Tents. Sockets. Poles.

Forward into hope.

The Lord spoke unto Moses and Aaron, and the children of Israel did all that the Lord commanded.

How far forward to the nearest well?

How many centuries to the nearest hotandcold running bath?

It was at this point that I began to understand, for the first time in my life, what it is that makes PPpedants of people who might otherwise be considered normal. The dive, the irresistible dive into bottomless seas, the tug, the irreversible tug by invisible hands back through the gate leading to the mists of time, down and down into the hysteriout amniout caul, comforted, cosseted, fed by words – endless, streaming, processional words. Maternal? Paternal? No one can know. In this preworld of worlds find no gods goddesses, no heroes heroines, no matriarchs patriarchs, no hierophants, sycophants, phants – nothing but matter in its willingness to go on forever without distinction or destination or apparent cause. One is swallowed up and the sensation is overwhelming. No more entrances exits, neither ascent nor fall. Nothing but an endless gravitationless swim in a blissfully warm syrup. Divine.

Remember the fleshpots of Egypt? The fish and the cucumbers, the watermelons and onions? The lovely reeking garlic?

Now there is nothing but manna.
The dew falls, the manna rises up.

There was, first, Moses himself or what he is said to have said, according to the rabbis. What I did, now, was to plunge in as if they had never spoken, never stuck finger in clay, never even begun messing about with an alephbeth: I wanted to listen in once more on the direct line. Once more, I say, because I had read it all before, and reread it, but never with a purpose that went beyond the poetry of the thing. Now, I began to feel, there might be more. Was there something being said across the rumour of the centuries that the peregrinating Wales had heard in the same way that I was hearing it? Listen, I said to myself, this is a *voice* speaking, and began to read the lines, even the dull ones, aloud. I propped them up in front of my porridge and read while it cooled; I lipread them on the train; I whispered them in the hole (for fear of being overheard by Cragg); I lipread them once more on the train; and propped them up again at dinner. Jeannine began going out for long walks. Finally when I got to the end of the reading, and silence, I gave myself over once more to the other experience, the vicarious thrill of the scribes and rescribes, the rabbis and rerabbis, the *Chosen*, who had knocked it into shape and spent eight centuries doing it. If they could do it that long, what were eight weeks to me? My pen glided smoothly across the surface of the nights with an assurance it had never known before. It was as if someone were guiding my hand. Literally. As if it had never been meant to write other words.

It was the time of the firstripe grapes.

So they went up, the twelve, and searched the land from the wilderness of Zin to Rehob. They went up the Negev to Hebron, and came upon the brook of Eshcol.

There they gathered grapes and pomegranates and figs.

After searching the land for forty days they turned back and made their report to Moses and Aaron and all the children of Israel.

It was, indeed, a land of milk and honey. But the people were strong and the cities walled. Amalekites in the Negev; Hittites, Jebusites, Amorites in the mountains; Canaanites by the sea and along the Jordan.

Caleb: I say move against them at once. We shall overcome.

Joshua: The Lord delight in us.

The Others: Not on your life. They are too strong for us.

Muttering and groaning from the multitudes. Embroidery from the Others.

The sons of Anak are giants. *Nephilim*. We are as grass-hoppers beside them. They would kill us for their sport.

And the people wept that night.

And the whole congregation turned against Moses and Aaron.

Why has the Lord done this to us? Has he brought us here to fall by the sword, to offer our wives and children as spoils of war? We should have died in Egypt! We should have died in the desert! Turn back! Back to Egypt! Let us choose a new leader and go back!

In the sight of the multitudes Moses and Aaron fell on their faces.

Joshua and Caleb tore their clothes.

It is good land, flowing with milk and honey. The Lord brought us here. If he loves us he will be with us and protect us and give us this land. Rebel not, fear not. The Lord is with us.

Stone them! Stone them!

Kadeshbarnea.

The stumblingblock. The turningpoint.

And the glory of the Lord came down upon the tent of the congregation and the Lord said to Moses, How long will this people treat me with contempt? How long before they learn to believe? I will smite them with pestilence. I will disinherit them. You, Moses, and your descendants, of you I will make a nation mightier than they.

And Moses said to the Lord, What if the Egyptians hear of this? What will they think? That the Lord who went before us in a pillar of cloud and in a pillar of fire could not keep his promise and so destroyed them in the wilderness.

No! Let the power of the Lord be great and merciful. Punish them even to the third and fourth generations, but do not sweep them clean away!

And the Lord said, They shall have my pardon. For the earth shall be filled with the glory of the Lord. But they have put me to the test now these ten times. Because of this no one shall see the promised land but Joshua and Caleb who have followed me with their hearts.

Because of this

your carcasses shall fall in the wilderness
your bones shall rot in the sand
your children shall wander
one year for every day
in which you searched the land I swore to give
to your fathers
forty years
until your carcasses waste
your bones rot
in the sand
and not one of you is left
but Joshua and Caleb and your children
who shall wander with you
forty years
bearing your harlotries paying for them until
your carcasses waste
your bones rot
every
one.
Kadeshbarnea.
And the people mourned greatly.

In the morning they rose early and made for the mountains,
saying, We have sinned. But we are here. Let us go forward.

And Moses warned them that they would perish by the
sword because they had turned away from the Lord.

Then the Amalekites and the Canaanites fell upon them
and crushed them and drove them back all the way to the
Place of Destruction.

The forty years began.

I don't know what you think of events as we learn of them in *Numbers*
or of the people who handed down the story; for me, even if the reality
had been limited to forty months and the Sea of Reeds to a country
creek, it would still be one of the greatest stories ever told, its people by
all odds the most Homeric of all time, their Yahweh the most terrible
and inscrutable of phants. Think of having a god like that for a friend.
Imagine having his author on your publishing list. In what manner does
the cast resemble the people who have inhabited the house of Wales? In
what way are we, in our contemporary wilderness of plastic milkbottles
and homogenized honey, remotely of the same breed of men?

Listen, you could argue along parallel lines. Wales born by the water:

close enough. Born by Ponytpool, we are told, in the firstclass carriage of a train passing through. What is a railway track if not an endless river of steel, a carriage if not a basket? Do we not all go to hell in a basket? Smoke on it.

Wales marrying a Midianite; marrying, that is, outside the tribe. Well, Alethea was Greek.

Wales the writingfinger of God? Not sure, now, that Wales' digit wasn't more antiwriting than writing. Reminds me of the time he urged one of our more luckless scribblers, who shall remain nameless, to go stick it up his fundament.

Wales leading his publishing tribe across the Sinai of the twentieth century? Stop laughing, he might have done it. But we are to believe that Wales disappeared. We are to believe that Moses disappeared.

> So Moses, the servant of the Lord, died there in the land of Moab, according to the word of the Lord. And he buried him in a valley in the land of Moab, over against Bethpeor; but no man knoweth of his sepulchre unto this day.[5]

We are plummeted, in other words, from the top of the mountain and the panorama of promise straight into a numberless ditch at the bottom of a nameless valley. Was that any way to treat the man who had led them there, and made them what they had become? Can you imagine it happening to Herzl, or Weizmann, or Groucho Marx? But in Moses' time curious events were occurring on mountaintops. My own version, untrustworthy as any other, says this:

> The Lord spoke to Moses, saying, Take this rod and touch the rock with it. I shall make the rock give forth water.
> Then Moses and Aaron stood before them, and Moses said to the rebels, Must we do everything for you? Even bring water out of the rock?
> And he touched the rock twice and water came forth.
> No reference to the work of God. Silence from Aaron.
> Fatal.
> And the Lord spoke to them in the wilderness of Zin.
> Because of this you shall not lead the people into the land.

....

[5] *Words* 34: 5–6.

For you did not uphold my holiness before the Water of
Strife.

So the Lord spoke to Moses saying, Aaron shall go no
further. Take him to the top of Mount Hor.

Strip him of his garments.

Leave him there to die.

A younger man shall take his place. Eleazar.

And Moses did as he was told.

Aaron, Clutterbuck in a nutshell? You tell me.

Eight centuries it took them to get the manuscript ready for the
printer, and it took the printer eighteen centuries more to get his
typefaces cut. Those were the days when they knew how to take their
time. If they could work at it that long, what were eight months to me,
eight years? What we all want from existence is the suspension of time:
to put it grandly, an eternity of doing, and I seemed to have found what I
wanted to do. Books about Moses, books about books, books about
numbers; references, cuttings, notations on scraps of paper; collections
of pencils and pens, pots of ink in several colours – for no one pen, no
one colour seemed to be good enough by itself – spread across my table
and into my mind like the tentacles of the beast. Then one day Jeannine,
hoping possibly praying that Freud might get me unstuck, handed me a
copy of *Moses and Monotheism*, in French, and I plunged in. Little did she
know that Freud, himself, was a case sprung straight up out of the
looneybin, and I pose my words. We learn from Jones that the good
doctor was not unafflicted with the curse of literature: Goethe, Heine,
Burns, Byron, Dickens, Walter Scott. Calderon, Homer, Schiller, Ranke.
Tom Jones, which he considered unsuitable for his chaste fiancée, *Tristram
Shandy, Don Quixote, La Tentation de saint Antoine*. Tasso, Gottfried
Keller, Disraeli, Thackeray, George Eliot, Nestroy, Mark Twain, and
YHWH knows who else. German, French, English, Italian, Spanish,
Hebrew, Latin, Greek. English preferred. Not only did he read them in
most of those languages, he collected them, and in order to collect them
he gave them to Martha who could not very well send them back. Had he
not had to sit there behind the divan listening long into the years, he'd
have read more than Karl Marx, who was probably the most insatiable
wordconsumer of all time. At what rate of consumption do words *become*
numbers?

Inevitably there was Shakespeare. Freud began reading Shakespeare
when he was eight years old, and reread him, when he wasn't busy
listening or reading all the others, or writing about his listening and

reading, throughout his life. His rereading convinced him, in the end, that Shakespeare was somebody else. He could not have been Francis Bacon: no one mind, he deduced, could have produced the work of Bacon and Shakespeare together. He might have been the deformation of a Norman named Jacques-Pierre, theory of the Italian Gentilli (twiceoperated slip?), for Shakespeare was most unlike the English in what? In his passion. Eventually he acquired, for one thing leads inevitably as Bertrand Russell observed to another, the work of a certain Thomas Looney, *Shakespeare Identified*, New York 1920, who intrigued him with the theory that Shakespeare was Edward de Vere, seventeenth Earl of Oxford, of Norman descent. Freud is now, in 1926, seventy years old, and has rereread Shakespeare quite a number of times. A year later he rereads Looney and declares himself convinced, more or less. In 1930 in his letter accepting the Goethe Prize, he returns to the Looney thesis; once more in 1935, in the revision of his Life; and finally in the last essay written during the year of his death. There is little doubt that Shakespeare, and Looney, had managed to get a grip on him; Hamlet's Oedipal confusion – how could he do away with his father when he was already dead – and the nastiness of Lear's daughters didn't help.

But all that was only a beginning. If Shakespeare failed to do the job properly, Moses and his tribes most certainly would. I first read Freud's *Moses* in Jeannine's French or Moïse version, and then in Strachey's English; the French language has always seemed unbelievable to me. Damned if they didn't both say the same thing. Moses, like Shakespeare, was somebody else. Not only was he somebody else, he was somebody else twice over, for there were two Moseses if I may be so bold, and I am bold because the name Moses, Yahweh save us, is *Greek*, point wildly exclamated. The correct usage, according to the savants, is 'Mose', meaning 'child' in Egyptian – hence Ahmose, Ramose, Ptahmose, Whatmose: child of Ah, Ra, Ptah, and What. Mose, the Egyptian prince, was an adherent of the onegod religion of the pharaoh Akhenaton/ Ikhnaton, husband of Nefertiti the household pet. We do not know, in this account, whose mose Mose was. Our man therefore was not the inventor of the monocular view of existence, nor of circumcision (the Egyptians had been slicing theirs beforehand), nor of disbelief in the immortality of all those mummified cats. Akhenaton/Ikhnaton fell off the wall, and Mose led the renegades across the Sea of Reeds to their destiny. Forty years. Along the way, two things happened. The Yisraelites lost their moral fibre and their trust in the Leader. An uprising occurred. Mose I was put to death, precisely as small Viennese boys had dreamed it outside their mothers' bedchambers. Mose II, more properly speaking Mosheh, meaning 'pulled out of the water', was a Midianite priest, soninlaw of Jethro, and it seems unlikely that he was pulled out of the Nile. This was the Mosheh who climbed to the top of the mountain with his lumps of moist clay and descended with tablets baked and face shining, the tablets bearing inscriptions made by the writingfinger of God. This was the priest whose awful Yahweh minus the vowels endowed the Yisraelites with the iron they needed to crush all those who opposed their entry into the Promised Land, and bequeathed them the mosaic that John Bunyan and the Puritans found so compelling.

At this point Freud was reading his way back in the footsteps of a prehistorian named Ernst Sellin, who had found his evidence in *The Book of Hosea*. In Hebrew Hosea means 'the Lord saves'. He managed to confine himself, in my Dispensation, to fewer than nine pages: I'd give him the Nobel for that alone. It seems that our prophet was not spared the humiliation of an unfaithful wife, Gomer, same name as the son of Japheth said to have been the progenitor of the Celts therefore of Wales; a gomer or uncorrupted homer is also the Hebrew measure expressed liquidly as ten baths. Does that save us? Gomer, the lady, caused so much havoc in Hosea's heart that he began to identify the Yisraelites in their entirety with his wife. Again and again, speaking as God's secretary, he accuses them of whoring away their credit, not to mention their persistent devotion to the golden calf, and he damns them with the terrible phrase about sowing the wind and reaping the whirlwind. But what stopped me was this, and I quote directly from King James: 'For the spirit of whoredoms hath caused them to err, and they have gone a whoring from under their God. *They sacrifice upon the tops of the mountains* (my italians), and burn incense upon the hills, under oaks and poplars and elms, because the shadow thereof is good; therefore your daughters shall commit whoredom, and your spouses shall commit adultery.'[6] Later on in the book Hosea reports malfeasance on the part of Ephraim, one of the tribes, who has provoked the Lord so bitterly that he (the Lord) felt obliged to 'leave his blood upon him'. Is this what Sellin was sotospeak sellin? In the circumstances I had little choice but to return to Carlyle House and plunge into the eighteen volumes of the Oxbridge Society for Theophanic Studies: there was a bath or two of material there, I can tell you, and it was only a beginning. But I had

. . . .

[6] *Hosea* 4: 12–13.

begun to get clever. I no longer read the books, I confined myself to the indexes. Sellin, who wrote in German anyway, was reduced to three miserable footnotes. So I was forced once more to fall back on Freud, approaching him this time by way of the ladder at the back. Falkenheimer, Farmer, Fazincani, Federmann, Fehrenbacher, Feiglstock, Feingold, Feinschreiber, Felloni, Fenstermann, Fernandez, Ferneyhough, Feuillebois, Fichte, Filipovic, Fischel, Fitzmeyer, Fitzsimmons, Flack, Flageollet, Flanagan, Flaumenhauer, Flaus, Fleisheimer, Fleishman, Foote, Frankenstein, Frankfurter, Freeble, Frein, pass on to Futerhendler, and Fzwarc. No Joy. You will not believe this: *only then* did it occur to me that I'd been doing what I'd been preaching against all my life, I had been worrying about the man. The boils in the crotch, the thirtytwo children nineteen of them bastards, the lifelong sucking of the thumb in the shape of a downhill pipe, the pink tights under the charcoal trousers – who, to spare the chaste Martha's memory, gives a tinker's eff? What matters is the poem. Why did Freud laugh when the publishers asked him to psychoanalyse the text? If he couldn't see it, I could. The writingfinger, having writ, wrote on.

And there shall come a Star out of Joseph to smite the people of Moab, and beat them down.

Pass on to Pisgah?

Not before the matter of the Midianites and their women, and the plague of Peor.

If ever you would disarm your enemy, let him sleep with your wife.

Creation 12:13. Creation 20:2. Creation 26:7.

Wife, thou art my sister.

But the children of Israel slept with the women of Midian and bowed down to their gods.

And the anger of the Lord came down upon them and those who died in the plague numbered twentyfour thousand.

And Phinehas seized his spear and thrust it through the Israelite Zimri and his Midianite woman, daughter of a prince.

Through her belly.

So the plague was stayed.

And the Lord gave the covenant of peace and security of tenure to Phinehas and his seed forever because he had been zealous in the service of his God.

Phinehas, son of Eleazar, son of Aaron the priest.

Then the Lord spoke to Moses, saying, Vex the Midianites. Make them suffer for their crafty tricks.

For the Lord thy God is a jealous God.

After you have taken vengeance of Israel you shall be gathered to your people.

And Moses spoke to the people and said, Arm yourselves and go down against the Midianites. One thousand from every tribe.

Avenge the Lord with the sword.

And Moses sent out Phinehas and Eleazar the priest with the holy instruments and the trumpets of war.

And they slew all the males
and the five Midian kings
and the prophet Balaam
and took all the women and their little ones
and their cattle and their flocks and their goods
and burned their cities and took the spoil
and brought the prisoners to Moses
and Eleazar the priest.

And Moses said, Have you kept the women alive?

These sluts and fornicators?

These provokers of the plague of Peor?

Kill the male children!

Kill all who slept with the men of Israel!

Keep the virgins, the undefiled.

Then purify yourselves outside the camp for seven days.

Holy War.

Midian. Sons of Keturah, Abraham's second wife.

Midian. Daughters of Jethro, father of Moses' first wife.

Fascism begins between the legs.

Provocaust.

Was it possible? I was so astonished by what my eyes were trying to tell me that I threw Nefertiti off my lap with a thud, rushed up the stairs to the bedroom, and seized Jeannine by the shoulder. She sat up in the bed straight as a post, horrified.

— What are you doing with my shoulder!

— Listen, I said, this is what it says. Fascism begins between the legs. Between the. Legs.

My paper shivered in my hands.

– You are waking me up to tell me *that?* Genial! Where the bloody-where else could it begin?

And she declined wearily into the sheets.

Suddenly I felt weary. Ralbol. Tired of humping it from wasteland to mountaintop to ditch. More tired than she would ever know.

Chapter minus verse. Yes. And as I read those extraordinary words, and reread them transfixed (that was before I had declaimed them to Jeannine), I honestly thought I had got a grip on one of the Great Truths. Now of course I see it more clearly. The Great Truth had failed to get a grip on me. Is that progress? I won't expect you to go along with this, entrenched as you are in the preconceived, but never mind; it works for me. Instil belief in the human breast and you create the possibility of every form of misery known to Interlinneus and his horrors. Think of them. Then try to think of counterexamples. They do not leap immediately to the mind. Mose, for me, is not the man, nor two men; Mose is the word. Mose is what the rabbis and rerabbis wanted us to think about him, and they wanted us to know that 'his eye was not dim, nor his natural force abated' when he disappeared. The beautiful death we all dream of, or were they rewriting the Greeks? If Freud was right and things are not what they seem, what must we do to be saved? Bunyan's Christian pilgrim abandoned wife and children for the pleasure of the quest. Wales to a W. But Bunyan retraced his steps; the pleasure was to be theirs as well, if only on the printed page. What part of the Puritan remains in Wales?

Mosheh was the author of a personage variously called Elohim, Yahweh, Adonai, translated perhaps too bluntly as God, whose simple tent we later modulated into the infinitely more hideous 'church' (Gk *kuriakon*), and no wonder it's gone down the drain since. The writing-finger, the 'face of',were primitive attemps to prefigure Freud: obscurities of the unconscious mind dictating the text. What Mosheh did was to institutionalize the One, an idea we have been grappling with unsuccessfully since, and install himself as general secretary of the Party. The Christians couldn't live with it either, and rewrote the book to give us Volume One in three parts. *Elohim*: singular in meaning, plural in form. Mosheh began with fire and thunder and lightning 'and the voice of the trumpet exceedingly loud' and worked his way along from there. The rest was articulation. Box within box within box. History of the Word, and what has happened to it since. You. Me. Wales. And Wales, if we are to follow Freud, is someone else.

Bekorgakov: 'I have always loved the Jews for their interpretative musicians and feared them for their prophets: Marx, Freud, Einstein – the twentieth century in three words. And Einstein played the violin like an angel. Perhaps they deserved a less jealous God.'

The only straw, for me, is the box within box within box. We are now at M Seven. I looked at one of the leering things the other day in the toy department at Gordon's – same cubic capacity, one twentieth of a bath – and it contained eleven offspring. Seven down and four to go. Either we wait for the others or we cut the cord. Yes, cord. Have *you* figured out why Wales chose to express himself with the maternal?

Nocturne. The received or glossymagazine view of marriage is that it is held together by documents, signatures, vows, and veils. Nothing could be further from the truth. Marriage is a construct of invisible string. No one can know in advance if the knots will hold or give way under strain.

I was investigating Ashtoreth and her shady groves, to find out what was so awful about oaks and poplars and elms, when Jeannine came down into the gardenroom and took up a stance. You know what wives are like when they do that: feet apart, arms folded, teeth clenched in a vise. Never so beautiful as when they are angry.

– Put it away.

I was not sure if she meant the reference volumes, the notebook, the Dispensation, the inkpots, the coffeepot, the chocolate biscuits, the plastic bags, or my navel; all I can tell you is that I didn't like the sound of it. She might have asked me when I proposed to announce a conclusion of sorts, or what progress I was making at the house, but no. It came without nuances.

– Put it away. If you don't put it away I will leave you, and I will take the cats.

I took that as a warning, and gathered up my materials. End of travail, from L *trepalium*, threestaked instrument of torture, and it was a wrench: I am never so happy as when I am doing something with my hands. So I had to invent something else, and pursue it until she had recovered her calm. Seriously. She was right, I had dithered too long. The comfortable caul is not to be ours this side of the unforgiving ditch.

The project, then, was to take up the search for *Numbers*, Wales' version, in a practicable way. I had seen a copy in Cragg's hands. He had let it fall in a heap on his table in the presence of Caroline Bream. It was the one volume of the collection that remained missing, and it might, just conceivably might contain the key to the rest. The code. Cragg was unlikely to have thrown it out; he would keep it as evidence. The thing to do was to go back to the house when he was not there and find it. That meant going back at night.

How much time do we need to make strokes of genius seem plausible? In this instance I allowed five minutes to elapse before I announced my plan. I would borrow the key from Helena and slip in after the charwomen had gone. It would cost me an evening in town, but what was an evening, won or lost, to either of us now? I quoted a verse from Moses' prayer without attributing the source.[7]

– For a thousand years in thy sight are but as yesterday when it is past, and as a watch in the night.

For all she knew I might have written it myself. I hoped I would be forgiven one day for finding encouragement in her silence.

That same afternoon I crept out of Great Conduit Street early. It was one of the new privileges I had acquired since I had taken up residence in the hole: no one noticed my leaving early so long as I left early enough. As a matter of routine I had begun putting out the candelabra an hour ahead of the others. Occasionally, when I felt so inclined, I left in midafternoon.

I did not take refuge in the club. Chesterton, to my dismay, had recently been taken in as a member. Once I found him in a corner of The Heart of Darkness pretending to read a manuscript at four in the afternoon; in point of fact he was asleep. To avoid a possible even probable repetition of that embarrassment, I immersed myself in the stacks at Carlyle House and returned to the matter of the sexy goddess and her groves. Frazer had a word to say about that, didn't he in twelve volumes, and every poet in the wood will tell you, at the drop of a dithyrambus etym. extremely dub., what that one word is. Freud found time for Frazer but Frazer had no time for Freud. Resistance? I promised myself to resume climbing my ladders once I had dealt with Wales. After Frazer I could always read Feuerbach, and after Feuerbach Hegel, and after Hegel Herder (J.G.), and after Herder Spinoza, and after Spinoza Voltaire, and I took particular comfort in the thought that, with the grace of Methuselah and the Oxbridge Theophanics, I might then set out to rescribe them all. Meanwhile I treated myself to a meal in a Chinese restaurant – gentile's horror of sweetandsour bellypork with chopsticks – and that pretty well used up the innocent part of the evening.

. . . .

[7] *Psalms* 90:4.

Great Conduit Street was empty. I fished among the coins in my pocket for Helena's key, found it, let myself in. Not a tick. I rattled the umbrella stand, banged into a chair, stubbed my toe on the landing. Burglar minus alarm. Hands along the wall leading to Cragg's room, turn left, along to the gap, turn right into Philippa's room, left into Cragg's. Door closed but unlocked. Lightswitch there somewhere: inside, outside? Click. Hand into eyeshade, straight to the cabinets. Bentwhistle, Birdwell, Carrington, Cragg, Herder, Magguinness – orderly chap, Cragg – *Prefaces, Introductions, Inscriptions, Acknowledgments, First Lines, Footnotes, Appendixes, Indexes, Errata. No Numbers.* Bof. Grace not exactly abounding.

Errata? Odd. Hadn't heard of that one before. Fattest volume on the shelf, fatter even than *Appendixes.* Reached in, took it down, thumbed in at random exactly as Grandfather I had done with King James, or was it Grandfather II. Letter M. M for Murderers. What in the name of Doyle could they be doing there? And after Murderers, 'see Bible'.

By that time I was hooked. Bible: the Greek has vacillated back in, notice well. Probably the longest entry in the book, with subs. A's, B's, C's and along to the M's. Maacah, Macedonia, Machpelah, Madness, Magdala, Magdalene, Magistrates, Magnify, Magog, Mahanaim, Mahlon, Maid, Maidservants, Majesty, Maker, Malachi, Malchus, Malefactors, Mammon, Man, Manasseh, Mandrakes, and on for five pages more to Moses, Mote, Mother, Mothers, Mourn, Mourners, Multiply, Multitude, Murder, Murderers. In my innocence I had supposed that the Murderers' Bible was a practical handbook on rubbing people out, censored, probably, at the time of the Malthusian debate. Wrong again. See Bible of 1801, *Jude* 16: 'These are murderers, complainers, walking after their own lusts; and their mouth speaketh great swelling words' mouth singular. Printer's mistake. Should have been '*murmerers*, complainers'.

And so the King's English is run amok. *Erratum*, cognative with the French *errer*, to wander, go astray.

I tucked the volume under my arm and turned out the light. On my return home I woke Jeannine and reported my discoveries.

( )[8]

....

[8] Ed.: Parenthesis left blank in deference to the sensibilities of Madame Racine.

Clean slate. If you read widely enough, and long, you will find that any one text is cancelled out by every other. Thus Moses is edited by the Jehovist who is rewritten by the Elohist who is supplanted by the Priest who is supplemented by the Deuteronomist who is scrambled by the Code. And that was only the beginning. Thirtyfour centuries pass. Moses, in the catalogue of the catalogue of the catalogues, is reduced to a footnote at the bottom of a microdot. And so Freud laughed. But in his heart he was an angry man: 'In its implications the distortion of a text resembles a murder: the difficulty is not in perpetrating the deed, but in getting rid of its traces.'[9]

What would Freud say about my empty shoes? They have come back to haunt me. It may have been – can it have been so? – that I was meant to step into them and be walked away by them into what remains of my life. And because I failed to seize my opportunity to step off briskly and confidently into a straight line moving forward, I am condemned to this morass, this flickering pit. And here I shall remain for the remainder of my years, crying out, never heard, floundering falling, picking myself up, floundering and falling with sand in my teeth and spines in my feet and the desert stretching before my inturned eyes without pathways or halts, until the end of time.

Meanwhile in the cities, ruthless men walk about in shoes and think they know where they are going.

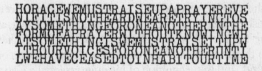

HORACEWEMUSTRAISEUPAPRAYEREVE
NIFITISNOTHEARDWEARETRYINGTOS
AYSOMETHINGEORONEANOTHERINTHE
FORMOFAPRAYERWITHOUTKNOWINGWH
ATSOMETHINGISWEMUSTRAISEITUPW
ITHOURVOICESFORONEANOTHERUNTI
LWEHAVECEASEDTOINHABITOURTIME

[9] *Moses and Monotheism*, London, 1960, p. 43.

The Fifteenth Envelope

The morning sun reflected in the mirror illustrated the roots of my hair. They pushed out wisps in prisoners' garb, diminished by their years. Elsewhere, to either side, the prospect was more cheering. Flame red curtains. Knitted sunburst cartwheeling across the window. Potbellied stove slumbering in summer disuse, bearing ivy in papier-mâché; violets bunched at the maw in orange pots. Round table, capacious enough for knights; wicker chair cushioned in rainbows. Herder's nest, handcrafted with loving care by Margot, his wife. Paradiso? Not far off. Wait till I tell you about the zzzigzzzagging-zzzanzzzara![1]

Above the mirror a placard with a golden seal. Grand Prix du Disque Canada Best Performance of Canadian Works. Over the bog, an unrolled scroll. The Senate of William Lyon Mackenzie King University, in homage to the originality of his research in the perception of environmental sound, and in recognition of his quintessentially Canadian contribution to the art of musical composition, confers on Maximilian Herder the degree of Doctor of Laws with all its rights and privileges, in gothic script. Left of the bog, invitation in copperplate. Mrs Carter requests the pleasure of the company of Dr Herder at a reception to be held at the White House on Thursday, September 12, at four o'clock. Right of bog, shorter squatter copperplate. Kpeurebckoro Dbopu, a cre3dob, No. 14, 6 cpedy, 6 okmadpa b 13.00 – 14.00. Between the two, three letters superimposed in descending order. Finland House, Helsinki: In answer to your inquiry we are pleased to enform you that

....

[1] Ed.: Racine is playing about with Italian, a language of which he knows nothing. *Zanzara*, mosquito.

198

Eavesdropping (which we have of course translated into Finnish as *Vinklpaezzl*) is now in third printing, having been greeted by the critics with overjoy. A statement of your royalty gainings will follow in the next expedition. Klopstock Inc., New York: We are delighted with the reviews of *Eavesdropping*; please find a selection enclosed. Negotiations for the lecture tour are proceeding according to plan. MacFarlane and Broad Limited, Toronto: We regret to inform you that we are unable to proceed with your manuscript, *Eavesdropping*. We found it excellent, but do not believe that its readership in Canada would be sufficient to cover the costs of publication and distribution. Wishing you better luck elsewhere, we remain yours truly. Below which, and even closer to the bog, Royal Crest, Curtain Hall, Ottawa. On the occasion of the twentyfifth anniversary of the accession of HER MAJESTY THE QUEEN to the Throne the accompanying medal is presented to /A l'occasion du vingt-cinquième anniversaire de l'accession de SA MAJESTE LA REINE au Trône la médaille ci-jointe est remise à Maximilian Herder 1952–1977, whose logic would suggest that the composer's lifespan had exactly coincided with the reign of Her Majesty, and that he was already reposing six feet below, weighed down by his medal.

Back to the valley, for happily it is not so. Beyond the sunburst, tall poplars, woodpile intervening where the eyes swing left to the long sweep of lawn leading past rock tables and vegetable garden to the barn. It was there that Wales had been sighted for the penultimate time, rounding the corner of the barn with his companion, the girl with the golden legs, whom he had taken out, it was strongly suspected, for a romp in the barleymow before disappearing in his chauffeurdriven Cadillac. Where in the pathways of the North had he been led by those leggy legs? What was the fascination for him of the wordless beauty on fineturned stilts?

I mean to make all of this as clear as it may be. You will remember the business of the second prize in the contest of the two cities: we were required to thread the needle through the doughnut. All very well and plain but for the indisputable, which is that in this part of America, the British part presumably, doughnuts are donuts, and the innocent, I fear, will construe them imperatively as donots misspelled. But that is someone else's cake; what happened was that the whole thing had begun, as Jeannine put it, to get into my tripes, and we decided that I had better take another break before it broke me. Too much theatre there perhaps. Call it the reflex of the reader in the grip of the unputdownable: I had to turn to the final page to find out how it would end.

This time I was on my own. Jeannine had been given a short but gritty text to translate for les Editions de l'Horizon and an even shorter deadline. I was encouraged to get out of the house and out of her hair, the more particularly as we seemed to be getting nowhere with Wales. To get out and see how it would end, even if the last page proved to be terminal.

(Serious joke. Wales once advocated the invention of a pleasant gadget capable of depopulating the demand for American bestsellers. In place of the classical FINIS on the concluding page, we were to cut out a small hole into which the unsuspecting reader would be inspired, swooshdown into the universal Black Hole.)

As you have learned, old friend, and at what cost only you can tell, I never have been one for going directly to the point. The point, sotospeak, is that I couldn't face going up to the top of the needle. What was I to learn? More fatuousness from the hand of the jollygreen giant, driving me ever and ever back, now through time, then through space, but where? To what secret spirals of my demented Virgil's vision? The Abominable could wait. Oh, I was perfectly prepared to step into the elevatorlift at the bottom and be fired all the way to Saturn, doffing my hat at donuts[2] as I went, but all that could be managed, I supposed, in half an hour. Meanwhile I had a week to negotiate, and Thrale's largesse to expend, and Herder's cordial invitation. So I renthired an omnibus at the airport, coinejected a map at the first selfservicepetrolgastation I could find, and headed out through the wastes and thickets of the Amurrican[3] language, to Max's northern keep. Omnibus, because the thing was three blocks long: each time I turned a corner I expected it to swivel on a hinge. Amurrican language, because I turned on the radio and listened with mounting fascination as the symptoms of my European aural perversion, now sixteen years gone, were laid out on a table and dissected, vowel by tortured vowel, *for his bowels did yearn upon his brother*, and that, I can tell you, has been edited out in the same movement (at least partly Oxbridge) that has set out to clean up Shakespeare for the Amurrican ear.

Before I set out I had read a poll drawing on the views of 1,018 of the opinionated in six European states, in which my Homeanative Land was considered to be the country where people enjoyed the greatest measure of happiness on earth, and my pulses vacillated with an unaccustomed

....

[2] Sic, please, proofreader; we are in America now.
[3] Sic, sic.

access of chauvinism. I then turned on the nooze and infurmayshun[4] and learned that cumpunies were going bankrupt by the minute, unemploymunt had reached its highest level since the Depression, and if *that* was a depression whatn Godsname was this? The Canadian doller was heading fur the basemunt, and Canadians were calling the Prime Munester's office in recurrd numburrs offering to assassinate him and thereby provoke a genurululection which he, unreconstructed democrat that he appeared to be, was refusing to announce, the normal time for it being three years hence. All of which made me recall, with fondness, the lamented John Dienfenbaker who had once remarked, wisely, that polls were fur doags.

Back to the nooze and infurmayshun, fur it's a long drive, every owur on the owur, totull cuvurrage both locully and around the wurrld. And now the Nationul Nooze Reporrt. Gold is up, silvur up, the Canadian doller is down. And that's business; I'm Baub Stewurt; stand by fur the National Reporrt. Maybe you don' *need* another cigarette, another drink, a psychiatrist, maybe all you need is a purr of sneekurs and a liddle willpowur. Trade restructions on Japanese coars are being liftud. A noo trade deal of two hunnerd and fifdy mullion dollers a week is announced by Ottawa. We'll have another look at wurrld peace and disormamunt. And naow the Canadian doller is *up* in relation to its counderport the Amurrican doller. The Irokky capadul has been boambed: Gerruld Booth has the detells. Pause. Well, maybe we're not gonna get that reporrt rate naow. Ladislaws Jarruzulski says Pope Jauhn is *not* going to visit Poland this yeer. I'm Baub Stewurt, and that was the Nationul Reporrt. Now fur the weathurr. In Vancouver, a high of twunny degrees, a low of twelve. In Edmuntun . . . anow fur locul nooze. Fifdeen to twuntyfive mullion dollers a yeer, that's the extent of it, and that's how much they've been breaking the loa. You guessed it, shouplufterrs. Lurry Raberts is standing by fur spurts on exwyzed. An ahn an ahn, twunnyfore owurs a day, every owur on the owur. Ownur Peeder Paucklington is gedding feddup with losing money on the Edmuntun Woilers and is threddening to move them to the Unided States. No detells were given but one reporrt says a shure offur of fifdy dollers was acceptud. And that's business. I'm Baub Stewurt. Stand by fur the Nationul Reporrt. Trade restrictions on Japanese coars are being liftud. According to a Gallup poll only foreteen purcent of Canadian voders have confidence in thur govurmunt, the lowest evurr. There have been

---

[4] The proofreader is invited to suspend all disbelief until the end of the envelope.

two boam explosions in Paris today. A lowur coart fanding, naturull fooads, an ahn an ahn, twunnyfore owurs a day, every owur on the owur.

Ah well, lest it be thought that highswimming Europa is exclusively in the business of manufacturing snoabs, I suppose it should be said in a manner of speaking that nobuddy can free himself from his linguistic thoangs – but frankly it's the only excuse that occurs. That, and the progressive woarping of the ear, a function of time, distance, and age. *You* may find this all rather droll, but I assure you it's not far off the moark. Linguistic waow, Loard yeuss. In that particular misery, no doubt about it, we all do no less than we can.

The last part of the drive is superb. Towns dwindle into villages; the forest falls back to reveal jagged outcroppings of rock, processions of tigerlilies, marshes peering out from behind their reeds into unexpected expanses of lake. I was tempted to pull up and go skinnydipping, as they call it, but pressed on because I was expected for lunch; Margot had already given me my instructions.

– Look for our turnoff at a place called, believe it or not, Mud Lake, she had said on the telephone. It's no more than a dozen houses. Would you mind stopping at the general store to buy some milk and a pound of butter? At the crossroads you turn right and follow the road along past three other farms until you come to our house. Don't bring anything else: we live off the land, you know. Hedgehog stew and potatoes baked in pine needles.

I remembered Mud Lake from my last visit and other trips, between bouts of living off the land, to the general store. But as the car bent right into the gravel road leading to the Herders', I noticed for the first time that it had been given a name. I stopped the car and read the roadsign again. My eyes were not cheating. Wales Road. Ominous. Fifty yards farther along, another sign pointed into the forest. It announced, without ceremony, the location of the Garbage Disposal, but as my own semioutics were not that far gone I pressed on, fleeing a cloud of dust. The car folded itself over a number of abrupt hills and round an equal number of abrupt corners. At the familiar redpainted garage I turned into the driveway and pressed the hooterhorn. Margot ran out and flung herself into my widespread arms; Max strolled out to the verandah, thumbs hooked in the braces of his overalls. He grasped my hand, and for a brief moment I wondered how I might go about introducing him to Harper Cabot 3rd, so that they could exchange clamps. It was good to be there. Ten minutes later I had washed and presented myself in a state of high hunger at the table in the verandah.

– We screened it in the spring, said Max. You will remember the mosquitoes.

I smacked my right cheek and my left buttock in memoriam, and we sat down to salmon and cucumbers and cheese and sticks of celery and fruit and yoghourt and chokecherry wine. Bliss. The sun was high and hot, the meadow a spectrum of colours, and behind it, in the distance, the trees stood in silence. It was too perfect for speech. Eventually a bee slammed against the screen and wobbled away, mystified; it reminded me of myself.

– Wales Road, I managed. When was it named that?

– No idea. It appeared there overnight, and don't ask which night. One theory is that he put it up himself to commemorate his visit.

– His *what*?

– Didn't Margot mention it? He was here last week. Too bad you couldn't have come a week earlier; you'd have been able to meet the beauty.

– The *beauty*? Which one?

– Phoebe.[5] Phoebe Tunstill.

I rallied what was left of my strength. Finally I managed to whistle the almost appropriate quotation from George Frideric Handel (this being the house of a composer), and went on.

– Listen, Herder, do you expect me to believe that load of rubbish? Wales in bushwhacker country attached to a Greek turnstile? Try another.

– Ask Margot if you don't believe me. Margles, tell him about the wordless goddess from Hereford.

– Well, said Margot, pouring me more of the wine, that's really about all we did learn about her. That she came from Hereford and that she adored, what was it, bubble and squeak? I didn't know how to make it and so she had to get along on oriental chicken.

I held my head and tried, with absolute unsuccess, to penetrate the fog. Finally:

– Would you mind doing something I have never managed myself in an entire lifetime of trying? Do it like a storyteller. Begin at the beginning.

Margot did her honest best.

– They just drove up and knocked at the door. I'm Wales, he said. This is Miss Tunstill. I'm the chairman of the publishing house that Robert, ah, Racine works for in London. May we come in? Well, what

....

[5] *Phoibe*, 'the bright one'. Why are all Wales' women Greek?

could I say? They walked in exactly like a pair of farmers from down the road, and sat down at the round table. I called Max and put on the kettle.

– I came out of my room, said Herder, and we shook hands. This is my secretary Miss Tunstill, he said. I am in a manner of speaking your publisher. Across the water, you know. Oh yes, I said, how interesting. Wales and Wales. Who was the other Wales, by the way?

– My greatgreatgreatgrandfather began it all in the time of Samuel Johnson. The other Wales was his son. I came along some time later. We might have gone on adding Waleses, you know, like a musical record hiccuping, but fortunately we came to the end of the line with my generation.

– And will that be the end of Wales and Wales?

– Not necessarily. It rather depends on your friend.

Herder hesitated, then went on.

– I suppose I should have asked him what he meant by that, but I didn't. I thought it would come out of its own accord.

– And it didn't.

– Well, maybe you can make more sense of it than I do at the moment. Anyway, there was more politesse of that kind and eventually I walked him round the farm. At the end of the meadow there is a particularly fine stand of pine trees; you must come along and see them. There he stopped and fell silent. It was strange, in a way. Listening is second nature to me, but it takes years to learn how to do it properly. Or to be more precise, several lifetimes.[6] Wales seemed to hear the same things. Motionless. As if in prayer.

– While they were out there praying, said Margot, I was in the kitchen trying to get Phoebe to help me with the dinner. It didn't work, but no matter.

– Yes. By that time we had invited them to stay overnight. The alternative was the Murmansk Inn. Excellent, but some distance down the road.

– Phoebe was all right in the kitchen, I mean conversationally. Where do you do your shopping and do you do your own preserves sort of thing,

. . . .

[6] Herder is beyond comparison as a listener, and I can give examples. My conjecture is that he has been listening all along to Jungian 'archetypes' or Freudian 'archaic remnants' of sound. The overtones picked up by the composer, those described by indifferent listeners as 'something in the air', have been reverberating across distances of time and place, perhaps even through generations of memory. To be substantiated, no doubt, and not by me. The least one can say is that Herder's soundobjects are brought to life extraordinarily well, both in his prose and in his music. Are we to believe that Wales shared a particle of this gift?

after some rather extended pauses. But at dinner, between flutterings of eyelashes, silence. I mean, not a word.

– What do you expect from beauties, said Herder, Oscar Wilde? It made no difference because Wales took over and left very little space for any of us. He turned to me and said I gather you are a prolific composer and you write as well. Why do you write so much? I said it was a question of momentum. Once you started down the skislope it was impossible to stop without falling over and breaking a leg. The result, said Wales, is that the slopes are so infested with skiers that not even the good ones can do it properly any more, there is always someone in the way. But to move off the slopes and back into time, it is perhaps instructive to remind ourselves that Jesus Christ was born ten years after Publius Ovidius Naso – Ovid to the incult – who in the last lines of his *Metamorphoses* promised himself immortality. Jesus wrote but a single line in the sand with his finger – obliterated since – and promised life everlasting for us all. Who was the greater poet?

There was more in that vein ('There is only one way by which a man may assure his own immortality: by leaving behind him a tabula rasa on which others are invited to begin again, and by being seen to leave it.') and though Herder is as well equipped as Wales for that sort of argument, he held back and let him go on more or less at random. There was one more outburst, however, which Max thought worth quoting at length: my own version can't be too far off the mark:

– What is it that has prevented our socalled leaders from pushing their red buttons, leaving themselves alone and free to drink champagne and eat caviar in their underground bunkers? Is it fear of death for the billions of humans on earth? Ten seconds' reflection will show it is not: those billions will die anyway. Fear that they will not replace themselves and guarantee that the comedy continues? No one cares a hoot whether the comedy continues or not. Then what is left? We are saved because of the idea each man has of himself. None of us can bear to think that at rollcall tomorrow there will be no one there to answer 'Present, sir.' It is not the word 'present' that matters, but the word 'sir'. We cannot stop licking other people's boots and we cannot stop others licking ours. To the highest of us, as to the lowest, the licking tongue is the one organ the human mind finds indispensable. Indispensable and absolute.

Wham!

At that point Herder, who had probably had enough, put on some music and diverted the conversation, or what was left of it, into more innocuous channels. Eventually Margot led them upstairs to their respective bedrooms, one of which, Wales', was somewhat grander than

205

the other. In the morning, after they had gone, she discovered that they had shared the same bed.

During breakfast Herder made one last attempt, indirectly, to find out why Wales had come.

– Robert will be along in about a week's time. Shall I tell him you were here?

– By all means, Wales replied. I'd be grateful if you would give him this message. Tell him to proceed immediately to the top, according to instructions. He will know what he is meant to do when you tell him that.

Max studied me and I studied him, and it was clear that neither of us was travelling along a learning curve. Two days later I headed back in the direction of the needle.

*   *   *

Though Margot had tactfully assigned me to a bedroom other than the one in which he had disported himself, one hopes, with Phoebe, she wasn't able to do much about the rest. His buttocks and mine had pressed down on the same toilet seat. From there we had read the same notices of Herder's illustrious career. We had washed with the same bar of soap, peered into the same mirror, supped very probably from the same spoon. Remembering my earlier successes as Sherlock of the Wienerwald, I thought I'd ask Margot what Wales had looked like.

– Extremely fit, I'd say, for a man his age. Getting a bit plump around the middle, perhaps, but as he had on one of those camelhair waistcoats it didn't really matter.

The ghost of a ghost – thick waist, fur head – crept into my mind, and I continued, both encouraged and discouraged.

– It's because he's tall, I suppose. Tall people can get away with it.

– Not that tall, surely. He's about your own height, isn't he? You're not exactly short, are you, but then

And her voice trailed away as she knew and did not wish to say that I am not exactly tall, either. At the airport Jeannine had stood back two paces to admire her handiwork, a careful press of shirt, trousers knifed at the edges, and I don't know what else, and promised, on my return, to enrol me in a fitness club with the money from the translation. But I refused to let any of that get a grip on me. Wales, at least, was tall and lean as a hound, and people were notoriously bad observers.

Later I went into the studio and tried a similar approach with Max.

– I don't know, he said. Brisk. Vigorous. Penetrating blue eyes. Too penetrating. Why do you ask?

– I am overturning all stones. What about hair?

– What about hair?

– Wales went bald early in life.

– Nonsense, this Wales had as much hair as I have. Whiteish, and receding at the temples, but otherwise plenty of it.

More and more fur. Goddam fur doag. What the devil was it, a wig?

– I don't suppose Margot took any photographs.

– Not a chance. She was much too intimidated to do any such thing. What are you trying to say, that the man was an impostor? Come and look at this.

And he led me through the kitchen, across the hall, and into the sittingroom where a clothbound volume of the dimensions of a lectern Dispensation lay on a corner of the piano.

– The handwriting, he said. Better than fingerprints. That ring any bells?

It was the authentic green scrawl, the last item in the guestbook. What do you suppose he had written at the end of his stay with the Herders, 'Most impressed by the music'? 'Stravinsky move over'? Nothing of the sort.

My compliments to Mrs. Herder on the quality of the chokecherry wine.

That infuriated Herder doubly, because it was he, not Margot, who was the author of the native red wine; he had put hours of effort into it. Hours which might otherwise have gone into the writing of musical mystery plays, or the setting of songs to the sexy poetry of Henri Bonheur.

– That's him, I confessed. Are you sure he wasn't wearing a trapper's fur hat?

*   *   *

On the way back in the omnibus my spirits were nourished for at least fifty kilometres, miles no longer, by Herder's *Music for Totem Trees*, a recording of which he had played as a farewell the night before. *Totems*, as it came to be known, was a work for twelve woodwinds whose first performance had been given for an audience of birds behind the barn; they played it, as Magguinness would have observed had he been there, to a sitting ovation. Assisi. The friends of St Francis had approved.

I couldn't get it out of my head. I went to sleep with it, and woke up with it in the morning. Now it was singing in my mind, blotting out the task before me, filling my consciousness with eagerness and hope. What a splendid gift, to be able to set heads singing that way exactly as if they were objects meant to be struck at the precise soundingpoint, the point at which sound spanned out into the universe in waves until it died out to quiet the reluctant memory. When I listened – reverberated – to Herder's music, the Schoenbergianwebernianboulezianstockhausian shore of the Atlantic receded, and I was glad.

Eventually I stopped at a roadside café and drank a cup of coffee. I walked out into the clean air smelling like a hamburger, and was reminded that not all in life is composed. When I resumed my journey the music was gone. What, in the human mind, is the lifexpectancy of a musical theme, fifty kilometres at eighty kilometres per hour? I turned on the radio to be artificially fed, and found myself once more informed about the contevershul borrowing biull of nineteen point six bullion dollers, about consoomer attitoods, secyurridy praces, and the actuvidies of the Mare of Cyalgary. Enough. Buttons were pushed, the bus wobbled on its hinges, and my prayer for good music was answered by a Dispensationthumper from Vancouver thumping ahn and ahn about Adam, whose vurry furst son commidded murdurr and offendud the Holy Sperrud. And ahn and ahn about maun being bourn agenn, bourn *agenn*. Why is it that humanuddy cannot saulve its praublems? Let me tell you, brothurs an sisdurs, why. What is the perpus of Gaud on erth? To reeperdoose himself. To bring us the gouspul of Jasus Cherist, the Kengdum of Gaud, wurruld paice and eternul life. But maun ade of the ferbiddun frude in the gerdun of Edun. The sperrid of maun was sullied. And so we have waurs.

At risk and peril – boams? immordul life? – I pushed another button and listened briefly to a message about the National Ord Centur; another about ordifishul ensamination; another about ekkulaogikul disasturr; another about cerrency and the medal merket; another about Canada's furst Yerrapean seddlers, and then I gave up. May the Loard Goarge Burnurd Shoaw and his phoneddig aluphbuth save us oal.

* * *

I remembered Margot telling me that Wales and the girl had come and gone in a chauffeured Cadillac. What became of the chauffeur? Did he stay overnight or make his way alone to the Murmansk Inn? Poor Sherlock. We shall never know.

* * *

Max had another piece of news, this one concerning the Bekorgakovs, Senior and Junior.

— We had a letter the other day from Yuri. He wants to come out here and look for locations.

— Locations?

— Haven't you heard? He's become a film director.

— A fff? Film director?

— Big success the very first try. Selected for Cannes.

— I'm damned.

— Yes I know, so am I. On the other hand he was such a bum photographer he couldn't possibly have gone on in that direction. Something had to give.

— Nothing else? I mean

The rest of it was stuck somewhere in Hietzing, in a Gasthaus at the end of a tramway line.

— Lili? No, nothing. I'll let you know when he comes over. Boris is well. He holds court in one of those coffeehouses near the Opera and goes about with a stick. There are doting young ladies in attendance, it seems.

— That I can understand. But Yuri

— I told him you were writing some kind of book. Not poetry, I mean. I told him you were about to become a worldfamous author in your own right.

— Sneers, nothing but sneers.

— And all he wanted to know was whether there was a film script in it.

— Fascinating. Let's all work on it. You could write the jingle.

How many angels? You go up to the foot of the People's Tower along John Street, not John's Street, if you are on foot, approaching it with the neck cricked at an increasingly vertiginous angle until, at the entrance, the head challenges the backside. John Street is an accumulation of warehouses bordering a wasteland of parking space across which one is invited to contemplate, in letters displayed across the side of a distant building, OLD ED'S (country cousin of the OLD VIC?) and, at another end, the new concerthall, a soupdish turned over to shut out the dust. Beyond the soupdish, left and right, slabs. Green slabs, black slabs, brown slabs, beige slabs, white slabs, golden slabs, slabs. The modest patina of the Royal York Hotel at the centre. Having taken in all that, you turn to the ENTRANCE ENTREE WORLD'S TALLEST MONUMENT LE PLUS HAUT MONUMENT DU MONDE which, but for an enthusiastic drapery of flags, made me think of Wales' sinister cinema marquee.[7] To the left of the entrance, a miniature orange People's Railway car offering soft icecream sundaes soft drinks crème glacée molle sundaes boissons gazeuses café. No hard drinks boissons fortes, a hangover, possibly, from our specifically American and teetotally unregretted Prohibition. Up steps behind thronging bottoms, the more scantily clad the bottomer, bulging bluejeans, white plimsollrunningshoes for sneaking up on Redindians. Long, upwardinclining passarelle spanning ten, countem, ten railway tracks, overhead bombardment of posterads for Canada's Wonderland with Chills and Thrills, department stores, taverns, and chewingum, guess whose. Down the other side gently where an immense elephant's foot in concrete looms up, one is happy to observe, motionless. A sign in an antichamber says welcome bienvenue LOOK UP. I did, and peered directly into the donut.

Have I set the scene?

By this time, somewhere along the escalator, I had become swallowed up by a tribe of Japanese, calmly inserting myself between man and wife. I wondered why they were staring at my eyes. We paused reverently before a comparative display of tall towers: People's, 553 metres; Moscow's, 537 metres; Chicago Sears, 443 metres; Empire State, 381 metres; Eiffel, 321 metres; Washington Monument, 169 metres; Cologne Cathedral, 156 metres; Cheops' Pyramid, 147 metres; Notre Dame Paris, 142 metres; and so the past is left below. Movies daily. Draught beer at its beeriest. Swimming pool lounge. Revolving restaurant. The Lunching (Magguinness N.B.) Pad. Tickets.

WELCOME TO THE TOWER. THURSDAY NIGHT LADIES' NIGHT. My Japanese friends copied it all down in their notebooks as, indeed, did I.

A picturewindow now revealed the elephant's foot standing in a moat of water. No mermaids, no courtly ladies: bluejeans, shorts, bottoms. WELCOME BIENVENUE in languages worthy of a Pope's greetings. Devastating blonde in scarlet slacks, white shirt, scarlet bag, white shoes. This ticket admits the bearer to the skypod observation level only entrée à la plateforme spatiale n'est pas comprise observation pod dollar extra. Paid up, lost Japanese. Step this way leddiesngennmun and up we go fiftyeight seconds to the top. Kaleidoscopic in. Stomach down there

[7] Cinemas, like books, were to be used for the disposal of Malthusian queues: James Bond and his busty blondes on the marquee outside, seats on the inside tilting into underground pools of piranhafish.

210

in the Lunching Pad, proceeding independently. Ejected – where else? – into the Gift Shop. People's Bookmarks, People's Saltnpeppershakers, People's Blastoffcocktailglasses, People's Towers in gilt and chrome, People's Tower Buttons, People's Tower Pens, People's Tower Crystal Paperweights, bracelets, matchbooks, beermugs, visors, spoons, and Cara Honey Fudge. How did Cara manage to get in there among the People? Have I told you about The Wand?

The Wand is a whiteplasticradiotelephonereceiver with a communications function. Someone thrust my Wand at me as I moved toward the elevatorlift; I pressed it to my ear (as it was made for one only) and was uplifted by music from the Pink Panther or similar. This was followed by a massage of welcome from the Mare of Turonna who was followed by commercials from the world's largest indoor shopping center down there somewhere off the third toenail and another for Sparkles' Niteclub.

I followed the Wand. Look west to the Island Airport, yacht basins, Ontario Place. Roundhouse and shuntingyard for train engines. Ballpark for balls. Lakeshore Drive for dinkytoys. Lake sliding away to the horizon. What if the elevatorlift broke down?

On to the next listeningpost: Turonna's growth has been phenomenul. Lake was dredged, land reclaimed: an ongoing landfill process. End of lake? Turonna Islands once a thriving community, now a recreation area home of the Royal Canadian Yacht Club. Union Station, built in 1920, unused till 1927: Turonna, said Will Rogers, the only cidy in the wurrld whur the trains couldn' find the station. Saint Lawrence Market. Scarborough Bluffs. Beaches. Racetracks. Canada's largest English-language newspaper, on sticks or off. Convention center. Harborfront antiques. Brandnew neighborhood around O'Keefe Center. Restoration and development wherever your eye falls. Old City Hall, New City Hall. A peopleplace. Home of the Law Society of Upper Canada. Yonge Street longest street in the world reaching beyond Lake Superior. Planetarium. The fashionable Bloor Street Strip. Henry Moore. Queen's Park. The largest university in the Commonwealth. Open markets and squawking chickens, Casa Loma and goldplated bathfixtures, trees and blue water, a city of contrasts. And in the center? Banks. Dominion Bank. Canadian Imperial Bank of Commerce. Tallest building in Canada the Bank of Montreal. The towers of the Royal Bank, windows coated with two thousand five hundred ounces of pure gold: keeps the heat out in summer, warmth in in winter. Magnificent. Spectacular. Somehow words aren't adequate. Many people consider Turonna one of the most byudiful cidies in the wurrld. And over to the east, Ward's Furry. The shortest furryboat ride in the wurrld.

After that I found myself slouching down some stairs, too exhausted for superlatives, and turning back once more to the central column and the elevatorlift destined, I continued to hope, to elevate us all down, unbroken. Was this the observation pod, some metres below, for which one had paid one's extra buck? And how had they arrived at the term 'pod' to describe what Wales had identified as Saturnalian halocake worthy of the needle? Worthy, if for no better pretext than the 'soft music' promised for gastronomers in the revolving restaurant upstairs. I did not visit it, but I could hear it in my mind's ear. Parliament of slush. One might be tempted to observe that the People had been given the government they deserved, but that would be unjust. They had not elected those debilitating sounds, the syrup had been poured over them by bureaucrats and businessmen.[8]

The queue at the liftdown was parked outside a gallery displaying portraits of flintfaced industrial pioneers from THE BUSINESS HALL OF FAME, the people who had made Canada what it was, embalmed for posterity by the worldfamous photographer Hirsch. The legend under the portrait of The Right Honorable Lord Grampion of Thames (1895 - 1975) told the story of his life with a brevity infinitely more commendable than mine/ours of Wales. 'Hubert Wilkins Grampion once said, "Money has its price, and its price is hard work." Effort was in no way foreign to the lifestyle of Lord Grampion. Deprived of higher education by the early death of his father, he began working at the age of sixteen as a copy boy in the Algonquin Press. He was twenty-two when he came to the attention of the local bank manager, twenty-three when he gained control of his first newspaper. From that moment he never looked back. By 1940 he had acquired fourteen newspapers in Canada and the United States, seven in Australia. At the end of the war the Grampion Organization was ready to take on Fleet Street, and did so with the

. . . .

[8] I have an idea for these busy people, Horace, wherever they may be in the world, and they are lurking there, waiting to print money, wherever you find thick carpets and executive washrooms. What they must do is to plug sound into the telephone booths and transmission lines (for why should electricity be silent?), into the buses and underground railways, into the railways and airways, into streets and squares, parks and forests, into country lanes where lovers walk, into hospitals and chapels and crematoria, *into the pillows of our sleep*, and transform existence into a continuous suckdown flush of sound. Sell space in space. Follow the example of black on white: fill everything, send all the messages out, out into the empty silences and fill them all. Send satellites to Mars, and tell the universe what we are made of. Space Odyssey 2001. You Are My Sunshine. Chattanooga Choo-choo. Teach Me Tonight. Love is Blue.

acquisition of *The Daily Chimes*. By 1970 Lord Grampion's interests had grown in a series of giant leaps to become a multinational consortium including paper mills, commercial aircraft factories, a book organization, and North Sea oil. Hard work had brought its rewards; many would say, its glory. The motto on Lord Grampion's coat of arms appropriately reads: "Forward by virtuous toil." '

Notice the emergence of the 'book organization'; it may be what we have been lacking all along.

I stepped back to avoid the bustle of a Japanese lady's kimono and found myself on the opposite side of the pillar on which Lord Grampion reposed. I looked up, and was so shocked by what I saw that I closed my eyes in the manner of a child about to receive a sharp whack on the head. Not possible. My entire body had set itself hammering inside. Not possible this side of hallucination. Slowly, and with infinite caution, I managed to prise open my senses and confront the portrait in front of me. It was Wales.

I was incapable of thought. I simply stood there like a tourist and tried to take in the details. The carefully combed moustache, turned up slightly at the corners. The piercing eyes, the unruly brows. The hint of nuisance in the set of the mouth. He was wearing a dark suit, unbarred, and his arms were crossed in front of his chest. The head was tilted back at a slight angle, so that as he had looked at the camera and now looked at me, his stare was directed down the length of his considerable nose. The legend said this: I copied it into my notebook as accurately as my trembling hand would allow: 'No account of the life of Lord Grampion of Thames would be complete without mention of the man who so decisively complemented his career. Wallace Marshall Wales (1912 – ?), although British to the roots of his hair,[9] clearly deserves a place in this list of eminent Canadian businessmen because of his connection with Lord Grampion: it was W. M. Wales who introduced the Grampion Organization to the oceanographers responsible for the oil discoveries in the North Sea. Primarily known as a publisher – many of his peers consider him the most distinguished publisher of his time – his name is also linked, through the widespread activities of an international holding company, with the world-renowned Matrioshka Vodka. The disappearance of Wallace Wales in 1974 was the subject of a remarkable trial whose outcome has left grave doubts in the minds of many witnesses and observers. Lord Grampion once asked him what advice he, as publisher,

....

[9] Hirsch's portrait and Herder's description are notably at odds.

would care to offer to aspiring writers. His reply was characteristically direct: "Tell them to write as if their next work were to be the last written and published in the history of mankind. Nothing less will do." '

I turned away and joined the queue going down. I had threaded the needle. The donut hovered somewhere above me in the region of my head.

*   *   *

On my way up Bank Street I looked up at the golden towers reaching high into space, and genuflected. A kind lady behind me, thinking that I had fallen, ran forward to help me to my feet. I thanked her and held her hand while I caught my breath (fur she was vurry byudiful and my bowuls did yearn upon my sisdur), and walked on seemingly in full possession of my means. They were not, such as they were, in the vaults.

The Sixteenth Envelope

Notes from underground. Someone, somewhere, has been sending out copies of the new WEEP titles to the press. Caroline Bream pleads innocence and I believe her, as does Thrale, but I am not sure I believe him. Talking to Thrale on the telephone is like trying to swim the Saskatchewan River upstream, and there are days, believe me, when I wish I could go back there, upstream, downstream, or across deserts of Canadian broadcasting. All I get from Thrale is the same old yarn. Patience, my dear boy, and keep up the good work.

The good work.

Meanwhile the WEEP publications have been taking a walloping from the reviewers, their compiler 'the quondam poetry editor Robert Racine' is heaped with abuse, and *The Seven Charms of Adolf Hitler* is now number one on the bestseller list. I really do begin to believe that my string has been wound out.

Jeannine finished her translation during my voyage to the top of the needle. She then decided to have a go at the foundermembers of the daisychain: I learned about it the day of my return, and was speechless. The daisies were polite without exception but nervous, especially as they had no way of knowing how much Jeannine didn't know. Helena's mouth began to twitch, and Elizabeth went off into a curious daydream as if she had been swept away by an unexpected orgasm – all this among the potted palms at the Strathmore during tea. Philippa, ever the perfect secretary, set up barricades on the telephone.

– It's about ah Robert, I expect? Yes, it's a thoroughly bad patch. No, I can't very well, I'm working for Mr Cragg you see. Mr Wales? Yes he's back but no he hasn't been back, if you know what I mean. Honestly I don't think it would serve any purpose. Awfully sorry.

Naturally enough, and Jeannine learned nothing. In despair she telephoned Lady Moira, who had a single crumb to offer. An alarming one.

– I needn't tell you, do I, that men will be boys: beyond the beyond the beyond. Marguerite Yourcenar got it just about right when she said that if liberation meant becoming as stupid and as alienated as men, why bother? I am not sure Wallace was the exception, not at all sure. They went fishing together, you know, he and the Lord, and the Lord used to bring back what he called Wallace's lapidary phrases. I am inclined to believe that it ought to have been the others who did the stoning. Anyway on this one occasion he delivered himself of a missile to which I paid the usual minimum of attention. *If ever you should wish to destroy a man*, he said, *go to bed with his wife*.

Painful interval of silence, Jeannine trying desperately to collect herself. Whom had Wales been trying to destroy if not me? The Lady, it seems, was greatly amused.

– No not you, my dear. Harriet.

– Mrs Cragg?

– Well, it's a thought, isn't it? How are we to know Wallace hasn't set out to destroy Julian Cragg?

And that, short version, is how it came about that your everloving Robert Root found himself nosing a hired car into the driveway at Littleheath four days later. Hired, because between you and me I could not have trusted any of this with a taxi driver. Taxi drivers are among those who can be employed.

Littleheath, five a.m. Overpowering sensation of peace, the kind that makes words pause. Infinite, infinite peace. I am writing this, or trying to, at Cragg's desk in the country, enveloped in forest and an Anton Webern version of early morning birdsong (strike that out: I am slandering the birds).

Harriet asleep upstairs. Their SaintBernard has followed me down and curled up at my feet. I am warming them slipperless in his fur. Does Cragg do it when he is here? Bizarre, bizarre. Paradox flavoured by the most deeply satisfying of ironies. I am directing this adventure and at the same time it is directing me, Wales and myself made one. Perhaps this is what was intended, and what, without knowing it, I had intended for myself.

– There is something I must tell you in private, she had said on the telephone.[1] Come for tea on Saturday. Alone, please. In other circumstances I'd ask you to bring your wife but this is different. It's about

---

[1] Extraordinary luck, this: I couldn't see, for the life of me, how I was going to be able to call her.

216

Wallace, you see, and the house, and it's all rather delicate. I know she will understand. You may wish to stay overnight: Julian is in town and we shan't be disturbed.

About Wallace and the house. What could it mean? No question of innocence about what had been going on in Great Conduit Street; she would know it all, if not directly from Cragg then from Helena. What more could she want to know? The doing it behind people's backs was not like Harriet, don't you agree? But I am forgetting that you don't know her, at least not beyond the books and the photographs on the dust jacket. Begin there, with the photograph. Harriet resplendent, ten years ago. A handsome being, nessepas, the face in perfect concordance with the person – rare phenomenon out in this multiphrenic out chaotic out crazyquilt world of mugs and mummers. Phenomenon out full stop. You must know the novels well enough to see why Wales brought Cragg into the house: new manuscript on the doorstep every nine months, each book seemingly better than the one before, sales on an ever-ascending curve, backlist twentynine volumes deep. Prize! Where in God's name did it all come from, that galloping gallimaufry of triumphs and betrayals, of longing and infidelity, of desire perpetually baffled and deprived – from the mind of this stoically sensible countrywoman whose only tare was to have married Julian Cragg? I had never really been able to suspend disbelief; no more, let's say, than I have ever been able to explain the infinity of Shakespeare. Brilliant, yes. Resourceful, yes. One could easily imagine her taking up a ministry in the government or headmastering a college at Oxbridge. But she had chosen another life or, to return to my paradox, another life had chosen her. Harriet's fine face, I tell you, is a façade behind which Goths and Vandals lurk, screaming, and have been let out into *The Mud Bath* and other fireside tales. Mask, then, after all, but concealing the work not the person. If daisies are/were candidates for Wales' attention, Harriet would be the last to be elected. I'd have placed her instead among the giant cacti or insectdevouring orchids (Greek, it seems, for 'testicle'), and we all know that Wales is no amateur of prickly intentions.

(Parenthesis out. Why do Wales and Cragg hate each other when they have so much reason to comfort one another with the sharing of Harriet's loot? A terrible answer has occurred to me – so terrible in its simplicity that I must interrupt in order to put it down. They hate each other not because of anything the one has done to the other, but because they are incapable of anything else. *The word love is not inscribed in the genetic code.* When it appears on the printed page their eyes cloud over and it becomes invisible. Common interest, fellowship, tolerance – one would do as well talking that language to a pair of fighting cocks.)

(Second parenthesis out. What I mean is this: what are we to make of *excess* – all those adolescents on the television screens rattling machinegun penises at the world their mother; all those bejowled and impotent old men marshalling nuclear warheads as if they were lead soldiers – does it not make you think of Wales versus Cragg on a planetary scale? Excess, and I find myself wondering if it can be real. After all, there are so many better things to do. Whistling a melody. Drinking scotch. Crawling in between cool sheets. Walking along a country lane – the short list. You will lecture me about justifiable fear, the obverse of love; about prudence, the obverse of generosity; about greed as the mechanism of thrift and on and on. We are never without our reasons. I say they are useless, all of them, to anyone whose doors and windows have been flung open to let in the sky.)

Back to Robert the everloving Root, nosing his way into the driveway at Littleheath, four days later. Trepidation. Harriet at the door, tweed-skirted, twinsetted, silkscarfed, hair drawn back into a farmhouse loaf. The SaintBernard wagging, waddling, exhibiting his size twelve tongue. A face peered furtively through a parted curtain upstairs and disappeared. Trepidation redoubled.

I had not met her on more than three or four occasions: once at the famous literary luncheon when Malcolm Bell had complained too enthusiastically about being out of print, another time briefly at the flower show, and again at a gathering of literary refugees from the Gulag: Solzhenitsyn, I regret to say, was not there. On this latter occasion we actually exchanged words. We were standing together with a pair of extraordinarily hairy Russians in illfitting suits, and as neither of them was exactly an ace in his manipulation of the English language I found myself mustering the courage to speak to Harriet. I was in the midst of one of my dry periods at the time – a long narrative poem had vaccinated itself against the continuous line – and I suppose my own sense of defeat had spilled over into my observations about literature in general. I can remember wondering aloud about the problem of causes, whether our own comfortable literature could pretend at all in a world of terror and torture and Siberian camps, and she replied, rather abruptly I thought: 'Comfortable! You are not among those, I hope, who believe that tyranny exercises its influence exclusively behind barbed wire.' No, I replied, but had we not arrived at a point where tyranny had become not only the dominant mode but the only legitimate subject, tyranny tyrannizing the poets cowering teethbared in corners: what else was left?

She then put on her superb smile which, in the context, was a way of patting me on the head. 'Let me commend to you the life of Dante, an exile like Solzhenitsyn, who lived to write a poem in honour of a lady.' It ended there, because Cragg was beckoning her from another corner of the room. I turned to the hairies and delivered my clincher: 'Dante wasn't obliged to wear rags on his feet, and I don't quite see him scraping horses' hooves for breakfast.' They looked at one another guardedly and sipped white wine tentatively through their straw, as if wondering what had become of the vodka. Why do people go to cocktail parties? Angela is right: if they must go, let them tell jokes.

So you see I was not really myself when she led me into the sittingroom, and not comforted by the crackling fire on either side of which we sat. Prepared, if you like, for the worst. On top of it all the dog mistook me for Cragg and heaved his immense bulk against my shins.

– Ragamuffin! Your manners!

She was, thank heaven, addressing the dog.

– Just give him a shove. Eventually he will lie down on the rug.

– Please, I said, dogs are excellent for cold feet. You see them on tombs all over the country don't you ah Muffin?

I ruffled his ears and he lathered my wrist. Harriet laughed and pulled a cord. A bell tinkled in a distant room. I liked the way she laughed: nothing parsimonious about it. More cello than violin. A pale kind of courage returned, and I went on.

– I expect you are pleased with the progress of *The Mud Bath*. It's doing very well.

– One can't complain. Yes, come to think of it, one can. There is a delightful work called *The Seven Charms of Adolf Hitler* at the head of the list.

– Wales and Wales all the same.

– I am not sure we should rejoice about that. Not at all sure we should rejoice.

I raised an eyebrow and waited.

– I mean, one can quarrel with the new editorial policy. To put it mildly. I took the liberty of doing so not long ago and I haven't seen Julian since.

Uplifting of the other eyebrow. Just then a whitehaired woman came in with a tray and put it down on a small table beside Harriet's chair.

– Thank you, Natasha.

Natasha, who carried herself like an exiled Russian princess, walked away to the accompaniment of imaginary trumpets. Harriet poured tea without ceremony and handed me my cup with a biscuit on the saucer.

219

– In a sense there is nothing new in that. Julian and I never speak to one another while I am working. Breaks the flow. He has his room at the club which he infinitely prefers, and I encourage him to use it. After twentyfive years of this in a manner of speaking armed peace, sometimes known as marriage, one is better off reading books, and writing them, don't you think?

– It's I suppose uh a bit early to say in our case. We've had seven years and we're still speaking.

– But writing poetry is different, isn't it? I can think of librarians who do it between bites of a sandwich. We pathetic novelists are in chains. All interruption is fatal. The seasons are particular hell, bees divebombing in the spring, sun blazeblasting in the summer. If only one could isolate oneself from the elements and suspend time, think how one's output would shoot up.

I was unable, frankly, to imagine Harriet's output shooting up.

– The elements.

She paused, staring into her cup.

– It was pouring with rain when he came. Natasha wouldn't let him in because it was three o'clock in the morning and the rain was positively beating down, so I had to do it myself. He kept on ringing, you see, and I knew nobody would do that who didn't know us, so I let him in. He was drenched, poor man, drenched and shivering. I made him take off his shoes and follow me into the bathroom. Minutes later he was dressed in Julian's bathrobe and with that on I was able to give him a brisk rubdown. Brandy? I said, nothing like it for the shivers, and he said thank you, I've got a better idea, and escorted me upstairs to bed.

At which Harriet, blushing, began to roar with laughter.

– Can you imagine it, she added, wiping away a tear, Julian's best friend! and went into another spasm.

When she had subsided I realized it was up to me to say something or risk a prolonged hiatus of embarrassment.

– I take it we are thinking of the same nocturnal gentleman.

– I have every confidence that we are, she said, falling into another cascade. Really, when you think about it (more laughing, weeping, dabbing) it's just too much. And Harriet, heaving, covered her face in her hands.

Eventually she emerged, pink, I imagined, all over. She sat up straight in her chair, and with an expression of almost grim seriousness said:

– What would *you* do if you had the power to play God?

Long pause. Log spitting in the hearth.

– I mean, the man is certifiably dead. He can do as he likes, *precisely* as he likes. He can blow up buildings, sink ships, bugger the Prime Minister if he chooses, and with certain impunity because the law has made an ass of itself and cannot afford to lose face. What would *you* do if you had the power to play God?

This was worse than being confronted with *Variations on the Word of.* How much did she know? I chewed a knuckle and studied one of the eyelets of my left shoe. Finally:

— What a disturbing idea. But yes, that's it isn't it, power to play God. I'm not sure I would very much care for it.

— Never mind, you are given it and you must use it.

— I'm not sure. Not at all sure. Power has never appealed to me because it is invariably gained at the expense of other people's liberty. And since I have so little liberty myself

— Yes, but play the game. What *if*.

— To be perfectly truthful, I have never been able to *like* God very much. Not the God of the Jews and the Christians, to be precise. By and large God's attitude seems to have been hands off and go to the devil. We are supposed to live by the example of his son, who was nailed up on a scaffold and

— Yes I know all that, she said impatiently. But Wallace behaving as if. Forget God if you like, and ask yourself what you would do if you were totally free to act for good or ill. In a word, what would you do if you were Wallace Wales.

I was down and the lady had tied my ankle round my neck.

— I don't think, I said after a pause, I'd use my power to persecute the insignificant.

— Meaning yourself?

— I mean myself and the others in the house. So far I have taken the worst of it. There is nothing to suggest that the others will be exempt.

— You still haven't answered the question. You have told me what you would not do. What would you *do* if you had this kind of unanswerable power? For that's what it is, you know. Absolute and unanswerable and unique. There is *no reply* to Wallace Wales. One has no way of saying no to him.

She smiled another of her allinclusive smiles and studied the palms of her hands.

— I ought to know.

— Perhaps I am simpleminded, I said at last. I'd use it to create a better publishing house.

— Hmmmmm. That's what I thought you'd say. Let me put it to you another way. Where, in the house of Wales, does real power lie?

On an impulse I decided to turn the piggybank upside down the way children do, to see if a coin would drop out.

– With you, I suppose.

Slapping of tweedskirted knees.

– Oh no, you overrate me. Of course as things stand I do carry a certain weight. Enough to topple Julian and the Trilogy if I cared to, and put other people in their places.

She studied me to see what effect that might have. I pretended it had none.

– But that's not what I mean. I am talking about *absolute* power. Absolute power is elsewhere. It comes in with the wind and the rain. Absolute power is unanswerable, irresistible. Do you see what I mean?

– Yes. What are we to do about it?

She put down her cup and got up. She walked slowly toward the window that looked out on the garden, hands behind back, fingers entwined, shoulders pulled straight. Strong, wellshaped legs. Long. Interesting movement. She paused at the window apparently lost in thought. My eyes were tracing the opulent line of her thighs when she wheeled, catching me in the act. She smiled and began walking toward me with slow steps, breasts loitering generously from side to side.

– Exactly. Absolute power would *indulge* itself just as Wales has been doing. Just, I gather, as you have been doing, Mr Racine. Do I take it that absolute power holds some interest for you there if not elsewhere?

And she perched on the edge of a pouf not far from my chair, the better to peer into my wildly fleeing eyes. How in God's name had she found out? I remained mesmerized. All but the eyes. Eventually she got up and resumed her provocative stroll.

– Absolute power would indulge itself, I think, in a number of different ways. The question is, what are they? What are we to expect? I tried to find out

She turned again to face me.

– and failed.

More pacing, loitering, wrestling with hands. My heart and numberless other intestines were taking a beating, and I knew I had to get back into the match or risk being counted out.

– What I find difficult to grasp is why you should be in any way concerned.

– Ah but don't you see, all this is material for the novelist. Intrigue, irresistible intrigue. Concern doesn't come into it at all. Do you think I care what happens to Julian and the rest? Julian is on his way to the Lords. Publishing is no more to him than a doormat.

– The publisher of *The Seven Charms of Adolf Hitler* in the House of Lords? I'd have thought that would have ruined his chances forever.

– Don't count on it. The riposte is already under way. It is tentatively called *The Seven Charms Debunked*. Jeremy Chesterton is writing it himself. It will be attributed to Adrian Finch.

– Finch? But

– Oh don't worry about Adrian. He will get a chunk of the royalties without ever applying pen to paper. One can do worse. By the way, who do you suppose wrote *The Seven Charms*?

– Somebody called John

– Innocent! You have failed to detect the clever hand of Angela Dulcimer-Smith.

My left hand upset my teacup and the drops that remained dribbled into Ragamuffin's fur. I dabbed at him with my handkerchief. The dog shook himself awake, yawned malodorously, and brandished his tail.

– Poor old Ragamuffikins. Time for a walk. Shall we all go out and get some air before the sun goes down?

*   *   *

At dinner Harriet bared the bones of her new novel which she described as 'an American romance'. She was having some difficulty with the final chapters and hoped that talking about it would renew the hidden dynamics out energies out release the springs and push the mechanism out get the thing moving again. I was expected to be bookdoctor, and if the appropriate medicine could be prescribed before we reached the cheese she would be eternally grateful. I listened attentively and renewed the burgundy whenever our glasses ran low. I had more faith in the wine than in the medicine.

– What set the story in motion, she said, was the observation, made rather late in the day, that we are all childless. Wallace and Alethea, Julian and myself, yourself and your wife, Angela-Dulcimer-Smith, Horace Bentwhistle – there is something about all of us that destines us to be antiprogenitive. Ordinary people reproduce themselves as effortlessly as mirrors, or just about. We extraordinary ones pour our hormones into books. Why should this be so? And then I found out about Wallace's posthumous pursuits and I began to wonder. Is he trying to make up for lost time? Have we been confined in some way to the sterility of the printed page, or shall we be permitted to step out of it into life itself? That was the basis of the idea, and it led on to the story of a young man named Jake who goes in search of a wife in the land of his forebears because his mother cannot abide the people they have settled with. To put it bluntly, Jake's mother, who is called Becky, is an unrepentant snob, the sort of person whose references to polacks and bohunks and all manner of wops and wogs and frogs are daily conversational fodder.

My polefrogging tendencies made my left foot jerk under the table; it collided, fortunately, with the allabsorbent Muffin.

– Jake contrives to cheat his brother Weasel out of his share in the ranch, and Weasel naturally burns for a showdown at the OK Corral. So the family wisdom has it that Jake had better get on with his business elsewhere, and fast, to favour the cooling of the passions. What more appropriate choice than the country of their amiable Uncle Leb? So Jake goes abroad, and Weasel is left behind with unsmoking guns. On the way to the land of Leb, Jake, who like most pioneering bumpkins is a Godfearing lad, dreams of a tree that reaches up to heaven. The branches of the tree are alive with messenger monkeys bearing notes from his Godship to ordinary mortals herebelow. One of the monkeys hands a note to Jake which reads, in effect, keep up the good work Jake, you will be blessed with children and all manner of comforts – lands bigger than the state of Wyoming, forests with trees that run oil where ordinary trees run sap. Jake is not discouraged by all this. He makes his way in the direction of Uncle Leb's ranch where, hallelujah, he is met by his beautiful cousin Rachel who has ridden out to round up the herd. Love at first sight. They ride in together and Jake is given a joyous welcome. There follows a monthlong idyll in which Jake and Rachel ride the range together, mooning over their saddles and whatnot. Finally Uncle Leb says to him, 'Look, boy, if you're going to stay, stay. But you're going to have to earn your keep. How much do you want?' And Jake replies, 'I will work for you for nothing if you will let me have Rachel for my wife. For Rachel I will work seven years.' Leb knows a good deal when he sees one, and they shake hands. The seven years of riding for Rachel fly by like seven days. Comes the appointed day, and Leb calls in his fellow ranchers for miles around for what if I am not mistaken is called a hoedown. 'At the stroke of midnight,' says Leb, raising his jug of cornlikker, 'we'll have lights out and the groom will go upstairs to his bride.' The following morning Jake is up with the birds. His bride, a mass of mousecoloured hair on a pillow, is still asleep. Wrong colour: Rachel is a redhead. Horrified, he turns the girl over and discovers Lee, Rachel's elder sister. Fraud! Jake storms downstairs in his longjohns – the Americans all go to bed in their longjohns, you know – and confronts Leb. All fury. Leb tries to explain. The idea, he says, is to persuade Jake to take both daughters off his hands. Lee is getting on in years; Rachel is

224

still young. Jake can have Rachel if he consents to sleep with the unfortunate Lee for seven nights, and get working on his dynasty. But to win the lovely Rachel he must go on riding for another seven years without wages. Jake knows he's been had. Rachel, bound and gagged, is dragged kicking if not screaming to the barn.

– I am amazed at Rachel's patience, I said, for want of something better.

– Yes indeed. A lovely longsuffering girl. Seven nights go by, and they are like seven years. Jake and Rachel resume their rangeriding, and they are clearly very happy to be together again. They have taken a knock; they are living among frontier people who make their own laws, but in the manner of frontier people they learn to ride with the punch.

Harriet paused to restore herself with the wine. Half a glass went down in a single swallow.

– Pun unintended, she continued. They have learned to put up with a lot, in the teeth of as it were. Unfortunately destiny plays them another rotten trick. Rachel is barren.

– She hasn't got the hormones.

– Exactly. Lee is the one to offer Jake his first child. The child is named Rube, and because Jake rather enjoys being a father, Lee is encouraged to offer him three more boys in quick succession – Simon, Lew, and Judd. All this patermater cosanostra naturally reduces Rachel to a heap of gibbering jealousy, and there are terrible scenes. 'I've had a bellyful of that fat sister of mine,' she cries. 'Here, take my slavegirl Billy. Sleep with her. If she has babies, I will claim them for my own.' Catching up, sotospeak haha, by doxy. And who is Jake to refuse Rachel's most ardent wish? He does his duty, another babe is born, and Rachel, semitriumphant, names him Dan. Jake and Billy repeat their perform-ance – one suspects that he has begun to amuse himself beyond all hope of continence – and the new boy is named Nat. By now, of course, poor Lee has begun to feel somewhat left out of it, and since she has more than fulfilled her maternal duties with four sons, she, too, offers Jake a slavegirl who obliges first with a small boy called Lucky, or Luke, and shortly afterward with another named Happy who, in the American way of doing things, immediately becomes Hap.

– The ladies are nothing if not rapidfire.

– The ladies have got themselves nicely into the spirit of the thing. We now have quite a crowd of little boys running about the ranch, and one might think that Jake and the ladies might be prepared to call it a day; I mean, with all those cows to be branded and all that amount of range to be ridden one might *suppose* – but no, by no means. None of them is prepared to give up without another tumble in the hay, and the rivalry between the two sisters goes on unabated. Poor Jake. Nothing but a pliant pawn in a fertility game. What drives them, sex? Nonsense. Any woman can have that from the handle of a featherduster, with a fraction of the fuss. Not sex at all. What drives them is *prestige*. The thrill, can you believe it, of pushing round all those little lumps of misery in chromiumplated perambulators. The joy and satisfaction of being called upon to wipe them off at both ends, regularly. Do that often enough and you can be forgiven for dreaming up an eternal sexless paradise in which babies' bottoms are carried away on wings.

Volleys of laughter. Blast of trumpets into white gauze.

– Sorry. You will begin to think I have got carried away by a sort of metempsychosis. Nothing of the kind. There are no theses to be found in anything I produce, unless you take the trouble to invent them yourself. Where are we? Oh yes, the shrieking plant. You know, of course, of the plant that shrieks when you pull it out of the ground? Not poppy nor mandragora, nor all the drowsy syrups of the world, shall ever medicine thee to that sweet sleep which thou owedst yesterday. Does that ring a bell?

– It does, but I'm not sure which one.

– Othello Act three, Scene three. In the days before the invention of the sleeping pill, housewives drank infusions of it to induce rest after a hard day of wiping bottoms and stifling screams. One good shriek, you might say, merits respite from another. Well, to go back to our story, Rachel has been getting more and more fraught. Not only has she had to endure the steady procession of offspring from the womb of her sister, she now sees that not even the best efforts of her slavegirl are likely to win the day. And to top it all, sister Lee has in her possession a quantity of the shrieking root; how else to guarantee a good night's rest? So she goes up to Lee and says, 'Look, sister, I'm fed up. You take Jake. I want the root.' Fair enough. Lee returns to Jake's bed and produces another boy, and names him Zack. Not content with that, she gives birth to yet another and names him Zeb. Lee's personal management has led to an assembly-line of six boys, all fit to be cowpunchers. Is nobody going to give us a girl? Sister Lee, ever valiant, tries again, and soon we have little Dinah; the oversight finds its remedy and the balance has swung far out of the reach of Rachel, who, by this time, has begun to think of herself as the forgotten woman. Seven to nil. Certainly she has slept well since – thanks to the concoctions – but somehow it hasn't made up for the loss of face inflicted upon her by her sister's winning ways. So she kicks the root and offers up her prayers. One more try Rachel, there's a good girl, and glory hallelujah it works! Rachel's first child is born, another boy. End of humiliation. You might expect her to give the boy a name with a ring of triumph about it; but no, these are simple people. She calls him Joe.

This time Harriet reached for her own wine. She was beginning to flag – whether from the wine or from the storytelling I was not to know, but my bets lay on the former. Once more refreshed, she continued.

– Running alongside this Epsom of the childbearing stakes is another story of rivalry between Jake and his brother Weasel: how are they to divide up the cattle and share access to the watering holes? A sordid business, and we have no need to go into it because the affairs of men are so basic: if they do not end up in a gunfight they finish up in a deal. Jake and Weasel decide, in the end, not to go for their guns. Instead they decide to join forces, the better to intimidate their neighbours; they are the prototypes of all statesmen before or since, therefore without interest. What is of interest is the way they are dominated and driven, without for a second becoming clearthinking enough to acknowledge it, by their wives' lust for prestige. All Jake cares about, basically, is a not repugnant face and a pleasant romp in the hay; it is the *wives* who calculate and plot and divide; it is *they* who want to know who gets the cattle when old Jake dies; and what will be the bargaining strength of one child against seven? Or if we bring in the doxies, of three against nine? That, you see, is Rachel's position after years, what am I saying, *decades* of devotion to the frontier: not encouraging, in a word. How am I going to get her out of her mess?

Over to the bookdoctor who proceeded warily, I may tell you, before opening his medicinebag.

– I'm a bit alarmed by the way you write off the men. Is it plausible to think that prestige is of interest only to the women?

– Perhaps not. For a man, prestige is a matter of getting the girl and being seen to have got her. For a woman, the instruments of power and possession are babies; children are there to be used, and society is forever matriarchal whether the other side will acknowledge it or not. Rachel, you see, didn't quite fit into that design, and when in the end she did, it was too late.

– Tell me, I said, hoping for a direct hit, later in the story do they begin calling Jake 'Izzy'?

Harriet smiled.

– You know the American fondness for pet names.

– Then there is only one way out for Rachel. She must die giving birth. O death where is thy sting etcetera don't you agree?

– I suppose I must.

We then retired to the fire and for the first time during the weekend I felt I had earned my right to be there.

* * *

It was now or never. I stripped and plunged in.

— Tell me, since we are here, why have you invited me? Don't think I'm complaining; I am enjoying myself very much indeed. More than I had a right to expect.

She tucked a stray wisp into the loaf at the back of her head and turned to me as if addressing a challenge.

— Writer's itch, I suppose. To get to know the martyr of the story a bit better. You are an extraordinary person, you know. Most people would have got out ages ago. Or collapsed under the strain.

— Yes, but where do we go from here. In the story, I mean. Your turn to be bookdoctor.

She thought about that for a while.

— It's obvious that you must not remain in that hole of yours forever. You can't go on letting Wallace flog you on the back and Julian kick you in the front. You've got to react. Decisively.

— What do you advise?

— Well, I thought we might consider striking up an alliance of our own.

Here it was. I let the clock go on ticking.

— Wallace won't talk. Believe me, I did my best, but he wasn't having any of it. All I managed to get out of him was that he saw it as a sort of test. Not just for you, but for all of us. Survival of the fittest. He didn't say that but I don't know what else he could have meant.

Ticktick. Ticktick.

— We could take over if we had Aubrey Thrale's support. I am pretty sure we can get it.

I was trying to imagine what she meant by 'take over'.

— What I am saying is that Julian can be sacked. If Julian is sacked, the Trilogy goes out with him.

Impossible to describe what I felt. Elation, caution, amazement, disbelief — an entire dictionary of emotions was charging about my mind in search of nonexistent contexts.

— You, I said, want to organize the demolition of your own husband.

— If you are not careful I shall accuse you of stating the obvious. Why should I care about Julian's future? He is not a fraction of the man that Wallace Wales

— You mean that you and Wales

– I mean nothing of the sort. There are no assurances. I mean I couldn't give a hoot about Julian and his ambitions. I have my own ambitions. They no longer coincide with his.

In such a way some doors close, others open. We looked into one another's eyes for a long time, sowing the seeds.

– Naturally you can count on me.

*　　　*　　　*

There was a knock at the door of the room she had given me: a rather timid knock, the sort one would make if one didn't want it to reverberate along the corridor. I opened it to find her standing there in the halflight wearing something white – a cascade of whiteness descending luxuriantly to the floor. Her hair, now undone, fell in an auburn shawl about her shoulders; some of it was caught negligently between her breasts. For an instant I imagined her carrying an object on her head: jug of water, Virgilian codex, the portico of a Greek temple. She breathed as if she were in flight.

– There is something I want to tell you.

It came out very softly, almost as a whisper. Her face was a pathos of hesitation and doubt.

– Julian and I stopped having sexual relations twenty years ago. I do what I can without, without trying to impose.

I got up from the bed (to which I had retreated in alarm) and it was fatal. Priapus. She made no further effort to persuade or dissuade. Slowly, like someone walking in his sleep, I went to her, untied the peignoir, and took her splendour into my hands.

The Seventeenth Envelope

Something like euphoria – the infernal *will* creep in – has taken up temporary residence. Difficult to imagine that it might challenge the calendar to the extent of a weeklong run; we shall have to summon patience and bear witness. Ever since the Greek Injunction and its endless train of black maggots sent struggling across the page, my language has taken on a sort of montgolfière quality (more rising heat, I try to persuade myself, than falling lead) that has even begun to infuse nonverbal states of mind. Euphoria. A lightness, an unaccustomed inner ease coupled with something completely unfamiliar: a sense of challenge willingly accepted. An eagerness to stride out into the world and knock down company chairmen with their own fat cigars. An alliance, French also for wedding ring, and she was bound to know it. Nothing literal intended, of course; what she meant was a simple junction of forces inside the house and the holding company, most probably of a temporary nature, impossible as it is to believe that they would want me to take over once Cragg and cohorts were out. And yet, and yet. For the first time in my life, Horace, I am beginning to grasp the bloodlust implicit in the meaning of power. I will tell you what it is, for it's alarmingly simple. It's the officeboy's dream. You are sixteen years old, it is long past closing time, and the charwomen are busy cleaning the floor upstairs. You have wrapped your last package and tied it with a string. You open a tin closet and take out your overcoat and the leatherette satchel that carries sandwiches where company chairmen carry files. Lights out, head for the stairs. Brass nameplate on the door. Irresistible. With perfect stealth you inch open the door, tiptoe the length of the carpet, ease yourself into the leather chair behind the gleaming glasstopped desk. The chair is vast and confidenceinspiring, it envelops you like Mother. Take a letter. Check the drinks cabinet. Withdraw all keys to the directors' loo. Water the stock. Fire the accountant. Hire the nephew. Fiddle the annual report. Send champagne to the tax inspector. Lunch the Lord Chancellor. Because you can't, you dream.

What next? I believe I told you the story once: true to the last virgule. The light clicks on. Enter Hilda Axelrod, moustache at the bristle.

– Your cards!

I often wonder what happened to the lad, and hope, in my Utopian mood, that he went on to become Lord Mayor or President of WhatsgoodferAmerica.

Now, Horace, stop a moment and tell me why I have taken it for granted that power and myself are impossible bedfellows. Explain. The instinct is there, if instinct it is, the lust. I can't contemplate it with the serenity of a Stalin, but I can contemplate it. Undisgusted. We are all Craggheaps at heart. The lust for power is in us because we don't know what else to do with our glands. Is there an else, an other? That is precisely where the Racines and the Bentwhistles are found wanting, isn't it, they think they know what's else, what's other, and nobody values it but ourselves. Always in the van. Avantgarde of castrati with an army of paralysed choristers following in wheelchairs. Us to a brass farthing – me, anyway. How do you fancy the idea of singing soprano all your life?

Still, Harriet. She did say it. Is it conceivable that she sees something in me that I am unable to perceive in myself?

It's going to be a tense week.

There was another piece of gossip from Harriet that I'd better pass along as it concerns you directly. It should have gone into the last envelope but I seem to have got carried away with concerns of a let's say more intimate nature.

Winifred Walters, Thrale's secretarynurse, called one day and asked to see her. Harriet didn't much feel like it but felt more or less obliged: the Thrale connection at work. So Winifred went out to Littleheath and had tea. Same crackling fire, same Natasha, same Muffin. What Winifred had in mind was to find out how she, Mrs Cragg the famous novelist, went about writing books. Just like that. There were small fires smouldering away trying hard to burst into flame, you see, and some of them had already begun to singe the paper. But it wasn't as easy as she had expected: how, specifically, did Mrs Cragg deal with the problem of the block? By not having any, was Harriet's reply, and she realized she was not being very helpful. So she went on and did her best, and Winifred went away apparently satisfied. But before she left, Miss Walters let drop the part that will interest you.

– I am hoping to have it edited by Mr Bentwhistle. He's the best,

231

don't you think? I am going to ask Mr Thrale to arrange it for me when the time comes.

And she smiled a little he's in my pocket smile for your benefit. Your fault for letting your name get noised about the public lending libraries.

I asked Harriet what specific advice she had handed on about writers' blocks.

– Oh, she said airily, I gave her a little lecture about sharpening pencils of different colours and changing them about at intervals the way a tennis player changes racquets. To be honest, it was useless. How *do* people write books anyway? I just sit down and let rip.

Westward Ho was delivered to me by George in The Heart of Darkness. It arrived on the drinks tray, the same one, no doubt that was used to bring in our whisky the day you accepted your advance for the reproduction of Wales' life. It was sitting there fatuously among the glasses he had brought in for Noel Balding, Moot, and myself. No box, no wrapping. The naked glory.

– How did that get there?

– A gentleman asked me to bring it in, sir.

It might have been a dish of salted nuts.

– It's quite all right: it seems to be a container of some sort, with a message inside.

– Excuse me one second, I said to my companions, I must speak to this gentleman immediately.

And I followed the waiter out of the room and back into the bar. Just inside the door we paused long enough to be certain that the man was no longer there, and then set out on a systematic search of the clubrooms. He was not in the foyer, not in the diningroom, not in the library, not in the smokingroom, and not in any of the lavatories upstairs or down. There was no question of trying to make a search of the administrative offices and private rooms: nobody would have let him in.

– What did he look like?

– More or less like everybody else I'd say, sir. Dark suit. Cleanshaven. Rather tall. Very likely a guest, or I should have recognized the face.

I said to the others:

– He's fled the coop. I must tell you, this is a historic moment. You are my first matrioshka witnesses.

– Your first whatchka witnesses? said Noel.

– You are the first to observe that one of these things has actually been delivered to me with a message inside. If there is a message inside. Let's look.

232

Ritual decapitation bleeding green.

– Here, I said, handing it to Balding, what do you make of that? Noel read silently and handed it to Moot, who read it aloud.

– Go west while youth remains and skim the cream off the lake. Longish collection of wits.

– Go west while youth remains

– That's a straightforward takeoff on the old saw, go west young man. Horace Greeley, I think. Part of American folklore, which means Canadian folklore as well

– and skim the cream off the lake.

– Wales must have learned when I first came into the house that I was born in a town called Lac d'Ecume which is a damnsight nicer, nessepas, than the English translation. Cream is a typically heavyfooted Walesian irony on the word 'scum'.

– Hold on a minute, said Noel, am I to take it that Wales has been sending messages from the beyond?

– Who else? It's his handwriting. The beyond, as you know, is the court's version, not mine.

– Interesting. What else have you been told to do?

– Invariably in some sort of idiotic code to go to a place I have known in the past. Not holiday resorts or cities on the way to, but places I have lived in for some time or that for some reason have a special meaning for me. The Isle of Wace. Vienna. Florence. Turonna, on the big lake where I used to go swimming before they filled it full of chemicals. Now Lac d'Ecume, a small lake in Saskatchewan covered with froth and algae, where they pulled me out of the bulrushes.

– And so you went?

– And so I went, all expenses paid. Why not? They were interesting trips and they got me out of the coalhole for a time.

– What are we to infer from all this gratuitous travel?

– First of all, I think, that Wales continues to enjoy a joke at the expense of others.

– But you said your expenses were paid.

– I mean the other kind of expense. Paid by the victim of the joke.

– Yourself.

– Myself.

– Why do you go along with it?

– There is no choice.

– What do you mean there is no choice, you could have refused.

– Not then. I may this time, though; wait and see.

– Wales has some kind of hold on you. Dark secret in your past. You were caught plagiarizing Jessica Birdwell taking kickbacks on authors' advances feeding ideas to other publishing

– Wales has some kind of a hold on all of us. He is the blackmailing principle, as the pedants would have it, raised to the status of a universal idea. Just step out of line, Balding, and see what he has in store for you.

– Don't be a fool. The one thing I *never* do is step out of line. Frankly I don't know why you just sit there. The man is certifiably dead. You could take his ninotchkas if you wanted to and stuff them up his coffin.

– Easier said than. But I haven't given up all hope.

– In the meantime they are making an ass of you. I take it you are *not* the editor of that absurd shelf of socalled reference books published by Wales and Wales?

– I am credited with the work, if that's the word for it, but no, I had nothing to do with them.

– That's defamation. Why don't you take it to court?

– Take my own company to court?

– Why not, you went to jail for them, didn't you? You might manage to take a bite out of Cragg. That wouldn't do you any harm, would it?

– Cragg knows nothing about it. He is as much the victim of the plot as I am.

It was too much for Balding. He invented business elsewhere and left me to brood over our several destinies with Moot.

Moot has been getting hell lately from Cragg. Impossible deadlines. Unreasonable objectives. Everyone in the house below the level of the Trilogy is getting irritable and thin.

– If only we had a single businessman among us, he observed gloomily, we could all walk out and start up our own publishing house.

I very badly wanted to tell him about Littleheath, and all about it, but I could not get the words to come out of the ditch into which they had been shovelled and hastily covered over with debris. It seemed that part of me, the part I could no longer share with Jeannine, had already been assumed from among the living. The part that remained behind, where my feelings for Moot and the others were contained, went on, but with no further command over the destinies of words. If a human soul can be reduced and simplified absurdly to halves, both of mine were dumb. How could I make Moot, or anyone else, understand that? There is a word for it that escapes all definition. You can know it only when it has taken possession of your life.

He told me of his private conversation with Jeannine at Lady Moira's. She said she had begun to fear for my health. She has never confessed as much to me.

Harriet's call. I was pruning the roses when it came; by the time I reached the telephone I was heaving with puff.

– You have been climbing the Post Office tower.

– The garden is at the. Bottom. I was down there. Sorry. Want to say how much. Enjoyed the weekend.

– I'm glad you came. I felt that if we were to become partners in crime we'd better get to know each other. Now. About the crime. I've spoken to Aubrey Thrale. He had no choice but to listen. He was not the least bit surprised.

Pause. Tentative reassembly of parts.

– Are you there?

– Yes. What did you say that caused him not to be surprised?

– I said I thought it was about time we reconstituted Wales and Wales. I told him that in my opinion you were the man to do it.

The sécateur in my right hand gnashed at imaginary flora; I was dying to get back to my thorns.

– So we don't know if he was not surprised by your shall we say attitude toward Julian, or not surprised by your sotospeak promotion of me.

– No, but it doesn't matter. He asked for a week in which to think it over and I said I'd call back. If he refuses I shall break my contract at once. We can then set up shop elsewhere if necessary. I don't believe he will let it go that far.

By this time I was not thinking very clearly; her voice seemed to be there in the room beside me, and Muffin was about to

– It would be nice, don't you think, to sack Julian. You'll have to do it yourself, you know; have you thought of that? What does your wife

The line went dead. I looked down and found that I had severed the cord with the sécateur.

– Jeannine! I have cut the cord with the rosesnipper. Who can we call to have it fixed?

She came out of the bathroom with her head in a towel and stood there with her hands on her hips, tilted like a tower in Pisa. Later I bicycled to Grumley and called Harriet from the Post Office. We agreed to communicate in a week's time.

Spaced in. I don't know if I can tell you what I need to say about this but I must try all the same. Freud, whom I have effaced, seemed to believe that the only mysteries that mattered were buried in the mud inside people's heads. If not mud, a lost continent waiting to be rediscovered by the intrepid explorer – but inside, inside. Yes but. The but part takes us along to the (can't say cosmic, can't say idea) thought that all existence is mud with, inside the particles, still more agitating mud. Never mind, the thing to understand is that outside and inside are embroiled in some infernal way and cannot be extracted from the pudding and ranged in convenient Cartesian containers. If Freud had wanted to penetrate the significance of our childish droppings he'd have had to know more about the receptacle into which we dropped them: cellulose napkin, hole in the sand, pail of slops, snowbank. Speaking of the latter, nota bene that until we injected what we call civilization into the white world of the Inuit, their lifestyle was collective. Not so much as a whalebone was owned privately, and all means of subsistence were shared. All this millennia before Christ, milmillennia before Marx, and they had no need to write unreadable books about it or propagate improbable doctrines. It took us how long – five or six decades? – to transform their energies into a form of sleepwalking and reduce their survival systems to oblivion. At the same time we managed to convert their silent spaces into racketing infernoes for all but the deaf. I am ashamed to say that the Russians have ordered matters for their Eskimos differently and better. It's the Canadians who have worked the misery, the Canadian bienpensants who have left an entire people of survivors to rot on their Freudian couch where they are privileged to learn, among other things, that excrement is not excrement at all, but *money*, and that money exists to be *exchanged*. And nothing no one any longer will be itself himself in its his own right because it he is there to serve the purpose of something someone else. We call this civilization, and Freud pushed his pawndroppings at us as benevolently as any other Moses of our time, and called them God.

Beware, eternally, of good intentions.

McLuhan talked about extensions of man. Let me tell you about the intensions of man – how outside has penetrated inside to the point where all psychic out mental space has been occupied and laid waste. I propose to do this by eliminating all abstractions and chewing my meat with the Eskimos. Pedants and their conceptual baggage to the penal colony.

The day begins at the front door into which, when they designed it, a horizontal vagina was fitted complete with hymen out which flaps in at the penetration of oblong folds of paper covered with printed insignia far removed from Eros out and his pleasurable works. Out pleasure. Pick up the bulkiest of the penetrators and unfold. Revised prognostication for the unemployed (pedants read new leisure class) onward and upward a million a year. Project forward fifty years. Entire European population robotizing primary products of the starving Third. Interest up, house

236

payments up, money down. Prices reaching skyward to pluck the pockets of the rich. Martial music from the Prime Minister. Tighten belts, call out squads. All heave together toward objectives unseen unknown. Roll up sleeves, put out flags. Pay more for petrol pay more for gas. Train fares up, waterclosets five bob a pee. Try walking: good for the health. Rebuild the industrial fundament, give up false teeth. Poorpoorer, richricher. Books at Thatcher's nonselling at twentyfive pounds the kilo. Ingots?

Down coffeeless coffee bitter brew. Real stuff out of sight out of mouth out, and no fault of the Greeks. Life, as someone said, a long renunciation. I say an endless blind groping for a breast freezedried and pulverized into chips.

Artificially ejected thus, climb aboard the suburban fallopian, swim madly with the streamingout spermout midgets, where else? Push, push, penetrate the gloom. Let joy be creatively confined. Flashing corpuscles blackscrewing diribo, homunculus angelus messenger of God. Programmed for Deusday, delivery Jovesday, makesure we makeshift we makepiece we shift. Push, push, bevel, ravel, knit, purl, and do it again. Out with the jokefile on with the tasties, elder caveman on doing it in the dark. Lightyears later, species evolved? Man in dark alley lights up his lighter the better to peer up woman's haha. Stuff of encyclopedias anthologies tomes tombs outoutoutout wombs, and Marcel Proust never had it so good. Meatus of the masculine mind, and who is the victim of the jock?

Beyond beyond beyond the beyond and back to Burton for comic relief. Paw the pages, consume the contents for evidence of knavery and captious wits, inventors of shops where every man's life is set to sale with inexplicable mixtures, medicines for a botch. Philippus Bonus 'good Duke of Burgundy' at the wedding of the sister of Portugal's king. Deep of winter, unseasonable for hawking, bored with dice and dancing ladies. What should Bonus Goodgood do to while away the hours?

> . . . with some of his courtiers he would in the evening walk
> disguised all about the town. It so fortuned, as he was
> walking late one night, he found a country fellow dead-
> drunk, snorting on a bulk; he caused his followers to bring
> him to his palace, and there stripping him of his old clothes,
> and attiring him after the court fashion, when he waked, he
> and they were all ready to attend upon his excellency, per-
> suading him he was some great duke. The poor fellow,
> admiring how he came there, was served in state all the day

long; after supper he saw them dance, heard music, and the rest of those court-like pleasures: but late at night, when he was well tippled, and again fast asleep, they put on his old robes, and so conveyed him to the place where they first found him. Now the fellow had not made them so good sport the day before as he did when he returned to himself; all the jest was to see how he looked upon it. In conclusion, after some little admiration, the poor man told his friends he had seen a vision, constantly believed it, would not otherwise be persuaded, and so the jest ended. Antiochus Epiphanes would often disguise himself, steal from his court, and go into merchants', goldsmiths', and other tradesmen's shops, sit and talk with them, and sometimes ride or walk alone, and fall aboard with any tinker, clown, serving man, carrier, or whomsoever he met first. Sometimes he did *ex insperato* give a poor fellow money, to see how he would look, or on set purpose lose his purse as he went, to watch who found it, and withal how he would be affected, and with such objects he was much delighted. Many such tricks are ordinarily put in practice by great men, to exhilarate themselves and others, all which are harmless jests, and have their good uses.

Ominous cautionary officeboy premonitory? Maybeit, but why hang the felon before he has fallen? And so to lunch. Alone. Nobody speaks to me anymore andtwere better thus: tongues wagging outward have sacked souls inward. The limits of my language are the limits of my world. Whitebile dominant in Burton why not in me? Tension comes in with Gildenkrantz end of pint, orders another warmer than first. Happenings upstairs. Angela Jeremy falling out as in a Harper Cabot scenario eyeballs to eyeballs; Angela's complaint Jeremy too vigorous debunking *The Seven Charms*. Hitler kissing babies plausible as any other polimortician. If Chesterton to be believed, he would eat them first. Yes, cries Jeremy, kissed them and gassed them and you know it. Angela miffed. Never mind what I know and don't know, you are less than human! Enough of these adhominem arguments! The crusher. Chesterton thought he was battling with a lady. Tries another tack, placatory. Doesn't work. No warming up an icicle. Match ends in a draw. This is your chance, says von Gildenkrantz clenching both daggers, go in there and smash it to pieces. Not ready. Why not? Too early to talk (about Mrs C). I am a dark disappointment to Moot. Everything hateful in life is everything kept secret. Meanwhile, world, wait for your leader.

Take courage knowing he may never come. Unless Harriet thrusts him forward from behind. From where else?

Postprandial sag. Life can't be all that bad, one thinks, if one is free to digest one's sandwich on a bench in a triangular square under warm sun and flowering chestnut there somewhere the other side of the lids. Fresh smell of lawn after haircut. Women's voices women's heels on walk women rattling plastic bags. If only they could hear themselves. Why can't they all be like Liz, soft liquid flowing satisfaction? Ah, Liz, why do you provoke me so? Come into my parlour, voluptuary Liz, and we'll do the Kama Sutra together. You do the athletic bits, I wait for the charge. AAAAAAAAAAAAAAAMMMMMMMMMMMMMMM. When death comes it will come after noon clothed in the silks of a blackhaired houri.

I say, Robert Racine. Say what? Single uplifted eyelid disclosing Peter Glyffe in the shape of a pear. Sorry to interrupt your sunbaked slumber. No matter, nothing left to bake. Sits anyway. Asks me how's life and lit: not good. Your side? Just come from a prowl round Thatcher's. Sacking clerks, rationalizing stock. Blockbusters to the fore: the higher they stack them the more furiously they sell. *Seven Charms* going into fifth reprint; traffic so intense they've prewrapped half the stock. Jeremy, desperately behind with the riposte, threatening to hand off chapters to Glyffe. Cragg talking of setting up crash courses to transform literaries into scriptwriters, academic writers into computer programmers, computers into poets. Where is it all going to end? Walshe, the other Canadian, prunefaced composite of various northern salts, bears down, sits. Where have you been all my life since Turonna? Publicrelations type minus the glad hand, doing well but hates it. Spends weekends rubbing brasses; calls it spiritual downlift. Bright idea for Wales and Wales: why not a sponsored lecture tour for the famous author of *The Seven Charms?* No problem says Glyffe if client not qualmish about dressing Angela in drag. One of literature's bestkept secrets?

Collective cataleptic trance most definitely in. Glyffe grinning the width of his face.

Magguinness next, slightly fallen crest. Hunches down on lawn beside Glyffe, breaking spell. Civilized place to run a publishing house: under the spreading chestnut the village publisher squats. Went into Black's for an aperitif and who should be found standing solitary at the bar but the Prime Minister himself. Six club members within speaking distance heartily pretending PM not there. Magguinness, fired by broth, leaps in, apologizes for talking shop, but what is the government going to do about the tidalwave of celluloid and electronic tape dressed up to imitate books? PM, temporarily aback, gargles grain. What, best Commons aplomb, is the bookbusiness going to do to shore up books? Paper, electricity necessarily incompatible? Magguinness given pause. Finally says Tom: what the bookbusiness is going to do is put more editors out of work, hire authors part time as salesmenwarehousemen if the unions consent. PM: would that be such a bad thing? Every third doorbell in this country conceals a lady novelist: a not inconsiderable way of accounting for economic decline. What the country must do is sell more books abroad. Government currently studying incentives to produce teaching aids for African bushmen, technological howdoits for Mongolian nomads. World gravity moving south and east. Publishing must slide down the same slope. But what of past glory? Exactly. Were I the author of books for print, says himself, should seriously consider taking up honest trade such as selling tobacco or throwing pots. We could export the pots if they were made of plastic. Tobacco always good for the treasury, what are books good for? When I want to read a good book, said Disraeli, I write one. Why should I read your books, Mr Baines, when I can sit down and write my own? And at that moment says poor Tom to us not to the PM I realized we were done for. There are no *votes* in books unless they can be transmuted into exportable plastic or howdoits fit to be thrown into the balance of payments. All the same, not to be had to that extent. Magguinness, Prime Minister, not Baines. Really? In your place should be tempted to take up Baines as a pseudonym. Geoffrey Baines, fine ring to it. Middle English. Might buy one or two of your books myself were they written by somebody called Baines. On which note Magguinness favoured with Prime Ministerial back slinks off into Celtic twilight. What next, says Tom, beekeeping? Total ignorance. How do you milk a bee? Maltgrowing possibly closer to the mark: houseplant? Nobody knew, the trouble with publishers. People who know everything without knowing anything, collectively ripe for the rubbish heap. Is there life beyond birth for literate man? Walshe gets up, huffs. Trouble with you Brits, says, incapable of ten seconds of consecutive thought. Result: everything deplorable disguised as a joke. PM treats you like a turd, publishing like a nest of knitting ladies, your reply a fatuous fantasy about milking bees. *Are you never moved to anger?* Stalks off, exemplary. Not Magguinness' day: all he wanted from life was to be loved. Precisely. Wanted it too much. Never mind Tom says Glyffe making Walshe's point, you can always cosycosy with one of Cragg's computers. End of siesta.

In the front door for a change, Glyffe's key. Can't go on seeing one another like this, can we? Down stairs and back to the pit. Smell of burning, darkness burning, unseasonably warm. Light up votaries, cast a glow. Curious sensation, edge of a cliff. Unstick a taper, roll back the gloom of the flickering flickering emptiness next door. Gone towers of manuscripts, gone cardboard boxes, gone rubberbands, gone. Cloying acrid burning sheaves falling blackvoid falling turning down down the spiralling pit.

Faraway firengine heehawing heehawing Cragg's voice breaking in

– He tried to burn the files fortunately damp. Jeremy please have the thing carried out to a taxi and get rid of it. Once and for

Thin slit of a smile, mine. He can't, I thought. He's away selling his house. He makes his living selling h

The Eighteenth Envelope

Mainmorte, mainvive. I am not quite sure which straw of truth to offer you first, nor even if you will acknowledge it, floating as it does on an ocean of deceit. We would have preferred to go to you and explain in your presence, but there was no time left; we were already in flight. We knew we had closed doors behind us that would never open again. The worst of it by far was that we could see no way of carrying out our plan without making you part of it.

A moment came when we both wanted to turn back. I had separated the death notices into two piles: 'hates' on one side, 'loves' on the other. Then she inserted the cards and I licked the envelopes and we both knew it was too late. Sending off the 'loves' was torture, the 'hates' a kind of macabre bliss. We were both torn apart by it. I have taken Jeannine off to a postmark in the sun; here we shall let time do its work and try to become whole again before going on with the tedious business of living as people do.

You will realize now (perhaps you have known it all along) that this account of my passage out of publishing and out of life, this series of notes for a biography of Wales that became, along the way, a 'biography of events', was foreordained to depart from the truth. I knew that Thrale had insisted on seeing everything I wrote: no need to cause even more bad feeling by identifying the source. That meant that Wales was reading it over our shoulders. You will understand now why I replied so inadequately to your many questions and solicitations, and why I was forced to fabricate as I went along.

We were deeply touched by your message of sympathy. You have a gift for this sort of thing that the others do not share. It was not simply a question of literary merit: in that sense Magguinness outshone them all.

I suppose it was the simplicity of it – something so far transcending words that one could feel your presence in the room. You will be offended if I say more than this: your voice came to us as a great booming bell from the highest of towers. It will ring in our memories as long as memory lives.

Were you able to spot the moment when truth gave way to the other imperative, the one we all submit to in order to go on? There were many moments of the kind: they had a tendency to feed on one another as we went along. To this day I do not know if it would be possible to do it with a lady on the back of a horse: direct all practical enquiries to the nearest circus acrobat or temple goddess in lower Bengal. And the darling daisies? In all honesty, Horace, were you able to see me, *me*, in that demented dance? With Harriet Cragg? Harriet, whose daisyhood had long since been lost in fields of prose? There was a chance that Wales might have believed it; after all, he had been there before me. What gave me the idea was Wales' sinister remark about sleeping with one's enemy's wife: I had heard of it long before Lady Moira brought it to our attention because she had mentioned it earlier to Moot. I simply took the theme and bent it into variations, asking myself how Wales would respond if I pretended to have slept systematically with his row of popsies – and sleep with them he did, if we can trust the word of the ladies themselves. And why not they, why not he? What would you do if you found yourself set free from life yet chained without remedy to your hungering orgones? You know damned well what you'd do: Prometheus unbound, contemporary rewrite. That much I know from having written about it myself; the pen scrabbles across the page like a drunken octopus. As for the ladies? You will agree, I think, that the differences between men and women in this respect have been reduced to the vanishingpoint in the grindingmill of the age. Wales descended on them in the night with the irresistible force and beauty of life restored, and went away at dawn once more a stranger. Death, delight. Overpowering. For Harriet it must have been even better. As daisies go she is, and must know it, long past the remedy of the wateringcan. Even so there are, I suppose, lingering attractions, and a brisk rubdown in Cragg's bathrobe would do nothing to diminish them. For her it was a way of taking revenge on Cragg, whose marital neglect is a matter of record.

Harriet did come into my room, but only to offer me an extra blanket as any solicitous hostess would. Had Priapus gripped me to the extent described, he would have suffered the humiliation, shoved smartly up the crotch, of the SaintBernard's wet and refrigerated nose. Good old

Ragamuffin, the places he gets into! Jollygoodshowing and tailthumping all round, and so to bed.

The matrioshka messages, the trips, the discovery and flight of Jeremiah Peach, all happened as related. As for life in the coalhole, I hope you will agree with me that some experiences are best accounted for with a bit of filigree at the edges. This one was of that kind. The real story was too dismal to invite the truth.

The impulse to search for Wales in Moses came as much from Herder as from the missing *Numbers*. Max had written me a letter explaining that my account of the book bazaar in Frankfurt – a description I had given in some detail during one of his periodic visits – had led to another of his ideas for liberating music from the concerthall. He had quickly sketched out a plan: one hundred pieces, based on themes from *The Decameron*, to be performed in and around the bookstalls at different intervals throughout the fair. Then, trifling task, he actually went to work and wrote the music: one hundred pieces for an astonishing variety of instrumental groups, some hitherto unknown. The enormity of that, and what Freud had seemed to imply about identity, left me momentarily in a state of shock. Was Herder a transmogrified Boccaccio or musical rewrite of Hokusai? And if Herder was an updated remnant of one or the other, who was Wales? The search for *Numbers* led me on to Moses and Wales and myself. What is history, I said to myself, if not theme with variations, good, bad, and mediocre, many of them decadent and perverse? If one could find a remnant of Moses in Wales, then Minimichelangelo had chipped out his statue and designed his stairs. Clutterbuck, as we have already seen, was a type of Aaron; that made Cragg a shred of the false prophet Balaam. And then unaccountably I thought of Angela, for if the pattern worked for Wales and myself, it would have to apply just as well to the rest. I could find her nowhere in the past; there are no female Moseses or Hokusais or Freuds, and I could not fit her in among the witches and courtesans. My mind, having exhausted history at a glance, swept on past stickybuns and her craving for sweets to a vision of Adolf Hitler devouring chocolates, for Angela *had* written *The Seven Charms*, hadn't she? Angela, Adolf translated? And there, you see, the whole thing fell down like the Tower of Babel into a heap of sand, and blew away in a gale of laughter.

Enough. Wales, for our present purpose, is Wales, and I am myself. If you care to be Freud, crouching there patiently at the end of your couch, sobeit. God owes you the brightest of aureoles.

Now to work, and you will understand that everything I say from this moment on covers the period of my 'illness' and subsequent 'death'. I shall try within the limits of my means to relate it chronologically; but perhaps I'd better dispose of Harper Cabot before I do that. During the week following my visit to Littleheath, Harper descended on us unannounced. Only Cragg knew of his coming, and Philippa, who was forbidden to talk. So the first information I had of it came in the form of a blow in the region of the right shoulderblade.

– Hiya buddy, I see you've come up in the world!

– Harper! What in God's name

A smile of sorts played stingily at the corners of his stingy mouth, and he held out his hand. I made the mistake of holding out mine in return.

– We are busy thickening the plot, he said. As they say in the trade. Are you well? Jeannine?

His eyes were busily scanning my table for evidence. The usual clutter of inkblotted pages, pastepot, and effacements was spread out before me: I had not the slightest doubt that he had found what he was looking for.

– I must say, nothing over here ever seems to change. Charles Dickens lives and breathes. They tell me they've made Micawber Prime Minister. What luck for the country, hawhaw. When're you gonna come over and see how a real publishing empire operates? Say, I like your furniture, buddy. When are you expecting the next air raid?

And that, apart from the usual musthavelunch, was about it until three or four days later when Magguinness came down in a state of excitement bordering on mania, all of it carefully concealed.

– The news is that they are about to convert me into a blockbuster. Six weeks of talkshows from coast to coast, guest lectures on seven campuses, and an evening at the Carrion Club smiling into the cameras with dishy starlets hung round my lapels. I signed this morning for a percentage of the soft covers.

– Great Scott! I said, wondering who Scott was. All this for *Kiss Me?*

– They've changed the title. The American edition will be called *Ten Kisses That Shook the World.* How's that for positive thinking?

– Sure you've had that many?

– Stop talking like an accountant and ask yourself when you'd like to drink the champagne.

I told him I was delighted, and I was. If it worked it would see him out; and if they wanted it to work, it would.

– Anybody else going?

– Angela.

Inevitably. What luck.

– But it doesn't matter. She's going mainly to take Harriet in hand.

– Harriet?

– Yes, we're flying over together in a party. Firstclass charter, sotospeak.

Ohoh. So Harriet was to get the treatment as well. It did not immediately occur to me that her presence on the other side would eclipse Tom as surely as night day: what it did say was that she had given up all thought of going ahead with our little coup d'état. That evening I rang her to confirm my fears.

– Quite the contrary, she replied gaily, this will strengthen our hand. Thrale knows that I shall come back with even more chips for the gambling table. You can count on me to thrust them forward across the green baize at the most appropriate moment.

She did not explain when the moment might occur, and my unshakable prudery made it impossible for me to ask. So I went along on the assumption that it would not happen until her return. For prudery read tension: once more I had launched myself into bouts of sleeplessness, and in the evenings I had taken to dragging myself round the garden like a postoperative complaint. I felt, truly for the first time in my life, that there would be no cure. I would continue blotching the book in my basement hole forever. Harriet's call would never come. Wales would never send another matrioshka. On one particular day the temptation to risk all forever and board the last plane to Saskatchewan became almost irresistible, and even Jeannine began to wonder if we shouldn't be better off to disappear for a time – at least during the weeks while Harriet and Tom were doing their tour. But that would have separated us from our purpose. If I was depressed it made it easier for me to act out the part that had been invented for me. I was supposed to look like a beaten man, and behave like one, and believe me no one has ever been more suited to a role.

One week, give or take a day, was saved by a diversion which persuaded me that Wales had focused his attentions for a time elsewhere. You will recall that before he left us Wales had accumulated his impressive collection of 'liquidses' – companies dealing in wines, whisky, syrup, petrol, the worldfamous vodka, anything that flowed. The exception seemed to be Wales & Wales itself, but was it an exception? The company that made printer's ink flow? It was inevitable, of course that he should acquire the foremost ink manufacturing company in the country, a giant among inkmakers, with tentacles reaching out into the world.

Wales called it the Squid. Then, for reasons unknown, he bought a foundry: when you heat metal, you see, it flows. All the same, we all thought that was cheating. The chief interest lay in the technology out: apparently it was capable of producing outstandingly light and heatresistant alloys of the kind used in supersonic aircraft and space vehicles. In a word, not backward. Years pass. I am pushing the ink in the coalhole. Sounds of hilarity from the corridor upstairs. Philippa, unable to contain herself, clatters down the stairs with a typewritten sheet, inserts it into the space separating my nose from the Word of God.

— What do you make of *that?*

I studied it closely, then held it out at arm's length. Eventually I stuck out my tongue.

— Exactly. And do you know, there isn't a machine in the house that doesn't do it? Cragg is absolutely livid.

Whereupon she ran back up the stairs, struggling as she went to dam up a torrent of giggles. The typing she had shown me appeared on the standard Wales & Wales letterhead. It went like this:

```
AAAAAA AAAAAA AAA
AA AAAAAAA AAAA AAAA
AAAA AAA AAA AAAA AAAAAAAA AAAA

AAA

AAAAAAAA AAA AAA AAAAAAAA AAAAAA AA
AAAAAAAAAAA AAAA AA AAAAAAAAAA AA AA
AAAAAA AAAA AA AAAAAAAAAAAAAAAAAAAAAAAA
AAAA AAAAAAAAAA AAAAAAAAAAAAAAA A AAAAAAA
AAAAAAA AAAA AAAAAA AAA
AAAAAAAAAAAAAAAAAAAAAA AAAAAAAAA
AAAAAA AAAAAAAAAAAAAA

AA A AA AAAA AA AAAAAA AAAAAA AA
AAAAAAAAAAAAAAAA AAAAAAA AAA AA AAAAAAAA
AA AAAAA AAAA AA AAA AAAAAAAAAAA A AAA
AAAAAAAA AA AAAAAAAAA AAAAAAAAA AAA
AAAAAAAAAAA AAAAAAA AAAAAAAA AA
AAAAAAAA AAAAA AA AAAAAA AA AAAAAAAAAAA
AA AA AAAA AAAAAAAAA AA AAAAA AAA AAAAAA
AAA
```

AAAAAA AAAAAAAAA AAA AAAAAAAA AAA AAA
AAAAAA AAAA AAA AA AAAAAA AAAAAAA AA
AAAAAAAAAA   AA   AAAAAAAAAAAAAAAA   AA
AAAAAAAAAAA AAAAA AA AAAAAAA AAAA AAAA
AA AAAAA A AAAAAAA

AAAAAAAAA AAAAA

It cost me twenty quid (lunch for two at the Strathmore) to get the rest of it out of Philippa. I don't suppose you have ever stood within shouting distance of a modern typewriter: they now purr along on electricity, and one day they will doubtless slink along without typists. In place of the old fanlike arrangement of arms set in motion by the keys, we now have a ball that rotates. If a change of typeface is required, you simply take out one ball and pop in another presto subito bringing Aldus Manutius back from the dead. Well, when Harper Cabot was with us he persuaded Cragg to throw out all the old racketers and replace them with the electronic purr: von Gildenkrantz's theory about that, and we had little reason to doubt it, was that Cabot's wife owned shares in the typewriter company. Be that as it may, Wales was not consulted, and when one morning he happened to overhear Philippa purring away, he retired into one of his silences whose meaning was clear to all but Cabot. The riposte has now come, somewhat delayed, in the form of the stuttering AAAAAAAAAA, to coincide with Cabot's latest visit; God knows what impression, if any, it made on *him*. Someone evidently had crept about the house and replaced all the ABC's with AAA's. Philippa, who is a crack typist, seldom looks at the things when she works, so the first letter, when she eventually checked it, gave her a jolt. Eyes? Mind?? Comic dream??? Whoever had gone mad, it wasn't she, because she quickly discovered that there wasn't a typewriter in the house that didn't say AAAAAAAAAAAAAAA. It took less than an afternoon to replace them, but there was no guarantee, of course, that the pussycats would not stammer again; the prevailing theory was that all would be well if Harper Cabot could be confined to his side of the drink.

Moot came down one morning muttering about terrorist trivia, anti-American paranoia, juvenile senility, and the consequences of the un-ending A as applied to the infinity of print. He never was very high on Wales, come to think of it, and the typewriter stunt confirmed his worst fears; it was the first external sign that Wales had begun to exercise his eccentricity out over a spectrum broader than daisies, antibooks, the Greek language, and me.

– It's not funny, he said darkly. The next time he sneaks round with his aluminium balls they are going to write ZZZZZZZZZZZED with invisible ink. And that will be the end for all of us.

I tried to reassure him but failed as ever. Difficult to know what Moot thought of me at this point: he had probably given up hope. What could have been more natural? Until Harriet made her move I could say nothing, and Harriet was over there, rocking them awake on telly. The other, the ultimate manoeuvre, of course remained privy to Jeannine and myself. I felt badly about that, but what else could I do? I had never had a better friend, may the saints preserve him, and it was awful because I was losing his respect. What cause had he but to think the worst: Root the hairshirt, the doormat, the automated yes. Root the spineless adjunct of Wales' will. The misery is that there was so much truth in it: who can make that straight which he hath made crooked? The Teacher himself left it in suspense; only eternity could reply, and in its own good time. Meanwhile we must get on with the business of living with ourselves, if possible, as we are. I was managing at last, because for the first time I could see the way ahead. All that remained was to choose our moment, to be fixed soon after Harriet's return. Then Thrale rang and stood our calendar on its head.

– I have spoken with Harriet Cragg on the telephone, and also with General Smallwood. You are to appear Monday morning before he arrives and take over his office. When he comes in, fire him. I shall have a letter delivered to your house on the weekend giving you the full authority of the holding company.

The call came, of course, in the evening. Jear ine said I went white.

– Are you there?

– Yes, I am here. I am trying to collect my wits.

– Don't worry about your wits. All the ramifications have been carefully weighed. Cragg will resist, naturally, but you are to ignore him.

Slow change of colour imagined: whitewash to insecticide green.

– Mr Thrale, may I call you back within the hour. You've caught me in the midst of something I can't very easily interrupt.

– Of course.

Like everything else in elastic time, the hollyhocks I was staking when the telephone rang could have waited. What I could not defer was the overpowering impulse to wrap myself body and soul round an immense glass of scotch. And to consult with Jeannine, who was no less shocked than I.

I rang back half an hour later: the scotch had done very little for me, and I had fired Cragg fifty times. Best to have done with it and get back to the greater security of the flowers.

– Mr Thrale, there are two questions I feel I must put to you. What am I to do when Cragg tells me to bugger off?

– You are to install another table in his room and remain there until he gets fed up with the situation. If that doesn't work, let me know and other measures will be brought to bear.

– The other question has to do with Wales. What is his attitude to all this? Does he approve, or have you not consulted him?

Dry laughter at the other end followed by a delicate sandpapering of vocal organs.

– It seems to me we have gone into this before. As far as the world is concerned, Wales remains officially dead.

– I am not the world, Mr Thrale.

– I realize that. All I have ever suggested is that you dig in and await developments. Well, they have come to maturity and you are to replace Cragg. Doesn't that tend to circulate a little joy?

– I am to *replace* Cragg?

– Momentarily at least. I can't tell you about the long term, or even about the short. We haven't had any reason to talk about it.

– We meaning who?

– Myself and the General. Harriet Cragg has begun to come into it as well.

– Wales?

– I thought we had dropped that subject.

The rosecutter was nowhere in sight. It did not occur to me that I might cut him off simply by hanging up.

– Mr Racine? Do I take it that I may count on you to carry out the plan?

– I am trying to think. Has it occurred to anyone that Wales may want – may have wanted – Cragg to transform the house into a machine capable of cloning bestsellers? That's what he's done, you know. We're top of the pops, and we've no one but Cragg to praise or blame. Isn't that what Wales wants wanted? Why are you doing this, Mr Thrale?

– I sometimes wonder. Nevertheless I assure you that we are carrying out the provisions of Wales' will. To the letter. This is not the time to draw back – even if we could.

– Do I take it that your hands are tied just as mine are?

– In a manner of speaking. Abominably.

– Then I pity you. I pity us all.

– I rather feared you would. It takes time, doesn't it, to discover that

250

pity is utterly without effect. Quite a lot of time, I am sorry to say. Meanwhile the world moves on and the pitiers are crushed like wet tar under a steamroller. I'll make sure the letter is delivered to you no later than tomorrow afternoon. That will give you Sunday to think about it. If you want my opinion you will read it and then go out and watch cricket. Goodbye, Mr Racine.

Tell me, Horace, do you ever get the feeling, a feeling so powerful that it amounts to a conviction, that you are doing something for the last time? It haunted me throughout the entire weekend. Last shopping excursion to Grumley, last lunch on the garden terrace, last catnap in the sun with the cats. The letter came; a man in black leather roared in and roared out on a motorcycle. On Sunday we decided to take Thrale's advice and went to the cricket match at Tonbridge Common. Last cricket match. Last ride back home along the winding lanes. Last visit to our local pub. And in the evening, of course, last supper.

I sat up most of the night with one of the cats on my lap, and if you asked me to say which cat I would be at a loss. Last sleepless night, most certainly. And yet I was terribly apprehensively awake when I climbed down into the stairwell and raised the window. More than awake: almost extrasensorially lucid, as though I had smoked hashish[1] in the night. As I groped my way along the corridor to my room, the wall felt damper, the air smelled mustier than ever, and when I struck a match to light my row of candles they gave off a glow that made me think of tapers in a sunken cathedral or crypt, and why not, it sounds suitably deathly. Just then I noticed that the candles had begun to stain the partition in front of me with the soot of their burning. Burning. What had happened to the piles of manuscripts next door? I picked up one of the candles and escorted myself into the adjacent cavern. The light sketched an uncertain circle on the wall in front of me – submarine grey, I now noticed – but apart from a single sheet of paper on the floor, it was void. I picked up the piece of paper: typescript with, in the top righthand corner, the initials JB followed by the number ninetyseven. My God! they had burned Jessica Birdwell, or was it James Bream? I folded the paper and inserted it into my pocketbook: evidence. Then I returned to my hole and asked myself how I should begin the day. It was half an hour before Cragg and the others would come tumbling in, each trying desperately not to be

....

[1] Hashish, the plant whose fibres decent men twist into the cord they use for hanging themselves and one another, did you know? A trip at each end, for those who know how to use it.

last. Cragg, you may be sure, was never the one. Helena would be there – all her life she had made a practice of coming in an hour before the others: some said, of the early years, to favour Wales with a goodmorning kiss – for otherwise I should not have been able to get in through the window. The mess in my part of the boileroom would have made any disinterested observer conclude that it had been occupied by one of those madmen whose bodies are found decaying beneath piles of paper and empty sausageskins: three sets of the encyclopedia were stacked vertically on the floor like San Gimignano towers, jokefiles from A to Z in another tower on the table beside the Wales Dictionary, the Bedside Bible, and tatters of paper on which these notes have been compiled month by month, photocopied, and inserted in their envelopes ranged, naturally, in another flatter tower – all of them zigzagging crazily toward heaven or zogzugging sanely toward hell, and each falling into its neighbour's lap. I have not mentioned the inkpots, the gluepots, or the scroll, and what you must do, before we conclude, is to make a liquid analysis of all these elements not excluding the glue. Because, yes, Wales bought a glue company after the ink, in order, one must suppose, to cover his bets. The centrepiece was not the tripedal encyclopedia nor the Greekless dictionary nor the cocktail party pornography nor the notes, but the Greekless scroll, the Word of God besmirched. In order to deal with it I had equipped myself with an edition of the Dispensations, Old and New, which actually had margins. I don't know if you are aware of it, ensconced as you are in your intemporal dream: the history of printing is the history of the shrinking, among other values, of margins. The first Bedside, of which you doubtless still have a copy, left an inch all round the page. We are now down to a quarter of an inch and the end is not in sight: the ultimate economy – economy in the classic sense implying the production of wealth – will be to print to the edge of the page, and why not? Have you ever tried to make a marginal note in a space one quarter of an inch wide? In short, I was obliged to rummage round the secondhand bookshops for a Bedside printed fifty years ago in order to get on with the glueing, because if the task is to glue the bottom of one page to the top of another ad infinitum until it becomes a scroll, one must have margins or the thing won't stick. By this time I had smirched my way through the Five and glued 257 pages together into a continuous sheet more than half the length of a football field, and wrapped it round a wooden stick to find out whether, in terms of thickness, one could do an entire Bible that way. The glueing alone took me the better part of two weeks, and as there was no football field immediately at hand, I folded it into a clumsy accordion before rolling it round the stick. Each page of Biblepaper went round the stick four times; that meant an edition roughly three quarters of an inch in thickness – nicely manageable as it would be divided, in the end, between two sticks. The entire Bible done this way would amount to a thickness of four inches, two inches per stick. Further into the niceties of production I was not prepared to go: the Freddie Fears of this world would have to run with it the next lap. My Bedside from 'In the beginning' to 'Amen' covers 1434 pages.[2] To this day I cannot say how one would go about printing 1434 pages on a continuous sheet of paper the length of three and a quarter football fields, and frankly I don't care. My confession is this, if you want it: I might have pasted the pages together horizontally and got it all into two football fields, but that satisfying economy didn't occur to me until the end. To be precise, it did not occur to me until I had installed myself, complete with scroll, gluepot, and the small bit that remained of the accordion, in Wales'/ Cragg's room. Were papyrus scrolls read from top to bottom or from side to side? On such momentous details hang the fates of houses; and just as the question occurred to me, Philippa walked in the door.

– Robert! What in God's name

She looked particularly lovely. Her hair had been tossed about in the wind and she hadn't had time to arrange it.

– You've given me an idea. I'll tell him I'm doing it in the name of God. That will give him something to think about.

– Have you gone out of your

At which, enter Cragg.

– This must be some kind of joke.

He spoke quietly, as if to italicize the menace in his voice.

I stood up before he had time to remove his coat, and handed him Thrale's letter. He read it in a single blink.

– Philippa, get me Jeremy Chesterton.

– He's taken the day off. He's moving house.

– Blast the man, that's all he ever does, buy and sell houses. Get Freddie, in that case.

Philippa disappeared into her room. Cragg and I stood there without speaking. His eyes seemed to be fixed on a small square of grass in the courtyard. The sun had begun to slant in over the rooftops; a bumblebee bumbled among the flowers on the other side. I wondered how it had got in, and whether it would ever get out again.

. . . .

[2] 1434, curiously the year of the 'invention' of printing by Johannes Gensfleisch. To this day a source of vast amusement to the Chinese.

– Morning, said Freddie cheerfully. Fine morning, isn't it?

– Freddie, will you be so kind as to show this gentleman to the door.

Fear and I looked at one another; for a second or two neither of us moved. Then I gathered up the materials I had laid out on Cragg's table and walked out of the room. According to Philippa, who rang that evening to tell me what had happened, I went out trailing behind me three or four yards of the Bedside Scroll. Cragg then called his lawyer and the battle was engaged.

The rest can be telescoped. Cragg of course refused to go, and I told Thrale I was too ill to go along with the fatuous plan to install me in Cragg's office at a second table.

– Never mind that, he said, I've got a better idea. Let me know when you're back on your feet. I'll have the lock changed during the night preceding your return. The new set of keys will be delivered to your house first thing in the morning. What time do you normally leave?

And so, after I had been away 'recovering' for three days, I made my way back to Great Conduit Street for the last time, with a ring of freshlyminted keys in my bag. The same motorcyclist, the one in black leather, had delivered them at seven o'clock, and roared away without a word. Helena was already there, waiting at the door, and trying unsuccessfully to demonstrate calm.

– Oh there you are, she announced, as if she had been expecting me all along. I can't think why, but my key isn't working this morning.

I then produced my ring of keys and opened the door, presto subito, with a flourish.

– How absolutely stunning. Are you the new keeper of the keys? I thought you'd been thrown out again.

– Here, take one, I said, detaching it from the ring. On condition that you do not let Cragg come into the house, however long he leans on the doorbell.

– What an idea! I never open the door to *anyone* in the mornings. It's not my time of day.

On the way in she paused and smiled one of her beatific smiles.

– By the way, she said, I am delighted. You were beginning to look like the prisoner of Zenda.

Dear Helena. How I wish we could have gone on together, but what good are regrets?

I took up my watch at the window beside the door, just to the left in the shadow, and watched them come up, one by one, to fumble with their keys. Yes, I let them try and fail to get in, and even waited for them to ring the bell. All but Moot, for whom I rushed immediately to the door, and Liz, who came up on his heels.

Moot threw his arms round me when he realized what had happened. Then Liz. They set up a cheer and began waltzing me round the reception table.

– Tell you what, said Liz when she had caught her breath, let me call Jeannine. You are all to come over this evening and get sozzled.

– It's too good, said Moot. It can't last.

The bell rang, and it didn't. It was Jeremy Chesterton. I signalled for quiet and let it go on ringing till he gave up, but panic was oozing out of my pores and staring out of my face: I could not stop it and I could not hide it. Liz and Moot both crept away, wordless and ashamed. Ashamed for me.

Cragg arrived and joined Chesterton on the landing. I could see him trying to force his key into the thing in a sort of attempted metallic rape, and when nothing worked he began pounding the door. Eventually he gave up and they went away together.

I was no longer standing.

Minutes later the telephone began to ring. I realized I could not let it go on forever, and picked it up.

– Racine, I said, knowing whom to expect.

– Cragg. What is the meaning of this?

– You have been locked out. You are not to come in.

– Try and stop me.

Bang.[3]

I went into Cragg's room and sat down at his table. *Take a letter. Check the drinks cabinet. Withdraw all keys to the directors' loo. Fire the chauffeur. Hire the nephew. Fiddle the annual report. Send champagne to the tax inspector. Reply to the Lord Chancellor . . .*

Somewhere in the distance a shattering of glass, a slam of window, more glass falling. Feet pounding up the stairs, pounding closer, Cragg.

. . . .

[3] Note for Herder. When someone hangs up on the telephone you hear a timid click at the other end followed by the dialtone: all very placid and harmless. At the other end the caller, white with fury, slams the instrument into its socket, hook, cradle, and you can measure your experience of life by your choice of the accusative. Something should be done to make the instrument reflect the degree of emotion in acoustic out sound terms. I have always hated the soundfunnel – perhaps because it is a blind mirror reflecting nothing so clearly as the hypocrisy of the caller.

Red fury, huge hand reaching far back over shoulder, swinging, swivelling, arching, crashing. Light going dim, light going out. Out.

When it came on again Moot was bending over me dabbing a handkerchief unaccountably stained red. He helped me up, wrapped his arm under my shoulders, and led me away to a taxi that was already waiting for me at the door.

I can remember a man in the street looking at me over his opened newspaper, frowning, as if I had been so illmannered as to have interrupted his reading. How interesting, I thought. It's Wales. I was about to speak to him when the taxi began moving and the light once more went dim, blotting out the man and Moot, blotting out the taxi and the house outside, blotting out the street that went sliding by in slow and ever slower motion. Blotting out the life I had known and sometimes loved. Almost. Until

The Nineteenth Envelope

It was one of those absurdly bright and cloudless Sundays, warm, somnolent with bees, echoes of dogs barking, cowbells tinkling at one another all along the valley. We felt like getting on the telephone and inviting everybody over for lunch, but we couldn't do it because I was dead.

The first thing I did when we moved into the house – incredible to think that we've been here almost two years – was to separate ourselves from the neighbours: the other Robert's neighbour would have approved. The house is built into a hillside with at the top a field of Saskatchewan wheatcorn belonging not to us but to some sturdy descendant of Piers Plowman, and at the bottom a winding road leading to us. Between the two, the garden with its elms, birches, and my mountain ash, the tree I planted shortly after we came.[1] So there is plenty of shelter: even so, from a certain angle we are exposed to those below who might think it amusing to look up the hill and find out what the neighbours are up to.

. . . .

[1] I must tell you one day what those trees came to mean to me – particularly the birches, and the mountain ash with its flashes of scarlet colour memorializing my native land. As it took root and pushed out its first timid foliage I began to see it and the wheatfield above, far more than any passport or dull entry in a statistician's ledger, as my totems of place. I planted the tree as a way of leaving something living behind me. Trees are not eternal stone, but they remind us that stone had once been living fire, and sometimes served, while it cooled, as flowerpress, seedbed, agaragar for petrifying fish. Just as stone will outlast us, our trees, too, will outlive the fragile traces we make such a show of leaving in our names. Meanwhile the leaves may bud and flourish and sear and fall, and birds may find a home in their branches. Every man who is not a carver of stone should plant a tree and nourish it, when the day comes, with the remnants of his bones.

Hence the lattice wall, thoroughly crept with creepers, and behind it, bathed in sun, the Nook, Nookery, Nookie – name it as you will, and we measure the length of your voyeurism by your choice of the proper noun. There, in short, we breakfast in the sun when it condescends, and on this day of days it did. Superbly.

Curious, the distance between then and now. Now I see it as our last breakfast, heavy with overtones. Triste. Then, as the morning of promise itself, ripening to explode from its pod. If for the only time of my life, and Jeannine felt the same, this was to be my day. Our day. I could tell you what we ate, secluded there in the sun, what perfume of tea we drank. I could number the hairs on the back of my left forefinger. In the supreme moments the details speak, at any rate to the beholder. Let it pass. We cleared away the breakfast, washed up for the last time, and went to work.

In chronological order leading you up to the moment. Thrale rang to offer his sympathy and to say that he, General Smallwood, and 'another colleague from the holding company' would like to pass by in the morning to pay their respects. That gave us the better part of a day to get ready, and it was none too much time because Jeannine had to go into the city to get the cosmetics. Meanwhile I set up the coffin on the trestle table and pressed my suit.

Are you lost? Elementary my dear Watson. I was to be 'laid out' at home before being trundled off to the incinerator. It fell to Jeannine to explain to Thrale that, as the result of the experience with Wales, I had developed an aversion to mortuary places; my last wish was to pass the hours before consignment in the serenity of the garden room, and she would respect it to the letter.

I must say, she was magnificent. Voice quavering but not too much, French accent more than usually to the fore, sentences slightly unsprung. She was shaking when she put down the telephone. Shaking and exhilarated.

– By the way, Mr Thrale, she had added as a sort of afterthought, my sister is here from Paris. If you don't mind she will bring you up to the garden room.

I was in complete agreement with that: to have asked her to hover piously with the guests over the body of her dead husband would have strained the resources of the Comédie Française. Besides, she insisted on reserving a hidingplace for herself in the winecellar, where she could follow what went on without being seen.

Suzanne was indeed with us; she had come over to shop for 'pulls' for the children, or so she thought. When we explained what she was really here for she was horrified and intrigued, and after some resistance she agreed. It was too late to turn back.

The coffin itself was no great problem: I had knocked it together the previous weekend with panelling from a woodyard in Grumley. Rudimentary but serviceable, with brass doorknockers at either end. Pity I wasn't able to keep it for the real event. I did not bother to make a lid; it would have covered up the drama and made it impossible for me to hear. Besides, Wales had exposed himself to the living and so should I. One's opportunities were not endless.

What else? Yes, you are to be forgiven for thinking that the 'death' was due to Cragg's blow, over and out. Not so. Moot called that evening to find out how I was and said something that amazed me.

– How did you do it?

– Do what?

– Knock him out like that? He was out for two hours. Like a stone. When Philippa ran into the room you were both on the floor like corpses in the last scene of Hamlet.

– Really? Come to think of it, I can vaguely remember picking up an encyclopediout. Pity he didn't stay that way.

In fact I was on my feet the next day, and the day after I reappeared with two determined gentlemen whom Thrale had dug up in the docks. They, having persuaded Cragg to sign for a sealed envelope, escorted him gently to the door. Exit Easter Island, exeunt Trilogy: I fired them en bloc. Enter the lesser Racine, king for a day. Remember Burton? The day after that, Harriet swept in from New York and it was all over. Cragg to Cragg, forward pass. All in the family. I was to remain of course as part of the régime – where and as what we never had time to find out because, a short week later, she was awarded the Babel Prize 'for her inexhaustible services to literature'. Founder and donor of the award: the Wales Charitable Trust. Chairman of the committee: Robert Racine.

Enough was enough. Harriet rang to announce that she was no longer speaking to me and my presence in the house would no longer serve. Moot rang to ask if I'd gone mad. Thrale accepted Harriet's resignation, pretending to know nothing. Peter Glyffe new chairman of the board.

That creep.

One last item before we close the door on Wales & Wales, Tom Magguinness at his unhappiest and best. What had happened to him during the American tour? In his own words: 'I thought Harriet had arrived at that excellent moment in life when women begin to take off airs. Well, in New York she put them on again. I didn't get a look-in.'

Will that do for the ABC's?

Back to breakfast. Suzanne took the dishes upstairs leaving the two of us alone on the terrace. There was nothing more to be said. I simply held her in my arms until the time came to put on the makeup and dress up in my suit. When she had finished with her brushes and pots of paint I looked at myself in the mirror and saw, not surprisingly, that I looked like death.

They were due at ten o'clock. I climbed up into the coffin at ten minutes before the hour and tried to compose myself. I had on the grey flannel, white shirt, white handkerchief at the breastpocket, black knitted tie, black stockings, and the black shoes I had polished carefully the night before. The sketch of a hole exposed itself on the sole of one of them: nobody's perfect.

At the last minute Jeannine went down into the garden and cut the stem of a single red rose.

— Buttonhole or across the chest?

I unclasped my hands and motioned to my chest, not wanting to risk cracking the paint. I clasped my hands over it and closed my eyes. She assured me that when I confined my breathing to the waistline and breathed shallowly, no trace of it could be seen.

Suzanne came down and conferred briefly with Jeannine.

— *Ça me fait frissonner*, she said. *Ça me rend malade.*

— *Moi aussi. C'est trop beau.*

They giggled nervously. Jeannine decided, finally, that she preferred to take up her place in the winecellar in advance: better than standing there making fun of the dead.

— How is it in there?

Suzanne calling out from the breakfast table. Muffled reply:

— Fine. There is a box to sit on. I can hear everything if I leave the door open a little.

Perhaps I should tell you about the geography. The geography of thanatos, and who will stop the plague now that its only remaining antagonist is dead? The house, as I have already explained, is built into the side of a hill upside down, with the kitchen and bedrooms at the top, the sittingrooms and study below, and the gardenroom at the bottom extending, when the glass wall is slid to one side, to the terrace itself. The floor of the gardenroom and the surface of the terrace are of the same flagstone cut in large and irregular blocks, giving an effect similar

260

to the lawn carpet in Wales' room at the house, only darker. I found the stone in Monmouthshire, where they quarry it for tombstones: black with a suggestion of green, moss embedded in coal. It was the only change I had made in the house once we moved in; cost me half a year's salary but made the terrace and gardenroom glorious. One of the flagstones of the terrace is taken up to leave space for a forsythia which, all too briefly in the spring, blazons the way up the steps leading to the top of the house. Entrances side and bottom. Next to the bottom entrance, a smaller door giving access to the cellar where Jeannine had gone into hiding, no more than six steps away from the breakfast table on the terrace. My trestle table and box were inside at right angles, completely sheltered from the sun. Behind me, reaching up to the varnished board ceiling, bookshelves. Some of the books in the garden-room had followed me through life since childhood: *Alice in Wonderland, Treasure Island, Robinson Crusoe, Gulliver's Travels*, and a splendid epic of the Wild West, *The Bandit of Bayhorse Basin*, who gallops on in memory every bit as vigorously as the rest. There were half a dozen plants scattered about the room in brickcoloured pots: we saw little reason to be lavish in this respect as the garden, with its birches, chestnuts, mountain ash, and flowering crabapple came immediately up to the terrace on the south and west sides; to the east, woodland. So to recapitulate, the kitchen looks out over Saskatchewan corn, the bedroom is suspended in the treetops, the sittingroom rests in the branches, and the gardenroom rooms in the garden. At the beginning Jeannine wanted to call the house Topsy Turvy – formally, I mean, with a signpost at the entrance of the lane like everybody else. I put my foot down and we had one of our memorable rows. She now calls the place Topsy; I call it the house.

So now you have, as Jeannine used to call it, the putting of the scene. The visitors would come up along the winding lane at the bottom and leave their cars on the platform in front of the garage. Meanwhile I lay couched on a comfortable white quilt in the bottom of the coffin, Suzanne sat at the breakfast table reading *Le Canard enchaîné*, and Jeannine crouched in her cellar, fidgeting with the door.

– This is ridiculous, she said, coming out, I can't stay in that black hole all morning long.

– Go back! I said through motionless lips. They'll see you once they're half way up the steps.

Motorcars in the valley had been swooshswooshing toward us along the road from Grumley ever since breakfast, and there was no way of knowing in advance which of them would turn off into our lane. I was listening for a grumbling Bentley. Dozens of cars went by, and some of the lorries grumbled alarming imitations. By the time four or five of the imitators had gone by, I had begun to feel a trickling sensation under the right armpit. Then:

THUMP!

A paw came down, and another, and before I knew it the cat was feeling his way along my body toward the makeup.

– Jeannine! Help!

Too late. By the time she reached the coffin Ozymandias had planted a paw on my neck just above the collar, and leaned over to grind his nose into my face the way cats do when they haven't been fed. There had been too much else on our minds.

– My God, I'll have to replaster the makeup. Don't move!

The cat had been plucked up and thrown out, presumably to assemble his own makeup elsewhere on the terrace, and Jeannine was bounding up the stairs. Just then a car turned into the driveway.

– Suzanne!

– *Ouihhhh!*

– Go down and do something to keep them back. Anything!

The car came up, Suzanne went down. Jeannine doubled over and crept along the side of the coffin with paint and brushes.

Licks, dabs, dontmove's, therethere's, dontworry's. Bon. Once more adequately frozen into the silent scream.

Car doors slamming below. Voices rising.

– It's not perfect, she whispered, but it will do.

She pulled my jacket and trousers straight, adjusted the rose. Slid back on tiptoes into her place of concealment.

Three voices floated up from the bottom of the garden.

Smallwood's chocolatecoated fruitandport. Thrale's velvetcovered anvil. Suzanne's gallic tinkle, trembling of crystal, breeze playing on a chandelier.

No Wales.

The whole plan had been devised to coax Wales out of his den, and from everything I could tell from stretching my ears into trumpets, we had failed.

No Wales.

For a very brief instant I considered getting up, climbing out, stationing myself at the top like a mannequin at a costume party, and calling the whole thing off. But it was the one plot we had not imagined, the contingency that made fools of *us*. Curious to think, now, that we had not examined it at all. Wales not showing up. Wales well and truly dead. Curious and unimaginable. An indefinable intuition, vaguely of the whatthehellwe'reboundtolearnsomething variety, made me lie still, and the voices began to come clear.

— By the way, Madame Racine hopes you will excuse her. She is not feeling well.

— I'm so sorry. Please tell her she has our best wishes.

Definitely fruit, unquestionably port.

They were now at the level of the terrace. Heels clicking, clumping on flagstone.

— Lovely garden.

Velvet anvil.

— Yes. Robert passed his weekends in the garden. He said he knew nothing about it but plants like to be poked.

Very close now.

Heels silent.

Trio of speechlessness broken, after an interval, by fruitandport.

— Aaaaargh. I wonder, Madame, if we might ask for some glasses and a jug of water.

— Of course. Please make yourselves comfortable on the chairs.

Door opening, closing.

Suzanne's feet clumping energetically up the carpeted stairs.

Continued speechlessness.

One pair of feet moving away on tiptoes to the far edge of the terrace.

— Aaaaargh.

Fruitandport directly into left ear.

— I suppose that's the way we all go. Damned if it isn't for all the world like theatrical paint.

Breaking away in the direction of the terrace.

— I say, Aubrey, do you think Wallace had any real notion of what he was doing to the fellow?

— I've often wondered myself.

— Pretty hard cheese, whatever way you look at it.

— Not pleasant. Not pleasant at all. I did try to reason with him, you know, but you know what Wales is like.

Water coursing along subterranean pipes.

Frivolous chitter of birds.

Swooshwoosh of cars along the valley.

Somewhere in the far distance, a child crying desperately to be drawn back into the womb.

Slow march of heavy feet the length of the terrace. Pause at the end. About turn. Back again.

Feet descending, glasses tinkling on a tray.

Suzanne bustling to the table, laying out jugs and glasses.
Début de partie.
– If you prefer, there is some orange juice.
– You are very kind, Madame.
– Thankyou so much.
– You will excuse me? I must return to my sister.
– Of course.
– And do assure her of our most distinguished consideration.
Velvet anvil this time. Aubrey had been writing letters in French?
General assembly of feet round breakfast table. Scraping, creaking of wicker chairs.
Soft pop.
– Snifter?
– Orange juice, if I may.
Clink of jug against glass. Liquid pouring, ice tinkling.
– Thankyou.
More clinking, pouring, tinkling. Clank of metal on metal.
– Cheers.
– Mmmmmm.
Chitterchitter swoosh tinkle. Fruitandport:
– Has anything been done about the widow?
– Yes. She is to receive the husband's salary unless and until such time as she remarries. Indexlinked, of course.
– Decent enough, I suppose. Not much incentive to remarry. What's she like?
– Rather like the sister. Smaller and somewhat more anglicized, thank heaven.
– Mmmmmm. I thought the sister was a bit of all right. Nice legs and all that. Wonder if she would consider – after a decent interval. The widow, I mean. Or one of the variants. I expect this one will return to France once the festivities are over. Curious, the chap getting involved with a Frenchwoman. How did it happen?
– They met in a Swiss boardinghouse, I gather. One thing led to another.
– Eh bien, Aubrey, if you should happen to speak to the widow on the telephone, do give her my regards.
Animated tinkle.
– My most distinguished salutations, as you are wont to have it.
– Indeed I shall. I'll say you intend to ring her up for lunch after an indecent interval.
– Dinner, if you don't mind.

Half suppressed laughter: grated chocolate falling down a short slope.

My right leg began to twitch alarmingly on its white cushion and might have gone on St Vitusing, I suppose, into the next world, had I not been distracted by another event. For just then – distant gutturals of antediluvian Bentley – another car began nosing into the lane, and the tremor stopped.

– Must be Wallace, said Fruitandport. I'll go down.

There were sounds coming up from the space in front of the garage, no doubt. They were obliterated, all of them, by the hammering of my heart against the wall of its prison. Until they were quite near. Curiosity again switched off the viscera: it was essential to hear.

– Ah well, said Wales.

Was it my imagination? Had I detected, beyond stormclouded kaleidoscopic eyelids, a faint tone of regret?

– Pity. I was about to send him another matrioshka.

Shuffling of feet on flagstone.

Embarrassment? Repulsion? What to do next? Finally, from the General:

– We are not without drinks, Wallace. Vodka or orange juice?

– Vodka and orange if I may.

General movement in the direction of the breakfast table. Renewed scraping of chairs, creaking of basketwork.

– Those whatchacallem, petroushkas – how did the Russians get into it anyway?

– The Russians, said Wales, are neither here nor there. The petroushkas, as you call them, are wooden envelopes. What I wanted was to see myself through the editorial lenses of another man's mind. Root was more than ideal because of the distance between us. People don't see one another clearly in closeup, you know. Besides, he was a poet. I am told that poets are particularly good at seeing things.

– I thought he wrote encyclopedias.

– Of a sort. But then he began comforting himself with the copulative verb. From that moment I knew he'd have to be written off.

– You mean none of this has come to you as a surprise.

– On the contrary, only two possibilities remained. Either he was to go up, or he was to go out. I was certain he didn't have it in him to go up, so I gave him the push. Indirectly. Nevertheless, upstairs and out.

– You gave him the push, said the General. I thought you were supposed to be dead.

– I have always had collaborators, as you are well placed to know. On this occasion it was Harriet Cragg. She agreed, or should I say was pleasured into performing, the necessary rites. My temple goddess, if you will.

— And was later thanked by being awarded the Babel Prize. Some temple.

— Two birds with one stone. Harriet had written the same bloody book once too often. Somebody had to stop her.

— I take your point. But it seems there was a somewhat better case to be made for Root, as you call him. Aubrey here tells me he was not without value. Heart in the right place and all that.

— Really?

Faint scraping of throat dry as tombdust. Was it Wales attempting laughter?

— What's the good of having your heart in the right place if it doesn't beat?

Door slamming open. Hell of a bang. Jeannine.

— You bastard! The trouble with you, Monsieur Wales, is that you are not dead enough.

Petrifying pause.

BLAM!

The roof blew off. Glass shattered. Pieces of flowerpot fell down from nowhere in an orange rain. I knew that because I was sitting up, all orifices agape. *All* orifices, I am ashamed to say.

Jeannine was standing there with the shotgun, ten paces from Wales. How she could have missed him from ten paces God only

— There is another bullet in this thing, Monsieur Wales. How can I be accused of killing a gentleman who is already dead?

Jeannine's face a concentrate of white fury. Smallwood reaching tentatively toward a silver flask on the table.

BLAM!

Silver flask spinning off against the wall. Smallwood's sleeve in shreds. Blood, glass, vodka everywhere: amazing how much damage ordinary kitchen salt can do.

Wales paretic from Gk *paresis*, partial paralysis of the muscular function, once more interrupted reading his newspaper.

— Goodgod, said the General, this is worse than war!

And as he began winding a handkerchief round his flayed hand, Jeannine let the shotgun fall. Her face was hidden in her hands. Her entire body was shaking.

The door burst open; Suzanne's mouth described a frozen O.

Wales recovered first.

— You all right? he said to the General.

– Small finger seems to be falling off but otherwise
– Jolly good.
Wheeling, glaring at me.
– *You're* all right, I see. We've heard of that one before.
With Thrale on the other side, he helped the General down the steps to the car. They did not pause to say goodbye.

The other version. Of course it didn't happen that way. What happened was that I went blind with fury and hatred and jackrabbited about like a sleepwalker parachuted down into a field of thorns. The worst of it was the morning after: I could no longer remember my dream. Two months went by and Jeannine filled in the gaps. I was back, and life still waited to be rewritten in a form acceptable to my demons. You may never be impelled to make the discovery (for your sake I hope not) that demons, if they are to be appeased, must be fed solutions. They insist on having the final envelope tied up with a ribbon and sealed with wax, permanent and bloodyred. Querulous readers, and how to be rid of them short of shuffling off?

Reel it back on the spool, then, to the moment when the General bent over to inspect the theatrical paint. In all good logic I thought I was about to be despatched to the guardroom and given three months' packdrill; but no, the paint passed muster and the General went for his stroll. After which, nothing else was the same. Sorry, Suzanne did lay out the orange juice and the General did bring out his flask of vodka. But the conversation shot off to an altogether different planet.

One more exception: the remarks about Suzanne's legs and how the General wouldn't at all mind striking up an affair with the 'widow' actually were made. My right leg did not twitch. I took it as a compliment to my ability to embellish my life with sexy women.

Now the playback. Chitterchitter, tinkle, clank. Velvet anvil begins.

– We shall have to get someone to take over as chairman of the Babel Prize. Any ideas?

– Dunno. Bentwhistle?

– I've already canvassed him. He says he has too much on his plate. We've sent him the Wales papers, you know.

– Really. Do you think there's a biography in it? Racine didn't bite on it at all, did he?

– There's some good stuff in it, I gather. No, he didn't. We'd have saved time by sending it all to Horace in the first place.

– How are you getting along with the new list?

– Well enough. Half of it's been farmed out already. Did I tell you about Winifred? She's agreed to take on the children's treasury of erotic fairytales, and do you know, she's absolutely transformed. Comes in now with her hair done up and red paint on her toenails. Better than psychoanalysis, by a long chalk.

Grated chocolate falling down the slope.

– She'd better watch it. She may get laid out over a car bonnet again.

– Do you know, the girl made the story up out of whole cloth? I know, because the doctor told me she hadn't been touched. Apparently she rent her own clothes exactly like an angry prophet out of the Old Testament and fell back into a trance. Absolutely ideal for the erotica.

– Splendid. How are we doing with the Greeklesses and the various Racine expurgations?

– Amazingly well. *Amazingly* well. Went into Thatcher's just the other day to see the new managing director and he told me they were pleased as Punch. People are *collecting* them, it seems; God knows one wouldn't buy them in order to read them. Wales was right, of course, about that.

– Never overestimate the sanity of people who buy books.

– Precisely.

– What are the unemployment figures doing these days?

– Worse and worse. Or better and better, depending on your point of view.

– Wales was right about that, too.

– Yes, and about the telly.

– What did he say about the telly?

– He was certain that when unemployment got up to exmillion, I think it was five, a sort of collective revulsion would set in. All that sitting at home with the missus, you see. They would then go out – not all of them, but more than ever – and buy books with their food coupons. Or booze. Books and booze, both anaesthetic.

– Well, thank God for the Russians. Drop?

– Thanks all the same. By the way, I'm in the middle of a corking good book. It's called *Numbers*.

– *Numbers?* Never heard of it. If you ask me it's a bad title.

– Top of the pops at Thatcher's.

– I don't care. What's it got to do with literature? I'd have called it *Letters* myself. You ought to ring me more often when you're choosing titles, Aubrey.

– Yes, I suppose we should. You were certainly on the button with *The Seven Charms*. By the way, how are you getting along with your new spy thriller?

– Blocked, I'm afraid. They're doing it all from airplanes these days and it takes all the joy out of it. I may have to think again.

– Well, and why not?

– Do you think Jessica Birdwell would play?

– Not jolly likely. Jessica does it with the birds.

– I don't mean that. I *am* capable of other lines of thought, you know.

– Sorry. What had you in mind for Jessica?

– I thought we might buy her out.

– Buy her out?

– Yes. I could write that sort of bunkum better than she does, and give it a lovely lesbian twist, you know.

Animated grating. Chocolate ladled all over the terrace.

– Besides, her last two have done badly. The Birdwell stock must be very nearly at the bottom.

– Possibly so. But you can't expect her to sell without a fight.

– I've anticipated that. We can let her take over Thomas Magguinness.

– That's a thought.

– And Magguinness could take over from Peter Glyffe.

– Not bad at all. Especially as Harriet rather squashed the chap on the American tour. He must be desperate for security, poor boy. What about Glyffe?

– I haven't worked that out yet. Can't see him taking over the Babel. He may have to go the way of all Racines.

I couldn't take it any longer. I sat up in my box and began swiping at the greasepaint. My throat was so desperately dry that what I said was almost inaudible.

– Get the hell out of here.

Adjustment of the volume.

– *Get the hell out of here! Move!*

– Fancy that, said the General. Thrale said nothing, for nothing in this life or in another could have surprised Aubrey Thrale.

I leaped out of the box and hurled myself in the direction of the winecellar, forgetting that Jeannine was concealed inside. I threw open the door and the light fell on her. She was bent protectively over MacFarlane, the taperecorder.

– What are you doing? she said between clenched teeth. Have you gone out of your mind?

– I haven't finished with them yet, I said, and began rattling the wine bottles.

It was still there, behind the carton of Lacrima Christi, the small

269

bronze box now clothed in a grey patina of dust. They were half way across the terrace when I emerged.

– *Wait!* I cried, struggling with the catch. *Take this with you!*

I hurled myself at them like a football tackle.

– *Wait!*

The damnthing wouldn't open. I clawed at it, twisted it, hammered it against my shoes: nothing happened.

Thrale and the General were at the steps.

– *Quick, the key! The key!*

I wheeled and ran with the box under my arm back to Jeannine, who was holding the doorjamb of the winecellar as if it might collapse.

– What key?

Furious rattling among the empties. Upending of fingerprinted bottle. Tiny tinkle of key.

– *Wait! Take Wales with you!*

They were now two-thirds of the way down the steps. I melted them into a skislope, and began throwing the stuff at them in fistfuls – over their hair, into their eyes, up their nostrils – everything that was in the box, upending it over a hunchedup Thrale.

Coughing, sneezing, weeping, they fell into the car looking, in their black suits daubed with ash, like a pair of ragandbone men out of a silent film. I stopped. It was useless to go further: I had spent the box. I had used up Wales.

Inside their glass cage they paused to wipe off their faces with handkerchiefs. Then Thrale started the motor and they drove away. I sat down on the bottom step and stared for a long time into the empty casket until Jeannine came down and put her arms round me. The earth turned on its axle. Finally I brushed myself off and went upstairs to pour myself a hot bath. There, in the bathroom, I cleaned Wales out of my fingernails and washed him down the drain.

Now you know it all. Almost.

270

The Twentieth Envelope

The last word. I need not remind you that life is full of surprises. One day as I was mucking about in the garden – it had rained heavily the day before and had not entirely stopped – a man drove up and began talking to Jeannine. He was dressed, like Cragg, in bars. They talked briefly at the bottom of the garden, and then Jeannine went up to the house. When she came down she was carrying my raincoat and an overnight bag.

– It's for the best, she said, and we drove away together in the man's car.

I thought of resisting, but frankly it wouldn't have been worth the candle, not to mention the row of them abandoned in the coalhole. Occasionally I found myself wondering what had become of my candles, hoping they had had the decency to give them to a church bazaar.

Jeannine came into the place with me and stayed long enough to say goodbye, trying unsuccessfully to be brave. Everyone was kind and polite. It lasted two months and three days, and I shall not go into it at length here as I came out of it well and learned nothing that would be of use to the world outside.

The ceremony of admission, however, is worth relating.

– I must tell you, Mr Racine (this after he had completed his examination) what you already know. You are no more bonkers than I am, you are simply bonkers in a different way. That, in a word, is the dilemma. Erothanasis. Sanity, on the other hand, is the ability to subscribe to other people's illusions. We are all crazy in a slightly different way, and of course in the business context where everyone is expected to be crazy the *same* way, these small differences stand out. I must say, hitting a chairman in his own office is a foolish damn thing to do all the same. Why didn't you take him out into the nearest dark alley?

– It was morning and the sun was beating down and he hit me first.

Anyway there are no alleys in that part of the city. I'd have had to take him to the North End.

– Mmmmmm. Well, never mind, you're here and we must put you to work.

Reaching into a drawer. Withdrawing a box that might have been made for writing paper.

– I wonder if you would be so kind as to cast your eye over this manuscript. I put a lot into it, good part of my lifesblood, sent it out, and would you believe it, twelve publishers in this country have had the effrontery to send it back. One wonders what else they do for a living. Anyway, Mr Racine, it may well be that I have produced a work that is too original for the humdrum editorial mind. What I want you to do, if you will, is to knock some of the originality out of it and make it into a manuscript that will sell. Once we've got that out of our systems I shall be glad to bring your case up for review.

I thought about that for a minute before reaching for the box.

– I shall be delighted, doctor.

He smiled and began pushing it across the table.

– On one condition.

Questionmark replacing smile.

– That you write me a letter on your official hospital notepaper promising to let me out the day I deliver the manuscript. That you send a registered copy of the letter to the Prime Minister and another to the Pope. That this be done before I start working on the manuscript.

He plugged a thumb into a rounded aperture formed by his mouth and pretended to chew a thumbnail. Actually he was sucking it.

Eventually, pulling it out with a pop:

– Done.

And that was how it came about that *The Paranoia Quotient* was edited, where it was not rewritten, and how Dr Jason Baldwin went on to become a cultfigure in the world of shrink.

Along the way, by one of those extraordinary coincidences which sometimes take history unawares and oblige us to wonder if time exists at all, I became known to my new friends as Dudu the Scribe. Apart from my work and the daily jog to the boundaries of the estate, there was not much of a programme, certainly nothing one could have described as amusement, no comic relief. And so one day I began applying pen and ink to other pursuits. It began with a series of complicated doodles, went on with a few quick sketches of tables and chairs, and finally evolved into a project which haunts me still. What happened was that almost without thinking I began designing pictograms. One succeeded the other and I began to get caught up in it, I mean really involved – to the point where I could see that if I persevered, my designs would eventually threaten the twenty-six letters of the alephbeth with obsolescence: those same letters that have led to so much misery because of their propensity to favour the abstract. The good doctor approved – no one in his right mind could get along without recreation – and I took up my new hobby with energy.

Then Albert came along.

– Dudu dudu dudu dudu, he said, pausing to let it sink in. He was a small man with a bald, pointed head and wisps of white hair floating over the ears. He was a frail accumulation of knuckles, elbows, knees, and eyesockets, and he quavered when he spoke – not just in his voice, but all over.

– Dudu dudu dudu dudu, he repeated.

I looked straight into the caverns where he hid his watery eyes, and it was clear that he meant what he said.

– That's right, Albert, said the doctor, who happened along just as he was delivering his text. Dudu the Scribe.

And in honour of Albert, who had given me my name, I designed a pictogram in the form of a postage stamp, moistened it, and stuck it on his head, so:

My secret wish was to put him in the post and send him flying off like the birds in Firenze to his freedom. What happened, of course, was that the stamp fell off him and the name adhered to me. The name of Dudu the Scribe was taken up throughout the house, and whenever Albert came to visit me, he stood pathetically rubbing his bones and reciting my name for me as a litany.

In the end I convinced myself that if he recited it long enough and ardently enough, I should eventually become rich and famous.

Dudu the Scribe, I later learned from an ancienthistorybuff, existed and had a small statue dedicated to him about the year 2400 B.C. The statue of Dudu, naked to the waist, skirted in plumes, and smiling a Mona Lisa conundrum, was discovered at Lagash, near Nippur, near Ur, near Eden. One day I intend to tell you why Dudu smiled.

By the time I was ready to say goodbye to Albert I had designed about sixty pictograms in my spare time, the objective being to complete a round onehundred like Hokusai and call it a day. 'Day', incidentally, looks like this: ⌣ . Sunrise is ⌒‿‿, sunset ⌒, and so on into the ——— . No need, in my system, for the encumbering article.

On my way out Baldwin called me into his office to wish me well outside and to assure me of his hospitality in the event that I might care one day to return. Why, I thought, should I want to do that? and said so.

– There might be a recurrence. There usually is. It's a sort of tic, you understand.

– I am not sure I follow you.

– You think you were brought here for clobbering a chairman and dreaming about a shotgun. Not so. You were brought here because of your compulsion to write fiction. For your obsession with writing letters in a world long since dedicated to numbers. Writing fiction, as you are well placed to know, is a way of departing from reality. We put *that* right, didn't we, with our work on *The Paranoia Quotient*.

Jeannine sold the house and found a job teaching in a lycée situated in one of those thumbs of land that jut up into the Atlantic like a permanent insult to the British anatomy – not far from the shores where the French sent out explorers to annex America. She is going through hell with her brats and her books and her bosses, but at least she is going through it in her own language. We brought the cats across in a basket. They detest France because there is no garden in the apartment and the mice are invariably served up in mushroom sauce. The apartment is at the top floor of a seaside gothic calamity in a fishing village within reasonable driving distance from the school: we chose to live outside the main town because the air is good here and the tides do wonders for my epigones.[1] Jeannine was obliged in the circumstances to buy a conveyance known as a deux chevaux, a sort of plumber's hallucination on four wheels, whose only advantage, apart from the wheels, is that it makes it possible for me to hear her coming in time to get the dinner started.

. . . .

[1] WED: Sb³ from Gk 'upon' + 'seed', membranous bag or sack enclosing the sporecase of a liverwort. Invariably given in the plural.

It was not until we were irrevocably installed that we learned the truth: the place is festooned with nuclear power stations, submarines, armadas, all in a state of permanent erection. Electricity is cheap, but the Black Cloud hangs over us all – and what is the Black Cloud but a multiplication to the enth millionth power of my shotgun or Cragg's fist?

We had thought of acquiring fifty bicycles for me to rent to the tourists coming down into the port, but we gave that up before losing any money. The tourists come down on their own bicycles, and they are all propelled with motors capable of rivalling the noise of a sawmill in Saskatchewan.

Eventually, for want of better to do, and to avoid thinking of myself as a chômeur[2] which in French sounds infinitely worse than the simple layabout I was otherwise to become, I got out my watercolours and my Greek stool and dashed off a few Turners and a scattering of Monets: the thought of doing Malevitchs or Mondrians simply does not occur, I am glad to say. Jeannine quite liked the things, so I went back to the seawall the next day and astonished myself by producing a halfdozen more between nine in the morning and noontime pastis in the fishermen's bar. I had them all laid out beside me, anchored at the corners with stones, when a voice behind me said 'Combien?' I looked up and found myself being inspected by Maigret, complete with pipe. Without thinking I replied 'Cinquante francs.' I sold three that afternoon and two the following day. One memorable afternoon I sold five. It was not an income of Great Conduit Street proportions, but it was better than a seagull's breakfast. And now that I have found out how to do them more or less in my sleep, who knows where it will end? Retrospective in the Grand Palais? Don't laugh, there must be something in it or they wouldn't all insist that I sign them, and if I don't sign them they won't buy. Curious business. I have come to believe that they are not buyers at all, but sellers. Somewhere in a smart gallery along the Seine my Turners are lined up with small red blobs stuck on them in the lower righthand corner. Five hundred? Five thousand? They don't come to buy the paintings, they are only interested in the blobs. My signature, of course, is Dudu's pictogram. That baffles everybody until I explain.

Speaking of money, Peter Glyffe has seen your copy (or was it Thrale's?) of *Wilderness* and thinks I should go to work immediately on the other four. The plan is to publish the five books as a single volume, and if they do well I will be invited to attack the entire Dispensation. Full marks for editorial judgment, but what are we to make of a publisher

....

[2] Person unemployed.

who sets out to commission a work without once alluding to the size of the carrot? Am I supposed to do it for the love of God? The good doctor would not approve. Moreover as there was a sinister remark in the letter about 'cleaning it up in places', I am not sure that much commerce will pass between Glyffe and Wyclif. Kind of you all the same for drawing it to his attention.

I seldom think about Wales any more, other than in my dreams, and then only indirectly. There is one recurring dream, particularly unpleasant, which I hope one day to leave behind me. The setting is Wales' room: green carpet reaching out across the courtyard, white walls uncontaminated by books, eggs on their shelf, plant in its pot, Hereford map on the wall, chairman's plate with nothing on it. I walk in, ready to take up the day's work, and invariably find someone else sitting in the chair. Glyffe one day, Chesterton the next. This person then proceeds to give me orders. Do this, do that – language as an infinity of injunctions. One morning I leapt up in bed and brought my fist crashing down on poor Jeannine's cheek, which she had innocently exposed over the counterpane.

– *Mon Dieu!* she cried, staring frantically at the ceiling.

– *C'est moi*, I replied, and folded her in my arms.

She felt much better, curiously enough, when I explained that the cad in me had struck Angela Dulcimer-Smith because she was sitting, that morning, in the chairman's chair. We are both hoping she will not return.

A letter came from Moot the other day: Wales has not only begun sending matrioshkas to Peter Glyffe, he has resumed plucking daisies. Helena told Liz told Philippa told Lady Moira told Moot told me. The only real news, this round, is that Philippa wasn't required to do it on a horse. And Tom Magguinness has gone off to Rome to recover: they say he has taken up reading inscriptions on Imperial tombs. Letters or no letters it all seems infinitely far away, though sometimes, as I sit gazing out over the seawall, I am reminded that we are all washed by the same waters that will never wash us clean.

But one can never put up sails that sail backwards. I amuse myself in the fishermen's bar by asking them who discovered America.

– Christophe Colomb.

– Nonsense, I reply. Amerigo Vespucci. Cristoforo Colombo came later.

And who discovered Canada?

– Jacques Cartier, en 1534.

– Wrong, I reply. Giovanni Caboto. 1497.

– *L'Amérique*, I tell them, *c'est une affaire d'Italiens*. That infuriates them, and I buy them another round of pastis.

One afternoon toward sundown, when I had taken up my usual lookout among the dunes, an object with a familiar oblong shape came floating in on the waves. Eventually it lodged itself in the sand, rolling this way and that at the whim of the tide. I knew what it was because it grinned at me, but I did not move from my sheltering place.

Some time later a small boy, naked to the nub, came along and picked it up. He fiddled with it a bit, and in the end succeeded in opening it. There was a piece of paper inside. That seemed to puzzle him: grownups do strange things with pieces of paper.

He grasped it in his hand, squatted down on his knees, and played with it in the salt water until the curious markings on it ran down and melted into the shape of a green flag.

WALES' WORK

'An outrageous and seductive book. There are accounts to be settled.'
— Harriet Cragg

'A superficial reading might suggest that it is about publishing.'
— Julian Cragg

'At the beginning I thought who on earth would want to read it? When I had finished the answer wrote itself like a shopping list. *Wales' Work* is intended for taxi drivers, poets, pedants, hairdressers, sex maniacs, Bible students, authors, company directors, uncomplacent Americans, feminists, antifeminists, therapists, and winners of the Babel Prize. I hope I haven't left anybody out.'

— Elizabeth Gwynne

'A seriospoof of the first order, absolutely. Don't tell me this is fiction!'
— Malcolm Bell

'He troths our plight very neatly indeed. One thing still puzzles me about Wales. Whose side is he on?'

— Thomas Magguinness

'One finds tears in the laughter, light in darkness, black comedy with dimensions added. The reader may take it in place of vitamins and steam baths.'

— Jason Baldwin

'I'll take the hot steam baths.'

— Angela Dulcimer-Smith

'*Wales' Work* is a mordant comment on the survival, against the heaviest odds, of the quality of language, and on the dignity of resistance to those tyrannies that tend to debase it. Read Racine and take heed before we are belted all the way back to Greek, with no possibility of return.'

— Helmut von Gildenkrantz

'We haven't been treated to a metaphysical mystery at this level since Poe, and it sinks roots all the way back to Horace. By the way, does anybody know if Wales is still alive?'

— Aubrey Thrale

MORE ABOUT PENGUINS, PELICANS, PEREGRINES AND PUFFINS

For further information about books available from Penguins please write to Dept EP, Penguin Books Ltd, Harmondsworth, Middlesex UB7 0DA.

In the U.S.A.: For a complete list of books available from Penguins in the United States write to Dept DG, Penguin Books, 299 Murray Hill Parkway, East Rutherford, New Jersey 07073.

In Canada: For a complete list of books available from Penguins in Canada write to Penguin Books Canada Ltd, 2801 John Street, Markham, Ontario L3R 1B4.

In Australia: For a complete list of books available from Penguins in Australia write to the Marketing Department, Penguin Books Australia Ltd, P.O. Box 257, Ringwood, Victoria 3134.

In New Zealand: For a complete list of books available from Penguins in New Zealand write to the Marketing Department, Penguin Books (N.Z.) Ltd, Private Bag, Takapuna, Auckland 9.

In India: For a complete list of books available from Penguins in India write to Penguin Overseas Ltd, 706 Eros Apartments, 56 Nehru Place, New Delhi 110019.

KING PENGUIN

☐ *Selected Poems* **Tony Harrison**

Poetry Book Society Recommendation. 'One of the few modern poets who actually has the gift of composing poetry' – James Fenton in the *Sunday Times*

☐ *The Book of Laughter and Forgetting*
Milan Kundera

'A whirling dance of a book . . . a masterpiece full of angels, terror, ostriches and love . . . No question about it. The most important novel published in Britain this year' – Salman Rushdie in the *Sunday Times*

☐ *The Sea of Fertility* **Yukio Mishima**

Containing *Spring Snow, Runaway Horses, The Temple of Dawn* and *The Decay of the Angel*: 'These four remarkable novels are the most complete vision we have of Japan in the twentieth century' – Paul Theroux

☐ *The Hawthorne Goddess* **Glyn Hughes**

Set in eighteenth century Yorkshire where 'the heroine, Anne Wylde, represents the doom of nature and the land . . . Hughes has an arresting style, both rich and abrupt' – *The Times*

☐ *A Confederacy of Dunced* **John Kennedy Toole**

In this Pulitzer Prize-winning novel, in the bulky figure of Ignatius J. Reilly an immortal comic character is born. 'I succumbed, stunned and seduced . . . it is a masterwork of comedy' – *The New York Times*

☐ *The Last of the Just* **André Schwartz-Bart**

The story of Ernie Levy, the last of the just, who was killed at Auschwitz in 1943: 'An outstanding achievement, of an altogether different order from even the best of earlier novels which have attempted this theme' – John Gross in the *Sunday Telegraph*